The ULTIMATE HUMANIST

Written By:

David Ben Foster

Library of Congress Control Number: 2017915853

ISBN: 978-0-9864010-5-3

Manufactured in the United States of America by

Blossom Marketing & Publishing, LLC
Post Office Box 1793
Medina, Ohio 44256-1793

Other works by David Ben Foster

POETRY

Anthology in Blue

A View of Ourselves

Meter, Muse & Rhyme

An Epic of Job, the Warrior-Priest - Nominated for 2017 Pulitzer Prize

SHORT STORIES

In Our Town

Market Street

AUTOBIOGRAPHY

Cute as a Button

BIOGRAPHY

Sweat & Blood, A Diary of a Civil War Soldier

Contents

Prologue

In May 2016, a tragedy struck the entire world. Nations were economically weak, including the United States. Its president, like European counterparts, had been soft on terrorists, and they had wide open borders to migrants. Military strength had also waned in the last seven years, even the United States could not wage a small ground war in two places. Nuclear might was yet viable, but since World War II, it had been unthinkable to use by most. In the face of this threat, whatever it had been, it took ten percent of the global population, mostly women and children.

Urie Lee Harrison, a Ph.D., is a thirty-two year old genius and is currently the second dual president of the European Union (EU) and European Commission (EC) in Brussels, Belgium. His offices were in the newly remodeled Europa Building. He had been elected in May, 2016.

Urie saw an opportunity and seized it. He thought of himself as the one human with the only practical answer to the world's woes. Without giving a second thought, he called a global summit of all world leaders. He asked the United Nations secretary general, Kobie Alber, to attend.

Urie had been the seven year old son of William Harrison, a South African diplomat who had been sent to China with his wife and son. While there, the youngster learned several dialects of Chinese. He soon liked the Chinese culture and studied their history. By the time he was seventeen, he earned two martial arts black belts in two of the hundreds of fighting styles in China: mimicry of five animals known as Shaolingquan, and in a sub style called Nanquan.

When he had graduated at seventeen, his father sent him to England to attend Oxford, and after graduation, he attended Cambridge for his law degree, and a Ph.D. Soon after he became involved in European Union politics. He was elected to various positions until being voted in as president of the EU.

Following the death of his wife Sun, who had died in a tragic airplane and boat accident, he makes an agreement with a being named Chu.

Urie calls a select group of leaders from the world, three weeks after ten percent of the global populations is missing. After the first half of the meeting, Urie goes back to his apartment and encounters Chu. Chu had Urie change his name to initials, UH, but more than that, transforms him, his relationships, and the world. UH is controlled by Chu.

In 2017, the world atlas is converted from seven continents to twelve Regional Zones, led by Regional Directors, and operated under the newly formed World Zone Coalition. No longer does any nation have prime ministers, presidents, or dictators. This transformation brings world peace for almost three and a half years, something that nations had failed to bring about.

The Global Summit

Wednesday in sunny Brussels was pleasant, yet there were scenes of angry people weeping, fearful of what they had been enduring with this new terror. Inside the European Union building was noisy with loud commotion, some people somber, others nervously moved about. Now they all moved toward the assembly room, a few bumping into others, but all rushing to get a good seat.

"It's ten o'clock, and we really must begin. Please find a seat. Welcome to this rather unfortunate conference. I hope that this summit will prove most beneficial. I am Urie Harrison, the current president of the EU and the EC. This past year that I have been in this position, has been quite challenging, but that all pales in light of what has been occurring around the world in the last couple of weeks, As you well know, I am from the UK. Before assuming my current position, I served as Chair of the Finance Committee, and over the years, I've watched the EU develop into one of the world's finest contributors to trade, commerce, and international law. We have wholly supported and embraced NATO and its role, and we maintained other treaties with our world neighbors.

"It has been almost two weeks since the world had turned upside down, yet it seems to be unifying—asking for answers, for on May 13th, we had lost nearly eleven percent of the planet's population. This is staggering to comprehend, but we are here in hope of making some sense of this tragedy.

We will begin a new program this week called *Diversity in Unity*. This is a little twist on our official motto, *United in Diversity.* Perhaps we could take a minute to consider this information.

"I will begin with the packet that you had received as you entered the this hall. The new motto is on the cover. We have a vast array of cultures, political differences, and international agendas, but it is humankind we must focus on this afternoon. Forgive the apparent rushed compilation.

Page one through twelve is an overview of opinions of world leaders. Not all, of course. The remaining pages, in outline form only, will be open for discussion. Our Parliamentarian, Joseph Travisee will strictly monitor these proceedings."

At times, loud outbursts of frustration were heard above the orderly meeting. By lunch time, 12:33 pm, everyone had been evolving into a consensus that global unity was now imperative. Safety and stabilization of the human race were paramount. Whatever it was, or whoever had caused this horrific attack on the world, could strike again.

That afternoon, reporters were questioning leaders.

"I am very pleased that the morning went so well," said United States President, James Rowe, who sat at the same table with UK's Prime Minister, Adam Weeks, Germany's Karlene Schmidt, Mexico's Carlos Rodrigues, Russian's Uri Koskov, and France's Peter LeFever.

"I disagree with you," said Rodrigues, as others at the table nodded in agreement. "We accomplished nothing concerning the alien invasion Urie mentioned."

Weeks said, "Harrison is quite right, although what you have said Carlos is correct. But Urie is the most capable organizer, facilitator, and speaker, so I am waiting to see what transpires this afternoon. He is rather a fine man, dedicated to his position, and always, to the good of the EU. I heard that he only had four or five hours of sleep last night with his phone ringing most of the night. Oh, here he comes." They all stood. Weeks introduced them all to Urie. Urie was handsome, thirty-two, over six feet tall; he had thick brown hair that he combed back, and was in excellent physical condition—his walk seemed to accentuate it. He spoke with skilled phraseology after all, he was a trained linguist.

"Gentlemen, I go by U.H. to my friends." They smiled and tipped their heads slightly. "I cannot stay. I have pressing matters in my office. Enjoy your meal."

"He is an expert in international law, and everyone seems to listen to him," said Weeks.

"Frankly, and regrettably, I don't know that much about him," confessed Rowe.

Weeks shared what he knew of UH. "He visits China at least four times a year. He stays with a man named Yen. He lost his dear wife, Sun about three years ago. Their son died in the same accident on the Kunyu River. There was a small plane that had run out of fuel, and fell quietly from the sky, and crashed into the bow of a yacht where she and their son were sitting. No one apparently saw the plane falling inaudibly into the yacht. She had been a brilliant scholar as well. Let me tell you something of this remarkable man.

"Urie Harrison had been born in Johannesburg, South Africa in 1984 to Bourgeoisie parents. His father became an ambassador to China in 1991. When a young boy in China, Urie learned that his great-great grandfather on his mother's side had been Chinese. He learned to fluently read and write Chinese. By the time he had graduated early from high school in 2001, with an IQ of one hundred and sixty. He had learned several dialects of the Chinese. He liked the sub-culture of old Chinese customs, traditions, and legends, and had an understanding of Mao Zedong dictatorship. The same year that he had graduated, his father sent him to England where Urie had studied at Oxford. He majored in history, pre-law, and political science. His father had been selected Ambassador to England since 2008.

"The year of his graduation from Oxford in 2002 with an M.A. in Linguistics, and political science, he went to Cambridge. Urie graduated Magna Cum Laud in 2005 with a J.D. and Ph.D. international law. His father died in 2006 of a brain aneurism, and his widowed mother lived off the comfortable pension and investment income from his father, and from his investments. He spent two years in China doing linguistic research, and studying early Chinese law.

"His parents eventually had become citizens of the UK, and his mother remained in the county after the passing of Mr. Harrison, but she adapted well. Urie had been an only child; his father's health had never been good; but his mother had been a mainstay to Urie. She loved London. In the fall of 2007, Urie married Sun Yen-Ming in the home of her father's friend, Yen Tse Zae, in a suburb of Beijing. Yen worked for the government as a spokesman in international law, and as a counselor to wealthy foreigners like the Harrisons."

"You seem to know a lot about this man," said LeFever.

"I have known him since his days at Oxford. We had become great friends then," said Weeks. "I had taught English literature there for thirteen years, before getting into politics.

"Urie began working with the EU in 2013, as assistant chair of the Humanitarian Aid and Crisis Management; one year later, he became chair of the International Cooperation and Development; in 2014 he ran for president. In an unprecedented move in 2015, the European Union and the European Commission decided, in an overwhelming vote, to have a single president over both. They asked Urie Harrison to be president. He immediately prepared a report on Global Capitalization to stimulate more discussion and to further greater international cooperation open trade. His knowledge of international laws, including maritime law, and his fluency in Chinese, French, Spanish, German, and Russian accentuated his charismatic charm. These were disarming tools. A flaw: he had a tough time with others who had not shared his opinions—'based upon fact,' he would say. Anyone not as intellectual did not become his friend.

"This last year as president, he visited more countries and had spoken at the United Nations. One such visit at the UN early this year, he addressed them with a stirring speech entitled, "Social Implications of Open Markets" and another in that evening, "The Creation and Enforcement of Global Commercial Laws." Standing ovations are common, especially after concluding that speech with, "I dislike referring to any region of the world as *third world*."

UH deplored isolationistic talk, and defended the Euro which was yet viable.

China took over Hong Kong in 1999—his older friend, Joseph Manning, the ambassador to China had helped with the negotiations. He vaguely remembered reading about it at Oxford. The United States under President Carter offered the security contract to the Panama Canal to the Chinese in the late 1970's. What he had liked most was that the Chinese had a foothold in the West. UH also crusaded regularly against nuclear proliferation.

"Welcome back to this historic event." That midafternoon, Urie delivered a passionate speech titled, "The Justification and Obligation for Globalism in Light of Current Events." All intently listened, for under the present conditions, he made sense. "Isolationism is a politically archaic term. We are moving past nation building, un-reciprocation in foreign trade, blatant disregard for international law, unequitable treaties… also, we must end factionalism between extremists on the right or left—in politics, religion, and national issues. This must change. There must be a synergism of ideas before we leave Brussels… On a more positive note, the World Trade Organization is diligently attempting to remove the wrinkles out of unequitable trade by asking certain nations to lift undue sanctions; this morning the World Bank is lifting a few restrictions for lending money; both are at work with struggling nations to help them take a more positive approach for their rightful place in the world community; maritime laws have been redefined, especially in the East; and by the way, the Cold War, which had only buried its head, is finally dying. The proponents of cross-culture ideas on finance, security, and safety are gaining ground. Sciences, technology, and satellite imaging, to mention only a few, are expanding every day, but we could do more.

"Past EU Presidents and members, United States president, especially Nixon and Carter, and yes, President Rowe, have been farsighted in matters of globalization. We must look at a more level playing field, as Rowe said, a few years ago.

"This week will mark itself in human history as an unprecedented international benchmark. For we must, this day, unify against the catastrophic disease, or alien violence, or whatever the hell it is. I favor alien attack because almost a billion people across the globe vanished, yet on a positive note, in the last ten days we have gained more than three million additional children. Once again the human race must be innovative to stabilize our planet. As Chancellor Karlene Schmidt, of Germany, said this morning, 'No one wishes to sit around and mull over this global crises, when there is much work to do.'

"There is no ripple effect, the shock of loss is over," concluded Urie.

Urie received a three minute applause, by most, after he concluded his one and a half hour speech until 3:00 pm.

While the leaders shook hands and said the sincere, and not so sincere, goodbyes, Urie asked Rowe, Weeks, Koskov, Yen, Yucura, Schmidt, LeFever, Jacobs, Rodriquez, and Alberto spend that afternoon in Brussels and to meet with him in that for dinner. They agreed to fly out later that night. UH had not felt that much positive energy since he had been with wife Sun Yen-Ming and their son, William Lee, in the last days during that late summer in China.

Out of the thirty-three points previously considered, the small group of leaders focused on seven:

1. The most gifted scientists, and exceptional technological intellects should meet in Brussels on June 12th, as well as skilled cybersecurity specialists, and military drone experts.

2. They all insisted on uncovering what caused the human losses.

3. Most leaders believed that the danger was not yet over.

4. Religious leaders from all faiths must agree to meet soon to discuss current issues from their particular spiritual point of view.

5. Terrorism should be dealt with forcefully and with swiftness.
6. Marshall Law should be enforced when required, as some smaller nations had already done.
7. Most agreed that local and regional officials are to quell any looting and/or law breaking, and the death penalty should be universal for any killing or murder in such times as these.

UH went home before everyone had left for their hotels. Many were still on the phone calling families or officials in their respective countries. He stood inside the door looking at the last picture taken of his wife and son that he had framed. It has hung the on wall above his couch since he had leased the place. He nostalgically remembered his last visit to China with Sun and William, and how playful and loving Sun could be, and how proud he had been of William. That evening he had been drinking more than he should have, and watching news on television. Missing his family became almost an obsession after work, and almost interfered with his job.

A thought passed through his slightly inebriated mind, and he laughed. "Seriously, what would I have to do to rule the world? Ah, be President of the United States or governor of the world." It didn't make sense, so He laughed. He looked again at the picture. "Sun, I would sell my soul—if I had one. Damn, I would do it even if it killed me. So what..." he said not finishing his thought, and reached for another drink of brandy. "Humans are the end in all. At least, they had been. No they still could be. I could be the top of the chain on a tiny planet. Sun, I miss you terribly."

There was a knock at his door. He composed himself, and raised his voice, "I'm coming." He opened the door, and there was a Chinese man dressed like an ancient priest or shaman.

"Many pardons for disturbing your evening Mr. Harrison," he said in perfect English.

"May I come in?"

"I see no harm in that," UH said. They made the customary bows. Urie asked him in.

"How can I help you?"

"It is I who have come to assist you. I am from Macao."

"How could you help me?"

"Yes. It is my understanding that you have had an interest in the arts of the theurgists from ancient times."

"Yes, but only as a scholar. Who sent you?"

"A mutual friend," said the stranger, closing his eyes while slightly and slowly bowing his head.

"Who's this mutual friend?"

"I am not at liberty to say."

"Look, I am not interested in the mystical, nor am I interested in contacting my wife or son through some séance. What kind of a priest are you?" asked Urie in Chinese.

The man began to speak in Chinese. "No. No séance, but yes, I am here to offer answers to your hidden or secret questions."

UH said, almost slurring his words, "I regret this situation, but I must ask you who this mutual friend is, or I must ask you to leave, for I am not a religious man of any sort."

"I will leave, if you insist, but our friend is from prehistoric times..."

"This makes absolutely no sense," Urie interrupted him.

"Nor am I. This friend has been in human history since the beginning, bringing light to a darkened humanity. You are a historian, who has academic expertise and would be invaluable to his wondrous ways. After all, he can make you a very powerful man. The importance of my visit cannot be underestimated. One thing, I am not an emissary."

"What you say is outrageous. What is it you want with me?" said Urie.

"Nothing more than to prove my genuineness. You have read about those who have transformed physical appearances of themselves or others. Allow me to come closer. You seem nervous. Sit in that chair by the table if you wish." Urie went to the chair, paused, looked again at the priest and then sat down. The stranger slid a chair in front of Urie, and sat down. Calmly the stranger said, "Look into my eyes." Urie's blood shot eyes reluctantly looked back into the eyes of the stranger. Suddenly the eyes of the priest became the eyes of a Bengal Tiger, flickering fire-like eyes. Urie almost tipped his chair backwards in fear. He wondered if he drank too much. He was frightened, but he liked what he was feeling, more stamina, mental acuteness, and a weird sense of power. Nothing like he had felt when first becoming president of the EU with aspirations that reached beyond the EU.

"What have you done?" asked Urie.

"I have fulfilled my purpose." The stranger got up and walked toward the door. He turned, lifted up his hands toward the empty fireplace, and it lit up with a whoosh as though the logs had ignited themselves. The overhead fan began to hum and spin, and Urie's chair began to move in circles. The chair then moved toward his bedroom. He quickly jumped to the couch. He lifted his bottle of brandy and swigged it, and then passed out. When he had awakened on the couch, he looked around for the stranger, but not seeing him, passed the experience off as a terrible dream. Rubbing his head, he looked at the cold hearth, the still fan overhead, and noticed that the chair in which he had been sitting was still in his bedroom.

An eerie feeling came over him. He picked up his glass and bottle and took them to the kitchen.

"It had been a dream," he mused, nodding his head up and down.

Urie noticed that it was almost time to meet with the various leaders at the hotel bar, and hurriedly began to get ready for his meeting, when he heard something and quickly turned, but decided it had been nothing.

"Well, when do you wish to rule this pathetic world?" asked a voice.

"Who are you? How did you get in here?" he asked looking up and down, going from room to room.

"Neither matters, but what does matter is that I can make you absolute ruler of this wretched planet. I was standing there in Beijing two years ago when you had awakened from what you thought was a dream, like this time."

"I must be tired. This is totally incredulous. You don't exist. Of course, I can't see you. This is another dream. I am an atheist for god's sake."

"Stop the gibberish. There is no time. Would you like a little wine?" asked the voice. At that, the bottle of wine on his a shelf uncorked, lifted deliberately as if someone was holding it above the wine glass; wine poured into the glass. The glass lifted in air like someone's hand was actually holding it and bringing it to him. He took the glass of wine.

"Who are you, I demand an answer."

"Very well. I am the mutual friend of you, and the old priest. I am your channel to absolute world rule."

"Now you talk gibberish!"

"I will empower your already brilliant mind. You will outwit, or outmatch any adversary more so in the near future, whether or not the person you confront is political, a religious, or a scholar like yourself. You will have supernatural abilities; I will teach you profound secrets; and I will be your private mentor. For the present, I will appear to you, but no one else will see me.

Astonished, Urie listened as the voice explained in part how this plan would work.

"My word, this is simply unbelievable. World leaders will not relinquish their powers to me."

"Ah, but indeed they will through fear, intimidation, threat of death, or even death. The times are right. All action taken will be preemptive, and everyone will submit to your power, even the hard to convince spiritualists, mystics, radical murderers, and malevolent leaders."

"This all seems surreal," Urie said pacing the floor.

"Listen Urie. I am offering you the very thing you had complained about; the very thing you have worked for so long; and your natural aggravation toward those who just don't understand you—that will be satisfied. This power will bring the world economy into balance, peace will be global, and the disenfranchised will find life more equitable. If ever you are uncertain about any decision, I will be there. Do you accept this power?"

"Yes, but..."

"Yes is sufficient. I will require two covenants: The first is an irrevocable verbal covenant between you and me. I have addressed some points of this agreement minutes ago, and I'm certain that you had understood. Secondly, you will secure a verbal pledge with Israel that will be initially sealed by the death of fifty people including Jews, Christians and Muslims. I say initially because later, thousands of Islamic terrorists, and leaders, as well as Jewish leaders in the Middle East will have to perish in order to carry out this plan. Prime Minister Jacobs must agree to include the removal of the Islamic dome over Solomon's Temple in Jerusalem. The dome is to be placed on the newly reconstructed Al Aqsa Mosque constructed in East Jerusalem, or taken to what they call a holy city in Saudi Arabia. I do not care; I realize that some prior stipulations must be addressed at the time of the drawing up of this particular agreement, but I must insist that this agreement be made, and there must be strict enforcement of it. This will bring lasting peace in this region. Anyone, mind you, who attempts to thwart this covenant will be dealt with immediately and forcefully. When you bring peace to this region, your stature and power will increase. Your fame will reach everyone on Earth. Your new ultra-modern technological equipped office will be more efficient than the CIA or MI6. I will draw in the best high-tech minds to install the latest and most advanced systems in your new offices in Brussels.

Is this agreeable to you?"

"What about..."

"Do you agree?" Chu bellowed.

"Yes." Urie sat down. "Answer me this..."

"I will not answer any questions at this time. Never again question my plans for you. You will answer me. Will you abide by my plans for you?"

"Yes," Urie answered, and when he did, he felt something surge through his blood. His eyes widened as his neck stiffened like when lifting his weights He looked at his hands and arms; they felt youthful again.

"Urie," the voice interrupted Urie's wonder at his unusually found strength and newness, "the binding covenant is in force. From this time forward, you will only use your initials.

"You will be known only as UH, for you are already known by many as UH, and this way others who now meet you might curiously ask what the initials stand for, and you will then have the opportunity to go beyond Urie Harrison, and who he was, to strike up a passing conversation about humanism—but only briefly. For instance, there is only one human race, and we should be one cohesive family, and convince them of great human endeavors by world secular humanists, like those in the International Humanist and Ethical Union, which you are familiar, for you have been their guest speaker many times. Make them sound like a good, middle-of-the-road type of organization by fleetingly referring to their youth program. You know of it, the HEYO. You will offer help to the youth organization.

"When you have your small meeting later, assure each of them that they will receive a call within the next seven days. You will use three days to convince and execute the second agreement I had spoken to you earlier concerning Prime Minister Jacobs.

"Tell Jacobs that you will call him around ten in the morning. By late next week, your office will have access to a new kind of webcam communication. You will have a twenty-four monitor hook-up on your office wall so that you may converse with that many people, if you wish. By the way, a new larger office is, at this time, being constructed for you at the EU headquarters. "

"What do you mean, 'a new kind of webcam communication'?" asked UH.

"It is a highly encrypted form, as is your email. You do not need to know about the encoded form of this advanced technology. Much more cybersecurity will be necessary, but I will have my team working on these programs. One more thing before I leave. I will be referred to as Chu, an ancient name in China."

Chu's voice was gone.

UH looked at his watch and realized that time was nearing for his meeting with the few leaders. He finished grooming, straightened his tie, and grabbed his brief case.

"Gentlemen, how good to see you again. I have chosen this small room for privacy. We are about to calm the fears and anxieties of our constituencies. I will give all of you an opportunity to go back home and give a report on this summit, which includes this meeting. Explain to them that this was the genesis of resolving our global dilemma."

Everyone tried to speak at the same time. UH lifted his hand, "One at a time. Yes, President LeFever."

"This summit has not given us any positive or conclusive information to take back to our countries."

"I'm afraid LeFever is quite right," said Weeks, "in that there isn't a bit of substantial, or any other type of counteractive information either. By that I mean, are we to return to out respective countries to label this worldwide calamity an alien invasion? Pure absurdity."

President Rowe waited to see if someone else had wanted to speak, and then offered, "Let's face it, this catastrophe has shaken the world, whether or not it is an alien invasion. I don't like that this supposed summit lasted just one day," he looked at UH, "ok two meetings. Now, we are to return to our citizens and tell them that maybe this or that happened."

"Does anyone else have anything to add?" No one did. "I can only say that the magnitude of this misfortune will provide us with more time. We can simply say that the summit was not able to come to a determination, and to be more prudent, we decided to teleconference or webinars with each other as we learn of anything new. This way we can all go home, and I will be in touch. I truly believe that within three to seven days, we will have a breakthrough for our peoples."

Alber from the UN, reminded them, "I have a major responsibility to look out for the less fortunate countries. My phone will not stop ringing, I sure like yours," he looked around the table, "and it is making me go mad. I hope President Harrison has something for us sooner than later."

As they departed, all felt the pressure from their citizens, the uncertainty in their minds, and the anger at whatever or whoever did this horrendous act of taking a twelve percent of the planet—somewhere.

As they left the meeting, Koskov, who served in the Russian Duma, said to LeFever, "I don't trust Rowe. He is weak-willed toward his external and internal enemies; talks from both sides of his mouth; and tell me, how he had won a second term? All he mentioned that made sense, 'We missed the G-20 summit for this?', and then sat down at our table."

Yucura from Brazil said, "You may speak about Rowe, but let me remind you how European leaders succumb to refugees as though it is really a way to produce jobs and bring talent to their countries, when it actually brings chaos and mayhem, more tax increases, free medical care and education expenses paid for by the governments who already feel financial burdens."

LeFever cut in, "Enough of this negativity, for all of this will change for the better, and for all world leaders as well. Our work forces have been depleted to some degree, that should help our economies. Now England may not pull out of the EU. You heard most of this kind of talk today. Many in the EU do not want out of it.

"One man said today that in one way or another, all of the past political problems will vanish like fog that evaporates in the morning sun. Perhaps we all share some blame, and we will be coming to our senses finding new solutions."

No one said another anything else; they each packed up their brief cases; and said goodbye to each other.

The Plans

Urie went back to his place. He sat on the couch and threw his brief case on a nearby chair. Usually at this time of the day, he was often tired, but not today. In fact, he was ready to get to work. Tomorrow he would call Jacobs in Israel to begin his plan for peace. Harmony, worldwide is the humanist's dream. He took out his iPad and began bullet-pointing ideas for his talk with Jacobs in the morning.

At seven that evening, the phone rang. "Hello, this is UH."

"This is Weeks."

"Yes. How may I help you?"

"Well, we have been good friends, I'd say, for nearly fifteen years since you were at Oxford, and this whole affair has me questioning my own senses." There was a pause.

"Go on Andrew."

"It's that I can't wrap my head around this catastrophe. It seems as though every religious sect or cult, political party, and even agnostics have some explanation. Do you think that we should ignore their speculations, and wait, as you had suggested?"

"Andrew, I believe that it is paramount that we not enter any kind of definitive dialogue for a short period of time. Time, at this point is on our side. I will keep you well-informed of any occurrences or developments."

"All right. Thank you for your time. As I have said many times, I trust you, UH."

"Andrew, I have always respected your judgment. Goodnight."

"Goodnight."

There was a shrewdness in his tone, that sounded secure and powerful, but with calm that came over UH. He was beginning to like this new role. He always had a vision, or sixth sense that one day he would play a major role in world affairs. He looked at his large apartment, but thought of a better place on the Mediterranean. He walked around the living room with his head ever so slightly tilted up, with a smirk on his face. Life was about to get even better.

He looked at the picture of his deceased wife and son, but didn't feel the downheartedness as before, but he didn't question the change. He was more invigorated, mentally sharp, and the virility he had seemed to have been losing—was back.

The next morning he called Prime Minister Jacobs of Israel with the plan Chu had given him.

"Prime Minister, this is UH. I know that this call is a half hour early; is that a problem?"

"Actually no, because two cabinet members were unable to meet me this morning."

"Good. When we meet, I have a radical proposal for peace, beginning in Tel Aviv. I will be rather blunt when we talk, for the world situation demands that sort of approach. I have several things I will ask you to do in a specific order in which I give." Jacobs just listened. "Don't be alarmed. You will see how well we will progress through these events. The outcome will be peace. I will explain more when we meet how, and how important it is that no one interrupts my plan, which I will clarify to you, for I need your blessing. I must stress that it is imperative that we move through these actions quickly—in less than seven days.

May I visit with you this late this afternoon or evening?"

"Sure, what time?"

"Say about 5:30."

"That will be fine. Are you in the area?" asked Jacobs.

"No, I'm in Brussels. I will fly in early this afternoon."

"All right then. Looking forward to our meeting. Always looking for a new peace plan."

UH contacted his friend Benjamin Singer, a wealthy Israeli businessman, who lived in the same luxury apartment complex. One day Benjamin had explained to UH that he traveled to Israel at least three times a month, and that he was flying to Jerusalem that particular morning.

Benjamin also works as a Senior Economist for the European Union.

"Good morning Ben, this is UH."

"Yes, I'm rather busy packing to fly out of here for a meeting in Jerusalem."

"I remember you telling me about that. I was wondering if I might catch a lift with you. How long will you be staying?" asked UH.

"Probably three days, and yes of course you may travel with me, but I leave here in less than an hour."

"I will be ready. See you at 10:00," said UH. "Oh, if we depart the airport at 11:00, we should get in at about 3:45 at the Ben Gurion International Airport. Right?"

Ben said, "Yes. I will meet you downstairs. Our cab will be prompt. He knows me."

Last week, UH mentioned to Ben that he would be looking for a townhouse on the Mediterranean, and that he would be doing some world traveling in the next year.

Ben asked, "Are you be traveling to Jerusalem for the EU?"

"In a major way, but not entirely," said UH.

At 5:33 pm, UH was escorted into the office of Jacobs. Jacobs stood and walked around his desk to shake UH's hand. Soon they dispensed with the politeness that these meeting required. Urie thought that Jacobs looked a little older, grayer hair, less of it, and a sadder face, although Jacobs had tried to hide the tiredness he had felt by smiling more. His slightly overweight body was slower because of the fatigue and stress. This was his second term as Prime Minister. He had served in the Israeli Army for fifteen years, attaining the rank of Colonel. He had served in the Knesset, was elected President of the body, and then elected Prime Minister.

"Urie, I am glad to see you."

"I am happy to see you, but from now on, I would like to be referred to as UH."

"Certainly," said Jacobs, but quickly changed the subject. "With the current world events, it seems that terrorism in Israel, believe it or not, has not been a big issue. A little unrest, yes. At first Muslims thought that Israelis had created the turmoil—thank god for television. Everyone saw what has happened and are worried. Human nature will stick its ugly head up sooner or later."

Sooner will be the case, Chu said into UH's mind.

"What is it that you really wanted to talk to me about? I might add, you came here the very next day. I'm impressed."

5:43 pm and Jacobs's phone rang. "This is Alon, what is it? What? When? Anyone injured or killed? Oh my god." Jacobs listened. "All right, keep me up to date." He paused, took a deep breath, then looked at UH. "Well that was short lived. I just found out that that at least thirty-three people, at a crowded restaurant in Jerusalem had been killed—just minutes ago.

"Al Jazeera had broadcasted two days ago that some Muslims believe that Allah had caused the global catastrophe, and that they would begin again to support ISIS, Hamas, Al Qaida, and the PLO. Peace lasted for thirteen days. Here we go again," Alon said throwing his arms up.

UH waited for the right time to explain his plan. "Alon, may I have a drink?"

"Yes, I keep a good brandy, that is what you prefer, correct?" said Alon.

"Yes, thank you." UH replied.

The two men sipped their drink for a minute or two, and then Jacobs said, "I'm sick of the cat and mouse killing all the time. Since I was a boy—killing, killing, killing. We have, perhaps, the best security in the world, and still they keep this provocation by any cunning means. My people are tired of jihad, and other Israeli terrorists, and so am I."

"Alon, my goal is to bring peace, even if it means by drastic measures."

"Maybe it's time for a shake-up, or extreme measures. What do you propose?" asked Alon.

"This is going to sound radical, but maybe that is what the Middle East needs. First and foremost, this plan must only be shared with a few key advisors," UH warned.

"Is this plan sanctioned by the EU?" questioned Alon.

Chu said, *Tell him yes, but that it is a security issue between only a limited group of individuals.*

"Yes, in a way, but I'd rather not say, yet, I understand your consternation and hesitation. We must, however, move with haste."

"What is it you are suggesting? I am open to just about anything," said Jacobs.

"Like I said, it will be dangerous, deadly to some, but that topic is nothing new."

"What are you referring to for god's sake?" Jacobs asked.

UH said, "The Dome of the Rock over the temple mount must be removed," at that Jacobs went to say something, but UH cut him off. "Wait a minute," UH raised his palm toward Jacobs who had tried to get a word in again. "I have a plan for you that will let Israel, and other peaceful individuals here, but more specifically you, to escape criticism and more violence, that far exceeds the likes of the successors of Yasser Arafat, or any of his kind."

"Violence has been like a cancer for my seventy years. Peace talks and cease fires have not cured it. Even modern security has failed." Jacobs cried out.

Tell him that natural events will loosen the dome tremendously, so much that it must be removed for safety concerns. Actually it will almost fall into the temple on the Foundation Rock. The event will bring down the Al Aqsa Mosque to a rubble. Also, tell him that minimally, three Muslim lives will be lost, three Christian lives will be lost, and one Israeli life will be lost. Explain that work will begin immediately. This will please Rabbi Peres who has worked with Muslims for years, to no avail, for a peaceful solution to the removal of the dome. Insist that Peres must not appear too enthusiastic for peaceful Muslims. You will tell him to begin now to put his chosen men in place. This will happen tomorrow," said Chu. "*There will be a total of fifty people to die in the earthquake in Old Jerusalem. He will find out soon enough.*

UH shared this information as though it was his idea.

"How can you predict such an event?" demanded Jacobs.

"It is unexplainable at this time even to me, but I would suggest that you privately contact the men who will be in charge of various operations. This event will commence at 3:00 am in Tel Aviv. This pre-information will help you be prepared and to act swiftly," said UH.

"This all seems so preposterous. You said that this will bring peace. The first knee jerk response from Muslims, and in a many countries, will be that we detonated small explosives to bring down the mosque and loosen the dome," complained Jacobs.

"After the site inspectors don't find any incendiary evidence or evidence of bomb residue, Israel will not be implicated," responded UH. "You will have to put up with a twenty four hour period of anger, and by then, Muslims will blame the earthquake, for earthquakes have happened many times before in that area."

He must understand that a lasting peace will be the eventual outcome, and that the next two to three months will prove that he, and you, are geniuses. Remind him of what Rabbi Peres has said for years, that Isaiah prophesied that the temple will become a house of prayer for all nations. He should like that. Assure him of his safety, if he cooperates, said Chu.

"I assure you that no one will stop the progression of this plan that begins at 3:00 am. It will be a 2.0 magnitude on seismographs. It will take place in the Silicon Wadi as a decoy, and will not cause any damage. Almost immediately, what will seem like a foreshock, and then, a 6.3 magnitude earthquake will do great damage in East Jerusalem at the temple area," said UH.

"How do you know all of this?" barked Jacobs.

"I know that you will be protected, Israel will be at peace, all radical terrorists will seek peace, and the world will be at peace. Doesn't that have a nice sound—peace, peace, peace?" asked UH.

"UH, I am an old man, and I would like peace to come on my watch. I have known and worked with you for many years, and I tend to trust you, for we need peace, but you are asking a lot." Jacobs said shaking his head, pulling at his whitish beard, and looking down at his desk. "I will call a few men and give them a heads-up," concluded Jacobs. He added, "I am worried."

Jacobs made seven calls to men he thoroughly trusted and told them of the coming 3:00 am events.

"You sound troubled Alon," said his closest friend Hassam.

The Risks

At 3:00 am, Jacobs was already dressed and waiting. Ten minutes later the phone rang "Good morning this is Alon," Jacobs cleared his throat.

"Sir, this is Hassam. I was just told that The Silicon Wadi had a 2.0 tremor on the Richter scale, but in Old Jerusalem, the temple dome has been badly damaged and loosened. The Dome of the Rock, almost but fell into the temple. The gold leaf held it from entirely cracking apart and causing extreme destruction. The Al-Aqsa Mosque is in ruins, and it looks as though dozens of people are dead. In three to four hours, I'm sure we will have many more deaths."

"I too felt the quake. I will contact Iman Amed, and probably Iman Azimi in a few hours," said Jacob. "You know well, we will be blamed."

The phone rang again. "This is Amed. Have you heard of the killing in East Jerusalem?"

"Yes, just minutes ago. The Silicon Wadi had tremors in Tel Aviv, and they told me of many deaths in East Jerusalem," said Jacobs.

"I am heading to the temple area in about an hour or so. When I assess the damage, I will call you," said Amed.

"Thank you Amed."

Jacobs began to think the worst. He was fearful that his second term would not end well. What would his family and friends think if word got out about UH and his plan? His phone rang again. "This is Alon."

It was 7:00 am. "This is Colonel Abel Hassam."

"Yes Colonel."

"I'm afraid that the dome will have to be removed as soon as possible, because if it falls, the dome will be damaged beyond repair, and perhaps, even some of the inner contents like the rock itself."

Jacobs said, "Iman Amed will be there soon. Get his advice or whatever, and then call me."

"Yes sir."

Later Jacobs called The Mamilla Hotel. "May I have room 333? Thank you."

"Good afternoon, this is UH."

"This is Jacobs. You were absolutely correct. Everything is falling down."

"I knew it would. I understand that the Dome of the Rock is about to fall in, and that the Al Aqsa Mosque is now rubble. Don't forget my promise: no one will stop your progress to peace."

"I am still puzzled, and worried, but I will keep you informed. How long will you be staying in Jerusalem?" asked Jacobs.

"I had planned on being in the city for three days. I will fly back to Brussels on Thursday," said UH.

"My cell is ringing, I'll talk to you later." Jacobs hung up.

Chu's voice said, *Good afternoon.*

UH looked around and said, "Chu, what happens next?"

I will tell you in the morning, for I have work to do in Tel Aviv and then back here to Jerusalem, the City of Peace. Try to get some sleep, for in the morning new measures will be taken. Remember that I had said that three Muslims, three Christians, and one Israeli would be killed—that takes place tomorrow, in the late morning.

By 8:30, UH had dressed, eaten, and began working on his I-Pad. His cell rang.

"Good morning UH. This is Russling from your new office in Brussels. We are combining two offices to make one large office as requested, but some of the technological and digital equipment won't arrive for four days." UH listened, his face frowned wondering who told Russling to expand his office. Then he remembered what Chu had said.

"Russling, just keep up the good work, and I'll see you on Thursday or Friday."

UH was beginning to wonder about Chu. Had he called Russling under some cloak or disguise? He thought that Chu was mystical, but after talking to Russling, he concluded that Chu was more powerful or tremendously potent. It made him rethink his involvement—but not too much, for he remembered his first covenant, and the very thoughts gave him a chill.

"Good morning UH," said Chu, and at that moment, he appeared to UH. He didn't look Chinese; he looked like a tall, handsome, well-groomed man from head to shoes. He was well-manicured with dark hair, and a small thin mustache. His suit was silk, modern, expensive, and quite fashionable.

"Good morning Chu. I must admit, I'm surprised by how Italian you look" said UH.

"I tried to look more Spanish," said Chu, "but let's get on with our meeting. Dire events will take place today. Three Christians, three Muslims, and one Israeli are to die. The Christians and secular Muslims will be conversing about the possibility of a third temple being constructed, and two of them feared that the PLO finally brought down the Al Aqsa Mosque, like Arafat had wanted to do to incite a global jihad against Israel. One of them believed that the Israeli government finally had it demolished. Christians believe it will set off the rapture of their church people. President Rowe had suggested, a third temple would provide a viable option for all three religions. He said, 'After all, there are still artifacts in the rubble of the temple since the Roman times, but no thanks to the Islamists who thought that they had retrieved them all through the years hoping to prove, in their minds only, that Jews hadn't really lived there. They forget the science of archaeology, historical records, and that they were the last of the three monotheistic religions—the youngest brother who feels neglected, unwanted, and are still throwing a tantrum through mayhem and murder.' Sometimes Rowe surprises me.

"There are museum pieces throughout the world that could be used in the third temple. Personally, I don't give a damn what they build, tear down, or reconstruct. The seven men will die at the same time in a café in the Jerusalem's Old City. Someone will walk in and toss a grenade into the small room where they will be meeting late this morning."

"I take it that you are handling all of these matters," said UH.

"For now," Chu said.

"I'm not doing anything today, providing that Jacobs or Russling don't need me," said UH.

Chu said, "Russling will call back with good information: your office is progressing better than he had expected; the items he had mentioned will come in on Thursday, and your twenty-four new monitors will be installed on Friday like I had said."

"Jacobs will be meeting with Iman Amed in Jerusalem this early evening," added Chu.

"Chu, it looks as though I have little to do," said UH.

"That will all change soon, for you will have a greater role in the coming days, probably in August. You will eventually be the face and voice to the threats that must be made, as well as ordering the pre-emptive actions that will transpire, and you will personally witness some deaths.

"I will appear once in a while as necessary and will act as your personal financial advisor and consultant. You will say that you had hired me because of my vast experience, not purely because of my expertise in other matters. This will accomplish two things: it will seem to be a correct choice on your part, and it will make you look more authoritative. I will explain this more fully as events unfold, and I will create a pseudo name and personality. I must leave for Tel Aviv; I will see back here in Jerusalem, but not until tomorrow." After that, Chu was gone.

UH thought about the possibilities, for they seemed exciting with unfolding potential, un-ending influence and control, and it seemed as though, this was his end of life struggle for power.

The next day, UH, Jacobs, Amed, and others met at the site.

"Good morning Prime Minister," said Amed.

Jacobs said, "Good morning, at least I think it is still morning."

The two men stared at the workers for a moment then Amed said, "You and Rabbi Perez must not be too upset, but the Christians are eagerly awaiting a trumpet sound. Anyway, this time the dome will have to be moved. The dome on the Al Aqsa Mosque, for all speculative use, was destroyed. On the temple mosque, it seems as though that dome has a crack on the east side of it, and some of the gold leaf has lifted up or peeled, and it is damaged in other ways, such as the bolts have loosened. Nevertheless, it has been loosened before at that same place during other earthquakes. You can readily see that the old Al Aqsa Mosque is gone. It looks as though the quake had only been centered around the immediate vicinity of the Dome of the Rock which is strange to me." Jacobs merely listened, trying to think of a good reason why it didn't go further into Old Jerusalem. "Why it didn't extend more than one hundred yards in any direction." Amed continued, "This is peculiar. Makes no sense. No bombs. No fire. Just destruction. What do you think?" Jacobs shrugged his shoulders intently looking at the workers.

Jacobs said, "This kind of thing has happened before with no damage to the dome. Now we have damage. I can't explain it. One of my engineers said that years of such tremors and quakes must have weakened the structure." He added, "The dome on the temple must be carefully removed."

Amed said, "I have several engineers from Dubai flying in today. I'm sure you won't mind if they work with your engineers. This kind of cooperation will be necessary for obvious reasons." Jacobs knew of the unrest of fundamentalist Muslims stirring in the streets.

At the same time, their cells rang. They received the same information. A small café had a small bomb, or grenade, thrown into a meeting room in the back, near a storage room. Seven people were killed.

Chu had been correct, UH thought.

The engineers worked together and agreed that the dome had to be removed and repaired. They took it down in large sections to protect the dome and the walls of the temple, after building supports had been constructed on top of the temple and outside its walls. They could see that the east wall had also weakened. No infidel was allowed to work inside to construct the supports. As they finished their initial construction work, great cranes began to remove a large section of the dome. Another aftershock occurred, as they had thought might happen. They began to take the main piece of the dome and swing it in the air away from the temple. Everyone held their breath as it slowly came to a stop, for the Holy Rock lay just below. They finally swayed it down to the ground, setting it next to the destroyed mosque. Muslims brought large tarps and boards to cover the opening over the rock.

Many Muslims, gathering all morning and late afternoon, were praying and crying out loud with shaking arms and fists waving. Jewish radicals simply watched and waited.

Jacobs said, "I must get back to my office. I have just received a third call. Keep me up to date on this massive clean-up, or whatever you decide that is important, even if it's late tonight."

"I will. The Islamic Council will be meeting tonight or in the morning. There are talks now as to what we should do. Everyone has an opinion. I will call you," said Amed.

Jacobs' cell rang. "This is Alon."

"This is Hassam. I'm in a police vehicle up the road. The body count around the temple and mosque came to forty-nine. We all agree, even Amed and his party agree, that there had been no foul play. The engineers are working together, or doing the best they can under the circumstances. Amed has tried to calm some of the radicals and especially the Fundamental Muslim Palestinians, like Hamas and PLO, who are complaining that someone, most likely the Israelis, had specialized weapons that could cause this horrible damage, yet these tremors are nothing new to this area, yet they still suspect foul play and claim that the Kach movement were behind this incident, yet that group had been banned in 1948 by Israel. When they had been told this again, they claim that a small group of the

Kach movement members are secretly meeting today of course, the toothless tiny group, plotted the entire attack in the Old City of East Jerusalem. The movement has no fangs. They, needless to say, deny it."

"Amed will calm the Muslims down. He has help: Amin Azimi and Amin Ashraf. I must admit, I too am at a loss," said Jacobs.

"Hold on. There's a fight down there, and on the rubble of the Al Aqsa Mosque. Let me get closer. Amed has been hurt. Someone stabbed him. Radical Muslims are arguing with fundamentalist Muslims, and some are wielding knives. Hold on. Here is Captain Isaac."

There was a long pause. "Isaac said that the arguing had been over the disaster; who had been to blame, and questioning the meaning of all this; then suddenly, it turned violent.

"Hold on sir," said Hassam to Jacobs. "Word was just given to me that Amed has been rushed to Shaare. I am sure that he will recover. Sir, I was told that the Islamic Council will not meet tonight, because of what happened to Amed. I will call you if anything else major happens."

"Very good colonel, thank you," said Jacobs.

The night did not pass quietly. Several groups of individuals talked, shouted in anger, and most were in saddened despair. Police drove through the Old City throughout the night into Wednesday morning, when another shift began. The Muslim workers found a body in a crumbled heap of stone—the dead man's foot had been noticed. The dead body count reached fifty.

General Goodman reviewed the scene, read the statistics, and read some of the complaints. He met with Colonel Hassam to compare notes.

"I don't care what the Islamic Council decides; this was an earthquake. The only suspicion I have, is why was it so concentrated? It was like a mini Epi center under the mosque, and under the Dome of the rock," said General Goodman.

Hassam said, "I get a little anxious when the groups meet for an Islamic Council."

"Why is that?" asked Goodman.

"I guess the paranoia that some of them exhibit. Their constant references to Israeli control over their so called Palestine ownership. It is historically our land." He waved an uplifted hand, "Forgive me, I tend to go off on a tangent. I guess that we will find out what is on their minds by lunch time," said Hassam

"You only have two hours to wait," said Goodman. "I better call Jacobs to inform him of the new body count, and give him my evaluation of the situation."

At the same time in the Mamilla Hotel, Chu and UH were meeting

"Would you like another cup of coffee," Chu asked UH.

"No, I've had enough caffeine. I'd rather press on with our conversation."

"All right," said Chu, "tomorrow you will be heading home. When you arrive at your place, before you unpack, call President Rowe, and tell him that you tend to agree with his proposal for a third temple. Feel him out. Most people don't know that he never intended to do anything with a third temple. Tell him that you just got back from Jerusalem, and that the situation there in quite tenuous. Assure him that his input is important. Tell him that Rabbi Peres will be in contact with him. I must admit that his self-importance is trying. I will clarify later as to your expanding role.

"There is a more pressing situation here. The Islamic Council is meeting, and Imam Ziv, a former underling of Arafat, is causing consternation to the group. Listen as I call him."

Chu speaking in Arabic, "Ziv, I understand that you are on a break from the meeting. If someone is near you, please excuse yourself for the most important call."

"Who is this?"

"I have a message for you. I suggest that you do not hang up the phone, it is hard on the heart." Ziv attempted to hang up, but as Chu spoke Ziv's heart began to race; his breathing became labored; beads of perspiration formed on his forehead. "Calm down Ziv. If you follow my instructions, you will live." There was silence.

Imam Ziv was calculating the risk of hanging up.

"Don't do it, for you will be dead before you hit the blue carpeting beneath you."

UH listened intently.

"What do you want?" asked Ziv.

"I want you to shut your mouth, and agree with Amed. Is that understood?"

"Yes," Ziv said wiping his brow.

"I'll be watching you," said Chu.

Ziv looked at his cell to see who called. It read, *UNKNOWN*.

Chu looked at UH. "That was quite easy. Once in a while this happens with a man who changes his course from agitator to one who lives with some degree of wealth and prestige—they want to live." Chu tilted his head back and chuckled—his own peculiar chortle.

UH said, "You speak excellent Chinese, which I understand, but I didn't know that you spoke Arabic."

"My friend," said Chu, "I am able to speak any language on this planet. This will be a bit different for you. I am giving you a new ability. You may speak in English to a man who speaks another language, but he will hear the words in his own language. When he answers you in his language, you will hear only English. This applies to any language or dialect. Do you comprehend?"

"Yes. That is amazing," said UH.

"UH, this ability will also help you eaves drop on conversations as you choose, even in international meetings. This is a powerful ability I give to you. You will have an opportunity to use it soon."

UH was shocked.

Chu continued, "Our work here will not be done by tomorrow, at least initially, but still, we will leave in the morning. Ben will be calling you today to explain that he is leaving on Thursday. We will be landing in Brussels at 9:16 pm." Chu looked out of the window of UH's hotel room. "Well the Islamic Council is finishing up, should I say, arguing down. They all agree on rebuilding the Al Aqsa Mosque. Most agree on placing the repaired dome back on the temple. There are two who wish to move the rock and the dome to a new, larger, and extravagantly Rebuilt the sacred mosque, like the Al Aqsa Mosque. This will take serious negotiations, but they will not move the Foundation Stone, as Israelis call it. I shall leave you for now. There is a problem with Ziv."

Thursday, at 9:16 pm, UH landed at the Brussels Airport. He arrived home at 10:30 pm. It was late, but he called James Rowe and told him that his idea of third temple was growing legs. He unpacked a few things, turned on the television, poured a drink of brandy, and sat down to watch the news.

"Israel is still in the news tonight. Imam Ziv was found dead in his home by his wife. He died of an apparent heart attack said a spokesman. He was with his wife at the time of death. His life in politics began when his was a young man. He had met Yasser Arafat during a demonstration in the Old City. He had believed strongly in a Palestinian state. Over the years, especially after Arafat's death, his views had softened in public. He liked President Clinton. Nevertheless, he has remained vocal especially following the earthquake in East Jerusalem. He was insisting that negotiations were off the table. He said yesterday, 'Repair the damage to the temple, specifically the dome and walls, and then rebuild the Al Aqsa Mosque. In other words, all must return to the same conditions, and we will continue our supervision.' Iman Ziv was seventy-seven."

UH surmised that Chu had remained firm to correct a situation with Ziv. He thought of the new power he had been given by Chu to understand languages he had never known before. *What exactly was Chu up to in Jerusalem*? he thought, and then UH went to bed.

The next morning at 8:30 am, when he was reflecting on the tedious negotiations that were still needed in Jerusalem, the phone rang.

"This is UH."

"Hello, this James Rowe."

"Good morning, Mr. President. How may I help you?"

"Pardon the time of this call, but I understand that you are working with all parties in Jerusalem concerning the earthquake that took down the mosque and damaged the gold dome on the temple."

"Yes," UH said hesitantly. "I was there when the quake happened. It was a rated as a 6.0 but all seems quiet and appears to be progressing."

"Well we have a few earthquakes, especially in California." UH took a deep breath. "You know, I have been interested in Israel building a third temple, not like the one in Brazil, but rather like the actual original temple," Rowe shared.

"That is a remote option, but the cost would be more than four hundred and fifty million dollars."

"There are a lot of people who agree with me, and the cost would be attained because of the wealthy Jews, and billionaires who look for such causes. What do you think?"

"Mr. President, it is not what I think. It's what Israel wishes to do. Wouldn't you agree?"

"You are right. Perhaps I'll call Jacobs sometime next week to float that idea again. The time seems to be right for such a thing."

"Good idea," *No so much* thought UH.

"Thank you for your time today," said Rowe.

UH said, "Have a good day Mr. President."

"Good day," said Rowe.

Negotiations

UH entered his new large office that was in disarray. Russling told him that it was a combined two and a half offices into one larger office. He said, "It is just shy of eleven meters wide and nineteen meters long."

"What is a half office," asked UH.

"Oh, it was a toilette and storage room," he answered.

"Where is my toilette?"

"Sir, we are constructing one for your private use at the end of the hall which you will enter from the back of this room on the left side. It is actually part of the end of the hallway, and that will give a nice size toilette." said Russling. "Your office will be done this evening, with minor tweaking on Saturday. The twenty-four, forty-two inch monitors are downstairs with your computers, speakers, and other items Eduardo wanted you to have. Your forty-two inch monitor for your desk is also downstairs. I hope that you approve the desk, files, and other décor.

"I did know that there was a highly specialized computer system technologist who is putting everything together so that everything will be integrated." He looked at a list in his pocket. "Yes, he will make sure that the encryption, Prism, and something else, of which I don't have an inkling as to how to properly put these things together. Does that make sense to you?" asked Russling.

"I'm quite certain that Eduardo knows what he is doing," said UH.

"I agree," said Russling. "Eduardo had contended with the technician about how things should be placed, set up, and that there would be no slip-ups. In fact, he fired that one and hired a new technician, but with the same five-man team."

"You saw Eduardo?" asked UH.

"No, I've never met him. The technicians talked to him over the phone several times, as I had." Chu said, *I am next to you UH. Let's take a walk.*

UH said, "Russling, I am going out to get a bite of food as it is almost noon."

"Of course, I'll see you later this afternoon," said Russling.

A taxi took Chu and UH to UH's apartment. Once inside, Chu appeared to UH, and the two sat down in the living room.

Chu began, "I had told you that your office would be ready today, and before midnight, it will; however, you will not be working there until Monday. I have work for you tonight and tomorrow. There is much turmoil in the world that I must settle, or shall I say, put an end to it. Let me explain: tonight we need to make some phone calls; tomorrow, we will make more phone calls; and we must speak with a leader in East Jerusalem." Chu saw the look on UH's face.

"Don't worry we will complete everything from your apartment."

"Chu, I will not question anything, but I am curious, and I can't wait to learn."

"It's just about time to make our first call. There is an Iman Ashraf who is picking up where Ziv had left off, which I knew would happen, but we must convert his thinking. This weekend will be the last time that we deal with one person at a time. You will understand more tomorrow."

Chu picked up the phone. "By the way, no one can trace my calls. I've taken care that issue, even for you on land line or mobile.

"Good afternoon. I'm calling for Iman Ashraf," Chu said in perfect Arabic.

"This is he," said Ashraf.

"I have a proposition for you: take a different position than Ziv had," said Chu.

"Ziv is dead, and I've taken up the same cause."

"I'm quite aware that Ziv is dead. Do not try me," said Chu.

Ashraf raised his voice, "No one tells me what to do. Who is this?"

"Oh, but I am trying to tell you what to do. There are two things that I would like you to consider. First, you will side with the Sunni leader who wants to build a new mosque where the Al Aqsa Mosque had stood, and you will do as I ask, or you will suffer the same fate as Ziv," said Chu.

"No. You cannot mean this." Without warning Ashraf began to perspire, and his heart began pounding. There was only quietness as he slipped to the floor. Ashraf was dead.

"What did he say?" asked UH.

"He said no, and died. The next call will be to a secular Muslim, Solomon Zarif. He is one of two who had wish to remove the rock in the temple to a new location, perhaps in the rebuilt, but luxurious, Al Aqsa Mosque, and then place the repaired gold leaf dome on top of it. This is something Rowe had hinted at, and what many world leaders wouldn't mind, even if concessions are made to Muslims in Israel and around the world. Jacobs wants the Foundational Stone to remain in the temple. Extreme Jewish radicals like the Kach Movement had also wanted that."

"You will make this call—with my help. Use your name."

"Hello this is Zarif."

"Good afternoon, this is UH," he said, in English, but Arabic is what Zarif heard. "I have a proposition for you that I believe would help you on the Islamic Council. I have reviewed several proposals for building a new mosque." UH shared the ideas Chu had given to him.

Zarif said, "This all sounds interesting, but the Israelis must make good faith concessions, for the Golan Heights and East Jerusalem. They must be willing to keep our stewardship rights over the temple, and of course, the Al Aqsa Mosque, and to expand municipal services. There are other points for discussions, but I think that we could at least sit down and discuss these issues. I will explain this to the Islamic Council. Most do not want a compromise such as this."

UH said, "I think that you will be surprised. I'll set up a time for us all to meet in Brussels. This sounds good to me. I will contact Prime Minister Jacobs, President Rowe, and others who will go along with this meeting and support some of your proposals. I will contact you soon."

Chu looked at UH. "We have work to do tonight. We will call three members of the Islamic Council who are more fundamentalist, and eliminate the three. This is what will be necessary around the globe to rein in those who oppose secular humanism and central control by you."

CNN: "Late evening, three Islamic Council members died of apparent heart attacks."

Chu said, "The loss of Ziv, Ashraf, and these three, should make this council fall in line, or they will, at least, listen to Zarif."

"Chu that is impressive," said UH.

"I'm off to visit South America. It will be easier than the Middle East to tether," said Chu. "I will be back by eleven a.m. At that time, you and I will make calls to a few world leaders."

Zarif called most of members of the Islamic council to set up a tentative meeting in Brussels. He had learned that five members had died. This made some of them eager to attend. They had no idea what was going on, but they did not want to die. Some felt that the deaths had been supernatural, and kept it to themselves. The meeting was set up for the first Wednesday in June.

Saturday, Chu came to UH at eleven a.m.

"On Monday, I am going to make calls to both Yucura in Brazil with his cabinet, and Cortes in Argentina, and his cabinet. Today we will contact Leaders in Chile, Columbia, and Bolivia. We will simply warn them to comply with our demands, and if they do not, death, obviously will befall on most of them, from their cabinets down through military generals in a matter of seconds. Many of their family members will perish as well." Chu continued, "Any factions like drug lords, will have their leaders destroyed in a swift eradication, and in a systematic fashion.

"To bring peace to the world, there must be a central leader, and that is you. Most leaders refuse to simply relinquish authority. They like the power and the money. So, I will simply offer each leader an opportunity to fall in line with our plan for peace. Many have grown into their powerful, or took it with force, and now lead with impunity, as if nothing can harm them because of the armed followers or some super power's military alliance. If that person refuses, instant death will come to all who are in his cabinet, all who align with him, and this includes his generals who support him." Chu concluded, "Within a few months the world will be yours."

"This all seems surreal, but it is very enticing and exciting," said UH.

By night fall, South America was wailing for its dead, and they remained in a quandary as to what had happened, and could not figure out who had done such a criminal act. Each country in South America had received an email or phone call that simply said: Stand down. Further instructions are forthcoming. On Sunday, all thirteen countries received Chu's ultimatum by phone or email. Those who had still refused, lost more leaders and their families. By Monday morning the remaining leaders had agreed to the terms that Chu put forth. Seventy-three leaders and their cabinets, generals and many of their family members died. When world heard the news about South America, the consensus was that aliens were now killing leaders.

"What happened in South America shook the earth again in less than two weeks," said President LeFever at a press conference. He echoed many western leaders. It had become clear after presidents to drug lords in cartels died in unison.

On Tuesday morning, UH had many calls. The callers were concerned that all the emails were untraceable, and that the phone calls (that Chu and UH had made) were not traceable either.

"Whoever called," the President of Brazil complained, that person knew every dialect in South America."

At the United Nations on Tuesday, a special Security Council meeting was called. They all decided to acquiesce to the demands made by the caller, but that did not convince some of their member nations.

"This is UH."

"This is Andrew Weeks. I am very concerned that whoever is calling and emailing these demands, is asking them to acquiesce to you. Why you?" UH thought for a minute. "To be frank, I just do not know. Perhaps, it is because of the ongoing work I'm doing in the Middle East."

"Well, I had to give you a call, my friend. This is odd to me, yet again. No one seems to fathom why this is falling on your shoulders. But, of course, it could be because of your efforts in Israel. In any case, I had to call. If this situation must fall on someone's shoulders, I am glad it is yours, and not someone like Rowe."

"Thank you Andrew. Have a good day."

Chu appeared. "UH, my, my, the phone calls you had this morning. I must say that you did very well. The UN Security Council is expediting this matter. The General Assembly has just agreed, one hundred and ninety to three, to funnel all requests, questions, and concerns to Brussels. We are making progress. If the three need further persuasion, I will accommodate them.

"This episode in South America has softened Central America, Mexico, the United States, and Canada, and has tempered most of Europe who will presently comply with us. South America made it easier to set the global stage. I am sorry about Yucura, for the Brazilian President did have potential."

"The parties in the Middle East are meeting in Brussels tomorrow," said Chu.

"I had thought that the meeting was to be the first Wednesday in June," said UH.

"What happened was that Rowe had spoken to Jacobs and Zarif, who had agreed last evening to move the meeting up, especially 'in light of current events in South America,' said Rowe This will move up discussions for a settlement over the Temple of the Dome issue." Chu said. "Of course, you see that this meeting will be to your advantage."

"I am expected to be there, but will you?" asked UH.

"Yes, without being seen or heard by others. You alone shall hear me," said Chu, "and you will have your language ability that I had given to you, but I will add something new."

Wednesday afternoon in the new large office of UH, they all assembled, but it was too cramped. UH had all of them follow him to larger conference room. Weeks, Rowe, LeFever, Koskov, Yen, Rodriquez, Schmidt, Jacobs, Colombo (Aldelfo Colombo, now the new president of Brazil), Fredrick Reed of Canada, Al-Hamid from Iran, Usama from Iraq, Mahram from Afghanistan, Prince Al-Karim Esmail Aziz from Saudi Arabia, Ghalib Hadi from Dubai, Nabil from the Republic of Turkey, and representatives from Palestinians, and from other Muslim in non participating countries.

They arrived in a room that would hold fifty, a little more than they had needed. Aziz said as they assembled in their seats, that he would speak for Kuwait and Jerusalem Muslims.

"Actually, President Harrison, I speak for most Muslims, as we are stewards and protectors of Mecca, Medina, and the Mosque of Dome of the Rock on the Temple." said Prince A-Karim Amal Aziz.

Nabil, from Turkey, said, "Although, I respect Prince Aziz, I will make my decisions based upon the wishes of my government."

"Of course, brother," said Aziz. "Everyone should follow the wishes of their government"

Chu reminded UH that he would not only understand the languages and dialects of each person in attendance, but when he addressed anyone, they would think that he was speaking their particular language. Also, to the amazement of Muslims, they would hear him speak in their language even with local nuances, and that greatly pleased them. UH would interpret for all who could not understand.

UH began, "I appreciate what the UN has decided to do, when questions or concerns arise. They agreed that we need a central command where all these matters can be funneled to my office in Brussels, for consideration, and dispersed to individuals who need that particular information. All recommendations will then be sent to the UN Security Council and the EU leadership."

"Because we are not part of the UN Security Council," Aziz interrupted, "nor the European Union, how will we benefit from this arrangement?"

Others listened intently, and thought to themselves, *He is correct. If I were not a member of either organization, how would we get information?*

Everyone understood in their own language when UH said, "The first line of defense, information, or assistance will be funneled through the UN and EU, but if it requires immediate response for a non-member, appropriate action will ensue. In other words, no one will be left in the dark. Please be clear on this matter. I had nothing to do with setting up this arrangement, for I had been told that because I am working with peace negotiations in Jerusalem, the Security Council had asked me to accept this new position of coordinator and observer here in Brussels."

Someone said, "Yes, but you are president of the EU and the UC." There was no response.

"I am encouraged by your command of my language," said Ghalib from Dubai. Many Muslim heads nodded. UH did not interpret this response, but gave a quick smile.

"I would like to begin these negotiations in reference to East Jerusalem, and the Dome of the Rock that had been damaged and removed for repair. Of course, I cannot forget the Al Aqsa Mosque. There have been unacceptable suggests, but I believe it would be more prudent if Prince Aziz to address this issue first."

"President Harrison" Aziz began, "someone has brought a matter to my attention concerning your name. You prefer to be referred to as UH, and I will do so from here out.

"I commend your efforts in East Jerusalem. I'm sure we will find a good solution. Whatever we decide, Islam must continue to be the steward of all Muslim sites. The dome must be repaired and placed over the sacred rock. The Al Aqsa Mosque must be rebuilt. The complete reconstruction will be more glorious, and will include earthquake proof construction."

Heads nodded in agreement, and a few arms shot up with a fisted hands.

Mahram from Afghanistan said, "I firmly agree, and money should not be a road block."

Usama, from Iraq, who favored secular Islam, said, "What President Rowe would like to see is a new temple in which all three monotheistic religions may visit. This would also provide income for the temple and the Al Aqsa Mosque, as many tourists would readily come."

"Yes," Rowe began, "a new temple would do just that." Aziz closed his eyes. Others, shook their heads and mumbled something in Arabic. "But, maybe it would do more for the Palestinians in East Jerusalem, if Israel would take the old temple, after the rock is relocated, and of course, Israel will make concessions, like national voting rights, and more participation in local governments."

"Mr. Rowe, this is an Israeli matter," said Jacobs.

UH began in English, but came across as Arabic as well, "This is first, and foremost, a decision of the Muslim and Israeli peoples. I am not dismissing Rowe's suggestion out of hand, so I would like Muslims and Israelis to meet for three hours, in our auditorium, and I insist— three hours. That is enough time to make peace concessions or new suggestions concerning the Jerusalem.

UH said, "I will suspend this meeting for three hours as the two principal parties meet. Please return here in the allotted time. This may sound harsh or cold, but it is paramount that we move these negotiations forward more rapidly than usual in light of what has transpired this last week in South America."

All leaders understood in their own languages, but the Muslims were pleased to hear their language spoken so often. Several questioned UH, but he said that it was his linguistic training and moved on quickly as they all existed the room to designated smaller rooms.

Rowe, North and South American leaders, European Union members, China, and Japan met in a midsize room down the hall to discuss their concerns.

Rowe said, "The rock must be moved, or maybe we can compromise by leaving it where it is, and allow both Muslims and Jews in to pray there."

Koskov said, "I don't think UH is going to settle for any shit from either group. They will abide by what is best—separation of both parties somehow."

Yen Zhang agree with Rowe, but understood Koskov's opinion.

Weeks offered, "This is not some either or situation. UH is seriously attempting to bring permanent peace. The world is unsettled; look what has happened in South American; someone is attempting to influence this planet; and we must begin somewhere. We must trust someone to lead, and I quite agree that that is UH."

Chu said to UH, *There must not be a turning back, nor an inkling of a slow process. Continue to be firm. It isn't pleasant, just like most of life. I will coach you later when they return.*

The participants all returned within the three hours.

UH welcomed them back. When everyone had seated themselves, he said, "I realize that I had been a bit abrupt earlier, but I believe that we are all a little anxious in light of world tragedies and recent killing of leaders," he stopped short of mentioning Jerusalem, "like in South America. I have brought in a stenographer and placed three microphones around the hall to expedite our conversations. Our wish is to be transparent in our proceedings and conclusions. Tomorrow morning each person will be given three minutes to speak. That alone will take us to 10:30 am. We will begin again tomorrow at 8:00 am. Coffee, tea, bottled water, juice, and pastries will be available.

The evening was a little tedious, but it did move along. They finished at 10:50 pm.

The consensus was as follows:

1. The temple dome was to be repaired; temple top rebuilt on the site; and at Israeli expense. (There would be shared Israeli

stewardship, only in the sense of military protection.)

2. Al Aqsa Mosque was to be rebuilt, but larger and with the Rock remaining in the temple. The repaired dome would be at the expense of Muslims. (Only under Muslim stewardship and with the leadership of Solomon Zarif.)
3. Israeli recommendation and concessions: None

The next morning when they were all seated, Prince Aziz asked to be heard.

"Yes, Aziz, go ahead," said UH.

"While we were meeting last night, two of our aged brothers suddenly died. That is why some of you heard the sirens. In two days they must be buried. Therefore, I hope that we can finish up this morning, so that we may all return to our respective homes. The bodies have been sent to their respective countries."

Chu told UH that the two that had died were fundamentalist extremists, and did not wish to change a thing in Israel. "As I told you many times—no one will curtail or stop our plans."

He explained that one other young man from Kuwait was quite vocal, but glad that he was put in his place by Nabil.

"We are saddened to hear of this. Were the families notified?" UH asked Prince Aziz. He nodded in the affirmative. UH looked at his watch, "We will get things finished up by eleven this morning. Gentlemen, the stenographer had transcribed her work from last night; my staff will pass out the recommendations and concessions, and print them up; and your consensus will be forwarded to the UN Security Council and the EU Board. I thank all of you for your participation. Have a good day." UH was not happy with the so called consensus.

Chu appeared at the apartment of UH. "I wish to give to you a heads up concerning the meeting in this morning, and my thoughts on their ridiculous failure to compromise. Prince Aziz is already surmising that what happened in South America has started here in Brussels last night with the death of the two outspoken fundamentalist Muslims. His brothers did not die in vain. He believes very strongly in Islam, but he is a practical man. He told his father, King Al-Qadir Rais Aziz, that he needed his advice. He advised the prince to 'hold tight the reins of Islam, but give what needs to be given to satisfy the infidels.' This will help you gain the leverage to broker the deal in Israel. All sides need to win in their own eyes. We will satisfy those needs. You understand these perils, I am sure of that."

"I have work to do tonight. The PLO leader, Qusay Fadi, is giving us trouble. I want to take the bite out of his words. If I cannot persuade him, Fadi will fade into history. The Hamas leader, Dawud Fajr, is another pain in our plan, as is his second in command, Fuad. I might be killing two birds with one whoosh. Nevertheless, the offer to abdicate their position is first. The profusely sweating, and the heart stopping refusal are the usual miscarry of their own justice. The same will happen to the two leaders of the Yechi Hamelech Hansashiach movement. Oh well, these kind of situations will cease once there is peace; however, we are dealing with human passion: greed, jealousy, lust from belief systems, love of self and money, and an evilness just below the skull. This kind of correction will not be over in a month. Men like power."

"Chu, this is all happening so quickly. I am speechless," said UH.

"No, that is something you will never be—wordless," said Chu grinning.

Later that night, before turning in, UH was watching CNN when a news flash announced the death of three top leaders in the PLO, and four top leaders in Hamas.

"Seven Palestinian leaders died last night in Jerusalem. The very outspoken PLO Ra'd JaFar and two of his lieutenants were found dead in the back room of a meeting house in East Jerusalem. Hamas said that Fuad Al-Latif, and three of his lieutenants were sitting a Fuad's home when they fell forward, according to a witness, and were pronounced dead at the scene. A spokesman from Jacobs' administration said that the Prime Minister would comment later, for ten Kach members died as well.

Our James Peterson in Central America said, 'After what had happened in South America, people are wondering if an alien or aliens had been involved. It seems as though only leaders are slain by some force.' We will keep you informed of any new events."

UH breathed out, "Chu."

Chu said, "Yes. I just returned."

"I see that. You startled me. I had been deep in thought. I understand, that you were busy."

"Yes I have. I must accelerate this process to complete what must be done by July 1st. I would like you in your office tomorrow. You will receive several webcams simultaneously from leaders, but Jacobs will help set the stage for upcoming actions, for tonight, he will be encouraged by the miraculous agreement of the PLO and Hamas. They will agree to all the proposals made by Israel, thanks in part to Prince Aziz and his father who made major concessions. Reconstruction and rebuilding will begin next week."

"Chu, how did you change so many minds?" asked UH.

"I must kill at least one hundred and thirty-three radical Muslims and ninety-nine Israelis to make them agree to our terms. I will kill thousands in a day if necessary. If any party agrees and then backs out, they will be annihilated immediately. On second thought, we are on a time table, so from here on out, no pussy-footing around. Death threats are out of the question. Only death itself will keep the negotiations on track."

The following day CNN reported: "Thirteen hundred Muslim leaders and some of their family members died mysteriously last night. Seven hundred and sixty-six Israeli leaders from around the world died last night. Are these deaths strangely related to the phenomenon that happened in May? This is exceeds any previous deaths or missing people since May of this year. Everyone in Israel and in Muslim countries are at a loss to explain this awful phenomenon."

New negotiations agreed upon came to UH's email the next day.

1. Israel agreed to lift some restrictions in Golan Heights and in East Jerusalem
   a. Muslims have a right to apply for citizenship again (1967)
   b. Muslims are entitled to municipal services
   c. Muslims have municipal voting rights, not national until they except citizenship (Must agree to Israel's right to exist.)
   d. Rebuilding of Al Aqsa Mosque: Israel will assist
2. Muslims agreed to certain concessions
   a. Will relinquish stewardship of Solomon's Temple
   b. Agree to move repaired gold leaf dome and place on rebuilt mosque
   c. Agree to not move rock
   d. Agreed to cooperate with Israel on all construction projects

UH forwarded the email from Aziz, Jacobs, Rabbi Peres, Rowe, Weeks, Yen, Schmidt, Koskov, Garcia, Valentino, Rodrigues, Colombo (new Brazilian president), and LeFever. He later forwarded the email to the UN Secretary General Kobe Alber.

Building in Jerusalem

Friday morning Jacobs sent a webcam to UH, as well a ten others at the same time. Chu was correct. He could speak in English, and all understood.

"Good morning UH," said Jacobs. "I noticed that there are several of us sending you a webcam, I can hear them talking with you at the same time. Anyhow, I am heading to East Jerusalem to meet with the PLO and Hamas leaders to clarify the building and reconstruction, so we can go on at the same time. I can't believe this, for I never thought that this was possible."

UH said, "I would suggest that the Muslims begin to clear away debris and rubble; study the enlarging of the Al Aqsa Mosque to see how much further away it is from the temple, so that the repaired gold dome will set on it quite nicely, as I would expect; the Foundational Stone or rock is not to be moved. That was an extremely difficult issue, but to prevent further deaths, the Muslims acquiesced.

"I hope that commercial contractors are being contacted."

"That seems simple enough, but when can we begin?" asked Jacob.

"Now, but you do not want to interfere with the work on the Al Aqsa Mosque. Your engineers may begin to look at what it would take to make the new temple earthquake proof. Secondly, because of the monumental task before the rebuilding of the temple, we need to estimate the building materials you will need, and also the costs. The temple foundation seems sound enough, but I was told that it would take five hundred to six hundred million dollars to completely reconstruct the third temple, which will include modern conveniences, and furnishings.

"Some of the building materials can be placed near the proposed temple site, but cannot interfere with the workers on the mosque. Does this make sense?" asked UH.

"Yes of course," said Jacobs, the verbal cease-fire has gone on for three days." Rowe, Weeks, Prince Aziz, LeFever who were also listening and agreeing with him.

Aziz said, "The Al Aqsa Mosque will be thirty-three hundred square feet larger. The refurbished golden dome, will set higher, and we will need a larger mosque to accommodate an area for education."

Rowe said, "This is what we have been trying to negotiate for decades." UH rolled his eyes.

"At least, it has actually begun," said LeFever.

"We have had a cease-fire many times, but never like this," interjected Aziz.

They all talked for about twenty minutes more, when UH said, "I must go now, but I would like all of you to know that I'm planning a visit to Jerusalem to see Jacobs and Zarif to assess the progress."

"When will you be going?" asked Rowe.

"In all likelihood, on Monday, because that will have given all parties about a week to have accomplished some progress, and I want to keep on top of this rebuilding. I must go, I'm getting a mobile call." The thirty-six screens went black.

"President Harrison, I mean UH, this is President Salvador Valentino from Italy. I was calling to let you know why I had not attended the Brussels meeting," he said in Italian.

UH responded, as Valentino understood in his own language. "That is all right. Many nations were not represented. I will be sending updates to all nations next week."

"Thank you. I will look forward to your update," said Valentino.

Egypt, Argentina, Kuwait, Norway, Sweden, and several more called with the same story as Valentino.

UH thought that with Chu's leadership and assistance, he would not have to work fourteen-hour-days. As president of the EU, it was unusual to work ten-hour-days. "I would like a weekend or two per month," he mumbled as he opened his office door. He turned and panned his large office:

tiny lights of red, yellow, green, and blue on monitors, work-center copier, printers, fax, and the array of thirty-three monitors on the back wall. His landline was ringing.

He closed the door behind him and went home.

Chu had been waiting. "Good evening UH.

"Good evening Chu. I thought that you had to see someone, because you were going to see me in my office today."

"Yes, I was there watching and listening to your conversations with people you had on your webcam, but I also had taken care of a few things in the Middle East as you know. It was a global cleansing of about a thousand unknown would-be leaders, agitating their citizens to do something that might upset our plans. Fundamentalists of various stripes had chosen the wrong decision.

"I had a small problem in Argentina with President Maximo Garcia. His vice president Bruno Fernandez is president now. Nevertheless, my friend, all seems to be moving ahead as expected.

"As far as your overworking, and less weekends to play, that will all change in your favor. That is, in about the middle of June, you will have regular holidays, less hours of work each week, and certainly two weekends somewhere interesting and fun," said Chu as he gave his notorious thin-lipped grin.

"Thank you Chu. I assume that you approve of me going to Jerusalem on Monday with a female companion."

"Yes, that will be fine, and by the way, she is quite beautiful and younger.

"As I was saying, the situation, I mean the difficulties between former combatants, are leveling off as they work. The rubble should be cleared and actual rebuilding should begin on Wednesday. We lose a day, because Friday at sundown is holy to Jews and Muslims, so they will begin again on Sunday." Chu added, "There is another possible problem, Moshe Peres, the brother of Rabbi Peres, is a fundamentalist Jew who isn't adverse to radicalism. Moshe is planning to sabotage the remodeling and the expansion of the Shaare Zedek Medical Center. I will call him on Sunday morning."

"You sure are on top of things," said UH.

"I have to be," said Chu. "We are on a tight schedule. How would you like to fly to the Mediterranean on the French Riviera and look at a house on the bay, with a view that is picturesque, and that has fifty-three hundred square feet of living space? It has four bedrooms, four and a half bathrooms, a chef's kitchen which is part of the living room, and one of the bedrooms will serve nicely for an office. There is a pool and a pool house. The owner had passed away recently and the family had wanted cash. They were asking for two hundred thousand euros." UH's mouth dropped open. "Don't worry," Chu went on, "I certainly can strike a bargain when I need to do so. Pack. I'll make a phone call for a funds transfer."

"Funds? From where?" asked UH.

"Two cartel drug lord suddenly passed on, and their funds went missing—I found them, and opened an account in Brussels with over twelve million euros. By the way, there are more funds coming. Take this twenty thousand dollars. You'll want to buy something there I'm sure," Chu smiled.

"Why are you smiling, Chu?"

"You will fly into the Nice Cote de'Asur International Airport tonight and leave Monday morning for Jerusalem. Your tickets have been purchased. When you arrive, you will find food, cable TV, the pool will be ready, and of course, your new clothes for play and evening enjoyment at the Casino De Monte Carlo."

"I don't know what to say," said UH.

"Say nothing. Pack your personal items, and call a taxi."

"Don't call anyone, just go. I will meet with you on Monday," added Chu.

When UH arrived, he was told by the airline that a taxi was waiting to take him to his new home. He was not surprised at anything Chu planned, even his itinerary. His new home was as luxurious as Chu had explained. He took his light bag and put it in the master bedroom. He opened the closet to find seven suits, twelve shirts, fifteen ties, and two tuxedos, with matching shoes for each occasion. At nine o'clock, a limousine driver came to the door to announce that he had arrived.

"You look very good tonight sir," said the French driver in rough English. UH was off to a night of excitement and fun. He won about three thousand dollars; drank brandy; and took home a beautiful younger women. He had met her at the bar of the casino. They struck up a conversation. She was beautiful, average height, soft brown hair, blueish green eyes, and spoke wonderful French and English. She had lost her husband two years ago to the Afghan war. She was twenty-five. He liked how intelligent she had seemed. She had completed a master's degree in fine arts. She had published articles in trade magazines concerning the world's lost art. She was stunning, and UH couldn't take his eyes away from her. He had attracted beautiful woman before, but she was out of any woman's league.

By Monday morning, they had swam; spent time at the private beach; and enjoyed each other's company in his master bedroom and elsewhere. On Monday morning, a taxi picked both of them up, first taking her to her apartment, and taking him to the airport. Jeanine would continue to visit UH on the Riviera and in Brussels with regularity.

As UH flew to Jerusalem, after stopping in Brussels to pick up the young woman that he had met. This put him a good mood, and then thought more charitable toward Chu, for he was grateful that Chu had looked out for him from towels after a swim, to his tux and shoes. The full bar in the living room was an added touch, but really all of the amenities were nothing short of magnificent. He actually felt indebted to Chu.

As the flight was approaching Jerusalem, while his girlfriend slept, Chu spoke to him. He looked around, but quickly realized that Chu was invisible.

Chu said, "You will find out that yesterday, Moshe Peres refused my first proffer. He is being buried on Tuesday. See you in East Jerusalem in about an hour."

Jacobs sent his armored car to get UH and his female guest from the airport. He soon arrived in East Jerusalem at the Al Aqsa Mosque rebuilding. He looked over at the reconstruction process of the temple. Even though only twenty-five to fifty yards separated them, Jews and Muslims seemed to be getting along. Commercial video cams from Al Jazeera and two Israeli TV stations were both sending live feed to their respective companies. There was high pitched screaming or hollering between a foremen and two project managers, but to UH, this was music to his ears.

Invisibly, Chu stood next to UH and said, "When these projects are completed in late July, peace in Israel, will make it a smoother transition to world peace. We have more work to do in the world: breaking it up into regions. I will explain later. Keep up the good work."

"Good morning UH, at least I think it is still morning," said Jacobs, in his habit of address people in late morning on the rebuilding site or in his office. Jacobs scratching his graying, but combed hair.

"Good morning Prime Minister. Good to see you again. I will be staying at the Mamilla again."

"Here comes General Goodman with Colonel Hassam from one direction and Solomon Zarif, from the other direction. Have you met Zarif?"

UH said, "No. Not officially that is."

"He is the new president of the Jerusalem Islamic Council. He brings a bit of fresh air to that group. He is a secular Muslim," said Jacobs.

"What does that mean?" asked UH.

"To simplify, a secularist has not as much knowledge of the Quran. Solomon also leans toward Sufism, meaning his is a mystic, and that means he is not as materialistic. God, I didn't think I could remember that stuff. I just impressed myself," Jacobs laughed.

Jacobs introduced every one present, Goodman, Hassam, Zarif, and UH.

Goodman said, "Prime Minister, we have had no incidents for three days. Colonel

Hassam is doing a good job here. Sir, if you don't need me here, I'm going back to Tel Aviv to work on a project I had started four months ago."

"That will be fine General."

"Sir, I'm going over to the other side of the temple area to look at the new supplies that had arrived this morning," said the colonel.

"Be sure to let me know of anything important. Thank you Hassam," said Jacobs, tuning to Solomon. "Solomon, how is everything going?"

"Very good. Small arguments that settle themselves. On the whole, Muslims are motivated to work on the expanded Al Aqsa Mosque. Of course, some fundamentalists still want stewardship over the repaired or rebuilt temple—primarily to spite the Jews. We are carefully watching for possible saboteurs," said Solomon.

"That is good," said UH.

Jacobs said, "Is there anything else?"

"Yes," Solomon answered. "The Islamic Council is especially interested and pleased with the expansion, updating technology, and the openness of services of the newly created Shaare Zedek Hospital. Changing this facility from clinic to hospital was a wise move, and all parties agree. I might add that there are no renewed discussions concerning the rock which is not to be moved to the rebuilt Al Aqsa Mosque."

"I hope that you had reminded them of their agreement we had negotiated in Brussels," said Jacobs.

"Yes I had. Keep in mind that only one Iman is complaining. He is from Syria."

"What is his name?" asked UH.

"Bassel Shammas," answered Zarif.

Only UH could hear Chu who said, *"I will look into this matter tonight."*

Jacobs looked at UH, "On a more positive note, Colonel Hassam told me by phone this morning," Jacobs continued, "that Jews are enthusiastic and motivated about the rebuilding of Solomon's Temple—the third time. The Romans had demolished the second temple in 70 AD, as you know. They are also overjoyed that they will acquire the stewardship of the temple. There is actually a ground-swell of support from around the world. Some collectors and businessmen have privately told me that they would donate large sums of money and some of their artifacts to the new temple."

"What kind of artifacts?" asked UH.

Jacobs said, "I can't say too much now, but there is a replica of a full size carved menorah, a bronze key ring, and a ritual cup. God alone knows of other artifacts that will show up. I should have mentioned that there are several wealthy US and European Jews who wish to plate or layer the silver reproductions with gold. Several wealthy Christian men and women are donating—three million dollars have been raised to assist in the cost of rebuilding."

"That is wonderful to hear," said Solomon. "We too are hoping for such donations from the world of Islam," He reached out his arm to shake the hands of UH and Jacobs. "I must be going. It is going to be another long day." The three men shook hands and politely smiled.

UH looked at Jacobs. "How long will it take to compete the rebuilding the temple?"

"Between you and me, UH, about thirty days for this reason. I didn't want Solomon to hear this, but, there is a multi-billionaire who lives in New Your City, for he is donating five hundred million dollars. By tomorrow, mega machinery, trucks, commercial backhoes, and whatever else is needed, will be working around the clock, just as those men working on the Al Aqsa Mosque are working around the clock. This whole area in East Jerusalem will be lit up like a sports stadium. All along, we worried about the money. Not any longer. Much of the money will be hear by Friday."

"I'm so glad for you my friend," UH said to Jacobs. "This will be a major tribute to your life as a decorated soldier, years in Knesset, and now as Prime Minister of Israel. It all adds up to prove to the world that your leadership has been significant, and will certainly bring great acclaim."

"Thank you for the kind words. I understand that you will be returning to Brussels on Wednesday morning, and that will be good because you will witness the genesis of the third temple. I am glad that you are serving as an outside advisor."

"I am glad to be a spectator to this grand effort by both religions, working together rather than finding ways to kill each other," UH said nodding at the hundreds of workers.

Jacobs noticed that it was almost noon. "I am going back to the office to work."

UH responded, "I am going to the Mamilla to eat, make a call to my office, visit a time with my guest, and, then begin to work on the notes I had jotted down this morning. If you need to talk later this evening, call me."

Jacobs said that he would, and the two parted.

UH walked back to the vehicle that he had transported him to the site. The driver was told to take him to his hotel. While on his ride to the hotel, Chu called to tell him that the two of them would talk in about an hour.

UH and his traveling companion had lunch, and went up to his room, and visited his *guest* on the bed for an hour. Jen was nice, beautiful, and a spirited twenty-five year old. He then retrieved several calls that he had missed on the hotel phone, and then he called his office in Brussels.

"Elsa, how is my favorite secretary?"

"Just fine sir. I do have a question, why isn't webcam working?"

"When I leave the office," UH began, "it is shut down until I get more help in the office. I guess I had forgotten to tell you."

"Yes, but I don't use the webcam here in the office."

UH asked, "Then why were you asking about it?"

"Oh, I had noticed that all the monitor screens are black."

"Any other questions?" asked UH shaking his head.

"No sir."

"Thank you Elsa. I'll be back Wednesday afternoon."

"Okay. See you then," she said.

After returning there remaining calls, he took his IPad and began to organize his notes from earlier that morning while Jen was in the shower, when Chu appeared.

He said, "UH, I hope that you had a good day. Zarif is doing what we intended him to do: lead the Islamic Council to abide by our deal. The third temple will be finished about the same time as the completion of the Al Aqsa Mosque; after all, we don't want to stir up competition. I plan to accelerate this building of both parties by making sure all materials are on time, and that adequate monies are donated to each group. I am watching the Kach movement—it's growing.

"There is a little stirring around in Somalia, and also in Italy. Valentino is being pressured to seek an alliance with his friend, Carlos Rodrigues in Mexico. So far, Rodrigues is not interested in losing his life. I will call Valentino tomorrow."

"How are we going to stop this nonsense?" questioned UH.

"My dear man, time and money is on our side, and things will be like this until the end of July. Even in the event of great peril, some greedy and powerful men refuse to change."

UH said, "I'm pleased with all that you are doing, and I know that your goal is like mine: world peace," said UH.

Chu said, "Is that Jen in the shower?" The shower turned off.

UH answered, "Yes."

"UH, I am happy with you. I have chosen you to be a commanding world leader. There has never been one like you before on this planet, and no one ever to be like you. In July, I will expand your abilities. By August, you will finally grasp your talent to lead mankind, for this will be paramount to bring about world peace. I will speak with you tomorrow. I regret to tell you that under the circumstances, Jeanine will call you later this evening, after your dinner with Jen. Jeanine seems to be well matched to your temperament. She knows how to be discreet, knows when to keep quiet, and can keep a secret—and she too is only twenty-five, but again, she is human. I think you like that age. You can make the choice between the two women, but personally, I would take Jen back to her home.

"I will be calling President Badri in Tunisia, the prime ministers in Sweden, and India, and also the presidents in Panama and the United States. Minor problems must be addressed too."

UH questioned Chu, "Why are you calling Rowe?"

"It is time to bring him to Israel on Friday, and to address some of the statements he had made to a few members of his cabinet."

"What kind of statements? I thought that he was with us," said UH.

"He is still resisting the idea of bringing all global complications and obstacles through Brussels," said Chu. "I'm going now. Do you need more money?"

"Not at this time."

Chu thought to himself, reached into what seemed a pocket, and then said, as a bank card appeared, "Here is a bank card. When you need an funds for an item or cash, use it. The account will always have money in it."

"Thank you," said UH.

"I will see you on Friday when you return to Israel." UH's face twisted a question. "Yes, because Rowe will be in Jerusalem, and the work that will have been done will amaze you."

Chu was gone.

Jeanine called after dinner, and UH explained that he would be in Brussels on Wednesday evening, but would leave early Friday morning for Israel again. She didn't like it much, and then told him that she would be in Brussels on Wednesday. She asked if she could go with him to Jerusalem on Friday. He was a bit reluctant at first, primarily because he had to drop of Jen in Brussels, and not knowing what Chu would think, but followed his instinct.

"Jeanine, yes I would love your accompany. I will make arrangements tonight for your room and any needs you require for Friday night. Saturday we will fly to my place on the French Riviera."

Jeanine said, "That sounds exciting. I will see you Wednesday darling."

UH had learned, later that night, that Chu had purchased, at a discounted price, a new Boeing 777-200 from a family that had ordered it, but in the delivery month, could not pay for the jet. He hired a pilot, co-pilot, engineer, and two stewardesses to work fulltime. The maintenance crew would work out of a hangar at the Brussels Airport. He had the plane customized with a full bar, sleeping quarters, and office. This would allow UH immediate access for travel anywhere on the globe, and at any time. It would be ready for Friday morning's flight.

Chu called UH, "I will see to it that Jen is flown back to Brussels tonight."

UH asked, "Shall I talk with her first?"

Chu answered, "Not at all. I will handle it cordially and as a gentleman." Chu laughed.

UH and Jeanine landed in Jerusalem on Monday in the new plane.

The next morning, at the East Jerusalem site, UH was astounded at the progress. The workers were busy from Monday evening and overnight into Tuesday. He saw mega dozers, mega hydraulic backhoes, and mega off the road dump trucks, and many other dump trucks, earth movers, and the types of construction equipment, he couldn't have imagined. Jacobs and, Aziz raised the money for the huge cost. Nevertheless, by Friday, they could begin reconstruction and expansion of the walls to the Al Aqsa Mosque. The upper level of the temple had been repaired where once the gold dome rested. All along the eastern wall Rabbis led people in praise and prayers.

At noon, UH was driven to the hotel to meet Jeanine for lunch at the Mamilla Hotel on King Solomon Street. UH helped her finish unpacking, and then they went to lunch in the Rooftop-Outdoor Lounge and Restaurant. Jeanine often exclaimed, "Oh my god, how beautiful is this place, from the first floor to the roof." They watched the news as they ate.

Local television reported that by this Friday morning, much of the preliminary construction had been finished. "Many of the residents both Palestinians and Jews were overjoyed with that the construction equipment mentioned at the mosque, had also been used for the temple. Great care is still given to this endeavor because the rock was still inside, which was a joy to the Jews, for it would not be moved. The Jews called the rock, the Foundational Stone. The construction of what used to be the Holy of Holies has begun in earnest."

Then they switched to Fox News. It stated that last Thursday in Tunisia, President Mohamed Ali Badri had died suddenly, and that the vice president Faris had assumed the presidency. The new president, Youseff slim Faris, a younger man, had been seen as more practical than the sociopolitical Badri. They also reported that "President Rowe has made an unexpected decision last night to travel to Israel, where on Friday in Jerusalem, he would witness the ongoing progress of the rebuilding of the Al Aqsa Mosque and the Jewish Temple." Fox reported that the rebuilding of the temple had been a three year goal of Rowe's to help bring peace in Jerusalem.

That's when UH explained to Jeanine some things about Rowe, "However, he, like so many others failed, and no one had ever provided particulars nor an outline as to how this would be accomplished," complained UH to Jeanine.

Fox went on to say that they had never seen such cooperation among antagonists in Jerusalem. "Presidents from Jimmy Carter to Rowe have attempted to bring peace to the Middle East—all had failed." They also reported that Jacobs had boasted about the progress on the temple, rather than seeing all the reconstruction as a peace project. Solomon Zarif suggested restraint, responding to Jacobs, "... for prudence is best. A spirit of compatibility is needed at this time," said Zarif to a reporter.

The Fox reporter went on to ask, "Will these two and a half weeks of ceasefire last?" Zarif quickly responded, "No one called a cease fire. This is a joint effort to show a sense of comradery, yet not by surrendering any religious dissimilarities."

"Leave it to the new media to keep pecking at the progress being made here," said Jeanine.

"You are absolutely correct, my dear," said UH about to eat his last bite of lunch.

UH said, "How did you like the flight?"

"Oh my god, the plane is beautiful. I loved the sleeping room with you," Jeanine grinned and leaned her head toward him.

UH took her hand, "My lovely woman, we will be at my place on the French Riviera on Saturday morning" His mobile rang. "This is UH."

"Had you caught the news this morning where they said I had bragged about the temple being rebuilt?" complained Jacobs.

"Yes. They know very well how to twist a story," said UH.

Jacobs said, "I'm not going to respond to their story. I think that even my enemies know me and laugh at such misinformation. I will see you in an hour or so at the construction site."

"Very well. See you then," said UH. Looking at Jeanine he said, "That was Jacobs. Later we'll meet him and Rowe, at the construction site. He came in two days early."

Jeanine squeezed his hand, "Do you think that I should go, or should I stay at this gorgeous hotel?"

"I want you to come with me, without question. From here on out, you will be seen with me on most occasions," said UH.

Jeanine was twenty-five, but was very astute; no children, and gorgeous both inside andout, especially out; she was as slender as a model, but was never pretentious; and she was already jealous of UH--she needed to be with him.

Pointing at UH and Jeanine, "They made a wonderful pair," said Jacobs at the construction site.

The construction site was noisy, dirty, with a slight breeze blowing fine dust around. Rowe finally arrived with Jacobs. They had continued to talk a short distance away from UH and Jeanine. UH was surprised to see two walls of the mosque going up, but noticed wide foundations using steel rods and bolts.

Solomon came over to UH, and UH introduced Jeanine as a personal friend, but "really more than a friend," he concluded.

"Over there," UH pointed, "what are those grey pieces piled at the end of the stack of beams?"

Solomon said, "Those big grey pieces are for the end of the beams, and when in place, they absorb energy. In other words, it helps make it earthquake proof," said Solomon. "We have also built a wider foundation reinforced by steel and rods and large bolts. They will not be visible in the stone. In addition, you can see that we have used many of the old stones for the foundation"

Rowe got into a little exchange with Jacobs concerning freedoms being expanded for Muslims. Jacobs decided to end the misguided statements of Rowe by quoting President John Adams, "'...those who trade liberty for security, have neither.' So Mr. President, as a former founder of the United States, and president indicated, we will guard ourselves while we expand the new agreements with the Islamic Council."

Rowe decided to end the conversation as the two approached Solomon, UH, and Jeanine.

Rowe said, "What is this renewed talk of Zionism?"

Jacobs responded, "Original Zionist thinking is not discussed. Today, Zionism merely means that we should keep the State of Israel, or protect its demise. There is talk that anti-Zionism is the equivalent to being anti-Semitic. Other than that my friend, there is not renewed talk."

Solomon said, "Zionism has angered Muslims, like Hamas angers Jews, because Muslims say that Zionists put forth the notion that Jews alone should govern the Middle East. They are expansionists, and support enlarging the Holy Land to include the eastern part of Lebanon and Turkey."

"That's what I was getting at," said Rowe.

Jacobs interjected, "They are a very small group, smaller than Hamas, or the PLO, and many Israelis do not adhere to their teaching. Today, they are not causing terror. They have their state—Israel."

"We have said enough about that subject," said UH. "Let's look at the progress on this site. Wednesday of next week, and I will be here for that momentous event when the gold-leaf dome is placed on the walls of the Al Aqsa Mosque."

"As will I," said Solomon.

"I will be standing here as well," Jacobs said sternly, with his feathers still ruffled at Rowe.

"I'm afraid that we must get back to the hotel to get our belongings, and then, off to the airport," said UH. "I am leaving tonight, and will return next week. Nice to visit with you gentlemen," UH added, and taking Jeanine's arm.

They all said their goodbyes, and Rowe, Jacobs, and Solomon remained speaking with the foremen and an engineers about the temple and mosque projects and about the installation of permanent furnishings, beautiful tiles on inner walls, outer walls, and floors.

UH and Jeanine flew to Nice, France, and landed at the Cote D'Azur Airport. They remained at his luxurious home, experienced the nightlife, and delighted in each other's company until Monday morning when they flew to Brussels. After going to his apartment, the taxi took them to his office, where Jeanine was going to work with UH. As he and Jeanine drove up to his office, he noticed some rioting down the block. They quickly got out of the taxi, and went into the building. When inside, he went to his office, and Jeanine talked with Elsa about what she does in the office.

Chu said to UH, "Good to be home?"

"Yes. What's going on downstairs in the street?" asked UH.

"Nothing much. A few young people spouting off about the supposed atrocities outside of Paris. Nothing to worry about. I see that Jeanine is with you." At that moment, Jeanine looked at UH through the glass wall, and wondered who he was talking to. "I will talk with you later," added Chu. She turned back to her conversation thinking the UH was on speaker phone.

That evening while Jeanine was showering, Chu came to UH. "Next week begins the third week in June. By July first, Al Aqsa Mosque will be completed, except for a few things inside. Zarif said that Muslim intricate art work for halls inside and out, floors, walls, and arches will take longer because of Arabesque." He explained that kind of art is taking very small pieces of colored glass and placing them in cement, which is tedious but "satisfying to the viewer" he said quoting a Muslim artisan. He added. "They also, use Arabic lettering which is important to them. This particular mosque will now have a madrasah," Chu smirked.

Chu continued, "The temple will be finished on July 1st, except for little touch ups. Both buildings are earthquake roof, and yet close enough to spy on each other," he joked. "Inside the temple there will be two artifacts found which the Jews will say is proof that God still cares about them.

"I want you on the East Jerusalem sites, from Wednesday through Friday. This way you will be there for the artifacts find, and viewing the excitement of worshipers around and in the mosque, for they will begin their Friday services, with the repaired dome, with its new gold-leaf that will be placed on the mosque, and the grand jubilation that follows. After which, you may return to Brussels. It will be the last week of June that will prove most interesting, and the most explosive since beginning these projects.

"I will speak with you on Friday, before you leave for France."

"Are there problems with world leaders?" asked UH.

"A handful of them lost their common sense, some time ago, but, as you know, some will find a bit of the lost common logic, but others never had it to lose," said Chu.

UH thought to himself, *I've never dared to ask Chu, but how does he dispose of people?*

Construction in Jerusalem

Wednesday, workers scurried around, putting finishing touches on the section of the expanded walls on the mosque which had been newly painted and decorated with Arabesque art. The repaired dome, in gold leafing, would be fixed with specially designed commercial steal bolts. Debris, which had been left after the reconstruction was being moved and hauled away. Visiting Imams were walking around encouraging followers to be patient and to pray to Allah for his guidance for the engineers, workers, and all others who had participated in this reconstruction of grandeur. "This mosque will be a destination for many in Islam," said one man.

Across from there, were rabbis praising Elohim for returning the Holy Temple to them. They prayed, asking God to grant special favor on all who worked on the Holy Temple, but also everyone who advised, gave funds, paid for mega earth movers, and who assisted in all of the two worship centers.It was time to place the gold dome on the expanded Al Aqsa Mosque. Everyone was tense, some praying, others whispering to those near them, but the new Iman Ammon stood near the crane as it lifted the dome in the air, and carefully moved it into place. Soon it was fastened down. The Muslim decorating was now moved to inner walls and arches.

A replica of the Holy of Holies had been build—less the Ark of the Covenant, and cherubim. It had been built over the Foundation Stone, with twenty-one stairs going down to the tone. Orthodox Jews still believed that the pierced hole in the stone was a well of souls, a junction between heaven and earth, and that the cave below it, also had spiritual implications. Jacobs said yesterday that the Foundation Stone proves that Jews were here twenty-six hundred years—no almost twenty- seven hundred years before Mohamed. That doesn't include the three thousand years before that. This kind of discussion would carry over into Friday.

Solomon Zarif and Rabbi Peres were talking, when a Jewish archaeologist approached. Zarif excused himself with a phone call, and Peres and

Dr. Isaac Benjamin began a conversation.

"Rabbi, I am Isaac Benjamin, an archaeologist, and I was hoping that my three-person team could look around in the temple. Be sure of one thing, actually two things. We will stay clear of workers, and we will not disturb or damage anything in the temple, in or around it."

"Yes, I know who you are," said Peres. "You called my office, and left a message. You teach at the Tel Aviv University International."

"Yes."

Peres continued, "You and your people may do some research on the temple, but not until tomorrow. They are putting finishing touches the on the Holy of Holies which is directly over the Foundation Stone where the gold dome had stood above it."

"That will be fine. We will begin in an area that will not disturb the workers. Perhaps near the steps by the east wall. Thank you so much sir, I mean Rabbi," said Benjamin.

UH walked a little distance from Peres, and was pleased to see so much progress.

"Do you approve of what you see?" asked Chu, invisibly.

"Why yes, most certainly. It is almost dusk, so I'm about ready to head to my hotel room to ask Jeanine to go to late dinner with me."

"That is fine," said Chu. "I'm going to be busy raising more funds, specifically from drug cartels in Mexico. Chavez was the number two man when his boss had been killed for losing five million dollars, which I had found and put in a private account. You have an interesting two days ahead of you. I'll talk with you on Friday."

"Very good Chu. I will look forward to Friday," said UH.

Chu said, "Remember, you may have your hands full on Friday." He vanished after that exchange.

Thursday seemed good. Jacobs, Peres, UH, and Jeanine had been there most of the morning and early afternoon watching cleanup. They were still in awe of the mega machinery like earth movers and other mega machines that had been loaded on mega trucks. The other dump trucks, backhoes, and smaller equipment would be finishing the cleanup after this had been done.

"This is so incredible," said Jacobs. "This has been accomplished in less than thirty days."

Peres said, "Yes, but unlike most projects, these men were worked twenty-four-hours around the clock.

"That is true my friend. I almost forgot, give my condolences to your brother's wife," said UH.

"Thank you."

In the temple, Dr. Benjamin found two coins from the Roman period which had been found in a crevice in the wall along the side of the stairway, and a twelve inch menorah was found in what appeared to be a wobbly stone in the wall close to the back of the stairs at the bottom. The menorah, a hand carved replica was fortunately found at a little deeper, but dryer area.

Benjamin quietly walked over to Rabbi Peres, and told him of their find. Peres was visibly overwhelmed with joy, but calmed himself. Peres said, "Let me get the Prime Minister on the phone. He walked over to the vehicle to get a water." He heard the mobile ringing a short distance away.

"This is Jacobs. I'm walking over to you."

Peres took Jacobs by the arm, and said, "This is astonishing. We found three artifacts in the temple."

"What are they?" said Jacobs.

"Two Roman coins, and a carved menorah," said Peres.

Jacobs stood quietly for a moment. "We must keep this hush hush. Where is Dr. Benjamin?"

"He went to get a cardboard box from his archeological items in his vehicle, and there he is, bringing a small cardboard box," said Peres. The box was folded to form handles.

Jacobs asked, "Are the items in the box?"

"Yes. Shall I give these items to you?" he asked Peres.

"Prime Minister Jacobs would you take these items to a secure place," said Peres.

"Someone is watching us from across the way near the mosque," said Jacobs. "I will smile, and the rest of you smile, and look like we had just shared a joke. I will then nonchalantly take the box and hold it as though it was of no importance, like swinging it a bit." They all agreed; talked for a moment or two; and said their goodbyes.

Peres said, "I haven't seen much of UH this afternoon."

"Oh yes he had been here. He came first to my office, and we came together this morning. He had a pressing matter, and had to leave minutes ago," said Jacobs

That evening UH received a call from his mother.

She spoke softly and slowly, "Darling Urie, this is mother. I'm in a London hospital, but I shall be fine. The doctor wishes to speak with you. I had to hear your voice first. Here is Dr. Perkins."

"Mr. Harrison, I would like to call you back. What is your mobile number?"

UH gave the doctor his number, and in about an hour, Dr. Perkins called back.

The doctor had stepped from Mrs. Harrison's room. Dr. Perkins began, "Mr. Harrison, your mother's condition is actually extremely grave. Her heart is weak, and the pneumonia had worsened. We are addressing both conditions simultaneously. She had waited too long to get herself into the hospital. She actually came through ER by way of a cab. Nonetheless, may I call you if I see a worsening of her condition?"

"Yes of course doctor. Should I fly there?'

"I will know more later-on," said Perkins, "after further testing."

UH said, "Thank you doctor for your kindnesses to her."

Thursday morning arrived: workers at the mosque were hoping to put the dome on today as they put the joists into place, with their grey energy absorbers on the end; Jews were cleaning out more debris from the inside of the temple; workers on the temple were rebuilding some walls with newly quarried rock and stone brought in during the last week; and officials from both parties watched vigilantly into dusk. Often, some people from both religious parties, remained until late because of the stadium-like lighting.

UH and Jeanine came to the site early enough to catch Jacobs, Zarif, and Peres.

Zarif said, “We have religiously planned and organized for our service tomorrow, and we have put in place needed items for the big ceremony tomorrow. The beautiful newly painted doom shines as the sun warms it. I feel poetic.

“At least we averted a nasty war over the destruction and rebuilding of Al Aqsa Mosque and temple.” The Muslims never referred the Jewish temple as the Third Temple. “This whole development has been designed by Allah, to make the old Al Aqsa Mosque a vibrant center for worship and education. The Madrasah is an exceptional addition; and he had made sure that spiritually, agreements by Muslims and Jews held firm; and that there had been rebuilding without conflicts.”

Jacobs responded, “Well, I would give credit to Elohim, but I understand.”

“Of course you would. I wouldn’t expect any different response,” said Zarif.

UH said, “It is truly remarkable how everything seems to have fallen into place, like the timing of a well-planned event. This is nothing short of miraculous.”

“Agreed,” said Zarif.

“It makes no difference how you describe these goings on, for this work is international news worthy,” said Peres.

The men talked and watched the workers and machinery.

UH was walking back to the taxi when Chu said, “Don’t forget about

Friday."

"I won't," said UH. He had to be brief because Jeanine was jogging up to him. They both headed for the taxi.

"Darling let's do lunch in that beautiful restaurant downstairs," Jeanine said getting into the taxi.

"Sure, I would like that, but they don't offer lunch, and they don't open until 5:30. We can go after I make a few calls. We certainly can go to dinner there," said UH.

Jeanine smiled and took UH's hand, "That sounds very good. First, let's go get washed up and change."

UH looked at the Jeanine, and said to her, "You are the loveliest, sexiest, and most adorable woman I have ever met."

"Oh my god. You are a wonderful, handsome, and sexy man."

At that moment, UH's mobile rang. "Hello, this is UH."

"This is Dr. Perkins. Your mother in now in critical condition. She is unable to talk, in large part because we have her sedated. I told you that I would call if things change, and they have, most gravely. I am worried about her heart, because the pneumonia is making her heart work harder."

"Thank you doctor. On Monday, I'll come up," said UH.

"Very good. I will share that with her, if I am able to do so because of her condition," said Dr. Perkins.

UH told Jeanine what the doctor had said.

"Do you want me to go with you on Monday?" asked Jeanine.

"Yes, of course I do. I need to have you by me," said UH, taking her hand.

That evening, Jacobs called. "UH, can you meet me early in the morning, say about eight?"

UH said, "Yes, I'll be there on the site."

"No, I mean in my office," said Jacobs.

"Certainly. See you there. Oh, is everything all right?" asked UH.

"I think so. I'll explain tomorrow." Jacobs hung up.

UH remembered Chu telling him that Friday was going to hectic.

Friday morning, Jacobs welcomed UH into his office. Jeanine waited in the cab because UH said that he wouldn't be long.

"Dr. Benjamin a professor at the Tel Aviv University, is an archaeologist," Jacobs began.

"He and his small group had been working in the temple, and they had unearthed these artifacts."

Jacobs opened the cardboard box and revealed the two coins and the carved twelve inch high Menorah. He explained that someone supervising the mosque construction, happened to see Benjamin hand the box to Jacobs. He added, that later that evening he had a phone conversation with Zarif, who had claimed that we were hiding something that perhaps belonged to them. "We were hiding these items because of their value, but more importantly, because of their intrinsic value to the temple and Jews. I haven't the slightest idea what is planned today when I meet Zarif and others from the Islamic Council."

"Let's not rush into judgement, for we don't know what they have planned," said UH. UH pointed out, "When we get to the site, the Muslims will be excited that they will worship under the golden dome in a new Mosque. There will be a lot of joyous activity."

"OK, I'll meet you over there," said Jacobs.

Shouts of joy and fists of defiance went up as Muslims circled the mosque.

Many others, like Jacobs, UH, and Peres, clapped. To see the morning sun gleam off the dome. Jacobs and Peres were clapping because two newly purchased, but pure golden palm trees had been attached to each side of the doors of the Holy of Holies as the morning sun made them seem on fire.

"Well, here comes Zarif," said UH. Every one turned to watch Solomon approach them.

Zarif said, "Good morning," as he nodded to each man. "Jacobs, yesterday we had seen you accept, what looked like a cardboard archaeological box."

Quickly thinking, "That my friend," said Jacobs, "was a box with magazine articles that Dr. Benjamin wanted me to read. The articles were written about the Temple by scholarly colleagues of his. Besides," Jacobs became a bit agitated, but thankful for his quick thinking, "I don't believe that there are any artifacts remaining, thanks to the hundreds of years of digging by Muslims, who had attempted to destroy every item that they could in the hope that it would disproved our existence back then. We have been here for four thousand years or more. Years before your prophet had been born."

UH said, "This is an obviously sensitive issue that we need not pursue at this time."

"You are right UH," said Jacobs. "I apologize."

"No matter Jacobs," said Zarif, "I was merely the voice for the Islamic Council. I am a mystic, and personally I don't get wrapped up in these sorts of things. I will tell them what you had said about the magazine articles that had been given to you."

Out of nowhere, a young Muslim man came running up the hill with a knife in his hand, running at Jacobs, screaming "Ali Akbar" as he neared him. As he approached Jacobs, UH quickly grabbed the man's arm with the knife, bent it backwards, and elbowed him in the face. As the man began to fall from the blow to his chin, UH took the knife out of his hand. The speed at which UH moved was shocking to all as they watched the a tragedy averted. Israeli soldiers came quickly on the scene, and arrested the man.

"Oh my god, are you all right UH?" yelled Jeanine. Zarif echoed her concern.

"Yes my dear. Not a scratch."

"Suspicion has always been part of the Middle East mystique," said Peres. He asked UH, "Where had you learned self-defense?"

"It isn't well known," said UH, "but my stay in China not only educated me on their history and culture, it offered training in martial arts, and I had received two tenth degree black belts from Yung, an expert, who has since died."

"I am surprised," said Jacobs, "that this incident happened, and at the same time, relieved that you saved my life UH. I had often wondered about your physique and your youthfulness."

General Goodman came from behind and had seen the entire altercation asked, "How do you keep in shape?"

"Until last year, I worked out with Master Chen in his personal gym. Anyway," UH said to Jacobs, "you are welcome my friend, but let's keep this martial arts ability under wraps, please."

"Of course we will," said Jacobs nodding to the other men, who also nodded in agreement.

Colonel Hassam called Jacobs. "Good afternoon Prime Minister. I just heard of your narrow escape from death, thanks to UH."

Jacobs responded, "Yes, it was a close call. I thank you for calling me colonel. I will talk with you later. Goodbye."

"Now that the gold-leaf dome is resting on it beams, the celebration is going on, and at sundown, they will be worshiping, I believe that Jeanine and I will return to the Mamilla Hotel for lunch on the roof top restaurant," said UH. He paused, "Jacobs, please join us for lunch. Zarif and Rabbi Peres please join us as well."

Zarif said that he must stay at the site, because of the attempted murder of Jacobs, and he needed to speak with Imam Amman, the new prayer leader of the Al Aqsa Mosque. He wished to speak with me about this matter. "Maybe, another time UH."

Jacobs, Rabbi Peres, UH, and Jeanine lunched at the Mamilla Hotel roof top restaurant.

Peres said, "That attack was totally unexpected due to the fact, we have had a good working relationship on the reconstruction site. Ammon called me on my way over here, and said that he wanted to apologize. The assailant had been frightened and frenzied about the thirteen hundred deaths to Muslims by perhaps aliens. He of course, blamed the Jews."

Jacobs said, "I too, am unnerved at the hundreds of Jewish deaths. I asked myself yesterday and today, when I think about it, why not me, when all the Jews had been killed?"

UH asked, "Now that the Holy Temple has been rebuilt, will the priesthood in some form reappear?"

"No." said Peres, "we will never have animal sacrifices, and thus, no priesthood is needed. Since the first century, meaningful prayer is the beginning of sacrifice to God, followed by other steps in making a sacrifice like giving to the synagogue, helping others, especially the widows, orphans, and so on. The temple has historical religious significance, but it now will become an important spiritual center for Jews, and I'm sure, will be a museum as well."

The conversation soon turned to Muslim concerns.

Jacobs said, "Muslims know one thing: hate of other religions and cultures. Look at the fifty-three meter high Buddhist carving into the stone. It was the world's largest statue. The Muslim Taliban turned a deaf ear to sheikhs attempting to stop them from blowing up this ancient artistic treasure. I notice these things. The oldest Christian Monastery was leveled in Iraq by Isis. I am not a Christian nor a Buddhist, but I know ancient treasures are needed for posterity.

"You can call it PLO, Hamas, Isis, Al-Qaeda, and Taliban, or any other name, but it is still Muslim. Jacobs face was flushed. "I apologize UH, and Jeanine. After sixty odd years of wars and terrorism, I guess, they all have accumulated in this old brain." He couldn't stop. "I remember my father talking about the Mufti, Haj Amin al-Husseini who convinced Hitler in 1941 to allow his twenty thousand Arab soldiers to join the SS, and go into Muslim countries to kill Jews. He, never mind, I'm done," he shook his head. UH just listened.

Peres said, "Historians know well that Islam has never had a moment that it halted its move to conquer the world, and it has marched throughout the centuries. From the seventh century forward, hate and death are part of their heritage. If the United States in the 1950's had not limited the its oil companies, and given the oil wells and refineries to the Arabs, they could not have financed their war of terror today. My god, don't get my started on women's' rights."

"I am sorry my friend, and Jeanine for taking twenty minutes of our lunch time talking politics," said Jacobs.

UH said, "More politics in the immediate future, when we go back to the site, but I assure you that there will not be another incident. Things will move just as planned originally. Noisy, dusty, and with a background of loud voices celebrating. The Al Aqsa Mosque will be completely done, inside and out on July 3rd. Your holy temple will be completed on July 21st. Men and machinery will be gone, landscaping will provide color, and lights in the landscaping will provide spot lights on the temple at night. Let's finish this fine lunch on this beautiful roof top restaurant." He winked at Jeanine.

They all returned to the busy site.

"Prime Minister, I must confess," said Dr. Benjamin. "We had found a broken or partial censer that had been used in the second temple. I didn't tell you until I ran some carbon testing and other data gathering, like on the partial engraving on the handle which read "Holines.., something, something Elo…"

"Where is it?" asked Jacobs.

"Wait, that isn't all." Benjamin continued, "We discovered a small, but almost crushed golden cup at the far east end near the cave area."

Jacobs said, "This is astonishing. I hope that you will continue searching the temple and surrounding grounds."

UH said to Peres and Jacobs that he would be back Monday to monitor the landscaping, lighting, the continued decorating in both the temple and the mosque, the progress on the Shaare Zedek Hospital, and the interrelationship between the Muslims and Jews. He and Jeanine walked to the taxi he had called only minutes ago.

UH thought to himself, *this is a nice ending for a Friday in East Jerusalem.* "Jeanine, I would like to go to the airport after we get our things at the hotel. We can eat on the plane or in France. What would you like my dear?"

They sat looking at each other at a table in the Casino De Monte Carlo, there new place to have fun.

"I am falling deeply in love with you," Jeanine said to UH.

"I don't need anyone but you," UH began, "for you make me complete."

Monday came too quickly UH thought. Jeanine fell asleep as they flew first to Brussels to stop in to his office.

"Good morning Elsa," said UH. "We are in today for about two hours. Jeanine will be assisting me in my office, I mean my glass enclosure." Elsa and Jeanine smiled at each other.

Chu called UH. "Next week I've hired a private secretary who will understand our relationship. He will only assist you when I need him to do so."

"That will be fine," said UH. "I could use the help."

"July is less than a week away, and it will be a busy month. That is the month we divide the world into twelve regions. This will make your life easier. You will deal with twelve regions rather than two hundred countries." Chu added, "I will assist you and will handle other calls, emails, or webcams, but we will discuss these matters in July."

"Very good. As you know, my mother is ill. I may be flying there tomorrow," said UH.

Chu said, "Why not skip Jerusalem and go straight to London. Spend whatever time you need to, and return to Jerusalem on Tuesday night or Wednesday morning."

"That sounds good. What is my new assistant's name?" asked UH

"His name is Jamison. I will have a complete file for him on your desk before July 1st. Goodbye for now. I'll talk to you when you return to Jerusalem."

"Chu, is everything going well in Jerusalem?"

"Believe it or not, there are some who are reneging among the parties, but talk is cheap as they say, so I'll just listen for now. Bye."

Jeanine asked who that was, but just then Elsa asked her a question, "Are you only going to be here when UH is here?"

"I'm not sure," said Jeanine looking at UH walking toward her.

"Darling, this afternoon, we are flying to London to visit my dying mother. On Tuesday or Wednesday we will be back in Jerusalem. I hope that you don't mind changing plans?

"Not at all, as long as I can hang on to your strong arm," she said taking his right arm.

"Elsa, would call a taxi for us?"

They arrived in London at 8:00 pm, and went directly to the hospital. UH asked at the receptionist desk for his mother's room in critical care. When he arrived at the room, no one was there. He went to the nurses' station, and they called Dr. Perkins who they knew was still in the hospital. He answered, and soon met UH and Jeanine.

"Mr. Harrison, I regret to tell you that your mother had passed about one hour ago. She never regained consciousness. One time, she whispered your name and the name of a William."

"William was my father who had died ten years ago," said UH.

"Thank you doctor for all that you had done for her. She was certainly a fine, lovely women. I will miss her," UH said holding himself back from crying. UH shook the doctor's hand, then he and Jeanine went to a hotel.

He knew his mother was a member of the largest Anglican Church in London, so in the morning, he called and made arrangements for his mother: cremation, buried with his father, memorial service Tuesday morning, and the vicar would care for all that UH had requested. He was paid handsomely in advance for everything.

He didn't want to see his mother dead, as he had his father. He wanted to remember the mother who raised him, loved him, gave him her wisdom and guidance, and always supported his decisions whether or not she had agreed.

That night UH didn't say much. He and Jeanine slept in each other's arms.

Tuesday afternoon, UH's plane flew to Jerusalem. That late evening they were back at the Mamilla Hotel where they had a late, light meal, and returned to their room.

Wednesday Jeanine called Jacobs to tell him of UH's mother passing. Jacobs said that he would make calls to several others so that UH did not have to address the matter.

Elsa called and said that she was growing concerned about the chatter led by EU's First Vice President Armanda Philips who was disgruntled about Mr. Harrison's traveling, especially to the Middle East, and the enlarging of his office at the expense of the EU. He also questioned vigorously the elaborate office. "I am so worried. The complaining is simply isn't helpful," she said.

UH called Philips and told him that the expanded office was at his expense, and that the EU building had several vacancies that they had normally rented out. As to the expense of the computers, monitors, and other technological equipment had been at his expense as well.

"By the way, my many trips to Jerusalem had been in the interest of the EU—not at any expenditure to the EU. Anything else I can clear up for you Mr. Philips?" asked UH. "I might add that my trip to London had been due to my mother's death. Again at no cost to the EU. Anything else?"

Philips quickly said, "No. No, UH, I was merely questioning a few things in the spirit of good will. I hope that this will not affect our relationship at the EU."

"It will not. Accept my apology for being impatient, and calling you before meeting you in our offices," said UH.

Later that afternoon at the site, Jacobs, UH, Jeanine, Zarif, and Peres met, while UH and Jeanine had arrived a half hour later. All turned as they approached, and Jacobs led them in giving their condolences to UH.

Jacobs said, "UH, we had found out yesterday, that you had hired the landscapers for both properties, and what they have done is nothing short of amazing. At first, no one could figure out who had ordered this costly work. I see that new palm trees and fruit trees have been added. There are two new olive trees situated between the temple and the mosque. What are you trying to say?"

UH said, "I had simply told them to be creative."

"I like the idea of such a tree. The Islamic Council is indeed grateful, as this was not in our budget," said Zarif. "The minbar was installed earlier this morning. It was placed, of course, so that women in their chamber could view the Iman as he spoke to the men in the main worship space."

Jacobs said, "Not to change the subject, but we would like to take you on a tour of the rebuilt temple whenever you wish," said Jacobs

"How about next week, when you have done more, on the second and top floors," said UH.

"That will be good. I appreciate your time and how financially charitable you have been during the entire project," said Jacobs.

"I would agree," said Zarif, as the others nodded.

As UH and Jeanine said their goodbyes and were walking toward their taxi to head back to the hotel, Chu called UH. "UH, how do you like the landscaping?"

"Very nice," said UH standing outside of his taxi.

Chu said, "That is not why I had called. Let's talk later tonight. There are problems we will face in July, and I would like to discuss them with you just as a heads up. Consultations and warning telephone calls, that usually turn deadly, will be part of the next phase. I'll see you later."

Chu came to UH, after Jeanine and he returned from dinner.

While Jeanine was in the gift shop, Chu and UH discussed a few things like how timing meant everything, and that UH would get more leeway in dealing with those who refused his offer of cooperation. Chu wanted UH to travel next month, and yes, he could take Jeanine along. "The last day of June," said Chu, "we will meet to discuss details about setting up global zones which I call regions. This will be tricky, often aggravating, but will happen. As I have said many times, men of means, coupled with power, never want to die. There are exceptions, like religious fanatics. One last thing, don't count on the EU, because it might splinter and vanish, but you will not."

UH said, "Chu here comes Jeanine."

"She can't see me," said Chu. "Tomorrow, why not take an early weekend? Leave for France, enjoy your time together, and have a good time at the Casino De Monte Carlo. I will come to you at some time Friday when Jeanine is doing something away from us."

"Thank you Chu. I am already looking forward to our meeting on Friday," said UH.

Chu made a frown as he watched the two lovebirds walk to the elevators.

Thursday UH and Jeanine flew to the French Riviera, first to his home, and then off to the casino. However, when they had returned home, they found that his office and bedroom had had been vandalized. Chu called him, and UH had wondered why just the bedroom and office, and not the whole house, unless *we had frightened them off,* he thought.

Chu said, "I didn't want to disturb you at the casino, but three men from the CIA had ransacked your home, but they found nothing. Rowe had nothing to do with this. They had been put up to break-in by the Director of the CIA, Paul Braden, who believed you were not treating America fairly, and he thought that you had something to hide. Let me assure you that if he gets out of hand, he will disappear. I will give him a call, as it is still June."

"Who was that at this hour?" asked Jeanine.

UH said, "It was a friend from the EU who called to tell me that he had heard that my mother had died."

"This is just unbelievable. Let's go to a hotel, and worry about this mess tomorrow," said Jeanine wrapping her arms around UH's waist.

UH called a cab.

They arrived back home the next morning to find the house put back in order. UH thought that Chu acted quite speedily. Jeanine thought that UH had hired someone to clean it up.

Jeanine went to the kitchen to prepare a late breakfast.

Chu appeared to UH who was in his office. Chu said, "I had the house straightened up. I knew that you wouldn't mind. It's Friday, and we need to talk. On July 4th, the Al Aqsa Mosque will be completed; on July 27th the temple will be done except for one or two things needed for the old Holies of Holy on top. You probably will want to write these things down." Chu paused. "Ready? All right, thirdly, I hired your personal secretary. His name is Jamison, and he will assist you, and he knows of our relationship and how it works; but you know that."

"How can that be? I had thought no one could know our relationship," UH said loudly.

Jeanine hollered out, "Did you call me darling?"

"Yes. I was curious as to how long before we eat."

"I will call you when it's ready," she answered.

"As I was saying, Jamison is different, you will see. He will take direction from you and me. You will have more abilities and expanded responsibilities, but Jamison will be handling all land line calls and mobile calls, and webcam communications. He will sound like you on the phone, and look like you and sound like you when using the webcam. I will expand your activity because of the nature of our next strategy. You will ask to rent your offices from the EU. This should resolve at least one of Philips' difficulties. Finally, by August, you will be increasing your traveling as we chop the seven continents into twelve regions. We will discuss this in detail at the end of July. I hear footsteps." Chu disappeared.

"UH, breakfast is ready." She stopped in his doorway. "Oh my god, it's Friday. Let's do something different," Jeanine exclaimed. "I mean after we eat." She went over to his smiling face and kissed him. "I felt a little impetuous darling," she said smiling.

"Do you want to go the casino, or rent a sailboat, or shop? UH asked her.

"That is unfair. I want to do all three before Sunday night," she said with a lift in her voice.

Chu called Paul Braden. "Director Braden, there was an unfortunate break-in at the residence of EU President outside of Nice, France. I would like to know why." Chu knew why it had happened.

"I apologize, but I don't know an iota. By the way, who is this I'm talking to?"

"That is not important, but you are the agent in charge in Paris, and has stuck his nose in something that will stink all the way to Washington. Please call me back after you speak with him." Chu gave him the number on a throw away mobile.

Later that evening in a Paris hotel, CIA field agent Jimmy Latrell died in a gunfire exchange. Chu was grateful that Braden had handled so quickly. Braden had heard that UH had been targeted because of his work with radicals while in East Jerusalem. Latrell hated anyone working with Muslims, and Latrell had been involved with turning over a Hamas leader to Jewish radicals in Paris. He also had embezzlement issues. He had been suspected of other gross misconduct, and had become an embarrassment to the CIA. The CIA had had an investigation of Latrell for six months.

Monday, July 4th came too quickly for them both, but especially for Jeanine. On the plane she held his arm most of the way to Brussels.

UH called Zarif. "Congratulations on the completion of your new mosque. Thank you for sending the pictures. The mosaics are spectacular.

I will call you when I get back to Jerusalem."

"That sounds good," answered Zarif.

UH called Jacobs. "Are we still on target for the temple completion by the 27th?"

"Yes, the workers are busy twenty-four-seven, except on Friday," Jacobs said sounding like he had a new lease on life..

"You sound as though something uplifted your spirits."

"Yes UH, we have contacted the line of Aaron, you know the priest line. We found several men who will dress in a linens, robe, breast plate, turban, and all, to be in our ceremony on July 27th. We also have twelve other Levites who will also be there. This ceremonial reopening of the temple, has electrified Jews worldwide who wish to attend this significant event. We plan to have more than five thousand people in attendance. I hope that you will come, for you have done a most gracious work with us," Jacobs then added, "that is all of us in Jerusalem."

"Thank you Alon. I will be there." UH wrote the date and time on his on his laptop.

His door opened. UH stood up. "May I help you?"

"I would hope so UH. My name is Fredrick. Jamison Fredrick a man with two last names. Chu had hired me."

"Yes, very nice to meet you Fredrick, or would you prefer your first name." UH examined him with his eyes.

"Sir, Jamison is fine. I hope that I am dressed properly."

UH walked back around his desk after shaking the hand of Mr. Fredrick.

"Sir," he started.

UH interrupted him, "Please call me UH."

"Yes. Yes, I actually knew that. Sorry."

"Don't think anything of it. Have a seat," UH said pointing to brown leather chair.

"You will not be required to teach me anything in the office. Chu taught me. I know all these machines and platforms. I'll be doing most of the webaming for you. And I will be answering your telephone."

UH interrupted Jamison, "How will you do that?"

Jamison said, "Chu said that I will look and sound like UH, when I'm on the webcam or the telephone."

"I see," UH smiled. "This was Chu-strategy. Correct?"

"Of course."

"All right, when do you start?" UH stood.

"Now. I'll be at my desk." Jamison walked to his large cubical.

As Jamison left the office, Chu appeared to UH. "Plans for the temple celebration have become well known in Israel, and of course, the new Isis leader in Turkey has been planning an attack for that event. I will let him strategize until July 20th, and then kill him, his cohorts, and their lieutenants—five deep. I will disarm all explosives that have been set, and also kill anyone connected to this plot of mayhem in Jerusalem. This should thwart their plans, and help keep peace.

"As Jamison explained, he will look and sound like you, only when necessary. This next week on the eleventh, we will fix our regions and make announcements to the parties involved. I will have this ready for us. Have a good week." As quick as he said that, he said, "I have it. Go to Moscow to shop, dine, and of course, visit Koskov. He would like that."

Surprised, UH said, "What about Jamison and VP Philips?"

"Jamison knows his duties. Philips will be told that you are doing EU work. Russian has always wanted in the EU. Of course, the UK is thinking otherwise. In fact, citizens of the UK are themselves wishing to exit the EU."

"That will never materialize. Neither will either ever happen," protested UH.

"Don't be so touchy. None of these matters are in your control" assured Chu. He vanished.

Jeanine entered the offices with three bags, and started back to UH's office.

As she entered, UH said with great spirit, "Sweetheart, how would you like to fly to Moscow?"

"Oh my god, you're kidding me." She dropped the bags, and stood on her toes to throw her arms around his neck. When are we leaving?"

UH told her, "Tonight."

"Oh, I have so much packing to do."

"No baby, we will purchase what you need in Moscow. However, we are not going back to the apartment on our way to the airport." He explained to Jeanine that he had contacted the Brussels Airport to ready the plane, and had them file a flight plan to Moscow. He booked rooms at the luxurious five star Four Seasons Hotel which was just steps from the Kremlin, Red Square, and the State Duma where Koskov works. Jeanine did not once stop holding his hands, nor did her beautiful smile disappear.

"Tell me how this happened. Is it EU business?" Jeanine asked.

"Yes, actually that is it," UH kissed her.

"Jamison, we are off to Russia for a week for the EU.

"I know UH."

"Would you explain this to Elsa and Philips?" asked UH

"Of course. See you when you return. Have a good week," said Jamison.

Jeanine remarked, "That Jamison is a man of few words."

"I know, but he is efficient," smiled UH.

UH and Jeanine took a taxi from the Sheremetyevo International Airport to the Four Seasons Hotel. When they got to their room, Jeanine looked at UH and exclaimed, "Oh my god, I had no idea Russia was so modern. Actually, I had never imagined that I'd be in Russia."

"I have never been in Russia either. We shall see things for the first time—together." UH added, "I am so glad I'm here with you." He took her in his arms and held her for a moment, then kissed her."

They arrived in their room, and as UH looked out at the city, he remembered his father saying how much he had like visiting Moscow with his young wife.

"Let's shower together, if you know what I mean you handsome hunk of a man."

UH began to undress.

Koskov called UH just as he and Jeanine had dressed.

"UH, how good of you to visit Moscow. Is this business or vacation?"

"Viktor, it is mostly, vacation. I have not taken more than four days off in more than five years. I leave on the eleventh, very early in the morning, for I have a meeting in the late afternoon."

"Good. We can have dinner tonight at the Lepim i Varim. It's a five star restaurant. You will be my guests. I will bring a good bottle of brandy."

"What time would you like us there?" asked UH."Not good. I'll pick you up at your hotel at 5:00 pm sharp," said Viktor.

UH said, "All right then, Jeanine and I will do some sightseeing. We will see you at 5:00."

That evening at the Lepim i Varim, Viktor lifted a bottle of brandy form his leather case. "I bought this bottle from a friend at the Kremlin, who had bought the bottle for a good amount of money, but decided he did not like brandy. This is called Mendis Coconut Brandy. It is all clear and natural they say. But it is the most expensive brandy in the world."

"Why thank you Viktor. I am impressed," UH smiled.

A waiter came to the table, and asked for a drink order. Viktor ordered a bottle of vodka, and a brandy snifter for UH. Jeanine had a French wine. They talked about wine, vodka, the brandy, and that Viktor downs his Russian vodka, Jeanine sips her Chardonnay, and UH takes the French approach to drinking—take your time. The food was exquisite, and they spent an hour and a half eating and talking.

Their next meeting was for lunch on Wednesday.

"I am alone today," said UH. "Jeanine wished to do some shopping."

"That is all right. It's good she could do some shopping. You must balance business with holiday time," Viktor offered as he pullout his chair. It is just as well UH, for I wanted to ask you about our membership in the World Trade Organization. It was brought up yesterday at a meeting in the Duma. I know that there are those in the EU that see us as part of northern Europe. What are your thoughts?"

"Well, it has a large measure to do with Russia's taking thousands of miles of the Artic Sea, and then, seized Crimea from the Ukraine." UH continued, "Russian had also separated two cities in Georgia. All of this worries Europe and the EU."

"Most of this is a farce. We lost a third of our workforce from these aliens. People never did understand Russia," Viktor raddled and exclaimed, as customers in the restaurant looked at the two men, then back at their lunch.

"Viktor, that is a miscalculation, try ten or twelve percent of your workforce. These moves by the Kremlin seem suspicious to EU and the paper tiger, NATO. I will speak to the EU Board, before I go both to the EU members and the UN."

Viktor interjected, "The UK doesn't look good. People want out of the EU."

"Yes, I've heard the rumors. Let's eat my friend, and enjoy this pleasant July day," said UH.

They congenially parted, and said that they hoped to meet on the weekend.

Saturday evening, at the hotel restaurant, Viktor, Jeanine, and UH met for dinner.

"I heard several times today that the Russian economy is not very good. Is that true Viktor?" Jeanine asked.

"Allow me to answer with a question. Was your shopping good, I mean did you find good prices, and were people nice to you?"

Jeanine answered, "Yes to both of your questions. I think Moscow is an exciting place to visit."

"What is on your agenda tomorrow?" asked Viktor.

UH was taking a drink, so Jeanine said, "Probably more sightseeing, and a swim in the hotel pool."

UH nodded in agreement, and Viktor said, "That sounds good."

Monday, the early am flight to Brussels was on time. Jeanine napped, and UH did some work on his IPad in preparation for his meeting with Chu. Jeanine remained at the apartment Monday, while UH met with Chu in his EU office.

"Chu, thank you for suggesting Moscow. Jeanine and I thoroughly enjoyed ourselves."

"You are welcome. Sometimes we must clear our thinking. We have much to work on today. We won't complete it all, but we will get our heads around it today.

"First let's get a world map that displays the seven continents." Chu moved to a table in the office. I will get the map I had made last week. Look at these continents. We will divide the existing continents into nine zones. North America is to be divided into two sections: the United States with Canada; and Mexico with Central America, governed by one person in each, with two superintendents or directors in each. South America will have Antarctica attached with one to govern and two superintendents to assist; Africa will be divided into two regions: Northern Africa and Southern Africa with one person to govern each, and two superintends or directors in each. Europe, excluding Russia, will be governed by one person with two superintendents. Russia with be governed by one person with two superintendents or directors. Asia will be divided into four sections with one person in charge of each of the four: Middle East, China, India, and Malaysia. Australia will have one person in charge with two superintendents or directors.

"Do you understand so far?"

UH said that he did.

Chu went on. "Now we must select those who will govern these regions. The U.S. and Canada will be governed by James Rowe. Mexico with

Central America with be governed by Carlos Rodriquez. South America will be governed by Alfredo Colombo of Brazil. Northern Africa down to the Congo Basin, and will be governed by Egyptian President Alim Jabir. South Africa, including Madagascar will be governed by Samuel Kingston of South Africa. Europe will be governed by Franklin Pierce from the UK. Russian will be governed by Vladimir Nikolin. Asia's four regions: the Middle East will be governed Adam Almon from Israel; China will be governed by Yen Zhang; India will be governed by Arnav Kapoor; Malaysia will be governed by Aiman Megat. Australia will be governed by Sherman Russel.

"These are the twelve men that will not find it easy to change, but power has its own reward, and the new found wealth is the bonus. They will cooperate."

"Have they all been informed?" questioned UH.

"Not yet, but by Wednesday, they will," Chu said refolding the map. "Keep in mind, that when these Regional Zones are set up, there will be no European Union, nor a European Commission, and the UN will eventually go by the way.

"My gosh, that's right," said Chu as though it was new to him. " Neither the EU or the EC will exist, and Kobie Alber, Secretary General of the United Nations will be out of a job," concluded Chu.

"Isn't Wednesday the thirteenth? I had planned on being in Jerusalem," said UH.

Chu changed the plan. "Ms. Swenson called from the UN and said that she had been asked to find a speaker for this Wednesday, because the original speaker had taken ill last week. She remembered you because at one time, she had worked for the EU. She actually works as head of the Development Agenda—nothing to do with speakers"

"Chu, what shall I talk about? Certainly nothing to do with the fracturing EU," complained UH.

Chu suggested, "Solar power. It is a hot topic, costly to purchase and repair, and not easy to sell. I think that Solyndra learned that."

UH thought for a moment, then, "I suppose that I could keep it under thirty minutes as Swenson had suggested. I'll have Jamison call her and tell her that I'll do it."

Chu said, "You will do fine. You always find a way to interest people."

UH went to Jamison and had him call Ms. Swenson. Then he called the Brussels Airport to have his plane readied for the transatlantic flight to New York. He called Jeanine to tell her that they would be flying to New York City on Wednesday morning.

Jeanine asked, "Must we leave early, I mean like 5:00 in the morning?"

"Yes," UH said, "but we can sleep on the plane. We will be staying at the Trump Tower."

"Oh my god, I have seen pictures of that hotel. I'm so excited UH."

Wednesday UH spoke to the UN Clean Energy and Climate Change Conference about global warming and the need for clean solar energy. "President Carter led the way..." He said

"Imagine, if cities began to go solar..., with businesses requiring large amounts of electricity, the excess electricity could sold for a profit to small businesses and non-commercial consumers... Cities and counties that put in solar panels and windmills could receive abatements and government assistance... windmill farms in conducive regions would ease the energy burden throughout the world..." After thirty-eight minutes, UH received a polite standing ovation. He answered questions, thanked everyone, receive a plaque, and he was thanked for coming on such short notice.

That afternoon, UH and Jeanine went to the Trump Tower's Jean-George Restaurant. He had their top shelf brandy, and Jeanine had a California fine wine, but almost choked on the first sip, when she saw the price of dinner for the Summer Menu: two hundred and eight dollars. When they had finished their appetizer, a waiter came to their table, and said that Jean-Georges Vongerichten, the chef proprietor had provided them with the soup of the day in a glass tapered shot glass.

"This is such a beautiful place. I love the elegance," said Jeanine to UH.

President Rowe had asked to meet UH on Thursday, when he had learned that UH was going to be in the city.

UH receive a mobile call. "This is UH."

"UH, this is Rowe. I just landed a LaGuardia, and tonight will be staying at the Lotte. I selected the superior guest room for our meeting. Will that be all right for you?"

"Yes, of course. We are at the Trump Towers."

"Would 9:00 a.m. be fine?" Rowe asked. "You're not far from the Lotte."

UH agreed, "I will meet you in the morning."

"Thank you UH."

Thursday, UH took a taxi to the Lotte, and was escorted by Rowe's security to the room.

President Rowe seemed a little edgy. The two men exchanged greetings and shook hands. They sat at a small conference table Rowe had brought in for the meeting.

"I will get to the point. Reed is not too happy that Canada will be part of my region," began Rowe. "May I offer him the supervisor position?"

"Of course you may," said UH.

"Another issue has to do with dividing the United States into two sections, west of the Mississippi, and east would extend to the Atlantic. Hawaii, Guam, and various territorial islands would be part of the west. The east would include Cuba, Puerto Rico and the islands that are around them. Pedro Sanchez of Cuba said that his allegiance was to Russia." Rowe was calming down as he had begun to speak with UH.

UH said, "Don't worry yourself about Reed or Sanchez. As far as Sanchez, Russia has been told, and the Kremlin will address it. Everyone will get in line. We are all thinking in the back of our heads, what a travesty it would be if the aliens returned. Look what happened after the initial shock of losing almost twelve percent of our global population; South America lost sixty or seventy leaders; and then think about the more than two thousand who had died mysteriously in the Middle East. We are not conducting a war, yet we all must work together for peace. Dividing the world into twelve regions will further help work toward this end.

"The directors are expected to hire two to three supervisors in their regions. They will assist you and the other directors primarily. So keep your finger on the pulse of each supervisor, and in that way, they will apply the right amount of pressure on the administrators, who in turn will give direction to the twenty-five administrators, men and women, who keep the people assured that peace is just around the corner. This will be the chain of command. What I am telling you now, will be given to each regional director."

"I see," said Rowe. "I can do this." Rowe thought for a minute, like a politician.

"Directors or superintendents are not elected."

UH agreed, "That is correct. The twelve directors have permanent positions."

Rowe smiled, stood up, hardily shook UH's hand, and said, "This was a fruitful meeting. I am grateful for your time UH."

UH left, went downstairs to find Jeanine sitting outside of the Palace Gift Shop eating a Hershey Chocolate bar.

Jeanine saw UH and stood up. "You know darling this bar tastes so different from European chocolate."

"Yes, I know that very well," said UH. "Let's take a cab back to Trump Tower and plan our day for tomorrow, for we leave on Saturday."

"How was your meeting with Rowe?" asked Jeanine.

"Rather interesting for me. Making a decision or two without my assistant back in Brussels."

Jeanine asked, "Do I know him or her?"

"Not yet my sweet girl." UH grabbed her arm in a playful manner.

Saturday, a sunny, but windy day to fly out of LaGuardia to Brussels.

Monday morning, at the office, Jamison shared with UH, that his last two days of the week were a bit hectic.

"What do you mean Jamison?"

Jamison went on, "Chu had sent me your order of command. You know, director to supervisor to administrator. I then emailed this information. You had explained this to Rowe. I merely sent it to the other eleven. Three of the directors emailed back to me. They were having disagreements with those who were having difficulty giving up a presidency or a prime minister's position." He took a dramatic breath. "And yes, I did send the information to all eleven from your computer. At the last minute, I send Rowe the same information, because he is Rowe."

"Thank you Jamison. Who were the directors that finding this arrangement problematic?" asked UH.

"It is President Alim Jabir of Egypt," Jamison began, "who claimed that the Nigerian and the Algerian President were angry that neither had been selected to be director of northern Africa."

"Had they given any other reasons?" UH thought about what Jamison had said.

"No, but each man thought that he was talking to you when I had called them. Nothing more was mentioned," responded Jamison.

Invisibly, Chu said to UH, *Pride. That pesky un-doer of men.*

"You are probably right," said UH.

Chu asked, "UH, would you go to your private office?"

UH told Jamison that he'd be back.

Chu said, "Vladimir Nikolin wants more territory, like Ukraine. Sherman Russel of Australia said that he is too old, and had planned to retire in December. Here is what you will do: give Nikolin the Ukraine, Belarus, and Kazakhstan; remind the presidents of Nigeria and Algeria what happened in South America last month; and explain to Russel that we will select another man to be director in Australia. In fact, tell him that he may resign now, and we will appoint Jeremy Leeds as Director. Russel is to bring Leeds up to speed."

Following the telephone call to these men, they were dissatisfied, but eventually agreed.

Tuesday morning, Jamison emailed the twelve directors from UH's computer stating that by the end of the work week, he needed the names, addresses, land line telephone numbers, and mobile numbers of their chosen supervisors. Further, the supervisors are to require the same information from their administrators. By Friday, UH had this information. He had Jamison put the new information into a new file called "12 Regions".

Chu appeared to UH. "We appear to be ahead of schedule, for this is only the fifteenth of July. You have done well UH. You and Jeanine should fly to France. I will see you on Monday. Next week, on Friday the 22nd is the Jewish Temple Rededication, They will invoke the blessing of their god in great praise for the prophet Ezra, and of course, Zerubbabel who had built the second temple. That information is for you, when Jacobs, Perez, and others begin throwing names around. For security reasons, the event has been moved up to Friday the twenty second. Have a nice weekend. Your plane is ready."

"Thanks Chu."

UH called Jeanine.

"My love, we are headed to France for the weekend.

"Our holidays, whether long or short, are grand. I love you," said Jeanine.

Rowe called UH. "I appreciate that you cleared up the matter with Reed. His unrelenting pressure on me was not something I was willing to content with very much longer. Well, thanks again. Bye."

"Goodbye Director Rowe."

The Third Jewish Temple

July twenty second, at three pm, East Jerusalem, Israel, the celebration began.

Jacobs whispered to UH, "My security tells me that five days ago seventy-seven men and women of the Muslim faith, primarily Isis, attempted to kill as many as they could during this celebration. I am not surprised. Unfortunately, a Kach member had planned the same for the Al Aqsa Mosque. The leader is Aaron Elberg. We will handle all of them."

UH said, "We too heard of this plot, but people like that engender hate, not peace."

Jacobs face frowned, "How did you know the extent of the plot, which had been conceived in Paris?"

UH leaned his head toward Jacobs. "One day Jacobs, I will tell you." UH turned his head back toward the speaker.

The Rabbi Peres spoke in Hebrew, and once he read a quote in Arabic. He announced before the reading from the prophets, that three men who had lineage to the priesthood were attending, although the kohanim ceased to exist sometime after 90 CE. He called them forward as he explained their white linen garments, the breastplate, and caps, and one who had worn a turban.. One kohein explained that rabbis preferred prayer, service to the synagogue, and giving to others as a proper sacrifice. There were songs and psalms sung, led by a cantor; readings from Ezekiel and Ezra were read; and speeches about the use of the new temple with references to the new school and museum. The Holy of Holies on top of the Holy Temple would be a prayer room. He concluded his remarks with the last verse of Ezekiel, "The name of the city is: The Lord in There—Jerusalem."

The actual ceremony lasted until 4:30 pm. The celebration went on until the Sabbath, but picked up on Saturday night.

Sunday, Jacobs asked UH if he would tell him how he knew about the saboteurs.

UH said in a rather frank manner, "By August, I will share with you and the nine directors just how this is done through informants." He also said, "Peace is paramount, and any person on this planet who refuses to adhere to our global goals, will be dealt with—speedily."

Jacobs said, "When I think of what happened three months ago I shudder to my shoes, but did you have anything to do with the deaths in South America?"

UH tried to avoid the truth, "I think that maybe it was an outcome of what happened three months ago when a twelve percent of the world had been taken."

They continued to walk toward a taxi waiting for UH and Jeanine.

"I am worried about the new temple because of the two month planning that these ruthless warriors of death had been working on. Am I able to ever find relief for Israel?" Jacobs hung his head and sighed. "Are you able to warn us through your informers, you will call us in plenty of time?"

UH took Jacobs shoulder, "I will be in touch regularly with the twelve directors and you, or whoever is Prime Minister of Israel. Each of you may call me anytime. There is coming a day, when thieves to global assassins will vanish, and drug lords and the mafia will cease to exist. There is hope for mankind."

Jacobs bid farewell to UH, as UH and Jeanine turned to get into their taxi.

In the taxi, Jeanine said to UH, "You are so smart and articulate. I see why world leaders listen to you."

On the plane, Chu told UH that what he had said to Jacobs was indeed the truth, but it would take months to happen. "Little skirmishes, I call them. We are going to use General Patton's methodology of attack. He said, 'Attack rapidly, ruthlessly, viciously, without rest.' We too will use speed to dispatch violent men, and murderous individuals by the thousands, and those who want peace will look the other way."

UH said, "I believe that in every place in the world, there are pockets of those who wish to keep resisting us with violence, hate, and bigotry. For instance, Rowe told me that he is investigating a group in Montana, and Zarif, along with Jacobs, said they don't know if terrorism will ever end."

Chu responded, "In August, we will set a course to eradicate these kinds of people.

Between you, Jamison, and me, peace is around the corner. We will focus the rest of July in Israel, for until we contain the killing in Israel, in fact, until we control the Middle East, we cannot clean up the rest of the world of such terrorists who directly receive the financing from Saudi Arabia, Iran, and others. Isis will be the first to go.

"Tuesday through Friday, be in Jerusalem, and then back there the on Monday the 31st when I shall lay out our strategy for August, and give you more ability to deal with issues, rather than just me. You will like that. You are getting quite a world reputation as a peace maker."

UH telephoned Jacobs, "Alon, this is UH. I will be in Jerusalem on Tuesday and stay until Friday."

"That will be fine. Could we meet sometime during your visit?" asked Jacobs.

"That would work, because I need to speak with you on Tuesday morning, if that is good with you. I am flying in on Monday afternoon."

"How about, let me see…" Jacobs looked at his schedule. "would 9:00 am be a good time for you?"

"Indeed. See you then my friend," said UH.

UH and Jeanine flew into Jerusalem on Monday.

Tuesday morning UH sat across from Jacobs.

"What can I do for you UH?" asked Jacobs.

"As you know, my goal is universal peace, but this cannot occur until the Middle East is first to experience it. So, I am here to explain, you will have reports of militants and terrorists on your watch list dropping dead, or will vanish." UH waited for a response as Jacobs scratched the side of his head.

"To begin with, I do not care how many of the monsters die, but how will this happen within the law."

UH said, "This will be under a time of unannounced martial law."

Jacobs said, "I do not want to know how this will be done. Allow me to simply reap the benefits." He continued, "Will all twelve directors eventually know what I don't, at this time?"

"Probably in late August or early September," a relieved UH said.

"That is acceptable to me. When will this begin?" asked Jacobs.

UH said, "This week. These terrorists are throughout the world, but that will not be of any concern, and this cleansing for peace begins tomorrow."

"You will be here until Friday? May I call you between now and then," asked Jacobs.

"Yes." UH stood. "You may call me anytime." They shook hands, and Jacobs followed UH to the door.

"UH, please step back in." Jacobs said closing the door. "I noticed that Jabir of Egypt is director over Muslim and non-Muslim countries, as is Samuel Kingston of South Africa. Is that wise?" asked Jacobs.

UH smiled, "Just as you are a leader of Muslim and non-Muslim in Israel." He opened the door and said goodbye to Jacobs, who smiled back in acknowledgement.

Chu contacted UH in his hotel room as he and Jeanine were watching a local network. "UH, meet me in the lobby, near the bar."

UH excused himself, saying that he had to meet with someone about their business in Jerusalem.

"UH, I will make this brief. Tomorrow at noon, this time zone, there will not be an Isis member, or sympathizer on this globe. This includes wives, husbands, friends, and acquaintances. I will not make any vanish, other Muslims will bury them. Directors and their staffs will take notice. I want other terrorist groups to comprehend what will happen to them in the coming days. When the news gets out, and it will, everyone with a television will know. I will talk with you tomorrow." Chu was gone.

UH called Jeanine to ask her to come down to the bar for a few drinks.

When she arrived, Jeanine looked at UH and realized that he was in deep thought.

"Darling, who was that who needed to talk to you?"

UH said, "An associate." Her voice made him feel better. "Let's get an appetizer."

Thursday, Chu came to UH.

"Chu, Jacobs tells me that the new Mufti at the Al Aqsa Mosque is stirring up a few Muslims."

Chu agreed, "Yes, I know, but I am letting anyone, as you say jibber jabber, until Saturday when I will reassess the next move."

UH questioned, "When did I use that word?"

"Only once, about three months ago," Chu answered. "Let's move on. Jamison called Rowe on your behalf and told him to destroy the KKK and other US terrorists, but he had complained that their constitution would not allow such a thing. Jamison told him that the Constitution permitted Martial Law in a national dangerous event that caused on-going harm to the citizens. Jamison reminded him of what had happened three months earlier around the globe.

"Rowe balked, but Jamison said that it must be done. He said to Rowe, 'On the pretext of violence through their rhetoric, find a way to instigate conflict with all such groups, and destroy them.' He still hesitated, "I am thinking that I will clean out these no-goods myself, all of them in the US that are anything like the KKK." UH didn't say anything, but his mouth turned into a frown. "UH, listen to me. It is either Rowe handling it, or I will."

UH said, "Give Rowe that ultimatum, and let him live with the decision."

"That is what Jamison did." Chu smiled, "I'll talk with him on Saturday."

UH and Jeanine left for France. On the flight, Jeanine asked, "What's this I hear on the news? Muslims throughout the world are burying dead Muslims. CNN asked if Muslims are turning on each other after such peaceful relations in Jerusalem.

UH said, "Muslims are burying radical extremists. It is still unclear why this happened, but I will say that there is a growing consensus, that peace will eventually come. If this is some alien force helping us, I don't know." He hoped that would satisfy her.

"What happens if," she hesitated, when UH interrupted her.

"Let's not talk about it now," UH took her hand. "I want to go to the casino tonight."

Saturday, late morning Chu found UH by the pool.

"Good morning Chu." UH said as he noticed Chu coming toward him.

"UH, the Muslim world has been a bit perplexed for the last two days, but so has Jews, as Jewish groups of terrorists have as they are burying terrorists. There are those who said that the radical extremists members should rot where they had died; others say that the Quran says that dead Muslims must be buried within two days; and many secular Muslims say good riddens to the psychopaths. After the slain were quickly buried on Friday, I had been listening and observing the remaining Muslim sects and Jewish sects. I hope that Jacobs and the Knesset realize that Israeli terrorists in Israel, and elsewhere in the world are having funeral services. I am sure that you had noticed that many Al Qaeda members who had sympathized with what Isis had been doing, are also being buried. In fact, other radical groups like Boko Haram in Nigeria died with Isis. This is one of two ways to deal with them."

UH asked, "What is the other way?"

Chu answered, "Rowe had been given the other way to deal with radicals by a military general, now dead, by warning all nations who support terrorism, that if a terrorist was linked to a county, or countries, that nation, or nations, would have a hydrogen bomb dropped on those participating countries. He believed that other nations who were directly, or indirectly, supporting terrorism would fall in line. He further stated that this process would continue until terrorism stopped. He also stated that any terrorist acts committed anywhere in the world, that if the investigation of that terrorist or terrorists could be linked to a country of origin, that country would suffer the blunt force of a hydrogen bomb. He didn't care if a country sponsoring terrorism was completely obliterated.

"This had been too much for Rowe and his world image, so he fired the general, who was found dead in his back yard, from a single shot in the back of his head. That is why my way must be chosen now."

Chu went back to what he had been talking about, "That Mufti in East Jerusalem came close to dying with Isis. He is plotting to do great damage to the new temple. Jacobs knows about this, but can't move until he breaks the law, even though he had been told about martial law. We on the other hand, may be preemptive. One word will describe our work: efficient. Plan on being in Brussels on Monday. We need to assure Jacobs that all will be well. Also, Rowe is meeting with a select group of US Congressman, his cabinet, his three supervisors, and Military Chief of Staff—yes he still feels presidential. He is discussing US Martial Law details compared to the World Zone Coalition. More information will be on Monday. Bye."

UH sat on his lounge chair, starring at the Mediterranean. Jeanine watched him for a time inside the sliding door.

She went out to him, "What is my man so deep in thought about," Jeanine asked as she stroked his hair.

"Thinking of us," he lied.

"Don't fib. You were too deep in thought with no thin smile." She kissed him. He pulled her down onto the lounge chair and held her in his arms. They stayed there watching the great sea together for a half hour.

"We haven't shopped together since Moscow," he said. "Let's go into town. I'll call a cab."

"A cab? Who's Mercedes is in the garage?" she asked.

"I'll check out the car, you get ready," he said walking through the kitchen to the garage.

Just then, Chu said, "UH I forgot—not hardly, to tell you that I had purchased that for you. The color, a deep blue, almost black. Do you like it?"

"Why yes, I do. Thank you Chu."

"You are quite welcome. Tell Jeanine that you had forgotten that you bought it, and had it delivered last week. The chauffeur should be arriving now by a taxi.

"See you Monday." Chu was gone.

They shopped in Nice and ate dinner there. On the way back, Jeanine asked if his mother had left him any inheritance. He said that she had left him no more than two thousand pounds, the same amount she had given to the Anglican Church in London.

Out of nowhere, Jeanine asked UH, "Darling please tell me what is bothering you."

"Sweetheart may we discuss this after Monday?"

She thought about Monday. *Is it an anniversary? Did his wife die on July 31st? Is he losing his job at the EU?*

"Jeanine, why are you so quiet?" UH asked.

"Nothing really. I was asking myself if Monday was an anniversary of some kind."

UH smiled, "No anniversary. It's the last day of July, and August begins a new task. I will be spending more time without you—I think. I'll be in the office, primarily. Even on our weekends to France, I will be busier. But, then again, I may not be that busy." He was thinking of Jamison's role, taking on his image and the sound of his voice.

Jeanine asked, "I hope that your thinking is ok. Darling, whatever it is, I understand. They got out of the car. UH walked toward Jeanine.

"Come here you sweet woman," UH said, as he pulled her into his arms.

Monday in Brussels, UH watched the news in his office. Jacobs called.

"UH this is Jacobs, this whole Muslim situation is greatly reducing terror activity. I believe it is because Isis is gone, Hamas as well lost men; some PLO and Al Qaeda followers died last week too. The only one rousing up people is the new Mufti. He was a pupil of Mufti Haj Amin al-Husseini, Hitler's friend, who died in 1974. He recently came from the Great Mosque in Mecca. He goes back there in January. He is attempting to start trouble. He's raising doubts in Imam Ammon and a select group of members of the mosque concerning the thousands of deaths of Muslims, and brought concern about the fewer death of Jews and Christians.

"They don't seem to care who is doing these things that they call reprehensible acts. They just blame others. What's next?"

UH said, "The less of fundamental radical terrorists in the world, the fewer incidents of terrorism occurs. All followers of terrorism and all of their sympathizers in other organizations died last week. If this Mufti causes a problem he will have seventy-two virgins to deal with. I don't know, but I have a suspicion that the Mufti will be included in next round of persons who find themselves in opposition to peace, and that is an unhealthy position. Don't be alarmed when you hear what transpires in Israel or Northern Ireland. Concerning such matters, don't be surprised what will take place in the United States."

"Some in the Knesset are asking if they are next," Jacobs interjected. "I assured them that this was not the case."

"That is true, but if any of them are in support of the seven Jewish terrorist groups, small or large, like the Bat Ayin, Lehava, or Shin Bet, it could go bad for that person," UH said.

"Jacobs, I must go, Director Rowe is calling me."

"Yes, this is UH."

"UH, over the weekend, I had a discussion about Martial Law with some members of Congress, Chief of Staff and two of his advisors, and my three superintendents, I mean supervisors. The consensus was that we impose martial law which in turn will aggravate the KKK and others radical groups to the point that they will see this as a provocation and will act out their hate, and take up arms. We are prepared to eradicate all such individuals in this region. Reed also in on board. We have completed burying the dead, mostly radical Muslim sympathizers." Rowe added, "The press will have a field day with this Martial Law business. We announced Martial Law this morning. I will keep you abreast of all that happens here."

UH thanked him and hung up, when he heard Chu speak to him.

"UH we have two more attacks to make on the radicals. One is in Ireland, the other in Italy, still another in Mexico, but this will make you richer, and the last one is Russia. Tomorrow we will send a message of death to all such gangs, thugs, and underground law breakers. This will send a message to Asia: no more gang activity. By the end of August we should have much of the world controlled. I plan on making you very rich when I shut down all drug lords, underground mafias, and other scoundrels in the world. This should bring in more than thirty billion dollars. Yes, billion. August will be good to you. Tomorrow, I would like you and Jeanine to take a short vacation at your area of France, not Paris, as you and Jeanine had talked about, because they are still reeling from last week, burying the dead.

"Wednesday could be a busy day, if the Mufti and others in Israel don't abide by our peace initiative. I will of course, keep you in the loop, as some say. Have a nice week."

UH and Jeanine flew to Nice that evening. In flight, UH thought, *I am going to be very powerful and extremely rich. I had never dreamed of that much money.* He looked at Jeanine, who was dozing. *My sweet lady will be by my side all the way.*

"UH, this is Chu. I decided to give you more than the language abilities. From now on, you will be able to speak in any one's voice. Not mine, but Jamison's, Jeanine's, or anyone else on this planet. I might add, that I will soon be your assistant—that people will be able to see. You will pretend to give me direction as you would Jamison. By the end of August, I will give you another ability. Enjoy yourself, Jeanine's beauty is breathtaking, and she is inviting. Good thing, I'm not human. Talk with you Wednesday."

UH didn't have a chance to respond to Chu. Chu did things like that to help UH think about what he had said to him, but today he learned that Chu wasn't a human ghost. Yes, he had suspected that, but reality of who Chu was, had begun to worry him—although, not much, for to a humanist, money and power dulls the senses of morality.

Jeanine turned her head and asked, "Are we almost in Nice?"

"We are about a half hour away my sweet." Again, UH couldn't keep his eyes off of her.

Jeanine said, "We have almost been together three months, but it seems longer, with all the travel, excitement, our times together in Nice, and our deep fondness for each other, or should I say how we've grown to love each other."

"What are you trying to say my sweetness?" said UH.

Jeanine didn't know where to start, so she said, "Well, we have both been married before, and I was thinking about that every time I hear your voice, or watch you dance, oh my god the way you fight. I want to spend the rest of my life with you, so that is what I was trying to say."

He just sat there starring at her. She got up, said that she had to go to the bathroom, and left him thinking.

He was uneasy about marrying again, but Jeanine was so full of life, extremely beautiful, yet not an academic like Sun had been, but highly intelligent in her own right. He believed that Sun would be happy for him to love someone. He thought to himself, *I must let go of Sun and William.*

Jeanine came back and sat down.

"I need you in my life," UH began, "for love does not come easily for anyone, but especially for me. You are a refreshing spirit in my life. I have been anxious about a second marriage, until you. I have traveled the world, met other women, but you have become my world. Just now, as I was thinking, the very thought of life without you would be shallow, without meaning, without the joy that I have found with you. Let's begin planning for a wedding," he said with a lift in his voice.

She jumped up, went over to him, pushed him sideways on the couch, and laid on top of him. She lifted her head enough to look into his eyes, "I love you so much. If there ever was a a handsome man, who was a man's man, and a romantic, I found him in you." She kissed him. Soon they got up and went to their bedroom.

They landed in Nice, a bus took them to their car, and they drove to UH's home. They talked about renting a yacht for a couple of days. When they arrived home, UH was about to make a call to the Port of Nice Yacht Club, when Chu called.

"You now own a luxurious super yacht at the Port of Nice. It is two hundred and four feet, and three inches from bow to stern. There is a large master bedroom, seven cabins, one of which is a new office I had set up with satellite connection for your computer, phone, and fax. It has a gym with equipment you like to use. Master Chen can travel with you, when you wish. I had the bar stocked. It is called the *Catherine Marie*.

"Take a week. I will still call you on Wednesday. There is a crew of eighteen, which includes the captain and his staff."

UH said, "Thank you for thinking of this yacht…" Chu was gone.

UH called out, "Jeanine, I found the yacht we had talked about on the way here."

"Good darling. When can we go?"

"This evening."

Jeanine came from the bedroom, "That was fast. How long do we have it for?"

"We will be gone four days. I had been working on the purchase for some time," he said.

"The global economy has been unsound for almost seven years, so this had been a good time to buy it."

"How much darling is a good price?"

"My price was one million, one hundred thousand dollars," he answered, not looking at her.

"Oh my god. Where does one get a million dollars to spend on a boat?"

"I will explain everything when we get on board," UH said. "I want you to have a good life with me."

"That is an understatement," she smiled grabbing his arm as they left.

They sailed down the coast to Spain on Monday evening and all day Tuesday. Nothing was more enjoyable than being with each other. He coveted their relationship, but still in the back of his mind, he feared leaving her alone in Brussels or Nice; he understood, that his thinking that irrational, but because of Sun and William deaths, the fear seemed real. Jeanine longed to spend every moment with him because of who she believed he was.

On Wednesday morning, Chu called.

"The Mufti has allies in Saudi Arabia, Kuwait, in Dubai, and even more such states. They are financing all of the Mufti's plans. After all that has transpired, they still hold on to a lie, that for some reason, Allah was behind all of the Muslim deaths. Today, the Mufti and his cohorts, in Saudi Arabia, or anywhere else on this miserable planet, will lay were they died. Israel will have no terrorists after tonight.

"Pierce, in the Europe Region is being informed as we speak, through Jamison as you, that no terrorist will survive tonight, anywhere in the Europe. The dead in Europe and elsewhere, will be buried by whatever city or town finds the bodies. Vladimir Nikolin will be called next. The Russian gangs, the mafia, like the Bratva, and all the Russian mafia arms that reach Asian, the US, and in another places others will die tonight. About fifty billion dollars will go missing—it's yours to find. That money does not include money from Asian gangs, mafia, and the underworld enterprises when we go there. They too will lay where they die, and cities in all these countries will bury them. I want every one of our directors, supervisors, and administrators to know that more deaths are coming until the peace we had planned, is attained. No religion is exempt. I will call you Saturday. You and Jamison will be busy answering questions from the twelve directors.

"I hope that you are enjoying yourselves. Just for your information, the yacht that you're on was only nine hundred thousand dollars. Bye."

UH decided to return on Friday.

At UH's house, Jeanine seemed anxious. UH went over to her. "Sweetheart, what is the matter?"

"Today while you were in the pool, I had been watching the news. All the networks were pretty much saying the same thing. Millions upon millions of people are dropping dead. This isn't like what happened three months ago, is it?"

"No darling. What the news failed to tell you is that all of these millions were against peace. They were vicious radicals and malicious terrorists who plagued the world with violence and murder."

"Ok, but who is killing these people or causing them to die?" she asked.

"The twelve directors and their staffs concur—they don't know for sure, but probably the same aliens who took people three months ago—but not good people this time." UH had no other answers.

Jeanine looked into his eyes, "I am scared darling."

"Sometimes I am too," said UH. UH didn't answer his phone.

Jacobs called UH and left a message "UH, I am elated, almost jubilant. We will be burying thousands of terrorists all over Israel. Knesset members are calling me. They are ecstatic that now we may worship in the Holy Temple, teach in our school, and do any archeological searches without the evil watchful eyes of those who hate us. Israel is at peace. Thank you UH. Shalom."

"Pierce called me to assure me that he is on top of everything that is going on," Jacobs added.

It just really hit UH. Peace in Israel.

UH's mobile rang, "UH, this is the UN Secretary General, Kobie Alber.

"Yes Mr. Secretary General. How may I help you?"

"I am calling to thank you personally for your efforts and success in Israel. I do not comprehend all that you had done, but you did bring peace to what seems to have been, an eternal problem. Because other nations are finding peace because of you, we had recommended to the Nobel Peace Prize committee in Oslo, Norway should go to you. The committee sent a letter to me stating that your name had already been put in the nomination process. You should be hearing from Oslo in the next few months. There is no doubt that you should receive this prestigious award. We at the UN would like to honor you with dinner to give tribute for your life of seeking peace.

"No one believed that the Third Temple would be a reality."

Alber continued, "Would August 30th be good for you?—that is a Monday."

"Certainly, I'll make myself available for that event," smiled UH. He added, "I don't really know what to say, but I am quite grateful and honored."

"I must say that you are such a strong candid that your age means nothing," said Alber.

"I must say that I had heard that political personages were not being considered by the committee."

"UH, yes that is true, yet all that you have done for peace is nothing short of astounding, said Alber. "I will let you go now. Thank you for your service to the world."

"Darling, that was UN Secretary General telling me that I have been nominated for the Nobel Peace Prize. He also said that on August 31st we are to be in New York for a dinner in honor of me." UH kissed her smile.

UH shifted gears, "Be sure of one thing my love, all I care about is an absolute monogamous relationship of love, now and forever. "

"I will confess something to you." Chu said in UH's ear, *Watch yourself.*

UH ignored him. "I am a very wealthy man thanks to investments made over the years. Whenever I'd get a bonus check, or a large check from my work and didn't need it, it would go into my investment portfolio."

"I don't know how much you are worth," said Jeanine, "how much are you worth?"

Chu said, *"Tell her one and a half billion. That will satisfy her."*

"Oh my god, you are a billionaire." She stood in the kitchen with her hands on her hips.

"My gosh! You could buy any woman you would have wished to have."

UH went to her, embraced her, and said, "I have the woman I wished for and I love her deeply. You are my sweet, sweet, beautiful wife to be."

"I had often wondered how you could afford weekends, or days at a time, or flying here and there. Now my love, you have a luxury yacht," said Jeanine.

"But more importantly, I have you," he said putting arms around her neck.

Saturday, Chu called UH. "UH, first things first, I am giving you another ability, the power to discern and hear what anyone in the world is contemplating to do, for good or evil. That includes directors and all of their people. When Jamison impersonates you, he too will have this ability. I realize that we are three days out from August, but it is necessary, for this will enable decisive pre-emptive action of whatever kind you wish to employ. Secondly, I split up three hundred billion dollars into twelve banks and put most of it into of your new accounts. The bankers don't have insurance limits for us, but I've spoken to them, if you catch my drift.

"Congratulations on your nomination in Oslo, and I hope that you and Jeanine will have a spectacular night in New York at the UN sponsored dinner."

Then the discussion centered around Jeanine yesterday. "I thought you had handled it well, switching your focus on money. I'll help keep you straight my friend. I had been concerned that our relationship was about to be revealed.

"From Thursday through today, three million bodies of the dead were buried and still being buried by cities around the globe. We are nearing our peace initiative goal. Good work UH. Talk with you later."

UH said, "Jeanine, on Tuesday, the 21st of August, I will be hiring a new personal assistant and financial advisor, Eduardo Casus. He will handle all of my highly classified business, like my investments, dealing with the staff for the plane and yacht, with updates and repairs. He will also care for my house in France."

"Well my darling, you certainly have the money to hire such a man," Jeanine laughed. "I have always seen you as an intelligent, driven, and successful man. I'm sure that Mr. Castus will meet your needs.

"His name is Casus," UH said, "There is no T. Thank you for having confidence in me," UH added.

Monday morning at the office, UH had a brief joint EU and EU Commission meeting. They congratulated him for his work in Israel that seemed to have positive influence on other nations in the Middle East. They all agreed that this will be financially beneficial for the economy. With the workforce depleted almost twelve percent in the Middle East and Europe, they were positive in the short term assessment. They wanted to adjust the EU pay scale for board members. There had been only two members who abstained. They thoroughly understood that he had to extensively travel to Israel, New York, and Moscow, and his work with the UK to keep them in the EU. They wondered if he needed an assistant—he declined an increase in pay and the idea of an assistant.

"Gentlemen and ladies," UH began, "the EU is facing seriously difficult times financially. Some members, as you are aware of, are contemplating withdrawing from the EU because of migrants, but that is to change under my peace initiative, but they also believe that we have a debt problem almost as bad Greece. The EU has been extremely good to me. Therefore, I want to ask my friends to match my gift of one billion dollars by December 1st. I have many friends who might want to give a a total of a few billion dollars, if they see that we are being more frugal. I don't want you to think that I am ungrateful, but I must take some leadership role in rebuilding this fine organization."

They all stood and clapped with approval.

"You have been our finest example of EU leadership since our inception," said a board member.

"Good meeting I assume," said Jamison. "A new personal advisor will be here tomorrow. You need one. You missed a call while in your meeting. I handled it. Carlos Rodrigues from Mexico."

UH said, "Thank you Jamison. He was probably upset, and happy. The cost of burying the dead distressed him, but he was pleased that the cartels and terrorists were dead."

"He also wondered where the money had gone from the various groups," said Jamison.

UH said, "Of course he did. Would you mind taking my calls today? I have several Regional Directors to call."

Jamison answered, "Not at all UH."

Jeanine called, "Do you mind if I come in today around one."

"Not at all love," said UH, "but I will be leaving at three. I had purchased a limousine today, it will be ready tonight, and they are delivering it to our apartment."

Jeanine thought, *"That is the first time UH said that the apartment was ours."* She, like most woman, paid attention to her man's words, because she was deeply in love with him.

"Call me when the taxi arrives, and I'll come down." UH was always happy to hear her voice, loved the feeling of anticipation when meeting her anywhere, and pictured her in his mind, every time he saw her smile in his mind.

"Ok darling," said Jeanine.

That evening, around five o'clock, the chauffer brought the limo. UH told Jeanine that he had found an small apartment on the first floor for the new chauffer, Anthony Piada. He had been recommended by Chu.

"Anthony, we are going to the Gourmand for dinner," said UH.

"You sure know how to spoil a girl," said Jeanine as she gave out her soft laugh, then kissed him.

Tuesday morning, UH introduced Eduardo Casus, his new personal assistant and personal financial advisor. Casus followed UH into his office. Chu said, "This masquerade looks good on me, don't you agree?"

"Indeed I do." UH sat at his desk after closing the door.

Chu said, "I believe this appearance I have put on will allow me to work in your office, talk with important people, go with you to EU and other functions, and not having to hide from Jeanine.

"By the end of next week, say by the Friday the fourteenth, Russia and Asia Regions will be cleansed of terrorists and thugs. This should bring your growing assesses to seven hundred billion dollars.

"Israel is complete, but China, India, Malaysia are still needing a good cleansing. Australia is less pressing because of the world news. Back areas in that country are less important, they will find out following Friday, the twenty-eighth, when some of them are to be in the death toll.

"The US is moving ahead nicely, Rowe is learning to be a little ruthless. By September 1st, Rowe will have completed his work.

"I understand that you and Jeanine are discussing marriage," Chu began, UH tried to interject his thought, but Chu cut him off, "Wait, I want you to be careful, for Jeanine is a very beguiling woman. You have been with many women, but this one, you fell in love with. Not all love birds end with happiness and bliss, for some get caged by their human desires. You must protect my identity for some time in the future. I realize that I sound like a broken record, that is a phrase from the 1940's, meaning to keep saying the same thing. Nevertheless, I will be watching prudently.

"I believe that you know well our arrangement. Material and financial possessions, I have given to you are tokens of that agreement. Please don't frustrate me."

"I won't disappoint you Chu." UH shook his hand, which was a tad warm. UH looked down at his hand as he walked to his desk.

Wednesday, UH worked in his office with Jamison handling his calls. Jeanine didn't want to disturb him until evening dinner. They both liked the Gourmand, and that is where Anthony took them.

Thursday, was uneventful, except the growing love affair with UH and Jeanine. They spent the day selecting a date, time, and venue, for their wedding.

Friday, Chu called UH in the morning before he went to work, "By the time Saturday rolls around, you will be worth eight hundred and thirty billion dollars. Next week, you will be worth one trillion dollars. The first of September, when the American Regions are compete, you will get another sixty billion dollars to enjoy in luxury for the coming years of peace as you travel the earth.

"The temple has been completed inside with the repaired floors, and the renovated twenty-one steps to the Foundation Stone; there are ornate gold overlade palm trees, cherubim, and symbolic solid gold goblets and utensils. Many museum artifacts have arrived from around the world from collectors. The archaeologists surprisingly found twenty-three more artifacts from the Roman period. The Jewish school is doing well, and the museum has been praised by art dealers worldwide.

Twelve men serve in the temple as guards. They are Levites by heritage. Al Aqsa Mosque is progressing with more energy spent on education; the teaching is about how one lives in a world of diversity." Chu continued, "The Jews and the Muslims no longer contend with radicals or terrorists. A new Mufti arrived to discuss education of adults. Three famous Jewish scholars are visiting the Jewish Temple. No more spying, just polite nods at their once arch enemies.

"All faiths use the newly remodeled and expanded Shaare Zedek Hospital.

"The Muslims think that Allah wanted peace at all costs. The Jews believe that Elohim gave them the temple back as prophesied to bring about peace. They don't question the why or how. Christians are also joyful that the Third Holy Temple is compete, and that they don't have to worry about anyone quickly coming up behind them to harm them. "Wow, three religions are jubilant in Israel. Who would have thought of such a thing?" asked Chu.

Jacobs called UH, "I would like to know how people on this earth, who oppose us that don't want peace, suddenly die, or are killed? It seems as though no one on earth can escape."

UH said, "I will tell you more when I visit in your office sometime. I have a call coming in. Be grateful for the peace we have."

"I am," said Jacobs.

Accolades and Wedding Plans

The office was especially busy this Friday. Jamison, Elsa, and staff were on the phones or sending emails. Jamison was skyping, off and on. The world was truly settling down from its chaotic life of terror. UH had been busy contacting his billionaire friends for matching funds for the European Union.

A billionaire in New York returned UH's call, "This is Ira Elderman. I had heard about your fund raising efforts. I also know what you had done in Jerusalem—building the Third Temple. In fact, I was there for the rededication. What a good time it had been to me.

"I realize the significance of the EU involvement, even though Israel is not a member of the EU, it is especially your connection that I am even thinking of matching your donation." UH did not interrupt Ira. "So my intention is to send in a billion dollars..."

UH called Ginger Adams in London. He explained to her what he had planned for the EU.

"How in the world did you make enough money to make this matching fund possible?" asked Adams from the UK, a real estate multi-billionaire, who had known UH for ten years.

"Well," UH began, "I simply fell into the right investments. Anyway, can you match my offer?"

"Yes UH, I will. I wouldn't turn you down." She waited for him to respond, but he didn't as before. "I will also speak with others who think like us, or like the notoriety of such a gift. I hope this works. I heard that the EU needs about a hundred billion to bail itself out. I guess that now you only need ninety-seven more matching funds. Thank you for thinking of me," said Ginger.

The morning had been good. UH had collected ten more matching funds. Jamison also had ten matching funds from various smaller donors.

UH stood up as he saw Jeanine walking toward his office.

UH said, “Jeanine, what are you here for, my love.” He had lost track of time.

“Darling I want to go to lunch with you. Anthony is down stairs.” She kissed him.

UH said, “Good idea my sweet. You pick the place.” He was in a good mood.

“What have you been up to darling?” asked Jeanine.

UH said, “Primarily putting out small fires with directors, and more importantly, raising money for my matching fund for the EU. Wow, its 12:30.”

“When did you start that?” asked Jeanine.

“This morning. I have raise twenty-three billion dollars for a fund I had started, to bail out the EU which is twenty billion dollars in unsecured debt,” he said.

“Oh my god, how did that happen?”

UH said, “I don’t know, but the reality is, that we must keep the EU a viable organization. I am trying to keep it from falling apart. The UK and others are talking about pulling out because of immigrants which is actually our fault, well primarily; nevertheless, I am sure we are able to remedy our problems. We need to reestablish trust.” He decided to say something more, “I don’t know why I even mentioned these dull business matters to you my sweet love.

Jeanine stood there, then said, “Does this have anything to do with your job, the peace prize, or your UN acclamations?”

“None of the above. This was a spur of the moment idea that came to me in the board meeting today,” said UH.

“Ok darling, you know what you are doing, and this is so far above my head. Billions, I mean, I can’t fathom,” Jeanine sighed.

“I have an idea Jeanine, let’s have Anthony take us to the airport, and we go to France,” said UH. ”I’ll call the airport, and the plane will be ready after lunch. We won’t even stop at our apartment.”

Jamison heard, and was on the phone with the airport, when UH asked him to call the airport.

Jamison answered, "Got it."

UH and Jeanine went to France for the weekend. Chu called on Sunday afternoon to tell UH, that he could stay in France until Thursday the 27th because *cleansings* were going on until then. Chu had called the yacht captain to ready the boat by Sunday. UH was elated and shared this information with Jeanine, who smiled and slightly shook her head.

"I love it, when you are happy." UH took her in his arms, gave her an ever so slightly squeeze. I haven't been this happy since…"—Jeanine quickly thought he was going to say something about his first marriage, "…I had been a boy in China." He further said, "but my sweet, that boyish happiness pales compared to my happiness with you. Everything diminishes in importance when compared to you my sweet, sweet love."

While in France, UH had raised an additional seven billion, plus, for the EU fund. The EU "Rid the Debt Fund" was going better than he had imagined—thirty billion dollars.

On the flight back to Brussels, he had three more donations. As the circled the Brussels Airport, he shared with Jeanine, "This far exceeds the funds I had needed is for my goal. Oh, did I tell you the EU board named the fund: "Rid the Debt Matching Fund" which I think is pretty much to the point." Jeanine shook her head. "I thought that I had. The board privately sent a communique to wealthy individuals in the EU asking them to give a billion, but if not, join someone else to split the amount. Think about this, the UN did a similar fund raiser among the membership. Darling this could be an enormous fund taking us beyond what we need."

Jeanine responded, "UH, people around the world recognize what you had accomplished. You are a determined man, who brought peace to Israel, and God knows how far this peace will reach. I will spend my life, telling you how proud I am of you. You will always amaze me."

They were chauffeured to the airport, after which, they had dinner on the plane.

During the ten days since the inception of the "Rid the Debt Fund", the world, grateful for UH's dedication to peace, the achievement of peace, and his uniting the Regions into a cohesive globe of peaceful cooperation—they raised money. UH had a total of one hundred and ten billion dollars. By the 27th, UH had been invited to speak to the twelve Regional Zones, to address peace organizations, and the EU was preparing an invitation-only-banquet which would honor him and the donors from around the world.

Later in their Brussels apartment, Chu called him, "UH, the tributes are coming in O great Caesar," he said laughing.

"Don't be trivial…" UH began, but was cut off.

"Don't ever call what I say petty, unimportant, or anything else equivalent to trivial," yelled Chu. "I mean what a say, and if the metaphor fits, because I say that it fits, wear it."

"I apologize Chu. Caesar was a great man, the first emperor of Rome. I understand the metaphor."

"All right, I forget that you are merely a man—but the one I had chosen," concluded Chu.

Jeanine came out of the kitchen to UH's office, "My sweet are you ready for bed?" asked UH.

"Yes, I need to hold you," she said.

"Jeanine, I must hold your beauty," said UH. "Speaking of your total loveliness, I must transfer some pictures of you from my IPhone to my computer, so that I my get them printed for my office, our apartment, our home in France, and for the *Catherine Marie*.

"You say such nice things to me darling," she said. "Wedding date is, if you agree, Saturday, November 7th. Well?" UH didn't respond at first, for Sun had died on the 7th of November. Jeanine added, "The weather is crisp, but there is plenty of sunshine."

"That sounds terrific. Sorry sweet, my mind wondered." UH picked her up in his arms and carried her into the bedroom. They undressed each other, and fell on the pulled back sheets.

Friday morning at breakfast, they had decided to have the wedding on the yacht with a few close friends and business associates. They would sail out about eleven miles, have the wedding ceremony officiated by the mayor of Nice. They invited the mayor's wife, the captain of the yacht, and a select few who they would invite to his home after the morning wedding. They could swim and drink and eat a catered lunch. *No gifts please* will be written on the invitations.

They were both happy to have this wedding planned—now the guest list.

Total Cleansing For Peace

"August 28th, was a great day," said Chu to UH. "The American Regions, and all other regions were completed. It looks as though the peace initiative has been a success. The rest of the money taken from men and women who committed crimes and had amassed the wealth like the thugs and murderers they were, and the alike are now penniless. This brought your wealth to a total of one trillion dollars."

UH couldn't believe his what he was hearing.

Chu continued on UH's mobile, "UH, take another fourteen days off. Be back on September 13th. The 14th, we will have another meeting when you return—you, me, and Jamison. I see that you had withdrawn fifty thousand dollars. Spend twenty thousand at the casino, and you will double your fifty thousand. Jamison and I will attend to your calls, and whatever needs your attention.

"Don't concern yourself with anything, and keep in mind, when it comes to the UN and the EU, you could say that you had walked on water, and they would not doubt it," Chu waited, then said, "what, no smart mouth with this metaphor? Wait, sorry, don't answer. I was being a smart mouth."

"You are probably right with that metaphor," said UH not falling for Chu's taunt.

"Thanks for the time off. As you probably know we are putting together our guest list that will not be over fifty guests. The captain said that we could accommodate that many, but not more than fifty-five."

"Sure that sounds good. You rest up for your many upcoming events."

"Thank you Chu. I'll call this morning to make arrangements for the plane and yacht," offered UH.

"No. I had Jamison take care of that. The plane as well. Have a nice time. God, I sounded like Jamison, short choppy sentences," he laughed. UH could imagine Chu's head tilted back, chuckling at his own joke.

Jeanine and UH flew to Nice, spent the night at home, and prepared for their cruise. UH did a lot of thinking about Chu's seemingly changed personality. Chu interrupted his thoughts.

"UH, I heard you talk to Jeanine on the plane about my so called personality change. I can't change. Well, my human friend, I guess I'll cut the humor. Have a good evening."

UH became more worried at Chu's attitude toward him, but he would not talk to Jeanine about it.

The days went quickly, and their love was more obvious to the crew. The weather was good enough to sail down to Porto, Portugal, where they had lunch and shopped. They purchased a few items for friends, boarded the *Catherine Marie*, spent the night on her, and then sailed toward France.

In the evening, they went to their favorite Casino De Monte Carlo. Throughout the early evening, UH bet twenty thousand dollars, and they were about to leave with one hundred thousand dollars, when the casino manager said again, "UH, you had an exceptional evening. It's still early. Why not try to win more." UH said that he couldn't that night. The manager thanked him and Jeanine for their patronage, and said referring to them, "Sometimes, I don't know when to quit asking patrons to stay awhile longer."

"We'll be back before we leave for Brussels," said UH.

They did return, but lost fifteen thousand dollars.

"Darling we still have four days to play. Let's eat, sleep, sunbathe, play rummy, or whatever," Jeanine said as she smiled that certain way suggesting intimacy. UH agreed immediately, and they spent three more days on the yacht, sailing, relaxing, and doing what lovers do.

Jeanine said, "You make me feel so young. I feel like I'm twenty again."

"My sweet, you are only twenty-five, and you look eighteen," said UH looking at the light blue two-piece swim suit she was wearing.

"Look at you, darling, thirty-two and you don't look your age. You're such a hunk, sometimes corny, but always romantic," said Jeanine as she rolled over to him on the huge towel they had been sunbathing on. "I love the sounds and the rolling movement of the yacht," she said kissing his cheek, "but mostly being with you."

EU Vice President Philips called UH who leaned onto his elbow to answer his mobile.

"UH, glad I caught you. We are firming up our Tribute Dinner, and the man in charge is Karl Schindler. He serves on one of the financial committees, but had been asked to care for this task. He will be calling you late today or tomorrow, if that is all right with you."

"Yes, of course, Philips. That will be fine. Thank you for the call," said UH.

"Darling the sun is getting a bit too warm," Jeanine said. UH didn't move. "I'm going below. Don't you want to follow me?"

UH sprang to his feet, as she scampered in front of him to their master bedroom below.

After their showers, Jeanine asked if UH wanted to have a steak dinner on board, or if he would prefer going straight to the casino. He asked her to call the yacht's chef, and smiled at her. They had enjoyed the dinner on the yacht, and afterwards, they returned to the bedroom and dressed for a night out.

At the casino, a casually dressed man entered who had known Jeanine, and spotted her at a table having a drink with UH. He walked over with a smile on his face, and said, "Jeanine, I haven't seen you for more than five months." UH stood and extended his hand. "Good evening, sir, Jeanine and I have something in common." UH sat back down, and sipped his brandy.

UH said, "Have a seat. What is your name?"

"Sorry sir, it's Randy Freeman. I served with Jeanine's husband in Afghanistan. Bob and I were in the same unit."

"What brought you to Nice?" asked UH.

"Bob and I had thought we'd get a job here, save some money, and maybe start a fishing business or something on the water. I had grown up on the water in south Florida." He turned he head toward Jeanine. "As you probably remember Jeanine when he had written."

UH said, "What are you doing in Nice, now?"

"I work for a company that transports goods from France to anywhere in the EU alliance."

"What product to you transport?" asked UH.

"We ship sugar beets throughout Europe. I don't drive a truck, I work on a ship. It's not a bad job," said Randy. "Well, I have to go, I have a meeting with someone in here. She will be here any minute."

UH stood and shook Randy's hand, who said goodbye to him and Jeanine.

Jeanine said, "I haven't seen him for almost a year. Wow, how things change."

"Yes my sweet, and in our case, for the better." UH smiled at her, and said, "He seems like a nice young man."

The two had a good time at the casino, and returned to the *Catherine Marie* for one last night before heading to Brussels.

On the 14th, UH, Chu, and Jamison began their meeting in the office of UH.

Chu began the 11:00 am meeting, "The world has been cleansed, no rather cleaned up.

No more small or large groups of hate and mayhem. It's time to call the Regional Directors to a meeting, so that an outlined directive called the Martial Law Agenda can be presented to the Regional Directors. The enforcement of that agenda will remain in effect for some time, and we will insist that there is no deviation from this ML, for that cannot tolerated—nor will it.

"Jamison has worked out some of the particulars; he will contact the twelve Regional Directors to inform them, making sure that they understand that the meeting is mandatory. He has set the date for the 26th of this month, which is a Saturday, and the meeting is here in Brussels. We will pay all expenses, including meals and hotel. The meeting will last one afternoon. We will fly them in on Friday, the day before the meeting; and provide dinner and lodging at the Hilton Brussels Grand Place hotel. They will dine at the Brasserie La Place on Friday evening, and in the morning have the hotel breakfast buffet. Promptly, at 1:00 pm we will meet in the hotel conference room. Naturally, cheese and fruit platters will be provided, and beverages will be made available.

"You will make the presentation and answer questions. Also, the expenses will be taken from the funds that I have in an account set up for such occasions. We will not be using any of your trillion dollars, at least, at this time."

UH asked, "Is that fund large enough for meetings in the future?"

"Yes, there in only a billion dollars in it." Chu reached into his pocket and pulled out a bank card. "Here UH, this is a bank card to that account. You will need it for some events that are directly related to the twelve regional directors, and you may wish to sponsor a meeting with the directors and their official staffs."

"Any questions? Good. Let's meet again tomorrow. Jamison will have written out the Martial Law Agenda. See you tomorrow morning at 10:00 am."

Wednesday morning Chu laid out the presentation for UH, and explained the three points: satellite monitoring throughout every nation, and social media like twitter, google, Facebook, and etc.; and WZC Martial Law requirements; with this caveat: no further gun laws are needed. The meeting lasted one half hour.

That afternoon Karl Schindler called UH.

"This is UH," who was with Jeanine at their apartment.

"This is Karl Schindler for the EU. Am I interrupting anything?"

"Not at all, Karl."

"Good. I have selected a date for the EU dinner tribute in your honor.

It is Friday, October 2nd. We will have the dinner in the newly renovated Europa Building. I am sure many guests will be flying in that entire week for sightseeing, shopping, or whatever. I will keep you up to date. If this date and evening is all right, I'll chisel it in stone. Ha, ha," he breathed.

"Thanks again UH."

"You're quite welcome," said UH.

UH spoke loud enough for Jeanine to hear him, "Jeanine, that was Schindler from the EU, concerning the tribute dinner. It will be the 2nd of October." Jeanine came walking into the living room.

"Darling that is wonderful, and you deserve it. I'll be there of course," she hoped.

"Yes sweetheart," UH began, "right next to me, where you will always be. Wow that pastel green dress looks like it was made for you. You are gorgeous."

"Darling, it had been made for me, in Paris."

Jamison said to Chu, "This total cleansing isn't total, but on the surface, it appears to be.

Chu said, "Humans deal with what seems to be real, or with things that suit them, not reality."

They both laughed.

Meeting with Regional Directors

"UH, time for another cruise, and I'd like to go. I'll work in your office on board," said Chu. "Get used to calling me Eduardo."

"This will be good," began UH, "for we can work on my speech for the 26th at the Hilton Brussels Grand Place. Are you calling from the office?"

"Yes. Jamison will email details of the meeting, and make sure that all twelve directors respond that they are attending; he will make checks out for flight re-imbursements—whatever a director claims that it is; limousines will pick them up from the airport, and take them back; and he will set up rooms, dinner, and the conference room." Eduardo continued with a perfect accent, "This will make it easier for you, so that we may work on what must be said. We do not want any slip ups. Tu comprendes. Sorry, I was practicing some Spanish."

"That's funny, knowing that you can speak any language fluently," UH said with a slight laugh.

"Don't worry, I will use English, like a Spaniard who learned English."

"No need to do that," said UH, "just do what you know is best for this situation."

"Of course I will," said Eduardo. "I thought that we might leave on the 16th, tomorrow, and return on the 24th, which is a Thursday, two days before the region directors meeting. They will be coming in that week to holiday on their own dime. Jamison has made the arrangements: plane and yacht will be readied when we need them. Talk to you in the morning. I will ride in the limo with you and Jeanine. Speaking of a limousine, how about renting one, with a chauffeur, of course, in Nice. Your car is too small for three of us."

UH said, "Sure, sounds good to me."

"Jamison will be on it today," said Chu.

The cruise was uneventful, but Eduardo and UH did put together the speech, the program outline, the details Eduardo insisted must be in the speech. They went to the Casino De Monte Carlo twice. Eduardo had made an impression with the guests and Jeanine. UH won three thousand dollars, and Eduardo won three thousand dollars.

Eduardo said to UH, "Peace is attained by force; lasting peace continues through the strength of powerful men and women. The reason we don't ask radical religionist terrorist why he or she does what he does, is because each of them answers the same, 'God wants us to kill the godless.' Their interpretation of godless varies from Christian, Jewish, Muslim, or cult.

"Seek peace, but first the eradication of religious radicals, murderers, and such, is the the ground work, so that peace can be established. This is first and foremost accomplished through secret preemptive action, destroying them, removing them from life itself. From the cradle to adulthood, generations of hate and murder generates more hate and killing. The majority of victims are lonely people.

"Recently, or perhaps in the last twenty years, but more specifically, the last nine years, leaders were jammed up with their own laws, so as not to offend the rights of the criminal, at the expense of ignoring the pain and suffering of the innocent. No terrorist is like a child, for the hate is too deep. What we will witness in the coming months is that Karma is a mean bitch.

"We will lay out in minute detail what is expected of regional directors, supervisors, and administrators. We will put this in writing; you will explain these things in your speech; and you will field questions."

UH said to Eduardo, "I think that we are ready."

Jeanine felt that Eduardo seemed cold and aloof at times, but she had not told UH.

The regional directors were picked up at the Brussels Airport by three limousines throughout the week, and brought to Hilton Brussels Grand Place on Friday, the 25th of September. Some of them, like Chu had expected, came early for a mini vacation, like Rowe and Reed.

They were given their rooms, meal designation at their plates: fish, chicken, or steak, and were told to meet the next day at 1:00 pm in the conference room on the second floor, after the breakfast buffet.

One o'clock sharp, the meeting began.

UH said, "Welcome everyone to this grand hotel and meeting. We will keep focused so as to stay within the time restraints, but we will save time for questions at the end of the first break.

"I have placed on your tables a print out of the agenda today, the outline of the regional director's responsibilities, and the meaning of Martial Law in today's global environment.

"Our agenda is simple: Welcome, Opening Remarks, Introduction of Directors, Responsibilities of Directors, Break, Meaning of Global Martial Law, Peace the New Action Word, and Q and A.

"Mr. Eduardo Casus is my personal advisor for many of my businesses and activities. He and his staff will take notes, and make a voice recording of this meeting for me. The EU and the UN is having this meeting filmed for our world citizens back home or anywhere in that it is requested."

Introductions of Twelve Directors:

Australia: Director Sherman Russel, from Sidney

Asia: Four Directors:

China: Director Yen Zhang, from Peking

India: Director Arnav Kapoor, from Chennai

Malaysia: Director Aiman Megat, from Ipoh

Middle East: Director Adam Almon, from Tel Aviv

Europe: Director Franklin Pierce, from London

Mexico: Director Carlos Rodriquez, from Mexico City

North Africa: Director Alim Jabir, from Alexandria

South Africa: Director Samuel Kingston, from Johannesburg

South America: Director Alfredo Colombo, from Rio de Janeiro

Russia: Director Vladimir Nikolin, from Moscow

North America: Director James Rowe from Washington, DC

UH said, "Let's begin talking about the responsibilities of directors."

1. You do not, nor do your supervisors, administrators, nor city officials, have the right to institute gun laws. In fact, you are prohibited from any new legislation or directive concerning guns. No New Gun Laws. However, all counties with strict gun laws may not keep them.
2. Directors are not Prime Ministers or Presidents, nor will they act like one.
3. Directors will follow the lead of my office and the UN Security Council.
4. Directors will be paid five-hundred thousand dollars annually.
5. Benefits include: all residence costs, the best medical care, costs for vehicles, a security force which includes your military, a secure airplane and helicopter, and a two-hundred and eighty thousand dollars for incidentals, and bullet proof vest for your personal guards; your is provided.
6. You may carry a weapon or weapons as you believe is justified.
7. Secure all sectors as you see fit to do using your military and any of your law enforcements, from township and counties, or any trained lawman.
8. There will be an underwriting tax of five hundred million dollars per year from each region.
9. No use of dirty bombs, atomic bombs, nor hydrogen bombs.
10. All directors will be monitored by any of the means available to the WZC.

"What about the extremely remote areas that most of us have?" asked Sherman Russel.

"We will provide the best equipment and satellite reconnaissance," answered UH. "Our satellite imaging is phenomenal. We have enhanced the entire satellite program. Scott Iverson, one of our expert technologist on satellites, will answer any of your questions after the meeting.

Also cell towers will be tripled or quadrupled in all regions.

"What in the hell is an underwriting tax?" asked Rowe. Nikolin nodded in agreement.

UH answered, "That will cover all satellite reconnaissance, improvements, personnel, the cost imposed on my office, lease, office personnel, and salaries to begin with. I won't ask, but I believe that you couldn't have functioned on five hundred million annually. I think that your region alone will require trillions. I have kept the cost down, so that all regions will be able to manage." There was not a rebuttal.

"It is 3:33 pm, so let's take a half hour break."

UH, and some of the directors talked about the responsibilities put on them. Eduardo approached UH who was talking with Karlene Schmidt; tapped his shoulder, excused himself for interrupting, and requested UH to follow him. They went into the open area outside of the conference center.

Chu began, "I don't like what I'm hearing from Rowe. He is insisting to press for more gun control. Because you are busy, I'm going downstairs to call him on his phone."

"All right, I'm using the men's room, and I'll get started on the next topic," said UH.

"Director Rowe, I am concerned with your attitude about how you feel about still being in control, like you were when President. There will be no further gun control."

"Who is this?" asked Rowe. "I'm heading into another meeting."

"James, if you don't alter you ego, give up on more gun control, and follow the plan, there is always someone ready to take your place. Have a nice afternoon," Chu concluded.

"Everyone please turn to your third page: The Meaning of Martial Law," UH began.

"Martial Law is an old historical concept where citizens worry about military rule, the lifting of rights of citizens like false imprisonment with no recourse in law. Habeas Corpus protects from the abuse of a state, but we will not abuse this right. Let it be recorded today, that no regional zone, no director, or any one under his or her authority may imprison a person without a formal charge."

UH gave the following as to the meaning of martial law today:

1. Directors will have final authority, monitored by my office.
2. Directors will abide by these rules:
    a. All murderers shall be executed
    b. All killers, which includes manslaughter, shall be executed
    c. All rapists shall be executed
    d. Child molesters shall be executed
    e. Kidnappers shall be executed
    f. Rioters and looters shall be executed
    g. Armed, includes any weapon, these robbers shall be executed
    h. An attempted assassination by any person, is punishable by death.
    i. A known terrorist shall be executed
    j. Directors, supervisors, or administrators not upholding these rules shall be executed.
    k. Mass murders, including terrorists, shall be executed as well as their cohorts and family.

"There are no exceptions. I realize that some countries no longer use a death penalty, but the WZC law is supreme and supercedes all regional zone laws. Securing peace overrides any of the previous laws in your regions. We will not tolerate any form of genocide. Should you have any question beyond the list given here, contact my office. It is not hard to figure out, guns, knives, clubs, cars, baseball bats, or any other inanimate object does not kill—people do.

"Frankly, we are at war to bring peace. Go to your radio and television stations to share these new martial law rules with your citizens. Have these rules published in newspapers on the front page, in larger print, but heed the spirit and the tenor of these laws—ignorance of the law is not an excuse. This is a global plan, so converse with each other regularly.

"I must repeat this, should we find that any director, supervisor, or administrator who has failed to uphold these rules in the martial law plan, that person will find themselves in a dreadful situation. By the way, quit talking to the press. Some of you have used the press in the past to further your careers. You now have fixed careers. The press has lost its power where you are concerned. The press will print what my office and ultimately your offices want them to print."

The directors sat in the seats like mannequins, not moving a muscle. Each fearing what was coming next, but thankful that directors were not in charge of the changes, and their careers were fixed.

UH continued, "'Swift justice' is our slogan. Any unsolved homicide after twenty-four hours, must be reported to my office. We will help solve all crimes. Remember, leaders were timid, worried about backlash of some sort, and feared using preemptive action. What they had only talked about, we have accomplished in Israel and elsewhere. True peace is only attained by maintaining vigilance to oppose anyone against our WZC peace initiative."

UH waited as directors read over the martial law rules again, and discussed the implications.

"Our next topic is Peace: the New Action Word. We are ahead of schedule, and this section will not be long.

"Sentimentality is not worth the emotional energy—it drains us of positive productivity. The world has no room for those who dreamily or nostalgically remember the good that was, because of all the evil that surrounded it, or clouded it from honest view. Let us be practical, level headed, more in tune with what could be. Peace from the callousness of unmerciful killers of every stripe.

"Peace, we shall use as a verb: a past participle, peaced; all criminals, villains, and terrorists will be *peaced*. They must be brought to face the consequences of their deeds, therefore peaced, whether or not the results in death. Peace is the absence of war, violence, and crime. It will be a new state of mind. Embrace it, share its importance, and let it be a goal in your administrations. Keep in your understanding that man is man, with the same passions, the explosive tempers, jealousies, and lust, so crime will continue, but it will be addressed swiftly."

"Violence has become the unwritten law in our lives, perhaps that is why people have continued to go missing, or died. Do aliens want us to be peaced? I don't know, but let us work toward that end. Since after these deaths of terrorists, immigrants are moving back to the own countries, and that should help overall."

When UH asked for questions about the topics, not one raised one. They sat in their chairs at the tables, as though unable to move, except for their heads.

UH said, "If there are no questions, we are adjourned. Thank you for attending, and I hope that your stay in Brussels has been pleasant. Your limousines are ready, your bags are packed and in the limousines."

The directors didn't say much to each other except like "keep in touch," or "nice to see again." For they all were in a state of contemplation about money and Martial Law.

"UH, this is Chu," he began, "That was a good meeting, and Rowe is going to fall in line. I believe he has a mental disorder of some kind, caught up in his past glory; nevertheless, I have your Black Hawk bullet proof vest in your apartment. You will wear it for most of your public engagements. It's thin, so you can wear it under your shirt."

UH stated, "I was about to tell them that mankind alone, could not bring peace."

"No matter," said Chu.

UH said, "I see that you are back using the other name of Chu."

"Just with you. Eduardo to everyone else.

"My next dinner engagement is for the tribute to me for my fund raiser campaign," UH said. "That will be on Friday night on the 2nd of October. My, that's less than a week away."

Chu agreed, "Yes. You had raised more money than was needed. The EU has been bailed out, and some of the members that were bailing out, are staying in. Good work."

The week sped by at work, as Eduardo, Jamison, and UH dealt with the Regional Directors. The World Zone Coalition Regional Director meeting for next year is February the 3rd at the Hilton Brussels Grand Place. A couple of the previous directors' countries had banned capital punishment, but they were finally convinced to follow UH.

On the night of the UN tribute dinner to UH, Chu suggested that he wear his bullet proof vest. He did, and the expensive vest was newer, slimmer, and more expensive. Jeanine said that it looked very good on him.

That night, everyone at the gala was beside themselves with gratitude for UH's efforts to make the EU debt free. The dinner had been exquisite, and as the speaker, UH, didn't miss a beat, and the applause lasted longer than usual. A publisher had been one of the guests, and asked UH if he could have one of his writers, compile a biography of him, but "at this time," he declined. Chu agreed with UH. At the end of the program, UH told board members, he had asked to join him it a conference room, that he would be resigning as president of the EU and the EC on the 2nd of November. They, of course were shocked and questioned his timing. He explained that by the end of November, there would be no need for either organization because the world was be divided into twelve zones. He further explained that they would be contacted by Regional Director Franklin Pierce from London. At first, no one believed what he was saying. Some snickered, others laughed or mocked, and but all were in disbelief. UH put his plaque under his arm and excused himself.

In the limousine, Jeanine said, "I'm sure that you are happy to put that dinner behind you."

"My sweet love, I am glad to have that behind me, because I don't like that kind of attention, but it was difficult to resign." He changed the subject, "You are all the attention I need. I'm sorry that this week had been so hectic."

"Darling, could we take a few days, by ourselves? I was going to say that we could take the yacht, but how about our home in Nice?"

"Yes, of course, grand idea. Let me call the airport." UH dialed, "Hello. This is UH. I know that it's late, but could you possibly get my plane ready to fly to Nice, France?"

The attendant said, "As you were talking I realized that the plane is ready. Mr. Eduardo Casus called in this afternoon. It's ready sir."

"Thank you young man." Then UH called to Anthony, "Would you just take us to our plane?"

"Yes UH. We're on our way."

Chu called, "This is Eduardo, UH. Please enjoy your trip to Nice. You really don't have to return until the 17th. I know that it's October, but you'll find something to do. Bye."

UH said, "My sweet, that was Eduardo, I had asked him to work for me this next week, and he agreed to do that for me. So we will not have to return until the 17th. Jamison had emailed the report guidelines to the Regional Directors, for each of them and their group. The reports are due on November 30th."

Everything was quiet and calm in Nice. UH and Jeanine decided to have a talk about all that is happening with UH, like finishing up with the European Union, his new lease that will not be required, for he will be purchasing the EU/EC building, and his evolving role as head of the World Zones Coalition. It would not affect their relationship, so Jeanine wasn't concerned. Chu warned UH twice during their conversation, for he worried that love would blind UH from his common sense and in particular, his covenant.

Jeanine and UH had time to discuss things about themselves that neither had shared before.

Jeanine's full name, prior to her marriage to the American Randy Roberts. Following his death, she had waited three years before changing her name back to Jeanine R. Bonnet. Her father, born in Nice, France, had died last year. Her mother, born in Madrid, Spain, died three years before that.

She had studied art, and received her Master of Fine Arts in Paris. She had written for several leading fine art magazines. Speaks and writes in three languages: French, Spanish, and English.

She said to UH, "There isn't much to my life at twenty-five, that is probably true for most individuals at my age."

UH said, "You have become an eloquent writer, and an untrained chef, but I hadn't known that until recently."

UH had told her about his life over the previous months; almost too much, according to Chu.

Former EU and EC executives and staff had been irritated and sent UH stinging emails and phone calls, but no one actually crossed the line for disciplinary review by Chu. One by one they resigned by the 9th of November. The European Commission, which actually owned the buildings, first thought about renting them, or turning the Europa back to a luxury apartment complex, and renting the other space out to businesses. Chu reminded them, that they were defunct, and made an offer to purchase the entire complex of buildings for a billion Euro's; EC agreed to two billion. They decided to give most of this money to charities across France and Belgium. Chu began to turn the newly remodeled Europa into a luxury hotel and apartments. UH wondered how Chu had managed to raise the money.

Chu said to UH, "I had made you a multi-trillionaire worth more than any man alive. I kept fifteen billion aside for this very reason. Besides, you will need more offices for staff who are to run the Regional Directorships, under the World Zone Coalition."

UH was not surprised.

On the 17th UH and Jeanine returned to Brussels. While they were gone Chu had made their fine apartment, into a lavish suite by combing an empty luxury apartment next to theirs. Anthony told them on the way back to the apartment, that they would be happily surprised when they entered their apartment.

"Here are your new keys to the two locks," said Anthony.

UH said, "This is a new door." Jeanine agreed. "It's heavier and more decorative," added UH. They walked in and their eyes could not believe the beauty, chef appliances, expensive art on the walls, and boxes of gifts for them both.

"Oh my god. Oh my god," said Jeanine. Other than those three words, she was speechless.

"Well, what do you think?" asked Anthony.

"I don't know what to think," said Jeanine, as a knock at the door was heard. They all turned to see Eduardo pushing the open door open wider.

Eduardo said, "Welcome home."

"How did this all happen in two weeks, and who is behind this?" asked UH.

Eduardo began, "A mutual wealthy friend who wanted thank you for your world peace initiative. He had called as you were probably in route to the airport on the evening of 2nd, and he made me swear to his anonymity."

"All right then, if you don't need me UH, I'm out of here. See you all later," Anthony said as he left to go down to his apartment.

They said goodbye to Anthony as he closed the door.

Eduardo said, "The gifts are from friends who heard of your wedding, but are unable to attend. Have you decided on the Europa or the Hilton?"

Jeanine answered, "Probably the Hilton. We had thought of a wedding in Nice on the yacht, but I'm an only child, and my parents are gone, so we thought that Brussels was just the right place."

"I like the Hilton, especially for informal weddings, official meetings, and sleeping," Eduardo said with his Chu chuckle.

"Eduardo, do you think that you could help me?" asked Jeanine. "I would like a Spanish and French décor if you could manage something like that being a well-rounded Spanish gentleman."

"Why of course, if UH can give me a little freedom for the next three weeks," smiled Eduardo.

UH answered, "Consider it done. For the next three weeks, Jamison can help a little more."

The next two weeks were not be very busy for Chu, UH, and Jeanine had the next two weeks to plan for the wedding. On the other hand, the EU and EC and their official boards were in the process of resigning; the Economic Committee were conversing with their lawyers about the sale of the Europa and the other two attached buildings, or selling them to clear up the question of ownership by a defunct organization. They had one other issue to address, at least in their minds: North Atlantic Treaty Organization which hasn't aged very well. With the EU and EC gone, the toothless old tiger will have to be put to sleep, for the Regional Directors, with the backing of WZC, UH and Chu will see to it that nothing goes awry.

Nikolin seemed quite happy, for he controls most of what he had wanted after the after the World Zone Coalition put the Regional Districts into place. Besides with NATO gone, Russia no longer felt abandoned by Europe.

The first week of preparation for the wedding had gone well. Jamison had told the twelve directors to write up their questions and attach them to the reports, after Director Sherman Russel, from Australia called to complain about the Underwriting Tax.

The smallest ballroom had been set up for the wedding. Eduardo had purchased two fifteenth century paintings from a patron of the arts. One was a French painting, and the other was a Spanish painting. The painters had depicted nude men and women in the fall of man in the Garden of

Eden. They were priceless, but Chu knew how to negotiate. They would be placed in the ballroom, and guarded by WZC security on the day of the wedding.

Jeanine was excited, and watched as UH had evolved from a cynic to a less pessimistic man. She had helped him look at life as he would a painting in progress; each stroke purposely placed on his original canvas. She was gentle with him, like her father had been to her mother, as she had watched him transform. She had thought that the wedding would be another step in the right direction for him.

UH called Jamison, "Thanks for your help last week, and for having the yacht serviced for the winter months."

Jacobs called UH, "I had meant to call you since my retirement. You had been an inspiration to us in Israel, and I cannot express my gratitude, for words fail me."

"Alon, thank you for your support, even when it was quite difficult," said UH.

"Your choice of Adam Almon as Regional Director had been a good one. Call me any time my friend," said Jacobs.

"May you have a good retirement," responded UH.

In reference to UH and his two calls, Chu said, "For god's sake is this a business call or a love fest?"

November 2nd arrived. Jeanine Rebecca Bonnet married Uri Lee Harrison at one o'clock in the afternoon. Jeanine cried, and UH looked at her with admiration and love. After the wedding, Eduardo announce the unveiling of the authenticated, two fifteenth century paintings. He had the guards unveil them, and he stated who had painted the canvases with the same theme: Man's Fall in the Garden of Eden.

Jeanine, crying again, and shouted, "They're real. Oh my god, they're real." She flung her arms around UH and whispered, "I love you my darling. Those were the most perfect gifts."

They met each guest, ate, danced, and thanked everyone for attending. Two hundred and thirty were in attendance, but fortunately they had switched to the large ballroom. Friends came from the World Zone Coalition, the office staff, and three friends from the closing EU. Even, Randy Freeman from Nice came, with his fiancé. Actually, Randy was hoping to ask UH for a loan on his new business: a trucking company.

Mr. and Mrs. Harrison took a honeymoon in and around Rome, Italy. When they had returned on the 27th, their suite had been filled with gifts from the wedding, and they discovered three specially trained armed guards in the suite and five on the street level who had protected the paintings. Both newlyweds were ready to get back to normalcy.

Jamison had received the Regional Directors brief reports before the 30th. He sent them to UH. The reports had been designed this simple way.

Asia: China: Yen Zhang: Supervisors and Administrators are satisfactory
Question: We have never paid a tax to any foreigner, so why should we now?
India: Arnav Kapoor: Supervisors and Administrators abiding by the rules.
Malaysia: Aiman Megat: System is working.
Middle East: Adam Almon: First time since 1948, peace; all is good.

Australia: Sherman Russel: All regional staff following directives.
Question: Why in god's name should we pay such a high tax?

Europe: Franklin Pierce: Thanks to good planning all is quite fine.

Mexico: Carlos Rodriquez: Struggling a little with financing, but OK.

North Africa: Alim Jabir: Surprisingly, we are doing very well.

North America: James Rowe: Doing well enough. Kind regards.

Russia: Vladimir Nikolin: Contented at present situation.

South Africa: Samuel Kingston: No comment.

South America: Alfredo Colombo: Gracias. We are great.

UH read the reports, and decided not to respond to Zhang and Russel, for they had this information explained in detail at the first directors meeting. He asked Jamison to remind them of this, and that they get a point by point explanation of expenses at the next meeting.

Chu said, “Let them stew. I know for a fact that they could afford more.”

“You are correct,” said UH.

Chu responded, “I am always correct.”

UH in New York

"Well darling, I guess we are off to the Trump Towers again," said Jeanine.

UH said, "Yes on the 10th of the month. Here we are in December."

"But look what you have accomplished this year. The World Zone Coalition for peace, your new offices at the Europa Building that you now own, and our wedding," she teased.

"Our new seventh floor suite at the Europa," said UH.

"Darling you mean the whole seventh floor, don't you?"

"My sweet," UH said to Jeanine, "you are correct. Eduardo said that it should be completed by New Year's Eve. When I told Singer that our apartment was for rent in January, he asked if he could have it. He said that he had grown his business in France and Belgium, and that it hadn't mattered if the EU dissolved. He would still fly to Israel twice a month to care for business there."

"Darling let's plan several days around the 10th. Our armored car will be flown in; Rowe is providing security SUVs to escort us; and he wants us to fly to Camp David. Before that we can go anywhere: New Jersey, D.C., or California," said Jeanine.

"California?" UH asked.

Jeanine answered, "Yes, I've wanted to visit there years ago."

"All right, let's do it," said UH hugging Jeanine.

They arrived in New York on December 6th; they secured the room at Trump Tower; ate an expensive, but pleasant dinner; and surprisingly saw Donald Trump, at least they thought it was him, walk to an elevator. The next day Rowe and the Harrisons flew to Camp David for three days.

"This is quite a nice place James. Do you come here often?" asked UH.

"Now that I have more time," Rowe began, "I come here, golf, and read."

"Directors hadn't realized the additional leisure time that they would have under the Coalition," UH reminded him that that had been one of the perks.

Rowe began, "The times have changed for the better. Crime is down, almost to zero; terrorists are gone or they are well-hidden underground; and for the most part my family is happy. I have more security now even though peace is more prevalent..." Rowe talked for about fifteen minutes.

On the 9th the Harrisons returned to New York. UH's chauffeur, Anthony Piada flew with the Harrisons from Brussels to chauffeur the armored car. Rowe provided armed agents to go with UH where ever he planned to go in the Northern Region.

At eleven am, UH and Jeanine were at the UN building, and were greeted by a delegation. He was introduced as the head of the World Zone Coalition, and a nominee of the Nobel Pease Prize, and as the last speaker at the UN because, under the new Regional Districts there was no longer a need for such an enterprise, shared Secretary General Kobie Alber. UH spoke on the Shrinking Violence on the World Stage.

"In the past, we launched empty words at terrorists, like hoping cancer would cure itself by talking it to death. We passed laws against our country's common sense, making it easier for criminals to commit crime again with the optimism that leniency was the solution... migrants never had been the answer to jobs, nor the solution to satisfy our thirst for doing good, at the sacrifice of citizens.

"Some of you had emailed me, and had called me, stating that the Coalition violated the 1949 Geneva Convention. Your enemies had laughed at your objections to your own militaries for an infraction of the Geneva Convention, but terrorists don't abide by laws of civilized people. We are under global martial law...

"A non-combatant who hides or quietly supports a criminal or terrorist is an accomplice, and should pay the penalty for the death of the innocent..."

UH spoke for thirty minutes. Not many said anything to him, for they all were losing their jobs, and he seemed radical to the UN.

UH, Jeanine, and their security detail passed through the UN doors, and onto the sidewalk, when shots were heard from across the street. The security immediately slammed UH to the ground. Within moments they realized that UH had been shot. The perpetrator was shot by someone, and he fell three floors with his rifle in his hand, and was pronounced dead. The security detail rushed UH to an ambulance parked near the UN building, as Jeanine climbed in, the doors were shut; it raced down East 42nd Street. UH kept his eyes closed, for Chu was saying something to him.

"UH, I knew this would happen, and I made sure a security person knew where he was, and I may add, guided his shot. The perpetrator was a loner, upset at martial law that he had said that you had instituted. We can't blame anyone for this buffoon. Open your eyes and tell them of your thin, Black Hawk bullet proof vest and how it saved your life."

Jeanine was in shock; couldn't believe that this tragedy had happened; and she thought that the reign of peace could prevent such a thing from happening.

UH opened his eyes, and said, "I love you Jeanine. I am just fine because I had decided to wear my bullet proof vest. We cannot stop a loner assassin, and that is why I had asked each of our Regional Directors to wear a bullet proof vest. The Coalition had purchased one for each director."

The ambulance driver was requested to stop because Chu told UH that Anthony was driving behind the ambulance. UH told the driver to pull over, that his driver was behind him. He thanked the paramedics. UH and Jeanine were helped out of the ambulance and escorted to the armored SUV. Anthony said that he had been a nervous wreck since the shooting.

Anthony said, "I sure am glad that you're alright UH."

Just then UH received a call.

"UH, this is Director Rowe. A security chief just called me to give the particulars of your ordeal."

"Thank you James. I was wearing my bullet proof vest. I'm delighted that the Coalition had paid for all twelve directors or reimburse those who have paid for one," offered UH.

Rowe answered, "Not yet for me, but I will now."

UH said, "I'll contact Jamison and have him send an email to all Regional Directors that because the Coalition had said that it would pay for the vests, they need to do that, especially after this incident. Thank you for the call."

Chu said to UH, "I will only protect you. Even though I know when a loner or a handful of assassins are about to take out a director or supervisor, I will not intervene. Maybe with your generous heart you could suggest that directors use part of their expense money to buy bullet proof vest for their supervisors. Have a fun time in New Jersey, no, I see you've changed your itinerary, and you are flying to San Francisco. Why not spend a couple weeks, and tour three cities in California: San Francisco, LA, and San Diego I'm sure Jeanine would love it."

"Eduardo, I will share that with Jeanine. I believe we shall, and we'll spend ten days here in California, and then off to New Orleans. After which, we'll head back to Brussels on the 24th."

"Good. You will be home to share Christmas Eve with your wife. Bye."

UH thought, *What is up with Chu? Does he not care for Jeanine? He speaks with a forked tongue from time to time, but ever since I had become engaged to Jeanine, Chu has been different.*

Jeanine asked UH why he was so deep in thought, but he lied, and said that it was about the New Year's Eve gala on the 31st. She said to UH that she was looking forward to their first Christmas Eve together. He embraced her, and told her how precious she was to him. She reminded him that although she isn't a practicing Catholic, she was Catholic, and that Christmas and Easter were important to her.

Jeanine said, "I know that you are an agnostic, and that after your wife and son were tragically killed, you became cynical, but you have changed.

I like to think, because of our love for each other, you have become tolerant of my faith." She looked at his face, "We'll stop talking about it now, darling."

They had returned to Trump Tower. They went to their room, had their things packed-up by UH's butler, Andre Le Shoot, who had traveled with them, and returned to the limousine where Anthony had been waiting to take them to the La Guardia Airport. They flew to San Francisco, then to Los Angeles, and the last stop in California had been San Diego, before going to New Orleans on the 19th.

They landed in New Orleans.

In the vehicle, Jeanine said, "After what happened in New York, it sure is nice to have the new and longer armored vehicle, and Anthony traveling with us."

"Why do they call New Orleans the Big Easy?" asked Jeanine.

"In 1970," UH began, as Chu spoke in his mind, "a gossip columnist compared the life in New York, The Big Apple, with the life in New Orleans, The Big Easy. The phrase stuck."

Jeanine said, "I just knew that you would have the answer, but what about The Big Apple?"

"That my dear was insufficient. I need to add something else. To make it simple I shall use the New York sports writer John J. Fitz Gerald in 1920 who used the phrase in a column to make a point about racing. The winning horse received the big apple. Keep in mind that there are other etymologists with other answers, but that one should do for now," UH concluded.

On the 22nd, they arrived back in New York. Rowe asked to meet UH in the Lotte Hotel. That evening UH and Jeanine had dinner with Rowe and his wife. Rowe said that he understood why the UN had to shut down its operation, but admitted that he had liked the UN even though a good number of Americans did not. UH said that he understood his sentiment.

Rowe shared, "Former UN Secretary General Kobie Alber, had informed me that he figured once the Coalition was formed, the EU, EC, and the UN would fade into history."

UH said, "Kobie finally told me that as long as the Coalition was thoughtful of the needs of developing countries, and that all regions had goals that included security, safety, and financial assistance in these matters, he reluctantly approved with demise of the UN. I explained to him that the second-guessing throughout weakened nations, the EU, and the UC, had made it difficult to govern, and had led to the formation of the World Zone Coalition. Many of the previous governments had been debt ridden, belligerent and xenophobic toward their neighbors because of human greed, power, posturing, or fearfulness. A nation would flex its military might, while their citizens were becoming desensitized, and led to accept political correctness which led to the growing violence especially in the United States, Canada, and most of Europe.

"We are in the process of reducing these tensions; eliminating organized terrorism; and reducing conflicts inherent to all governments, like angst of scheduled elections, political corruption, cronyism, and in the Middle East the over-throwing of those in power through a coup, or radicals, and putting in place a totalitarian and oppressive governments. Under your watch, the Middle East became unstable and terrorism grew. There are many more reasons for the Coalition. Nations collectively could not function to bring about peace because of pride, lust, power, financial gain, and other human flaws.

"Be honest. What do you think James?"

Rowe said, "I'm afraid that I must agree. I cannot stand alone, and I did not like the limelight; but I did favor the many perks of being president; yet, I'm grateful to you for appointing me regional director. At least for my salary increase."

UH said, "I'm indebted to you for your security as I traveled in you region. Europeans are always intrigued with the vastness of this continent. I am fascinated by New York City."

December 24th, Jeanine and UH were back at the luxury suite. There was a ring at the door bell, and UH could see who it was at the down stairs door.

"May I help you?"

"I am here from Antwerp," the man said.

When the man said Antwerp, UH remembered that he had purchased a two hundred thousand euros necklace: diamonds and rubies. "I'll have my one of my security men come down to get it."

UH's chief security man went down to get the gift for Jeanine. He retrieved it and gave the wrapped box to UH. Jeanine had been in the kitchen.

"Darling," she said leaving the kitchen, who was that?"

"My sweet, I had purchased this gift for you before we had left for New York, but I had not remembered it in the last week. Here my adorable wife is a Christmas Eve gift," UH said handing it to her.

As she opened the wrapping, she noticed printing on the box *Antwerp Diamonds,* and it peaked her enthusiasm. UH stood there looking at her beautiful eyes, noticing every movement in her gorgeous face.

"Oh my god. Urie, what have you done? This is beautiful, just beautiful. You are so wonderful." Lifting her hair in the back, Jeanine latched expensive necklace on the nape of her neck, and quickly went to the mirror in the living room. "Oh you are a darling man. These are Christmas eve diamonds." She turned to each side in the mirror to see the variable light gleam of the necklace.

UH said, "That necklace was made for you, or should I say that your diamonds had been made for the necklace. You and your necklace deserve to be together—with me."

Jeanine, with tears in her eyes, and running down her tender face, she threw her arms around him and said softly, "You are wonderful to me. This is the best Christmas Eve—ever."

They spent the night, in their private sitting room, away from the security who sat in the living room, security changed shifts every four hours.

UH had hired an additional sixteen men, for his safety, and for Jeanine.

The next day, culminated their Christmas season in Brussels. When UH came out for breakfast, Jeanine was baking, moving about in her chef's kitchen. The aroma stirred a memory in UH, of his mother during Christmas season.

"Good morning darling. What are you baking?" asked UH.

"Your birthday cake for January 3rd. One like your mother had made for you, a devil's food cake with butter cream frosting.

"Thanks my sweet. I had a delightful evening, and an enjoyable night," she smiled.

"I still can't get over the stunning necklace. I like how you spoil me."

UH said, "You are quite easy to spoil, my sweet."

They ate breakfast, talked about moving into the Europa Building.

Chu called UH. "This is Eduardo. Your seventh floor suite will be ready to move into on the 28th. The entire floor is yours, as I had said before. You will have a nice sized ballroom on the sixth floor, and by the way, your suite will have a large office and conference room. In the center will be a sitting room, adjacent to that is the formal living room. The kitchen will have fully equipped Chef's appliances, two sinks in the large work island, with a walk-in pantry and refrigerated wall of doors for easy access. The island also has a four seat eating area at the end. The formal dining room is off of the kitchen. You have a guest room, and enormous master bedroom with a private living room that has several three feet by eight feet windows from which you may view the city.

"Inside the main floor on the right of the elevator is the security detail flex room for sleeping, watching television, and eating. The room will have small kitchen appliances, and there is a three-quarter bath.

"I have hired the movers, to begin in the morning. I booked a room at the Hilton for you and Jeanine for the 27th. Your security team will care for the paintings, and watch over the movers. Any questions?"

UH answered, "Not at all. I am again impressed with your efficiency."

"I'm not done telling you what has been done. I had taken the liberty to send out invitations for your New Year's Eve gala, seven weeks ago. Your guests include Regional Directors, their wives, and four of them are bringing their area supervisors. Your friends from New York and here in Brussels will be attending. I think, so far, you have seventy guests who had sent an RSVP.

"High tables with high chairs, or to stand at, will be place in the ballroom; a wet-bar at each side staffed with five servers, and seven attendants for refreshing the food and the hors d'oeuvres. The bar will be completely stocked with fine wines, champagne, and of course, your new choice of brand Remy Martin Louis VIII brandy. There will be beer and other concoctions for mixed drinks, and a small band of fifteen will provide music for background to socializing and for dancing. I've hired, and I'm flying in a world renowned chef from Paris, Enrico Petit, to prepare dinner for you, Jeanine, and guests."

New Year's Eve: Networking

Huge television screens were located around the ballroom. Television and radio stations were from New York, Los Angeles, London, Paris, and Hong Kong, and from many other major world cities. CNN News was broadcasted live that night from New York on the television two screens were and Fox News was reporting on the other two screens.

"Three former justices of the Supreme Court were complaining today about martial law.

Chief Justice Burble said, 'We cannot function like this.' A protester from the steps of the Supreme Court, said, 'Well at least they ain't gonna make any new laws now.'"

The network went on, "Justices around the world are in the same situation. Gosh, these people just don't get it—we are under the World Zone Coalition martial law," said Jamison passing behind UH.

UH demanded, "Change those stations. I want festivity not news."

Jeanine turned and yelled, "Thank you darling. This is New Year's Eve, and I want to remain happy. We will never again see 2015."

Eduardo had entered at six o'clock to make sure all had been going as planned: the chef, Enrico Petit; the band in place; bartenders and servers on time; and the hors d'oeuvres were be set up properly.

Jeanine went to the bedroom to finish getting ready. UH had been ready for early guests, and began trying to find Chu again.

"Eduardo, I'm glad you were able to come early. We are about to have dinner, and I won't ask you to join us because you never do, but at least this time, I recognize the reason why," said UH.

Eduardo smiled in acknowledgement of UH's statement, "I will remain out here, to meet and greet the guests. I imagine that our first guest will be Rowe. He never misses a free meal, nor ever shuns a money gift; and he will always look for the limelight; and he seems to crave praise. Anyway, he has been in town since this yesterday morning. Actually, there were twenty-three guests at the Hilton Brussels this morning. I suppose that it is obvious that I don't like Rowe, and I seem to find even the most insignificant negative that I can imagine, then label him or pick on him."

UH asked, "How many guests are there at the Hilton at this time."

"All of them—seventy-two," Eduardo said walking away.

The celebration of another year gone by, started a nine p.m. and went as planned, except for the originally uninvited guest from France, Randy Freeman and his female friend, that Chu had invited again at the last minute. With the current information that Chu had, it was necessary to invite Randy.

Randy made his way over to UH, without his female friend, and UH was surprised to see him. Randy explained to UH that at this time he didn't need the money, but he wanted UH to look at a new opportunity to make money. UH frowned in thought, for he realized that he hadn't called him as he had planned. Randy had been drinking heavily, so UH wasn't sure that Randy knew what he was talking about.

Chu interrupted the conversation, by telling UH in his mind, that Randy's scheme will make several million euros for himself, but much more for the criminals he was now involved with. Chu asked UH to tell Randy that you will get back to him, but we won't. Thank him for attending, and that you hope that he is enjoying himself. Randy's scheme involves a new Vietnamese drug gang that is not known to Director Yen Zhang. They have been under the radar of Zhang for about three months, and yet they have the opportunity to amass nine million dollars next week. Randy had been told that he would make three hundred thousand euros for the use of his truck in France. He is desperate, so we will snuff out the gang, take the money, and send Randy the three hundred thousand euros, and tell him to expand his trucking business. I will warn him not to get in trouble like this again. I will be sure that he views it on the news that Zhang busted a new drug gang.

A gentlemen from Los Angeles was introduced to UH by Rowe.

"UH, I would like you to meet, Jimmy Landerwood. I've known him since my days in Chicago. He left for LA right after I had been elected president. He is an investment broker."

Eduardo walked over to the three men, and offered, "I heard part of your conversation, and when I had heard the phrase, 'investment broker', my ears perked up. Eduardo asked Jimmy if his business was solvent, after all, Eduardo was the financial advisor to UH. Jimmy assured him that his portfolio was thick. Eduardo thought for second, and asked him about the fraud charges that had been brought against him last year, knowing that they had been dismissed. They talked for a while, when Eduardo agreed to call him next week. Then he added, "What you say makes profitable sense. I will call you on Wednesday.

Although most had been inebriated, everyone had a good time, so they had said. The guests, the band, the bartenders and servers, and Eduardo had left by one-thirty a.m. Jeanine rolled over onto a sleepy UH. "Can we talk about us, tomorrow?"

She seemed a little tipsy, so UH breathed, "Sure."

"Darling, wake up it's 2016."

UH blinked his squinting eyes open the best he could, and said, "My sweet..."

Jeanine jumped off the bed, flung on a robe, slipped on her padded socks, and headed for the kitchen. By the time brunch was finished, UH was sleepily ambling up to the table.

Halfway through their meal, Jeanine asked, "Can we talk about something that I have a hard time talking about?"

UH said, "Of course my sweet—after we eat."

In the afternoon they were watching television in the private living room, and talking about what 2016 had in store for them, the Coalition, and the peace initiative. They had a life of financial independence. This led to the discussion of Jeanine's quandary about having a child.

"UH, I don't know where to begin, so I'll just begin. Now that we are married, I thought of having a baby as well."

UH shut off the television, took Jeanine in his arms and said, "Following the death of my first wife, and of course my son, I was reckless at a high speed boat race, and crashed into a retaining wall, throwing me feet first as I twisted and landed on my inner leg and scrotum. I was out cold and later told that I had been in serious accident, and that is why I had been in such pain. The point that I am making is that I had permanently damaged my reproductive system. Months later my doctor told me that I would be as infertile as an old man." He held her closely and stroked her soft blonde hair. "My sweet one, I will gladly check out this problem again. There might be a way. I am healthy."

In the next few weeks they contacted doctors, the best of the best, flying to Paris, London, New York, and Berlin. Their new year, was not promising when it came to having a child. A Berlin doctor heard of their plight and contacted UH.

"I cannot promise anything," Doctor Burgerhin, a male fertility specialist, began in German, "Are you able to see me next week on Thursday the 21st?"

Doctor Burgerhin could not help them—UH shot blanks.

Coalition Interactions Broaden

February 5th, the regional directors assembled in Brussels for the Second Annual Meeting of the World Zone Coalition. The meeting was again held at the Hilton Brussels Grand Place, and the accommodations were also the same. They met this time to discuss the new duties of the supervisors. They had all agreed to these duties in the in 2017 meeting, supervisors would be invited for a special program for them.

The directors confirmed what Chu had said and was now taking place. More interaction between directors, like sharing ideas as to increase revenue, offering opinions concerning the work of administrators who work with mayors, charities, and councils, and were shone how to watch for or find loner terrorists. Some directors shared resources like gas, oil, commodities, and new law enforcement gear. Military technologies, surveillance equipment, and vehicle improvements were the Coalition's responsibility to approve.

The meeting centered around the problem of identifying a terrorist who is a loner.

UH opened the meeting, welcomed everyone by name and region, and other pressing considerations.

He began, "I am going to address a concern that is a common predicament that has plagued nations more recently since the 1970s, like a hijacker on airplanes, a political assassin, or a berserk man down the street. They are all pretty much unstoppable. I suggest that when a loner commits murder, the friends and family who know about that murderer's intention, must be seen as an accomplices. Under the Coalition's martial law the collaborators, or individuals who knew what had been planned or was being planned, would be viewed as guilty, and put to death as well. This may or may not deter most crimes of this kind, but it would send a message.

"When an administrator hears of a developing incident, or a loner, he must advise the authorities, and his supervisor. Covert surveillance then begins, and remains until that potential perpetrator purchases a gun, explosives, or seeks an active accomplice. Our action is to be preemptive. We cannot wait until he commits a felony. His purposeful intent is enough, and he is to be picked up, charged accordingly, and executed along with accomplices. This international malignant cancer must be stamped out, and it will be done on my watch. Will this prevent others? Human passions will create such problems, so we must be diligent, direct, with meticulous detail gathering. Preemptive, is the key word. By the way, all of you know, the United Nations is obsolete. It may have had a function at one time. World War II gave birth to the UN in October of 1945, to prevent such a conflict from ever happening again. Its fifty-one member states had grown to one hundred and ninety three. I must add that due to its demise, there is no Security Council—thank god.

"I'll stop here for questions."

"Mr. President, I have a question," said North African District Director, Alim Jabir. "Has the Coalition ever found out what ever happened to the people take by aliens, if that is the reason?"

UH responded, "We have adjusted the people missing from thirty-three percent to ten percent. Secondly, during the peace initiative in Israel, there were two percent more taken, which brought the total missing to twelve point two percent. Although we replaced your satellites, we have put up twenty-three more than had been in space. We also sent an unmanned space vehicle to outer space in hope to discover life. We enhanced the Hubble telescope with ours, which is a tad better; we improved all large telescopes of three meters, or one hundred and twenty inches or greater ones around the world. Yet, no other life has been seen. We are working at a heightened pace, but we will inform our directors if anything changes in November or in the WZC Newsletter we will send electronically. Deep space will be probed before next year. Our press agent John Boudreaux will have a news release as soon as it happens. Directors will be informed the day before we have lift off.

"We should have answers next year around August as to what happened to the almost thirteen percent of the global population."

Rowe asked, "Will we ever dispense with martial law."

UH responded, as Eduardo rolled his eyes, "Not for the foreseeable future. Peace must become the norm. Coalition Martial Law is harsh, but more so are the actions of genocidal maniacs and suicidal murders. Please accept this: life is better under the peace initiative than what had been under any nation's watch.

"Anyone else have a question?" asked UH.

"Yes," said Pierce, "well not quite a question as it is a statement." UH waited, as did everyone else. "I'm not sure how to frame this statement, but here goes. My country, as well as others, have kicked and scratched at the thought of a central world government, or in this instance, a World Zone Coalition. It's high time we all simply get on board. Let us finish cleaning up the bloody mess of mayhem and terror. Thank you UH, and the other directors who had approved your leadership. That's it."

"Director Pierce, I am pleased that you have brought that issue up," said UH. "It has troubled me, but only to the extent, that prior to this meeting, I overlooked much of the gibberish, as someone had once said, and I somehow believed we could come to an accord before the RD Meeting concluded. How many will agree with me, and the other three directors, that this issue of a central executive, is agreeable to all present."

There was a full consensus. The regional directors were ready to follow UH from 2016.

Chu told UH that the meeting cemented the Coalition, and that now perhaps, Rowe will "shut up." He told UH to increase the RD's discretionary expense accounts to three hundred and fifty thousand dollars. RD's would have their salaries increased by fifty thousand dollars to five hundred and fifty thousand dollars annually. Nikolin, the Regional Director from Russian said that he was very pleased—this too was a consensus with the regional directors.

The RD's and UH agreed that supervisors would be responsible for holding meetings with administrators to observe more closely any covert activity, especially loners. Each salary for a supervisor increased to two hundred thousand dollars, tax free—like other Coalition officers.

UH called Jeanine to tell her that the meeting had gone very well. He told her that next year the Regional Director's Meeting will be in Europa Buildings."

"What do you mean by buildings?" she asked.

"They are all attached. Eduardo said that the left building, that is as you face the buildings; it will be for business offices and conference rooms. The building on the right will be a hotel, restaurant, and apartments. The center building is for private use. Our suite is the entire seventh floor. The third floor is a ballroom. The sixth floor is our personal gym and Olympic swimming pool. I'll tell you more later."

"Oh my god, that is great. Every meeting is within walking distance from our suite," said Jeanine. "UH, are you on your way home?"

UH said, "Yes my sweet, Anthony is at the wheel."

Jeanine began to spend as much time with UH as she could, so she went to work with him in his office, doing things UH didn't want Elsa to do. She continued to travel with him during February and March. They visited China, Japan, Brazil, and Turkey. In March, she began to assist Eduardo, UH, and Jamison with busy things. She published two articles in the new provocative art magazine, *Can't Trust Your Eyes,* and *Art—not Always Pleasant.*

Jeanine's main concern was that a medical breakthrough would help UH, so they could have a child.

On March 29th, UH received a call from Doctor Martin Baldwin from the National Infertility Association.

"Mr. Harrison, this is Dr. Baldwin," he was sorry for the late night call, and he explained where he was from and that he had been looking at the records that were sent to him from Doctor Burgerhin in Berlin. He believed that the major vein leading to the scrotum had pooled blood, like a hemorrhoid, and left untreated it was like it had caused varicocele. This of course lowers sperm count to practically zero. I don't think that this is caused by the type of injury you had in the boating accident. I believe that your condition can be repaired."

UH said, "When can you see me?"

"I can see you on April 7th at 1:00 pm, at my office Cleveland Clinic's main campus. This procedure is controversial, but many men have been helped."

"My wife and I will be there. Thank you doctor." UH shared this information with Jeanine.

"Oh my god darling," she said sitting straight up on the couch were she and UH had been holding each other. "I will pray, and pray, and pray. You have been so faithful to our wanting a baby. I love you beyond measure."

Chu spoke into UH's mind. "Just a heads up. Be careful what you ask for. Bye."

A Morning Sun of Hope

The next seven days were both daunting and exhilarating. Jeanine worried that if the operation was not successful, UH would be upset or concerned for her well-being. She thought about her parents; how happy they would be if they were alive.

UH privately thought that if the surgery was ineffective, Jeanine would be terribly upset. He thought about his son William and what a joy he had been, and that it would be thrilling to have a child with Jeanine, and maybe it would be a girl.

UH decided that they should leave on April 5th. They flew from Brussels to Cleveland Hopkins International Airport. Their personal driver Anthony, who now carried a Glock, traveled with them as well as his five armed security detail.

The armored limousine left the airport and drove to the main campus of the Cleveland Clinic on Euclid Avenue.

Dr. Baldwin finally arrived, and asked the Harrisons to come into his office.

"The report from Dr. Burgerhin," Baldwin started, "made me think about a controversial, yet viable procedure. The repair is not just for sperm count. Let me say it this way. The large varicoceles can block sperm count. I must say this again, the problem you have could not have been caused by your accident."

UH asked, "This is what other doctors suggested; but you mentioned that this operation is controversial."

"Yes, the procedure has been around for many years. The most recent studies have shown success with the larger varicoceles, not so much with smaller veins. The new microsurgical repair techniques eliminate potential damage to the testicles. This condition has been with you for several years. Varicoceles is much like varicose veins. They appear as small veins under the skin, and some get so large that surgery is the only remedy, like yours.

"Microsurgical varicocelectory improves testosterone levels and normal semen which allows for a natural pregnancy or minimally upgrades the semen of adequate quality for intrauterine insemination."

"When can we schedule this surgery?" asked UH.

Baldwin answered, "If you are able to get some blood work done for me, preferably three days, because you must fast ten to twelve hours before the blood is drawn, and because I have to schedule a surgery room. Are you able to stay in the city for a week?"

"Yes," said UH. He would need to call Chu and Jamison.

"On Tuesday the 12th, I will do the surgery," said Baldwin.

UH asked, "What is the surgery time, when can I go home, and how long before I am able to go to work?"

"The surgery itself is less than an hour, and you will leave the hospital the same day. The recovery time is three to four days, after which you may return to work," said Baldwin.

Jeanine asked, "When can we expect to get pregnant?"

Baldwin smiled, "It will take between three and nine months for the spermatozoa to appear. In other words the sperm count level must be high enough."

The 12th, at 8:30 am, Dr. Baldwin did the varicocele repair in thirty-five minutes. A nurse in the recovery room, said to UH and Jeanine that she loved his English accent and her French accent.

They returned to their plane, and were in flight to Brussels at 3:50 pm. They arrived in Brussels at 8:55 pm, and Anthony took them to their Europa suite and dropped them off.

Chu called UH, "I hope that you are feeling better."

"Yes, I am quite fine, and anxious to get back to work," said UH.

"Good to have you back. The Europa Hotel will be ready the first of June. The office building is almost completed, but renting the office space will take some time. Jamison reports that the RD's are acting more cohesive, like a championship soccer team.

"Well, I'll let you go," said Chu

Jeanine was watching Fox News and unpacking. She said, "Darling can we go out to eat?"

"Yes, as soon as a make a call to Jamison."

At dinner, Jeanine asked if they could hire a chef fulltime. UH said that that would be fine, but thought that she had wanted a personal valet. They had two maids and his butler servant, Le Shoot, and currently twelve security men.

"I would like for us to have three maids, two valets, and an executive chef," she smiled at UH.

Chu said in UH's mind, *I think she's right. The additional help will assist her in the coming months, say after August 9th. Have a good night. See you in four days, unless Eduardo drops by.*

UH worked in his home office; caught up on his mail and emails; went next door to check the progress on the Europa Hotel; and worked on plans for a vacation in Nice the first of April. By the weekend, UH was feeling good. Let's leave for Madrid next weekend and stay for a week. Jeanine agreed. Their marriage "honeymoon" was still bright, with a hopeful future.

Chu called with a Coalition update, "UH, one fatal stabbing in Jerusalem, one handgun death in Brazil and in El Salvador, and three deaths in India by a machete waving idiot who was on an illicit drug. The stabbing is said to have been done by an emotional wreck, I mean a man suffering for years from a mental disorder. The four directors have apprehended the murderers, tried them today, and tomorrow they are to be executed. The South American Director Colombo said it best, 'A death for a death.' A brother of the shooter in Brazil knew about the gunman who had wanted to kill the lover of his wife. He too is dying tomorrow on the charge of complicit accomplice. Other than that, enjoy your weekend."

UH said, "Thank you Eduardo," so that Jeanine would know who it was that was calling.

The Harrison's had a nice weekend talking about how positive they felt about having a child together. They busied themselves with work, and met their new staff members, who they had made apartments for on the eighth floor for security apartments, souse chefs, and any other staff that wished to live near their workplace. The off-duty security detail, who wished to have an apartment on fourth floor were provided one as well. The valets were working out, meals were provided by Enrico Petit, and the rest of the "staff were great," according to Jeanine.

On the 21st, India Regional Director Arnab Kapoor, skyped everyone with distressing news. Rebels, outside of the city of Badrinath, had amassed fifty or more guerrilla fighters. They were spotted through satellite imaging. He sent security forces by train to quell the uprising.

Chu told Kapoor, and everyone else who was skyping, not to lose lives of his men, and should take out all of rebels with heavy ordnance, delivered by our specialized drones. He added, "No one is to survive."

These types of incidents happened less and less in ensuing months.

On July 28, with the summer dressed in green, Jeanine and UH finally made plans to take a vacation in Rome. They flew down to Rome, Anthony drove them from the airport to the Stars Hotel in Vatican City. UH's security team searched the hotel, and took the Harrison's cases to their room.

Jeanine cried as she looked from her hotel room at the Vatican.

They were not typical tourists, for their entourage was armed, walking in front and behind them. They ate at a fine dining restaurant several times; visited the Vatican, where Jeanine had a Cardinal bless her because of her famous husband; and held each other for hours in the hotel room.

On Sunday, they attended mass—much to the chagrin of Chu, and UH was uncomfortable. Chu said to UH, *My, what a women can make a man do.*

They arrived back in Brussels on the 26th of August, after traveling to Sidney, Australia where Regional Director Sherman Russel met them, and took them to a Regional dinner.

"That last visit was enchanting," said Jeanine. "I would like to visit again sometime."

The next day, Eduardo came to UH's suite to take him and Jeanine through the Europa Hotel. The tour included most of the Europa three-building structure. The Europa Hotel had turned into a luxury hotel. The ballroom could accommodate five hundred guests. The guest rooms had unique features and/or upgrades that made them appear more like stepping into 2030. An Olympic size swimming pool was built on the first floor of that building, as was the complete gym. Benjamin Singer was to be the Europa's first apartment lessee. In the beginning, word of mouth was the main way tenants found out about this fabulous hotel/apartment complex.

The office complex was filling up, in part, because of the nice gym, swimming pool, and locker rooms for men and women. A small restaurant was added when all other rooms were finished. The three attached building in the center of the complex became an attraction when a swanky night club was built on the on the first floor of the this section, the same section where UH and Jeanine lived on the entire seventh floor. A special code was needed to stop at that floor.

The Harrisons were impressed with all that Eduardo had accomplished in such a short time. Eduardo said that the revenue from the partially occupied complex was beyond reassuring.

"This is so exciting to me," Jeanine began, "darling I love you." She stared at him.

"What, my dear, are you staring at. Do I have something on my face?" he said brushing his hand over his mouth and chin.

"Just you my love. All that we have, the yacht, the plane, the luxury we live in, and all the money we could never spend, but none of it can buy intelligence, drive, respect, common sense, trust, class, or love. You darling epitomize them all."

UH responded, "The life I've lived this short time with you, is more satisfying and peaceful, than my previous life without you."

"*Wow. How poetic,*" retorted Chu into the mind of UH.

Jeanine said, "Do you think that we could take the yacht somewhere?"

UH said, "Of course, my sweet. Of course. Please know, from the second month of our relationship, I had already been deeply in love with you. I'll call the captain, the pilot, and Anthony."

On Sunday the 28th, they were enjoying the August sun in Nice on board the *Catherine Marie.* They talked about the prospect of being parents.

Monday morning Chu called UH, "Scott Iverson and his team have almost perfected a new satellite program. It allows us to monitor any activity on the planet—no blind spots. Heat sensors can penetrate twelve feet below ground and further in the oceans. He said that it should be operable by November. Realistically, they are more than merely satellites capabilities, they already have high power laser beams that will kill anyone or anything. We used this laser to kill rebels in India, near Badrinath. A few had scattered, but we shot them.

"I had no intention of disturbing you on your holiday, but I believe that it is imperative to keep you in the loop. Have a good week. Bye."

On September 16th UH and Jeanine were back at their suite. Let's work-out together, shower, and go to diner next door at Petit Restaurant and surprise Enrico. I miss him, but our new chef, Franco Russo, is superb.

On Monday the 26th, Jeanine went to see her gynecologist, Dr. Dubois.

On Thursday, the doctor called back.

"Hello, this is Jeanine."

"This is Dr. Dubois."

"Yes doctor."

"I'm calling to give you results of your pregnancy test. It was positive, the doctor said.

"Oh my god, it happened, it worked, I'm pregnant," Jeanine shouted.

"Oh, thank you doctor." She hung up and called UH at his office next door, and told him through emotional crying and eagerness. "Come home when you can. I am pregnant," she exclaimed.

UH said, "I'm done for the day with that kind of news."

They sat together in the living room, UH, embracing her in his arms.

UH said, "I guess Doctor Baldwin knew what he was talking about. I am flabbergasted after all of my early doctors following my accident that I would be sterile." He gave her a tight squeeze and released her to look at her sweet face. "I am so happy."

Chu ruined the moment by, *Congratulations is in order. My, what a lucky couple. See you in the morning.*

The next morning the butler served UH and Jeanine breakfast, and left for his room.

"I feel like a dark shadow lifted from me," said Jeanine. "I'm officially pregnant.

UH looked at Jeanine's glowing face. He said, "I see life as a bright new morning like when I was a teen, and the morning sun warmed my skinny face. Today I have an abundance of hope. I actually said hope."

Anticipation

For Jeanine, October rapidly turned into December, working, traveling, writing magazine articles, and buying her first maternity clothes, even though she hadn't really been showing. She had often thought about how Urie had been changing into such a kind man and husband. "He will make an exceptional father," she said to their chef Russo one afternoon.

A Christmas Party was planned for December 23rd in the Europa ballroom. Franco hired two sous chefs to assist him. The guest list was shortened to fifty-three, which included his friend Benjamin Singer. The head butler, Andre Toole, hired three servers to assist his staff. Eduardo wanted a band that could play swing, eighties and nineties favorites, and a good singer this time. Eduardo was disappointed, but not the guests.

The next evening, on the 24th, Jeanine had been looking forward to attending Christmas Mass, but wasn't feeling well enough to be there alone, so UH had decided to go with her. Chu was not pleased.

New Year's Eve event had been planned to be a larger event. The number of guests on the list was two hundred and twenty. The staff, of course, was larger, the thirty piece band had a main singer, and a quartet had been made up of band members. Jeanine and UH danced, as did most of the guests; UH drank as everyone else had, except Jeanine. Benjamin Singer made a toast to UH and Jeanine for the party and for the couple's "child to be".

The evening was full of expectancy: the world had settled into a peaceful habitation of sorts; last year had the lowest global crime rate, for there had been only twelve hundred incidents; the regional directors were achieving more than the thought was possible; and Chu had great hopes for UH in 2017. Chu would also attempt to keep UH from dwelling on Jeanine's due date which was June 22nd. Chu assured UH that in 2017, his income would increase by one billion euros. No one expected a down turn in the global economy. Because of the peace initiative and the World Zone

Coalition, unemployment was less than three percent.

The guests at this New Year's Party were imagining only "positive karma" as one guest put it.

The next day, Eduardo met with UH in his home office.

Chu started the conversation, "It is time for us to have a talk. I know who you were and what you became because of me. Did you believe for a moment that I would not continue to be involved with your decisions?" UH attempted to say something. "Shut up. Wait until I am finished. You do not decide anything apart from me. Understood?"

"Yes I do comprehend the situation. I got carried away by…"

Chu interrupted, "A woman."

"Not any woman for god sake," UH stated.

Chu laughed, "What a shocker—a woman. The same ancient story of man."

UH said, "What is it that you expect of me? What is it that I'm not doing?"

"Don't play dumb with me. You are to regulate your life as I dictate," Chu answered with his fist slamming down of a stack of paper.

"All right. I would like to take a week off this month," said UH.

"Just say it. 'Jeanine and I would like to take a week off this month.' I don't care if you take a week or two, for that matter, take the damn month."

"Thank you, Chu." UH smirked.

"Don't get insolent with me. All I am asking, is for you listen to my lead, advice, and demands. Got it.?" Chu said, when there was a knock at the door.

UH said, "Come in Jeanine." She entered. "Eduardo and I were discussing 2017, and I think he has the right idea about this year."

Jeanine smiled at Eduardo, "You do have good ideas and plans."

"I thank you Jeanine, you are most kind," said Eduardo. "I really must be going, so I'll bid you both a Happy New Year." Eduardo left.

"My sweet pregnant wife, my beautiful Jeanine, this weekend we are flying to Mexico City for a week, and then off to Guadeloupe for another week. It is an exotic place I have wanted to visit. After we return on the 23rd, I will be preparing the Annual Regional Directors Meeting."

"I didn't know what we would do this January, the dreariest month of the year, even in our beloved Nice," smiled Jeanine. She left to see what Chef Russo was planning that day.

"Chu, did you hear our plans?" asked UH said out loud.

"Yes, and thank you for letting me know. See you when you return," Chu answered, then added, "After your visit to Guadeloupe, why not just go to Nice to stay at your home until the 28th?"

"Thanks again. We will just do that," said UH.

Mexico was pleasant, hospitable, and warm.

At their home in Nice, they talked about their parents missing the birth of the child; about the life of privilege the baby, he or she will enjoy, and how they would handle it; and about the hopefulness most children would have, in a world of peace.

Suddenly, a shot rang out, then another in the back yard near the pool. Anthony ran into the house and said to UH and Jeanine, "Joe, the chief security guard, had shot and killed a male assailant who had attempted to enter your back door. I will call the local administrator, and I will write a report for you and Pierce. I hope that this didn't ruin your evening."

UH asked, "Did he have a weapon?"

Anthony answered, "I don't know. Joe is running his picture through the Coalition's data system.

There was a rap at the door. Anthony let in Joe, who said that the older man had been on a watch list because of vocal opposition to the Coalition, but that was eight months ago. His name is Franz Duval, a retired dock worker. He had a five inch pocket knife." He looked at Jeanine, "Sorry Mrs. Harrison for the situation tonight." Jeanine nodded.

UH thanked the men, and said goodnight.

"My sweet, even with this global peace, we cannot control human nature, passions, and hatefulness," UH said before kissing Jeanine's forehead.

The Harrison's were home in the suite on Sunday on January 29th when Chu called UH.

"Please excuse yourself from Jeanine, for I need to speak with you."

UH told Jeanine that he had to take a call in his office. She was a bit sleepy, so she reclined on the couch.

"Go ahead, I'm in my office."

"Over eagerness is silliness when considering anticipation. I won't explain—figure it out. We have the Coalition Meeting for regional directors and the supervisors, who will be focusing on the duties of the administrators on the 3rd of February. I had sent them the topic, agenda, and the place of the meeting. They had already known that we are meeting in the left building of the Europa Complex. We, of course, are sending limos to the airport on Thursday. Anyone arriving early, like Rowe and Reed, will not be expected to use a taxi. We'll send a limo. They are staying at Europa Hotel, and I explained the amenities in my email.

"The world is free of terrorists, but misguided teens and college students tend to look for grand causes. There is always the prospect of loners. God, I keep repeating these things to you, but then you might want to remind the World Zone Coalition guests about these things.

"Is there anything that you would like to discuss, other than what is on the agenda, if not, I will see you there. Bye."

On February 3rd, at 1:00 pm, all were present, and one Supervisor brought his best administrator with him. The administrator had had the lowest crime rate over the last seven months. The entire Coalition went to dinner at the Petit Restaurant, after which they were on their own. Several discussions evolved around the topic of the next day's meeting: Positive Expectations.

At dinner, Reed said, "How can we be positive at all when we are in the mindset of vigilance, catching Criminals, and making sure that murders and accomplices are executed?"

"First of all, it is important that we anticipate our goals in a positive way," said UH. "To expect your people to be the best that they are able to be, is to anticipate a favorable outcome. It's simply nonsense, to view ones vocation in a negative manner. When an athlete trains, is he merely hoping to be the best, or does he believe he will be the best. That is anticipation."

Reed responded, "You are absolutely correct. One must see the cup half full."

Rowe added, "When I was a young man, my only sport had been chess, and then I discovered golf. That is where I had learned to expect the shot. I'm still not very good."

Eduardo privately said to UH, *How in the name of sense did that man win two elections? I am quoting Nikolin, but I had to repeat it. I am sure that the press had been in his pocket.* UH smiled at him.

UH began the meeting after dinner. "Look over the agenda. The heading of the agenda is: Expectations for 2017-2018. Let me introduce our regional directors, who will in turn, introduce their supervisors. Following the introductions, UH started his remarks on "Positive Expectations".

"We anticipate cooperation amongst the regional directors, supervisors, and administrators to maintain global peace. We have had enormous success with the Coalition's peace initiative, and we dare not rest on our laurels, for next year we will add new policies, unlike in the past when each nation had promised peace, and called peace accords or peace treaties which were utterly false hopes, usually one-sided, and lasted thirty to sixty days. These peace agreements were more corrupt than some of Mafia families or politicians. The World Zone Coalition will define more methods to develop lasting peace. In the past, political leaders and parties negotiated away from the core of the initial treaty through meaningless and lengthy compromises to make their nations believe how difficult the process had been. When in reality, it was more profitable politically. Yes, fixed ideas based on fraudulent political agenda.

"Let's continue to address corruption: the press corps and any other private agenda. Regional Director Franklin Pierce asked earlier, why we avoided the press and the media for two years. When the Coalition replaced the UN, the EU, and the EC, the press around the world leaped like jackals hoping to find as undercurrent of political fraud, or a possible negative deception to write a commentary of twisted truth—lies. . We refused to talk to them, so they invented their own scenario and wrote the pieces as they imagine—the WZC was evil. All because we had the UN, EU, and EC agree not to talk to the press. They received nothing to screw into a story. We had found, as most of you know by now, the reporter, John Boudreaux. He writes an article, and passes it over to the various press organizations. At first, most of the press corps had refused his reports. Now most of them grudgingly accept his information—that is what we stipulate. He is our press agent, correspondent, and reporter for the Coalition. Only regional directors and supervisors may speak with him about Coalition business in your regions.

Rowe asked, "Why not allow key or productive administrators to talk with him?"

UH responded, "The general media has always been corrupt, like snakes that crawl around to find a bit to eat. There had been good, fair-minded reporters throughout history, but they have drifted down to a minority over the last century. No administrators are permitted to speak to the media. Rowe, if anyone has taken advantage of a corrupt media, you have. Sorry for the frankness."

"Our meetings usually last one day, but perhaps next year we may invite key administrators who have been awarded like Roy Hart. Regional Director Frank Watson, would you please come up here and tell the story of Roy."

Watson brought Hart to the front of the room, and began to tell the story, "My administrators have done a superlative job. They must attend my mandatory meetings for them, and be prepared to offer suggestions to ease my job. They must have their reports in on time. Roy Hart does this.

He is the administrator from section two: Arizona, New Mexico, and Nevada. He found the man that shot a mayor in Tucson, Arizona. His mother failed to report a warning of her son. She had told him not to kill anyone. The mayor, Juan Menendez, was the first administrator killed in the Coalition. Gosh, Juan had done an outstanding job. The man who shot him, and his mother, were executed after a speedy trial. Roy this plague and certificate is our appreciation for a job well done. Here also, is a check for three thousand dollars."

Everyone applauded as the two took their seats.

UH said, "Thank you Frank. You have done an exceptional job in the North American Region, more specifically, division three." He then read the names of the supervisors and their divisions.

Eduardo and UH had a discussion after the Coalition meeting ended.

"I talked with Jimmy Landerwood, the investor from LA last week. He was at the New Year's Eve party. He called again this morning," Chu explained. "He wanted you to invest five hundred thousand dollar in an oil and coal conglomerate. I did some investigation into the Liquid Process Incorporation. It owns a refinery, three oil wells in the Gulf of Mexico, ten oil wells in Texas, fracking business in many former states. They also bought out a huge cosmetic company which brings in close to a billion dollars annually. Their net worth is sixty billion dollars. I sent him the money this morning."

UH said, "That sounds fabulous. Thanks Chu."

"Not so loud, there are several men in the back. I'm Eduardo, here." He went on, "I will tell you now that you can expect to double your money.

"I'm headed to the office next door. Talk with you later." Chu was actually going to visit a friend in China: Shaman Chen.

"Chen, how pleasant to see you. I see that you haven't changed," Chu chuckled throwing he head back.

Chen said, "I see that he is doing well for the most part, but you know how to handle him."

"Yes I do," Chu said, "I anticipate that the next year and a half will prove most interesting."

"Indeed," said Chen. "Will I play a role in your scheme next year?"

Chu said, "Not until the fall of 2018."

"Very good," said Chen.

"I'm headed to my plush office in Brussels," said Chu with his famous grin.

UH said to Jeanine, "I had been thinking how wonderful it would be to have a girl in June. What name should we consider?"

"I haven't thought of a name yet. I had been named after my grandfather John. In French, a variant of John is Jean. My father insisted on Jeanine."

UH said, I was thinking of Jeanine Nadine Harrison. Nadine means hope or anticipation."

"I like that," said Jeanine. "My name, her name, and our name." She added, "I have never been as hopeful in my life."

UH called Chu. "Would you mind if we took time off this February and went to Miami and the Caribbean. We will return March 4th?"

"Not at all. I appreciate that you checked with me."

"Thanks, Chu."

"UH, I saw one of our mutual friends this morning."

UH asked, "Who was it?"

"Chen, the shaman from Macao," said Chu waiting to hear his reply.

UH paused for few seconds, "Ah, yes I do."

"He was just wondering how you were doing, and said tell Urie that I said hello. He would like to visit in 2018."

"I had only met him once, but I do remember him," said UH.

Chu said that Chen wished him and his wife best wishes in that Jeanine was expecting. UH and Chu hung up. He sat back in his office chair and thought, *I had spoken to the RDs about positive expectation. What in the name of sense is going to happen when Chen arrives next year. How can I truly anticipate hope for me, Jeanine, and our baby?*

Countdown to June

March 6th, UH went to his office. Elsa, Jamison, and Eduardo were in as well.

"Intolerance to evil is a good thing," said Regional Director Arnav Kapoor to UH over skype.

"In North America, we are learning this, and that is what is bringing peace," added Supervisor Reed from section one.

Regional Director of North Africa Alim Jabir said in Arabic, "It is too bad that my Muslim brothers had not learned this sooner. We are moving ahead with a better economy, cooperation between the sects has improved dramatically."

Adam Almon said, "My radical Jewish brothers and sisters had not learned until all were gone. Radical extremists had never really belonged on this planet."

Pierce skyped, "Laws went too far left to protect the criminal and terrorist. Liberalism just about got all of us killed."

All twelve of the directors and three of the supervisors skyped early that Monday.

Every one that morning discussed the difficulty with capturing a loner criminal before that person commits the crime.

UH again reminded them that cybersecurity, from the beginning of the World Zone Coalition, is more sophisticated. Cameras are more advanced in every city, more efficient than had been used by the CIA, and that there are more of them, even in new rural areas around the world.

UH said, "In only a year, we had doubled our satellites and cameras. They are more efficient and extremely advanced because of our forward-looking technology. We now have less loner activity, more peaceful conditions, and better communication." He completed his skype meeting and send an email to all RDs and supervisors reporting his remarks so as to eliminate misunderstanding.

Jeanine called UH, "Darling, I am almost six months now, and I would like to visit the Lady of Lourdes in France. We will only go for two days, and return to work."

UH said, "Of course sweet love. Let me look at my calendar, it's right here; how about Monday and Tuesday, the 13th and 14th?"

"Great Darling. Thank you. I love you. When will you be home?"

"You just talked like Jamison," UH laughed.

Jeanine said, "Don't make fun of me."

"I'm not love. I'll see you at three o'clock."

UH and Jeanine arrived in Lourdes, France on the morning of March 13th. Anthony drove them to the Hotel Jeanne d'Arc where the best suite had been available. The next morning they ate breakfast, talked about the birth of their baby in June, and Jeanine's need to visit the Grotto of Lourdes.

A young priest met the Harrisons, and introduced them to a sister who took them to the shrine.

"I see that you are with child. May I pray for you and the baby?"

Jeanne looked a UH. He whispered, "Yes."

The nun took Jeanine's hand, and in front of the shrine, and recited a prayer, "O Mother of mercy, comforter of the all mothers; you know the suffering, and her needs. Look upon her with loving compassion. Most of all, O Mary, may she embrace your will.

"There my daughter, go in his will."

"Thank you sister," said Jeanine. She wiped her eyes.

UH didn't say anything as they walked to the armored vehicle. Anthony got out and opened the door for Jeanine and UH. One security guard rode in front with Anthony, and the other four followed in two other armored vehicles.

Instead of returning to Brussels, they went to Nice, to spend the rest of the week.

"UH," said Chu, "I thought that I'd bring you up to speed. Our cybersecurity picked up a warning that Zhang had passed on to Woojin who had been dictator of what was North Korea, and warned him to get in line with the Coalition. He is the supervisor of the Korean Peninsula. He, at first, refused, but quickly accepted Zhang's advice, when he was informed of the alternative—death. Zhang also reminded him that his section had the highest loner attacks than any other section in the Coalition. Woojin promised to do better; he could because he had ruled the area with an iron fist before.

"How are you doing? I see that you are in Nice."

"Yes we are," said UH. "We will be here until the weekend. I'll see you on Monday."

"No. Just take it easy. I understand that Jeanine isn't feeling well this week, just like the other five hundred and thirty thousand pregnant women. Take off until April. I'll see you on the 3rd. Bye."

UH ignored the remark about other women, and hugged Jeanine.

He said to Jeanine, "We do not have to return to Brussels until April 2nd, so that I can be to work on Monday the 3rd."

"That is wonderful darling. Let's just stay her in Nice, after all, we love this house too."

Chu hired a local chef to cook for them, so that Jeanine could take it easy. The Harrisons were surprised to have the chef coming in; he had called to come over that late afternoon."

"Wow. That Eduardo is amazing," said Jeanine.

"Indeed he is," said UH.

"Let's watch a Netflix movie after dinner," suggested Jeanine.

"Good with me," returned UH.

UH and Jeanine returned to Brussels on the 2nd of April, UH went in to work on the 3rd, or at least to put in an appearance.

Jamison said to UH, Jeanine is probably counting the days. Hope she is fine. I believe that you are probably anxious. Well, better get back to work."

"Thank you Jamison for asking," said UH.

Eric Everson, the cybersecurity expert, called UH. "Would you come into the Cybersecurity Room, I have some good news."

UH left his office and went into the CR to talk to Everson.

"UH, our cybersecurity in Coalition had been developed from other highly technical countries, like the UK, Israel, Russia, China, Japan, and the United States, but, now we have the capability to be faster, more reliable, than they had been, and we are able to pinpoint a problem in seconds, and find the person who sent the message in nanoseconds."

UH said, "Thank you Eric. To keep peace at the level we have attained is imperative, and I believe you have raised the bar."

Eduardo came in to say that he was quite impressed with impregnable cybersecurity, that the tech team developed.

He said, "The Coalition had two hundred and seventy sophisticated satellites. The drone program had thirty-five hundred units with military striking ability and five thousand for surveillance only. Fighter planes, flown from the ground do exceptional strikes every time they are deployed. We do not permit any such technology to Regional Districts. In fact, the former nations Eric just mentioned and a few others were shut down, and some were confiscated when the World Zone Coalition assumed global control. We control every army and navy in the world."

UH had not known these improvements until that moment.

"This has been a very enlightening day," said UH. "We are grateful Eric."

On his walk from office building to the middle building, or number two section, where he lived, UH got a mobile call, "This is UH."

"Yes, I am sorry for the intrusion," He said in Chinese. "This is Chen from Macao, China. We had met in your apartment near Shanghai."

"I am not sure."

"Do you remember the shaman at your door?"

"Yes, but why in the world would you be calling me?" UH said with a raised voice.

"UH, this is not to be a stressful exchange. Perhaps, I will call you at another time. Have a good evening. Bye."

UH was going to call Chu, but changed his mind.

"UH, this is Chu. I understand that Chen had just called you. He will be working with us this year, so I thought that I would bring him into our little circle."

UH knew he dare not get involved in a conversation with him at this time, because he feared something was up. "All right, that sounds good. I had just been taken back by his call that was out of the blue."

"I see," said Chu. "He thought that you were upset. I'll explain to him that you were surprised to receive a call from him."

"Thank you Chu. I can always count on you. What will be his role next year?"

"I will explain more in September of 2018. See you tomorrow. Bye."

When UH got home, he was visibly upset; hollered to Jeanine that he was home and going into his office; she yelled back that she was resting on the couch.

He sat there, turned in his chair with his head resting on the back, staring at the ceiling fan over him, thinking how his life was spinning somewhere—but where? He needed to get away. That, of course was not going to happen—the covenant. He went out to Jeanine.

"Sweetheart, how are you feeling?"

"UH," Jeanine said sitting up. "I feel good today. Dinner is almost ready."

UH said, "May I talk to you for a moment?"

Jeanine smiled, "Of course darling."

Even when Jeanine didn't feel her best, like now, she never displayed those feelings.

UH began, " If Eduardo doesn't need me, which he shouldn't, our staff is now thirty-five, and I would like to visit Edinburg, and visit a professor friend of mine, and then on to Istanbul, the former Constantinople, until

May 6th."

"I would love to do that. I don't like sitting around—neither does our baby," she said.

"Should we check with your doctor first?" UH asked.

"No darling, I'm fine."

Later that evening, UH called Chu, but before he said a word, Chu said, "Thank you for asking again. Spring is nice in Istanbul, and you may want to go to Shanghai for another two weeks. How about vacationing until May 20th? That is if Jeanine is up to that kind of vacation."

"That is grand Eduardo," UH said in front of Jeanine. "I will share this with Jeanine."

They arrived in Edinburg where UH met with his friend, Dr. Stanley Moore at The University of Edinburg. Jeanine waited in the library looking at some of the University's art collection.

"It's been about ten or so years since we've talked. How pleasant to see you Urie," said Moore, shaking the hand of UH.

"You understand the theurgists", UH started, "and how they supposedly work their magic, so I thought that I would get your understanding of real magic as you teach a course on this particular subject."

"To begin with, I do not believe in real magic, I teach it as a mythology course," said Moore.

UH responded, "Had you ever met someone who thought that they could perform magic?"

"No. Well, yes some years ago, maybe two years ago, a female student who dabbled in Ouija Boards, and other magic paraphernalia. One day she told the class that a man, a shaman, had come to her and told her where her murdered father had been buried. I never saw her again. I take that back. I graduate student told me that she had joined an occult."

"You personally have never witnessed magic," stated UH.

"Not really," said Moore. "Why all these questions?"

"When I had been in China, I witnessed such things as a séance, and an unexplained magic act at a party that had made a man vanish, who had been standing at my side. No one ever saw him again."

"Well, at least I had never witnessed any real magic," said Dr. Moore.

UH, said to Moore, "Thank you Stanley," shaking his hand. "We are flying to Istanbul for a week of sightseeing. Then we will head to Shanghai. My dear wife has not seen either place. Thank you again for your time, and it was quite nice to see you again.

The Harrisons spent ten days in Istanbul, and flew to Shanghai. Jeanine had a few difficult days; the baby had been moving more; and she was missing her father for some reason.

In their room at the Radisson Blu Shanghai, Jeanine laid down for a nap. UH received a text, asking him to come down to the bar. He wrote a note and put it next to Jeanine, and thought that he would call after sometime. He went down to the bar, and there sitting at the table was Chu and Chen. He walked over to their table and sat down.

"Gentlemen," UH said, "how interesting to see you two together. To what do I owe this honor?"

Chu said, "I'm not sure it is an honor, but I am grateful that you view it in that way. We dropped in to say that, first of all, I am glad you are having a great holiday thus far; and secondly, the next time Chen calls, be courteous, don't be acting like you are tired or confused. OK?" UH nodded in the affirmative. "You have everything that you have, because of me, except for Jeanine. Anyway, I wanted to clear up this thing with Chen." He turned to Chen then back to UH.

Chen said, "I would only call you, UH, to keep in touch, or to ask if you needed help or some assistance with some problematic situation."

"Very well," said Chu. "We will be going, and do enjoy Shanghai." Chu stood, as did the other two men. They shook hands, then Chu and Chen walked together toward the parking lot. UH discreetly watched them. As they moved toward a row of cars—they vanished.

UH slowly turned and walked toward the elevators, thinking about what a true theurgist is capable of doing. Suddenly he felt something happen, not to his psyche, not to his strength, but to his blood. He could feel it coursing through his body. Just then Chu called.

"UH," Chu said, "enjoy the new ability—you can now decide who lives and who dies. Bye."

UH thought that this feeling of his blood surging in every vein and artery. It was a small rhythmic pulse. He decided to jog outside, but it didn't change. He went up to his room and did twenty-five pushups, then twenty-five more, but there was not a change in the quiet, cadenced pulse.

Jeanine came out of the bathroom and saw UH getting up from the floor. "Are you alright?" she asked.

"Yes, sweetie, I was doing a few pushups. I'm hungry. Are you?"

"I could eat something like peanut butter and radishes," she laughed.

UH went to the telephone and called down to the kitchen. "Do you have peanut butter? OK. Do you have radishes. Good. With the peanut butter and radishes, would send up a cheeseburger, rare, with the works—whatever that would entail? Thank you. How long will that take? Very good thanks."

They sat on the loveseat and talked about the countdown to June 22nd.

"I am so excited," said Jeanine. "Oh my god, I'm really to be a mother." She squeezed the arm of UH as she snuggled her head on his shoulder.

UH couldn't get Chu and Chen off of his mind. *What the hell is so special about the Fall of 2018,* he thought.

June 1st brought them closer to the due date.

"Jeanine found out last week that the baby is a girl," said UH to Ben Singer. Her name will be Jeanine Nadine Harrison."

"That is poetic," said Ben.

"We chose the name Nadine because it means hope or anticipation," said UH.

"That is really nice, but before I forget, I'm flying to Jerusalem in the morning, so I won't be around this weekend. See you next week. Congratulations on the little girl."

"Darling, we have three weeks exactly until our sweet darling baby girl arrives," said Jeanine. I am so glad that you wanted to name her after me."

"So am I my sweet. Your complexion looks heavenly. Of course, it always has," said UH.

Chen called, "Yes, this is UH."

"I called to let you know that I'll be in Brussels next week to visit the Europa Building complex."

UH responded, "That will be fine. Eduardo and I will give you the grand tour. You can stay in our hotel."

"Good. I will be referred to as Alphonso, Eduardo's brother. Everyone will see the resemblance," said Chen who gave a quick chuckle similar to Eduardo's chortle.

"Excellent," said UH. "I look forward to your visit."

"Darling who was that?" asked Jeanine.

"It was Eduardo's brother. He is coming in from Spain to visit Eduardo," said UH with an inaudible sigh.

The next week, Chen, as Alphonso, came to Brussels. He settled in his room at the Europa Hotel, and he, Chu, and UH had a late lunch at the Petit Restaurant. They discussed nothing about 2018, but Chu made a suggestion, which was never a suggestion.

"I was thinking, that if Chen wished to relocate here, it might prove helpful."

"Sure. He could live at the hotel, or in one the apartments," offered UH.

"I was thinking," started Chu, "that he could reside at the twelve floor of your building."

"Sure," said UH.

Chu said, "Quit thinking of other matters. I can see you're not listening. Tell me what you think."

UH began to say something, but changed his mind, "I apologize. Yes it is a grand idea."

"Fine," said Chu. "I will hire him to run the office of forty-seven. I saw that look. Yes, we had hired twelve more bodies as assistants which adds to the thirty-five. Chen will take the large vacant room at the other end of the office next to yours. These days, you're not in the office that often, so, as I had been saying that we would hire him, we'll do that on July 3rd. He will move into his new apartment on June 29th."

"Questions?"

UH and Chen had nothing to add. They finished lunch, said good-byes, and UH wondered what Chu was up to now. He thought *sometimes these two spirits or ghosts, or shamans, if that is what they are, make me wonder what the covenant really means.* UH never spoke out loud again, for he knew they could hear him. Thoughts were still his.

Chu called UH, "I wanted to let you know that your investment with Landerwood paid a handsome return of four hundred million from your billion dollar investment. I told him to keep the billion, and send the earnings to our bank. That's it. Bye."

UH thought that he was falling out of favor with Chu, but dismissed the thought when his mobile rang and saw that it was Jeanine. "This is UH."

"Darling, I'm not feeling well. I'm ok but, a little queasy,"

UH said, "I'm walking in our building as we speak." UH ran to the elevator that came rather quickly. He felt antsy, as he entered, and as soon as the door opened he went directly to find Jeanine.

"Jeanine, I'm home."

"In here darling." UH followed her voice.

"What seems to be the problem sweetie?" UH asked, sitting beside her on the bed.

"I just don't feel right, like I'm more tired than usual," Jeanine said closing her eyes and falling back on her pillow.

"How is the baby doing?" UH asked as he gently rubbed her stomach.

"She isn't moving as she had been, probably because I am so tired,"

Jeanine said.

"I'll call the doctor for you tomorrow, my sweet."

The next day, UH called Dr. Dubois. He wasn't in, so he left a message. He called again in the afternoon.

"Dr. Dubois is not in today. If this is an emergency, call 107."

In the early evening, while eating dinner, the phone rang. UH picked up the phone.

"This is UH."

"This is Dr. Dubois. I'm returning your call." UH explained Jeanine's recent condition."

Dr. Dubois asked, "Can she feel the baby move at all?" UH asked Jeanine, who claimed to have some movement of the baby. "Ask Jeanine if she can see me on Thursday the 9th at 9:30?" UH said yes.

On Thursday, Jeanine and UH visited the doctor. He was optimistic, for he heard a heartbeat, felt the baby move, but not to his liking.

"I would like to see you at the hospital tomorrow. A few tests, and an ultrasound, should give me a better idea as what to do next," said Dubois.

The ultrasound revealed an active, but little smaller baby than he had expected, but she seemed quite healthy. The other general tests suggested that all seemed well. UH and Jeanine were glad to have this over with, because they both had feared a small unhealthy baby.

Anthony drove them home, as they planned for a quiet weekend.

"It's hard to believe that we only have about two weeks until our sweet little girl is in our arms," said Jeanine

Chu said to UH's mind, *Medical science has come such a long way. Give my best to Jeanine.*

"UH, what are you thinking about?" asked Jeanine.

Anthony cut in, "Miss Jeanine, UH is always thinking."

Jeanine responded, "I would have to agree."

After they arrived home, Jeanine said, "Let's go to the Petit Restaurant tonight."

"That sounds terrific. I am very glad that you are feeling better my sweet."

They enjoyed their dinner; UH had brandy; Jeanine had no alcohol, and they lingered at the restaurant until 6:00 pm. They watched the news that was reporting a commentary on *Why Peace Occurred.* UH was quite interested until Rowe had been given most of the credit.

"Darling, don't be upset," Jeanine said, "it's a commentary on CNN, who helped elect him president twice."

"Again you are correct my sweet."

Jeanine said timidly, "Do you mind if I go to, or we go to the Sacred Heart on Sunday?"

"If I do not go, I'll have Anthony take you, but I will consider it love," said UH.

Sunday the 17th, Anthony took Jeanine and UH to the Basilica of the Sacred Heart mass.

Following the mass, as they left, Jeanine heard Father Summers tell a man that the church needed about one million euros just to properly repair the organ that had been made in 1899.

At the Petit for lunch, Jeanine asked UH if he would consider helping her church with some repairs. He asked her how much would this cost? She knew that it was at least a million euros. He was at first, shocked.

UH began, "I don't mind helping your church my love, but a million euros."

They discussed it further, the UH said that he would call Father Summers in the morning.

"Father Summers, this is Urie Harrison, my wife attends your church. She mentioned that you had repairs and refurbishing needs."

"Yes Mr. Harrison, we are in quite a dilemma. Our building committee indicated that we cannot raise the kind of money necessary for all the required repairs, for years down the road," said Summers.

UH said, "Give me some idea what all these items would cost."

Father Summers recited the list: the dome has a small fracture; the 1899 pipe organ must be repaired; the boiler furnace is old and had been repaired many times; and a few of the stained glass windows were damaged by an Islamic extremist riot two years ago. The cost is estimated at two and a half million euros, but could easily reach three million."

UH said, "Let me give this some thought, and I'll get back with you."

Father Summers said, "Thank you UH, and many of us here at the parish, are grateful for the global peace we now experience."

UH shared this information with Jeanine. She said, "Darling, of course it is up to you, but three million euros is nothing to us. Would you please consider it?"

UH smiled at Jeanine. "For you I will. Actually I had planned to go to the bank today and have a demand draft drawn for the church's bank. I'll call Father Summers now, before I go to the bank and tell him of the seven hundred and fifty million euros we are donating."

"Oh my god Urie, you are so wonderful. I love you," she said leaning in, to hug UH, reaching above her stomach.

UH called Father Summers, who became ecstatic, and must have thanked UH four times.

"We were at a cross roads in the time remaining time for us to raise the funds was nearing. We had raised about three hundred thousand euros toward the organ. My lord, what a relief this is."

They talked for a short time, and UH hung up, then Chu called UH.

"Aren't you the kindest, most interesting person, daddy-to-be in the world?"

UH didn't say anything at first, then, "Why thank you Chu. Sometimes you say the most amazing things."

"To begin with, the money means nothing, but, UH, just be careful. We have a covenant," Chu said sternly. "Bye."

The next day, Jeanine asked Father Summers to come to their suite for dinner. He accepted. When the table had been set, Franco had them reset it with good china, when he heard that Summers was coming to dinner.

They had a pleasant dinner talking about the Coalition peace, the Church, and Jeanine's due date. It soon turned to the most generous gift of seven hundred million euros that UH had given the Church.

Anthony returned the priest back to the rectory.

UH and Jeanine were alone.

"Jeanine, you are so beautiful. May I listen again to the baby?" asked UH.

"Sure my darling."

The day has arrived—June 22, 2017, Jeanine Nadine Harrison was born.

Tension as Basilica Is Repaired

Father Summers and Bishop Biladou called UH to the Basilica for a brunch. They talked about what would be repaired first. It was decided by the building committee and the Bishop, that the furnace would be the replaced to begin with because winter would soon be coming, and the air conditioner needed fixed as well.

The old pipe organ would be dismantled and sent to Berlin. The company was still in business after one hundred and eighteen years. The company will send workers who dismantle the organ and truck it to Berlin where it is completely restored. These two items alone would cost one and a half million euros. The three toured the facility for an hour.

The Harrisons called their child by her middle name. They bought her the most expensive—everything the child needed or that the parents felt that they wanted Nadine to have.

Bishop Biladou and Father Summers baptized Nadine: Biladou said, "Jeanine Nadine Harrison, I baptize you in the name of the Father, the Son, and the Holy Spirit…"

Eduardo and Alphonso attended the reception. They bought gifts, very expensive presents, for the infant: a perpetual mother's love necklace made of gold and diamonds; three personalized pillows and matching blankets; and complete sets of monogramed clothes including onesies.

All in all, it was a great day for Nadine.

UH explained to Father Summers and Bishop Biladou that he preferred to be addressed by his initials. They both agreed it was not a problem and would explain that to the staff at the church. UH would be asked to come to the church for his input as to the repairs, after all it was his money, but there were many times he could not go.

"Time seemed to run past us," said Jeanine. "It's almost Christmas.

The holiday season was in full swing, and Christmas was days away. Nadine had been the perfect baby. No colic, projectile vomiting, nor any other infant difficulties. She was to have her sixth month birthday, and Jeanine reminded everyone many times that month. Nadine looked more like Jeanine, but her hair and eye colors were UH's. Jeanine and UH had been working on the last minute Christmas items, and planning the New Year's Eve event. Eduardo told Jeanine that the guests would number one hundred and sixty. Some of the European, Russia, and Asian Coalition directors were attending this year. He also informed her that he and Alphonso would get the food, band, and security for the event.

The church had installed two new furnaces, two air conditioners, and the stain glass windows had been repaired. The dome was still being repaired, and the pipe organ would be delivered until February. UH refused to have a plague hung in his name, and no other public recognition.

"UH, we are going to the Christmas Eve Mass, aren't we darling?" asked Jeanine.

"Yes of course, this is one of your must-attend-services, my love," said UH.

They attended the mass, and arrived home at 1:30 am. Nadine fell asleep in the limo, and went promptly to sleep in her crib. Jeanine and UH talked for a while, had a drink, and reminisced about their becoming a couple, their marriage, and Nadine.

Jeanine asked UH, "Would you ever consider joining the Catholic Church.?"

"Well, I'm an Anglican, you know, Church of England. We are almost Catholic, so I would consider it," said UH. His response was what Jeanine had wanted for a year.

Jeanine responded, "Thank you so much darling. I just am the luckiest woman in the world."

Tuesday, the 26th, Chu went to UH in his office and closed the door.

Chu began, "UH, I think that we, no, you, are going too far with this church business, with Jeanine, Father Summers, and Bishop Biladou. I must insist that you remain an Anglican." Chu thought for a second.

"What the hell, Anglican or Catholic, there is not much of a difference. All the damn religious members are the same: emotional, psychological, or pathological, or all three. Go ahead and join the Sacred Heart Church, for I know that you are an agnostic, the maybe-or-not, wishy-washy, uncertain man. I found you. I made you unbelievably wealthy and powerful. Don't ever forget that, no matter if you think of becoming a saint or remaining an agnostic. You are a brilliant human—that is why I had chosen you. I have allowed you additional privileges like falling in love, marrying, and producing an offspring, but, enough is enough. It stops today. Do not become cozy in the church, like being a buddy to the clergy, or asking how you could help the seminary, or whatever else they need—always need.

"Do you have anything to say?" added Chu.

UH answered, "Not really, for I have been an intellectual ass, that is before Jeanine."

Chu dropped his eyebrows, "Let's not go there. A love bite from any woman, can change a man."

UH saw Chu's demeanor change, "I understand the frustration. I can't fathom your mysterious behavior I've witnessed these eighteen or so months."

Chu smiled, then said to UH, "I never cared if you comprehended the activities of my coming or going, my ability to end a life, or spare one for a purpose; you're a piece of my plan, not the design itself, for the design is on a grand scale.

"I will explain every detail of this scheme next year, in November of 2018. Let's do away with the stress between us, and once again work as a team," proposed Chu who knew quite well of his ulterior motives. "Tension is only good for high wire walkers.

"I can't say that I've taken too much of your time, because, that is what you have the most of—time," Chu then laughed like he always does: head tilted back, chuckling at his own humor. He walked out of the office.

UH sat, swiveled his chair to face the window, and stared away at a cloudy sky, lost in his thoughts.

Jeanine called to say that the Christmas presents that Nadine received from Eduardo and Alphonso, are displayed on her dresser. "I especially love the perpetual diamond-studded mother's neckless," she said. "Should we insure the gold and diamonds trinkets?" she asked.

"No sweetie," said UH, "I'm leaving here in a few minutes. Did Franco say what was for dinner?"

"Yes, darling, and he calls it Russo All Natural Prime Pork Roast with red potatoes and asparagus. He is surprising us with desert."

"I'll see you in a few minutes, love of my life," said UH.

Chen called UH as he approached the elevators.

"UH, Eduardo and I am excited that we will see you at the New Year's Eve gala."

"I'm glad you are coming. I knew that Chu would be attending because of his tireless care and work in setting up the event, and since we started this tradition, he has attended. Good to hear from you Chen," lied UH.

Father Summers called from the Basilica, "UH, I am returning your call about membership to Sacred Heart."

"Yes, Father, thank you. I was wondering if as an Anglican, I could transfer my membership?" asked UH.

"Actually, yes. I will conduct an orientation for you, after which we can convey to the Anglican Church of your new membership with us for their records," explained Summers.

"I am grateful that you will do this for me," said UH. "I know that Jeanine will be happy. I hope to see you and Bishop Biladou at our New Year's Eve gale."

The priest said, "Yes, we plan to be there."

New Year's Eve: many friends of the Harrisons attended; the four regions of Asia came—Adam Almon from Middle East, Yen Zhang from China, Arnav Kapoor from India, and Aiman Megat from Malaysia; from the European region—Franklin Pierce; and from Russia Vladimir Nikolin. Rowe had planned to attend, then cancelled. He called three days after that, to say that he would be attending. At the last minute, Alim Jabir, the North African Director, said he would be attending, as did most of the other directors from the Coalition. This year, Ginger Adams flew in from London, a billionaire friend of UH.

Ginger said, "UH, I was not going to miss this party this year. I believe that 2018 will be a great year for us all." He knew what she was implying.

Many guests returned from last year like Jimmy Landerwood, the investment broker, and new guests like Dr. Baldwin from the Cleveland Clinic, and Dr. Dubois, Jeanine's gynecologist. From the Coalition office, Elsa, Jamison, Iverson, and Everson.

The new twenty-six member orchestra played, some of the orchestra members sang, and led the guests in singing, until one pm.

Jeanine was happy that Nadine's live-in nanny, Louisa French, who she had found at the Sacred Heart She had hired her some time ago, and she enjoyed the party. Jeanine was able to freely walk around and talk with the guests. She had purchased a special brandy for UH, a bottle of Remy Martin Louis XIII for only $2,500.00. UH watched her walk about in her new gown, and thought that she looked like an angel.

On New Year's Day, everyone slept later, except Nadine, Miss French, and Jeanine. Nadine had her own schedule, but it was not as demanding, for now she sleeps through night, and as a six month old, was playful. Jeanine made a quick brunch for everyone, and played with Nadine. UH finally got up; the three of them played with Nadine, until French left for the day.

"She is beautiful like you my sweet," said UH.

Chu, and then Chen called to wish UH a Happy New Year.

UH said to Jeanine, "Let's go to Rio de Janeiro for ten days."

"Should we take the baby there?" asked Jeanine.

"Yes. We fly in our own jet, ride in our own limousine, and will stay at the Windsor Miramar Hotel, in a deluxe room with Nadine," said UH.

"If we go out, we will go in our limo. We are taking Nadine's nanny, Miss French, so everything is covered. What do you say?"

"Yes darling," said Jeanine, "this sounds wonderful. It has been eight months since we did any vacationing. Besides, I like going away from any winter weather.

"Good. I'll call Eduardo, so that I am not forgetting something," said UH.

"This is Eduardo. I appreciate the call UH. Your little vacation to Rio sounds good. Why not go to South Africa, after Rio, for several days and meet with Director Samuel Livingston, who wanted a visit from the Coalition President. That way you would be back on the 25th. That week we can prepare for the Annual World Zone Coalition Directors Meeting. This year all Superintendents are permitted to bring with them a notable administrator, that is one who had proven himself wise and innovative."

"That sounds good," said UH. "I'll see you when we return."

Eduardo said, "Have a good time. Bye."

As they arrived at the Windsor Miramar Hotel in the limo, three men who had planned to assassinate UH for over a year watched him. They claimed that the slaughter of South American leaders and their families had been the work of UH, and that he had been behind other killings. Chu knew about this plot, and waited until the last minute to tell the security team where the assassins were hiding and the weapons they would be using. The security team had positioned themselves, and when the assassins were about to shoot at UH, security marksmen took them out. Anthony, Jeanine, UH, and his personal body guards heard the shots fired. UH ducked back into the limo. In moments, Anthony said that all was clear for them to enter the hotel.

The three were part of a larger group of families related to the slain leaders in South America. Within weeks, the murderers had been found, tried, and executed, and so were the other conspirators.

The Bishop called from the diocese of Brussels. "UH, this Bishop Biladou. I was wondering if we could meet next week."

"If I were in Brussels, yes of course, but I'm on vacation in Rio de Janeiro, but when I return, I'll give you a call," said UH. "Is there something urgent that we must address?"

"No. I simply wanted you to know that your private classes with me concerning membership had gone quite well. I have contacted the Anglican Church in London, but they did not have any record of your membership. Is there another Anglican Church that I can contact?"

"My parents were both Anglican. Let me do some checking. I'll get back with you soon," said UH.

Chu called UH, "UH, let me save you some time. You were baptized in the Anglican Church in Johannesburg, South Africa. You were a young man attending Oxford, when they moved to London, and they transferred their membership shortly after moving to the UK. Your membership, however, had not been moved from Johannesburg."

"Again you are right on top these things," UH said with appreciation in his voice.

"You sound grateful, and that is an improvement," answered Chu.

UH said, "I sure didn't want any tension with the church."

"Not yet," Chu quipped.

"What do you mean by that?" questioned UH.

"Nothing, other than you don't need any more pressure in your life," lied Chu. "I'll see you on the 25th. Bye."

The Harrisons had a pleasant vacation in Rio. They did some sightseeing, ate at fine dining restaurants, and visited the Museum of Modern Art. Later that month, Jeanine wrote an article for a new art magazine, "Truth About Art".

While in South Africa, visiting with Kingston, UH made a new friend of him. He was pleasant, and a scholar. His expertise was in Ocean Acidifications and he was fascinating and interesting. They talked for hours about international law, and marine ecosystems. Jeanine had waited in another room with Mrs. Kingston drinking tea and conversing about motherhood. They visited the Absa Money Museum, the Adler Museum of Medicine, and the Apartheid Museum. After the state visit, Kingstons and the Harrisons kept in touch.

"I look forward to our Coalition meeting in February," said Kingston, "and this time, I'll bring my wife, if that is all right."

"Of course, and do come a couple of days earlier so that the four of us can have some private time. We will show you around Brussels," said UH, and Jeanine smiled in agreement.

The Harrisons returned home on the 25th; Chu told UH not to come in until Monday the 29th, that he had the agenda for the Coalition meeting in outline form; and that Chen has helped immensely. There will be some unexpected changes this year.

UH was not sure that he was glad to be home, for in their conversation about unexpected changes, Chu left a feeling of uncertainty for 2018.

Chu, Chen, Jamison, and UH firmed up the World Zone Coalition Annual Meeting Agenda:

Greeting

Introductions

Mentioning of the all who had attended the New Year's Even event.

Honoring of Fallen Administrators

New Safeguards for Regional Directors, like bullet proof neck brace, and upper leg cover: no cost to directors

Discussion of possible law proposals

Next meeting: November 2, 2018 (likely new month for future meetings)

Adjournment

This year all participants had been notified that after the WZC annual meeting, they are invited to a formal gathering with entertainment in the Europa Ballroom in building two. They had been instructed to attend the two day event, rather than the one day meeting, and anyone attending could bring their spouse, or significant other.

At the meeting Rowe asked if the Coalition was picking up the tab for November's meeting. UH told him that he already had been told that any required meetings were paid for by the Coalition.

UH explained again to superintendents and administrators that their positions were permanent as long as they abided by the Coalition's rules and WZC Martial Law directives. There had some tension surrounding the continuation of WZC Martial Laws. Pierce had been the most vocal, but after UH had addressed the issue, especially about loner activity, it remained the same.

The Europa Ballroom was alive with music from the eighties and nineties; servers were hurriedly moving around tables; and the entertainment: three comedy routines from Europe.

Rowe was thinking of retiring at the end of the year, and said to UH that Reed would be a good choice as the North America Director. He then said that he would probably would not retire, but Chu had disagreed with the Reed suggestion. The event lasted until 2:00 am, because of lingering conversations among the directors and UH.

There was anxiety bordering on angst in the office on Monday. Chu went in to see UH who was sitting at his computer. Chu said, "What hell is going on in this office, I could sense it when I came in?"

"I know nothing of what you are asking about," snapped UH.

"Well, well, notice that tone. It has affected you as much as anyone else," retorted Chu.

UH said to Chu, "We had seven directors skype today and complained that they wish to resign because of Martial Law."

I know that. Following their tirade on skype, I called each of them. All changed their minds, following my explanation that there is no future in such a drastic move. Now, what else is bothering you?" asked Chu.

"Nothing really, I have been slacking off with my exercise and training programs," UH said.

Chu questioned again, "No, there is something more. Is it your membership transfer? I had already handled that. The priest should be calling today. My god the Basilica is completed, and everyone is happy."

"No. I knew that you had taken care of the membership problem." UH went on, "It's a woman who said that three months ago I had an affair with her. She has threatened to call Jeanine. Jamison tried to tell her to quit calling, and so had Elsa."

Chu said, "I remember this gorgeous woman. You were depressed—too little sex at the time. She approached you at the bar in the Petit Restaurant. You had a couple of drinks together, after which she kissed you. That was the only *sex* she could be talking about. She knows that you are wealthy, and part of that wealth is owning the Europa Complex. You poor silly, sensitive, man. I'll handle that situation, now," Chu said in a mockingly way.

UH offered, "I just worried that she would call Jeanine."

"What is really wrong in the office? Chu asked. "I can't get into your skull."

"I don't know what to tell you," complained UH.

"Damn you UH. You will tell me." Chu began to change from Eduardo, but stopped himself. "I must know. An entire office is upset. Your moping around had upset them. I saw you, the demeanor, the short replies worse than Jamison, and the way you seemed down when you talked with Jeanine."

UH said, "I have been thinking that I am not the man you thought I was."

Chu leaned toward UH, and in a quiet, forceful voice, almost venomous, "What the fuck are you talking about? I get it, you got too close to Father Summers, Bishop Biladou, members of that church, and Jeanine. You are a prick, a self-centered human, but you are tied to me tighter than a hang-man's-noose. You damn fool, you made a solemn covenant with me. You had better snap out of this fucking thinking, because you and I are closer than identical twin brothers.

"I have a blueprint for 2018, and no human is going to prevent this design, and my dear Friend—neither are you. Now, shape up, screw on you head a little tighter, whatever it takes, it better happen this second." Chu's eyes were filled with red fluid. "Have a good day. Perk up, things are getting better my human assistant.

"I am calling Miss Suzy Q when I leave here. You will never hear from her again. Watch those times of selfish depression. Got it. Bye.

UH sat almost motionless staring at his screen.

"Hello, Alice, this is a friend of UH, and he wished to meet with you."

She agreed to meet, but was not ready for Chu's eyes of red and threatening tone of warning if she did not leave UH alone. She left town with a man who promised her love and lavish living.

Jeanine called, "UH someone called this morning, but hung when I answered."

UH assured her, "Don't worry sweetie, this happened at work today. It will never happen again. I'll be home for lunch. I love you so much."

"I love you darling," said Jeanine. "So does Nadine."

UH said, "Give her a kiss for me."

Jamison entered, "Excuse me sir."

"Yes, what is it?"

Jamison said, "Chu said that he needed you at the Petit Bar. I told him that you were on your mobile." Jamison left, closing the door.

UH called Jeanine, "Jeanine, tell Franco that I will be a little late. Maybe fifteen minutes."

UH entered the Petit Bar and found Eduardo sitting at a table in the corner.

UH sat down. "What is it Chu?"

"I hope that my conversation with you this morning made sense. You still seem a bit down," said Chu.

"I'll get my head around it. I feel like a pawn," answered UH.

Chu sharply said, "Oh, you will never be a pawn, because you are human. You were raised an only child by a doting mother and a stern father who insisted on providing an exceptional education and developing a man who finds himself attracted to only intelligent, or superior men and women who helped feed and nurture your self-centeredness, over-confidence, and futuristic goals of power. I required a man like you; someone who had no shackles of parents, siblings, or spouse," but after mentioning Jeanine, Chu quickly added, "I adjust well to change within reason. In 2018, I must ask you to stay focused. There will be a requiem for the world beginning in November. This lament will cause the human race to look inward. I'll explain what all of this means in November. No one knows any of this, except you and me—not Chen nor Jamison, but Chen does now, he is sitting next to you, Chen appeared. Everyone does as I command.

"I believe a little vacation is in your near future. I believe that Honolulu, Hawaii is most excellent in February. Following that pleasant stay, you can go to Barcelona for two weeks in March. When you return in mid-March, the yacht can be prepared for the Mediterranean. What do you think?" asked Chu. UH was a tad slow in answering. "Listen to me, damn it. Straighten up, smile, and be quick about it."

UH smiled, "Ok, I'll be fine. Thank you for the pep talk." He began to get up.

"Sit down you ungrateful fuck." Chu added, "Don't move until you are sure we are in agreement. I know that it takes you about an hour to work out thoughts in your mind that seems disparaging or upsetting. Well, it's been one hour and fifteen minutes since we talked in the office. Times up. Get with it, or we will have another difficult talk."

"All right, I'm fine. I'll stay in the correct mindset. I'll see you when I return in March—or sooner if you feel it is necessary," said UH. He stood, "By the way, thank you for the peptalk."

Chu looked at him, "You are welcome smart ass."

This damn pressure, I need a long vacation, UH thought to himself as he left the restaurant.

As he reached the elevators in the center building, Father Summers called, "UH, you are now a member of the Sacred Heart Church. We are so fortunate to have you as a member. A member who is actually responsible for all the repairs and the refurbishing of the Basilica."

UH said, "You are most welcome Father, and thank you for settling the issue concerning my membership. See you soon, goodbye."

Another call, but it was Jeanine, "Are you almost home darling?"

"I am at the elevator. I have very good news for your winter blues. We are all going to Honolulu."

Jeanine replied, "That is terrific. Oh my god, Nadine will love this trip, and you, my perfect darling, need to release some of the stress I detected in you lately."

Vacation but No Escape

"Honolulu is delightful, enchanting, and warm," smiled Jeanine. UH, Miss French, and several bodyguards were with her on the beach. Anthony was no more than twenty feet from UH when he heard some shouting people behind him. He turned and reached for his gun, when he noticed everyone was smiling.

"UH our hero. UH our hero," they repeated running by Anthony who had tried to stop them. Five security guards circled UH and his family.

One person said, "President Harrison, we are grateful for your leadership and what you have done to bring about peace."

Another person said, "I had never imagined that I would live long enough to see real peace."

Many were there for autographs. Jeanine took a pad of paper from the diaper bag, and ripped off the top sheets, then handed it to UH. He wrote on each page, *Best wishes, UH* with the date, then handed out each of them until there were no more sheets of paper.

"I didn't get an autograph," several complained.

Anthony said, "Perhaps you can look for us on the beach again, and we will be ready with paper."

"I have a piece of paper... Take my hat and use it... write on my hand... UH signed many items that afternoon.

UH thanked them, about one-hundred in all.

"See darling you are appreciated for what you have accomplished," said Jeanine. "Of all the hotels, I like the Hawaii Prince: the beach, the food, the accommodations. How long will we be in Hawaii?" she asked

UH answered, "Until March 3rd."

"Wow, that is wonderful sweetheart," said Jeanine. She touched the cheek of Nadine, "You do too, don't you honey doll?"

They packed up, walked to the hotel, changed, and went to an early dinner. While there, UH had to use the men's room.

A man came up to him as he left the men's room, and extended his hand to shake hands with UH. As he did this, he said that because of his peace initiative, and Rowe was a better director that he had been as president. "I always knew that there would be a cost for peace, and WZC Martial Law is that cost," he said.

It seemed as though people were beginning to realize UH's worth, leadership, and reasons and conditions for world order.

As the Harrison's dined and Miss French was with Nadine, a reporter from the Honolulu Star newspaper, came over to their table, after Anthony had permission from UH.

"UH, I'm happy to meet you. I understand that you are staying at this hotel."

"Who told you that?" asked UH.

"Some people that had received an autograph from you, had followed you here," he answered.

"Can we meet later in the bar?" asked UH.

"Yes, just tell me the time," the eager reporter said.

UH and Jeanine finished dinner, talked about the beauty of Hawaii over a drink, and about the sudden recognition in the media for reporters from the Washington Post, Boston Globe, Le Soir in Belgium, and the HLN station there. UH received calls from around the world: Fox News, CNN, and on and on. He would have to choose which of the journalists to accept for an interview. He would have to call Chu later.

Chu called UH. "UH, what a difference a day makes. I believe that New York would be the best approach. Belgium, your home base, would be next. We can decide after those two initial interviews. I am coming to you as Eduardo of course. I'll be there tomorrow. I am staying in the same hotel, three doors from yours. See you in the morning. Bye." Chu smiled, because he was already at the hotel.

UH explained to Jeanine that Eduardo was flying into Honolulu to meet with him because the explosive celebrity, and he wanted to discuss a strategy to professionally handle the situation. Eduardo hired the following: Chief of Staff, Deputy Chief of Staff, Press Secretary, and Senior Advisor. This was not to be a top heavy administration, if fact, like Chu told UH, "This is merely a subterfuge to satisfy the public. With this staff, and each of our WZC staffs, we will be at one hundred and thirty-three people in the Europa Building Business Complex.

Chu said to UH, "I will get right on this situation, and in less than a week, it will be done. I will select individuals from around the globe to fill these positions."

UH went back to his room, and talked with Jeanine about continuing their vacation in Honolulu. Chu went back to Brussels to get the offices ready, and to call a few former world leaders in order to fill all vacancies in the personal staff of UH. All of them would be vetted by Chu.

A reporter from the New York Times called UH as he and his family got off of the elevator.

"Hello, UH, this is Stanley Daniels from the New York Times. I would like to do a short interview with you in a few minutes, if that would work."

UH responded, "Give me a half hour, and I'll meet you at the table in the back of the bar."

UH explained that he would be in the restaurant, but for about fifteen minutes, he would be giving an interview to a reporter from the New York Times. He would sit with Jeanine, Miss French, an Nadine, but when the reporter came in, he would excuse himself, and they could wait at their table.

Chu had given him a list of answers to basic questions.

Daniels began by thanking UH for the exclusive interview.

"Mr. Daniels, I will begin to give interviews in Brussels, and my new press secretary will provide daily reports shortly thereafter," said UH.

"What drove your passion for world peace?" asked Daniels.

UH said, "This passion, as you call it, began after I had finished my PhD. at Cambridge. Later, when I was fortunate enough to work for the former EU, the desire grew. Within several years I was elected President of both the EU and the EC. As president I was able to work closely with the former United Nations. These organizations also sought world peace, so I had been right at the correct place to further my plans for world peace."

Daniels asked, "Why were you selected to be the World Zone Coalition President?"

UH responded, "My ideas and my work are securing peace in the Middle East, caught the eyes of world leaders."

Daniels said, "I realize that I only have fifteen minutes, and I will shorten my questions. Why did you select Brussels as the seat of global government?"

"It was a logical decision. I was there working at the EU," said UH.

Daniels looked at his watch. "You have had seven attempts on your life. Why? UH glanced toward Jeanine. "There are individuals who are born and bred in families that hate, and/or who have been taught bigotry as a way of life."

"How is your family holding up with all these changes?" asked Daniels.

UH stood up. "My wife is very supportive, loving, and has her hands full with our baby Nadine. Thank you Mr. Daniels, but I must get back to my family for lunch."

Jeanine said to UH after he sat down, "There is no evading the press."

"No sweetheart, and the Soir Newspaper in Brussels wants an interview," UH continued,

Eduardo said that he wanted the New York Times and the Soir to be the first two interviews. Noah Lieven, from the Soir, said that he would like to skype the interview. So I told him that 2:00 pm today would be fine. I am sorry that this is cutting into our vacation time."

"Darling, I am just happy being in this warm weather and escaping winter in Brussels."

Jeanine said touching Nadine's little cheek, and Miss French agreed with Jeanine.

While UH conducted his skype interview, Jeanine and Miss French took the baby to the pool at the hotel.

"Good afternoon President Harrison. It's good to see you again," said Lieven.

UH replied, "Yes indeed, it has been about eight months. It was at the Petit Restaurant."

"I believe so. Anyway, I don't wish to keep you long. Just some general questions. How many are there on your staff at present?"

UH said, "There are one hundred and thirty three, including my personal staff of six."

"How are they funded, or how is the Coalition funded?" inquired Lieven.

"We set up a World Zone Coalition appropriation tax for the twelve regions. It's a flat tax, and everyone finds that fair. The more prosperous regions pay a little more," UH said.

Lieven pressed him, "How do you keep a lid on the violence that had once been so prevalent?"

UH cleared his throat, "Our superior technology: three hundred more hack-proof satellites that are able to spot a tennis ball from three hundred miles in space; we have just developed stealth drones; and our ability includes our ability to read any one's email or mobile texts. We have a great network of people from twelve Regional Directors to the thirty-six superintendents, to three thousand administrators. We have eyes and ears on the ground to seek out the loners. We, of course, cannot stop crimes of passion or manslaughter caused by some altercation, but we do enjoy global peace—no wars."

"Mr. President, Thank you for your time. I would ask a few more questions, but I realize that you are on vacation. Have an enjoyable afternoon in Honolulu," Lieven concluded, and signed off following UH's goodbye.

Chu called, "Good job on the interviews. Having no hardball questions makes interviews pleasant. That sounded like I was talking about Rowe and his softball questions from the press. These are the type of Q&A meetings that Rowe enjoyed at his first and second run as United States president. These are the kind of interviews that will propel you into the hearts of people. Talk to you later. Enjoy. Bye."

It was never imperative for UH to reply to Chu, for it was Chu's information that mattered.

It was March 1st, and the Harrisons and company, flew to Barcelona, Spain.

"It isn't Honolulu, but the temperatures are usually in the upper fifties in March," said Anthony, as they flew to Spain.

"Wow, sixty-one degrees, and it feels cold compared to where we just came from," said Jeanine leaving the plane.

"Well, we could have gone to South Africa again," said UH.

Anthony drove the Harrisons and Miss French to the hotel as the security team led and followed the UH's armored limousine.

In their hotel room, UH receive a call from Fox News.

"President Harrison, I am in the hotel bar, could I trouble you for one or two questions today?" said Harry Simpson.

"I could come down now if it is only two questions," responded UH.

UH told Jeanine that he'd be back in fifteen minutes, and why he was leaving.

Simpson stood up as UH entered the bar. There were television crews, cameras, and other necessary paraphernalia.

"I told you that I only had fifteen minutes," warned UH.

"Yes, and we only need that much time. Please stand over here with me," Simpson pointed to two chairs arranged in front of a camera. They sat down. "Mr. President, do you have a staff, or are you pretty much running the Coalition yourself?"

UH answered, "I have always relied on the several key people that I considered my staff, but we are expanding that initial staff of personal advisors to..." UH waited for Chu to reveal to him some names. "Chief of Staff David Retsoff, Deputy Chief of Staff Ben Somerville, Senior Advisor Eduardo Casas, Press Secretary Robert Davis, and Military Chief of Staff Angelo Petiti. Keep in mind, some of these people could be replaced, and there could be additions to your staff," said Chu.

"Why do you need a Military Chief of Staff when there are not hostilities?" asked Simpson.

"To oversee our more than three hundred satellites and stealth drone programs, and to monitor all in-coming global cybersecurity," said UH.

"Where will your office complex be?" inquired Simpson.

UH answered, "In the Europa Business Building, which is building one. The staff, their assistants, and general employees will require this size of building.

"How many people will that require?" asked Simpson.

"Three hundred or so, but we are still working on this issue." UH looked at his watch.

"Just one more question Mr. President. What is being done about the individual who acts on his own to kill, or to rain down terror?"

"We are developing a tighter, more effective anti-loner program with our administrators on the ground and increasing our drone program. Acting completely alone is a rare act. Peace is the norm today—there are no wars. Thank you, but I must go." UH got up, smiled at Simpson, and hurriedly left the bar.

UH, Jeanine, Nadine, and Miss French left the Grand Marina GL Hotel and visited the art and design museum Fundacio Joan Muro for Jeanine, and also the Museu Picasso. She had planned to write another article for the *Nova Fine Art* Magazine.

Miss French remained with Nadine, while UH and Jeanine had an early dinner.

"Darling, could we stay another week?" asked Jeanine.

"I'll check with Eduardo right now."

"Hello, this is UH."

Chu said, "Good answer to Jeanine. Of course you can stay another week. Jeanine had mentioned to Miss French, that if the weather was pleasant at the end of the month, she would like the take the *Catherine* back to Nice, and fly from there to Brussels on the 30th of March. I'll call the captain and have him and the entire crew sail to Barcelona. They will be there on Friday the 23rd. Anthony will meet you in Nice with the limo. Ten members of the security force will sail with you.

"See you on the 30th, or before. Bye."

UH explained to Jeanine the itinerary.

"Oh my god baby girl we are going yachting," Jeanine said to Nadine, who simply smiled. Miss French agree with the itinerary as usual, "UH, this will be wonderful," she said in French to Jeanine.

On March 23rd, Anthony took the Harrisons and Miss French to the Barcelona Marina where the captain had docked the *Catherine* earlier in the day. Once all were aboard, including the ten security guards, Anthony took the limousine to the airport and loaded it on UH's newer cargo plane, and flew to Nice. He waited at the home of UH for word from UH or Chu.

"This yacht is more beautiful that you had told me," said Miss French. She had her own cabin next to the Harrisons.

UH asked the captain about the weather, and the Mediterranean.

"For the middle of March, we are lucky. The temperature today is to be sixty-five with relatively calm seas. Mr. President, this mega yacht is fit for heavier seas and rougher weather. At two hundred and two feet, this is considered a ship. Eduardo told me that in April, we will be looking at a four-hundred, and forty-four foot vessel. That is a ship."

"I look forward to that new ship," said UH.

"You should. The crew size will double, you will have a helicopter pad, two swimming pools, luxury beyond imagination, and of course, this will more than double the cost of sailing," the captain said.

"Thank you captain," who had continued talking. "Talk to you later captain," UH said leaving.

Chu called, "Sorry UH, this was to be a surprise in April. The deal is closed, for we now own the *Somerville,* a four-hundred and forty-foot mega yacht. The *Catherine Marie* was sold to Director Franklin Pierce, the self-made billionaire industrialist. I also purchased you a new Augusta Westland AW101 VVIP Helicopter for only twenty million euros. I will give you more details when I see you on the 30th or 31st, you decide. Bye."

"My ever beautiful Jeanine," said UH, "we have purchased a ship which doubles the size of ours, and it will have a state of the art helicopter and helicopter pad, of course. We have doubled the size of the crew. Her name in is the *Somerville* which is a private palace. The *Catherine Marie* was sold to Director Pierce."

Chu called UH, "I will send you a text showing the *Somerville* and the world's number one private helicopter with a new seal emblem and the letters, UH, on both sides. Hope you like them. Bye."

"Darling, why do we need a ship?" asked Jeanine.

UH responded, "Eduardo thought it would be good for sailing on the ocean, and when we dock the ship, it becomes a private meeting vessel for directors to meet with me, and it is a perfect mega yacht for vacationing. Each February and November when we have the bi-annual directors meeting, we can sail to these regional zones to have these meetings. It will provide, at least in a sense, a different venue, for wherever we dock, it will be an exotic, or pleasurable experience to visit each city.

Chu called again, "Beginning in April, you will have weekly briefings with your presidential staff. Your press secretary will be traveling with you from time to time, but on each Monday morning, he will give an update to the press. Now that there is world peace, and you are the ultimate humanist, the reporters will like you and will treat Davis like a comrade. I will set these meetings up. Bye for now."

Chen called, "Jamison told me, in five short sentences, that District Director Megat called and said that the Malaysia Region has a small island of dissidents on the north east side of Sabah. They have been vocal and amassing more followers. They had found a stockpile of guns, rifles, and missile launchers in Sarawak."

"Why has no one found them before?" asked UH.

"For one thing it is a sparsely populated island, but because Military Chief of Staff Petiti, had ordered more stealth drones, we spotted them moving some heavy weapon. Petiti just found out about this situation, and has ordered a unit of drones to attack and destroy all on the island. This should be done before I hang up."

"I appreciate this information, Chen. Keep up the excellent work," said UH.

Jeanine said to UH, "I think that you have worked more on vacation, than ever before. You just can't escape from work, the attention is stimulating to me."

UH responded, "But sweetheart, this presidency, as Eduardo phrased it, is consuming at times. Having a good staff will lighten some of the work load."

Arriving home on the 30th had allowed for some relaxing time before the workweek. Miss French told the Harrisons how much she had liked caring for Nadine, how gracious they were, how wonderful to live at the Europa.

Chu called as Eduardo, on UH's mobile, but he knew Jeanine would pick it up, "Good evening Jeanine. This is Eduardo, is UH about, I need to speak with him."

"Hold on, I'll get him," she said.

"Hello Eduardo. How may I help you?"

"UH, on Monday, I need to talk with you about the rest of this year. Nothing earth shaking. Just a few items which relate to your staff, weekly meetings, and Monday morning press conferences. You will have your first staff meeting on Thursday.

"One other matter, explain to Jeanine that she should now let your mobile go to voice mail because of the complex nature of new callers. See you next week. Bye."

UH asked Jeanine not to answer his mobile now that he is president of the Coalition. She thoroughly understood, and kissed his cheek.

A Wonderful World Thanks to the World Zone Coalition

The first Coalition cruse would be in July with invited directors, superintendents and their spouses for a private cruise with the guest speaker: The Top Rated Director, for he is the most improved and most effective in serving his region—Yen Zhang. This information was published in the April WZ Coalition Newsletter which went out on the 10th of April.

The *Somerville* arrived in Belgium at the Port Oostande on the Voorhaven docks on April 12th, and Chu was able to secure a permanent private dock there. The Harrisons, Miss French, Anthony, and other security flew to the ship on the AW101 helicopter from Brussels on the 15th. The ship entered the North Sea turned right into it and continued north west to the Atlantic Ocean; or at other times, it makes a left into the Strait of Dover proceeding to the North Atlantic. On their first voyage they proceeded south along France and Spain, then along the west side of Africa in the South Atlantic down to South Africa to Sierra Leone, and anchored at the Port of Sherbro Island. They went to the Sierra Leone National Museum. Jeanine concluded after an hour, that she would write an article for her new magazine on the indigenous art, but more specifically on the 1898 Rebellion known as the "Hunt Tax War", and on the Kamajor Mast and other Kamajor military items.

Jeanine and Miss French could not stop talking about the mega yacht.

"This ship is simply grand. Oh my god, UH, how did you find this sailing palace?"

"My sweet excitable wife," said UH. "Eduardo found it for a very good price, as he did the helicopter."

Anthony said, "Man, that is one huge chopper. I would love to learn to fly."

"May I say something to you UH?" Miss French asked.

"Of course," UH said.

"I appreciate my employment. I love Nadine, you, and Jeanine for all that you have done for me. Then, on top of that, you let me travel with you, and make me feel like family."

Jeanine answered first, "You are family."

UH said, "Most certainly, we consider you part of our family."

Chu called, "The press conferences went well on Monday, but I would presume that on 26th you will be in the your staff meetings, and then on Monday the 30th, you will be doing a press conference before David."

"Yes, that is a good plan. I will see you on the 27th, unless you think otherwise," UH offered.

"The 27th will be fine. I hope that you had enjoyed your expensive toys. Did you receive the WZC newsletter I had sent to you?

"Yes, and it looks great," UH said with enthusiasm."

"Good. We'll iron out the details of the voyage with the directors next month. Bye." Chu was gone.

When UH arrived at his office on the 25th, Chu went into see him about the staff meeting that had been scheduled on the 26th.

Chu began, "There is really nothing of importance, after all the world is at rest, enjoying the peace that the WZ Coalition has created. Humans alone could not have accomplished this feat. They are too selfish, self-willed, self-important, like Rowe. That's why he is a good dictator, I mean director. The last time I had shaken his hand, it felt like I was holding a limp, dead fish in my right hand. Enough of him for now.

"Military Chief of Staff, just to run by you, is that Angelo Petiti's idea that the defunct NATO, in some fashion, could be revisited to serve the world as a global force. What do you think?"

UH said, "At first, I thought that this idea was ludicrous, because we are doing fine with local military from former nations. Hearing you say that makes me think that perhaps a global military would be far more conducive to our goals." UH thought to himself, *What the heck did I mean by that?*

Chu said, "You took the words right out of my mouth. Let's meet with the staff tomorrow and make this a focal point."

At the staff meeting all were present. UH welcomed them, apologized for not making the previous three meetings, and set the agenda for the morning meeting.

The discussion was orderly with Angelo leading the discussion. They all favored the plan. It made sense to reorder all military and para military forces into one Nonpartisan Alliance Task Order for world security and order under the direction of the WZ Coalition. New uniforms, advanced weapons, protective gear, with rank designation that all will recognize, and would demand meetings with the ranks of major, colonel, and general; they will meet with me, in the field as well. Innovative equipment and vehicles will all be the best available. Angelo stated that he would need a larger staff of about seven hundred divided among all senior officers; some stationed around the world would have less need of a large staff; but more would be needed working with him; and about fifteen working with Scott Iverson with satellite development and Eric Everson and his staff working closely in cybersecurity. He requested a budget increase. He added, "With superior equipment and weapons, vehicles, sharp uniforms, and authority to take-out enemies of the WZC, will entice our new recruits."

The vote was unanimous. Afterward, Chu said to UH that that was perfect timing. UH asked him what he had meant by that statement, and Chu said that he would soon see.

Jeanine called UH, "How are you darling? How did your staff meeting go?"

UH responded, "I'm fine and the meeting was good."

"When will you be home?" she asked.

"In an hour," answered UH.

"Also darling, the cruise was magnificent, and you plan such great holidays. I did notice how safe it was off the coast of Africa. There were no pirates or terrorists. Thank you for making the world a safer place. See you when you when you get home. I love you darling," Jeanine added.

May 3rd staff meeting had a new member, Alphonso Casus, as Director of Finance.He wanted to raise subsidy payments from the regions by one-quarter of one percent, and said that this would "quite easily relieve the financial burden of equipping for the newly organized NATO of the WZ Coalition." This measure also passed unanimously, and the regional directors also agreed. UH was surprised to have Chen on the staff, for Chu had told him nothing about his addition to the staff, but he said nothing.

Each Monday in May and June was a scheduled press secretary conference, and twice a month, UH gave a televised press conference, unless he was away. The Thursday staff meeting was reduced to every other Thursday because of the absence of global unrest. UH continued to give television and radio interviews, but not that often, except to HLN, Soir, CNN, and Fox News. Sometimes these interviews were in his office, at home, or on the *Somerville*.

He listened to Chu's advice about all social media: use it, for people will follow you. He adhered to the saying that Chu made him put to memory: 'Reinvent yourself regularly, for humans are fickle.' Chu often had private meetings with UH following a staff meeting in the conference room.

July 2nd Chu told UH in his office that the staff wanted a new safeguard: a vice president. This was certainly all right with UH, but he wondered who will fill the position. Chu had a suggestion—Sidney Barnsfield from Canada. A seasoned politician who knew how to say yes to any liberal ideas; any humanistic endeavor or ultimate humanistic organizations; and had been easily persuaded by Chu to take the VP spot. He had been a prime minister, interior minister, and minister of defense. When taken to the staff on the 5th, it was unanimously approved.

Barnsfield said, "This should not be a difficult position because of UH, the staff, the WZ Coalition itself, and the world slumbers beneath the umbrella of peace. It is almost heavenly." The staff was glad to have him aboard the good ship "Alliance" as they all sailed into a brighter tomorrow."

Chu told UH later, that Barnsfield reminded him of Rowe, right down to the handshake.

All of the regional directors, all but one of the superintendents, and twenty-five of the administrators responded to the WZC newsletter, that they would be attending the seminar on the *Somerville,* some with their wives. UH and his staff, Jeanine, Miss French, Anthony, and UH's security team with automatic weapons.

This planned cruise would begin in Amsterdam where everyone would embark for the voyage to Da Nang, Vietnam. The ship would make stops in Alexandria, Egypt, Colombo, Sri Lanka, Singapore, Republic of Singapore, then on to Vietnam.

Rowe said to UH, "I see, we are taking the *back roads* to Vietnam."

UH replied, "Yes, but I like a scenic route from time to time. At least we found ports to make stops in interesting places."

"That's true, and in today's climate of peace, it will be a rather pleasant trip," said Rowe. The *Somerville* sailed into the Mediterranean Sea, through the Suez Canal to the Red Sea, then into the Arabian Sea which bordered the Indian Ocean. They sailed in between Indonesia and Malaysia and headed north toward Vietnam.

They made port in Da Nang, and after a short visit, returned to the ship for the first seminar.

UH welcomed everyone. Introduced once again, the regional directors, and asked them to stand to pledge allegiance to the WZ Coalition flag. He then introduced the speaker, Franklin Pierce who had led the most improved region, and the most effective with no loner attacks.

UH added, "Pierce is not an outspoken, in-your-face, audacious man. He is a measured leader in that what he does is thought out well. Most of you directors have met him. Franklin please come up." There was a respectable applause.

Pierce introduced his remarks about the successful efforts of the Coalition, and that the New subsidy contribution amount had been nothing compared to former nation taxes. He supported the military Nonpartisan

Alliance Task Order, for he thought that this new army called NATO that would tighten our control of each region by using a united military technology and force, against all who would attempt to subvert peace.

Franklin's speech lasted for forty-five minutes. All had cocktails, or wine with hor d'oeuvres prepared by chef Franco Russo, the personal chef of the Harrisons. The *Somerville* was at its capacity, so guests ate on deck as well.

For another dinner, they went into Da Nang and ate at the La Maison 1888 Restaurant. They could not all be seated in the same area, but everyone seemed to understand.

The voyage back, took them around the bottom of Horn of Africa and up the coastlines of Spain and France. They made port in Nice. Many guests wanted to visit Nice. All in all, it was an interesting voyage. Chu and Chen wondered why UH had skipped China with smiles on their faces.

They arrived in Amsterdam on the 29th.

"My, Nadine is certainly a world traveler, and she's a baby," said Jeanine to Miss French, as she was lifting up Nadine to disembark.

UH said to the guests, "I realize that this trip was to be a ten day affair, but it lasted for two weeks. Of course, this was a cost to the Coalition that was certainly happily paid. Have a fine flight home." He received a loud ovation of gratitude.

UH had given two press conference via skype, the Coalition reporter gave updates, sent pictures and videos of the events during the two weeks.

On the 30th UH gave a press conference from his office. This was followed by a Q&A with Robert David.

On August 2nd, UH met with his staff.

"Alphonso remarked that he had thoroughly enjoyed the seminar cruise. All clapped in agreement. He also said that by the 9th, he would have a new budget with the expenditures listed that the staff had requested.

Eduardo said the he had enjoyed the voyage, but believed that everyone had agreed that they could have had one more seminar speaker, or some entertainment. UH agreed, and said that that will certainly happen the next time.

UH commented on the voyage as quiet, peaceful, and refreshing. We couldn't have sailed the "the back roads" as Rowe's tongue-in-cheek statement, but if we had tried this even last year, loners, terrorists, and criminals were too rampant everywhere on this globe. I want to thank my personal advisors, Edwardo, Alphonso, and Alon Jacobson, former prime minister, for assisting me in Israel when I had first addressed these issues around terrorism and war."

Military Chief of Staff, Angelo Petiti, had spoken to the staff by saying that he had personally worked with Scott Everson on the satellite program. "I authorized thirty-seven more satellites to be deployed. I finally had our laser experts come together from around the world to complete the work on several fiber lasers to knock out meteors, missiles, and unwanted satellites. I should mention that all satellites that did not belong to the WZ Coalition were blasted into oblivion. We also have hand held fiber laser weapons.

"As to cybersecurity, Eric Everson has made it possible to get into any computer or mobile phone. This was an overdue development.

"I might add, that all of this had been done within my budget."

"That is fantastic," said Rowe.

UH adjourned the meeting because he had an interview to do.

"Good evening Mr. President, this is James Torline from Fox News. Thank you for your time. I'll get right to the questions. It has been ten straight months of no threat of war, and terrorism is something we used to cover regularly in previous years, and now there is a sense of tranquility throughout the world. I had been a history major in college and my MA was in American history, before turning to journalism. I don't believe there has ever been a time in history without war, or mayhem of some kind. How do you account for this situation as leader, or president of the world?"

UH answered, "To begin with, this all began in Israel where I had Jews and Muslims deciding to find peace. This overlapped into South America, North America, Europe, and Asia. It was the free will of these leaders to accept the peace initiative we had begun in Israel."

"That process sounds so simple, yet it took almost a year and a half to attain. You must have had good advisors. Who were they?" asked Torline.

UH carefully answered, "Eduardo Casus, Alon Jacobson, Solomon Zarif, and Rabbi Peres. Later new advisors helped me. James Rowe, Peter LeFever, and Francis Green, who has since died."

"I must leave at this time," said UH, "but we will do this again. Thank you," he said standing up.

Eagerly Torline said, "No sir, I am grateful for your time."

Chu called UH, "Who was Francis Green?"

"I made him up, just to have one more advisor. Chu, truthfully, you were my only advisor."

Chu laughed, "At least that is an accurate statement."

UH asked Chu if he and Jeanine could take the *Somerville* to England because after the last three weeks, he could use a little rest and recreation. Chu agreed and told him that he and VP Barnsfield would hold all the staff meetings. If something came up that he needed to know, we would contact him.

"Why not take off until the 14th, that way you will be here for the staff meeting on the 16th. You can do your press conferences and interviews on board the ship. I'll call the *Somerville's* new captain, Dudley Bigalow, and have him get the crew ready. Are you taking the nanny?"

"Yes," UH responded.

"Good. I'll see you the 14th. Bye," said Chu.

UH decided to go to Scotland as well, on his trip to London. Jeanine looked radiant on the deck. *No women is as stunningly beautiful,* UH thought.

UH stated, "Jeanine, your timing is impeccable walking in the sunlight, for as I came on deck, you stood there looking at the ocean. You are truly a gorgeous woman. I love you my sweet."

"Nadine is sleeping," began Jeanine, "so I had thought I would come up and look at God's beautiful ocean."

"Indeed, it is beautiful. I have to do an interview with CNN in my office at 3:00, so I'll come back up when I'm finished." UH kissed Jeanine, then held her head for a moment, as his eyes told him how lucky he was to be married to this beautiful woman.

The CNN interview went well until the journalist, Sharon Gleam, asked, "Now that there is no such thing as privacy, what is next?"

"What do you mean what is next?" snapped UH.

"I mean that there is nothing you cannot find out about anyone. Cell phones, internet, drones, and whatever else you have, makes us nervous, paranoid, and insecure," she said.

"This is nonsense," UH cleared his throat, and took a drink. "We never intended to make anyone suspicious or anxious. We are unable to simply rely on informants, reconnaissance, or satellites. It takes every effort and means possible to maintain peace. Besides, some countries, like the former United States had a crude form of surveillance that you complain about now. "

"Your system is perfected like you imply. In light of these intrusions into our lives, when can we expect to have the martial law lifted?" asked Gleam.

UH took a visible deep breath, and said, "The bright light of these intrusions is an all-out tranquility worldwide. Nevertheless, my staff and I will be considering this in our November meeting. Perhaps we could schedule another interview in the middle of that month." UH ended the interview.

The Harrisons made port in London; met with Director Pierce; and Jeanine visited the National Gallery of Art. Their trip ended with a three city tour of Scotland, and they headed home. They arrived on August 14th .

On Thursday the 16th after the staff meeting, Chu met with UH.

Chu harshly started the conversation. "I needed to go over some issues with you that will make a difference in the months leading to the holiday season. I will now begin to tell you in advance of all events that I am involved in. But let's take this a bit farther. I assure you that you shall always be a multi trillionaire. You shall always be the President of the WZ Coalition. Something new: before the holidays, you shall speak, and all will listen as though they are hypnotized. You shall command and all will follow like sheep. Your word will become law, and there will not be a witness or witnesses summoned against you. You will masterfully address any controversy."

UH responded with trepidation causing perspiration on his forehead. He had never heard Chu speak with such measured potency. His eyes focused on UH's eyes like he had once before when they had turned blood red.

UH cautiously asked, "Are you all right Chu?"

"Yes, I'm quite good. I simply desired you to focus on what I had been explaining. This design is still unfolding," answered Chu. "Damn it, you, Chen and Jamison will work together more so than before."

UH thought it best not to ask about Chen and Jamison in relation to the great design.

"What must I do to help Chen and Jamison?" asked UH.

Chu looked into the eyes of UH, and said, "Most of our hints seem to zip over your head. I understand and explained to them that your brilliant head is so thick, you are a human. Hints don't faze you." Chu raised his voice, "Chen and Jamison are to help you in your new role. I see that question on your face. Your new role will begin around the holidays." UH went to say something, but Chu raised his palm toward him. "Don't ask me one more damn question. I'll talk with you next week after the staff meeting." Chu disappeared.

At home that evening, UH wrote a note to Jeanine so that Chu would hear him talk. *Don't say anything out loud. I think our place is bugged. I am worried about Eduardo, for he seemed upset today after the staff meeting. He didn't look like himself.* UH decided against notes, but concluded, *Let's just use small talk.* "I love you.

UH tore up the paper and said, "That was a delicious meal tonight."

"Franco labored over it for hours," said Jeanine.

UH questioned Jeanine, "How was Nadine today?"

"She was her adorable self as usual," smiled Jeanine.

Jeanine asked UH, "Is keeping the peace and serenity of the planet wearing you out darling?"

"Not at all, for I get many times away from the office, and others help with duties and responsibilities. It's just this design ..."

Chu called, "Watch what you say damn it. Change the fucking subject. You don't know the first iota about what you are talking about to Jeanine. That matter is between you and me. Got it." Chu hung up.

Jeanine didn't question the phone call, but instead went to check on Nadine and Miss French.

During the next two weeks, there appeared to be tension between Chu and UH. In Chu's opinion, UH spent too much time going to church with Jeanine, giving too much money to the church, and getting too friendly with Bishop Biladou.

Biladou once said to UH that there had never been a period in church history were peace prevailed—especially in the known world.

On September 3rd, Robert Davis was about to start the press conference, when UH motioned him to come over to where he was standing.

"Davis, there has been a change. I will be giving the press conference this morning," UH said taking out a note card.

UH spoke with decisiveness, directly at them, doing what he had never done before. "I have never appreciated the fact that the press is so prompt to banter, ready with unfair questions, and eager to splice my sentences into their own interpretation. But that was last week and the weeks before. Today we begin a new era. We are looking at a new world of promise. No negativity, no more nonsense, for we have no more wars or chaos. So, what is the point? I must admit that most journalists have been fair with me, yet from this day forward, I will answer only prewritten questions, as well as Press Secretary Davis will do. I will make an exception from time to time, and allow the old rule of open questions.

"My staff has enlarged to seven, with each staff member having three to five assistants.

"The Coalition budget is at thirty-one trillion euros, funded solely by regional subsidies or flat taxes as some refer to them. We are switching over to dollars next week, and dropping all other forms of currency used around the world, so as to have one unified currency.

"The New York Stock Exchange will be the primary exchange, and this will be reflected next week. Countries will no longer have a stock exchange. We are setting up regional ones.

"We will continue to be transparent, and you will receive updates as things change. Our budget is rather small, but we are not dealing with gouging prices, political corruption, or lost revenue from some unforeseen reason.

"Keep in mind that regular updates, both in print and in person will be weekly. Mr. Davis will keep his Monday press conferences, but from time to time, I will lead the press conference.

"Thank you."

UH and Davis exited the quiet press room.

UH, received his expected call from Chu, "UH, that was a fabulous, and enlightening press conference. You took the words right out of my mouth—the note card helped I'm sure.

UH felt his blood pumping through his body with each heartbeat. It was warm and unnerving. He was now sure that Chu had something to do with it. He couldn't talk with Jeanine—Chu would know what he said. He couldn't talk with anyone, for Chu would know.

Poco Por Poco Learning the Truth

On Monday the 20th, Jamison asked UH if he was feeling all right because of the look on his face. Then Chu called UH into his office.

"How can a man of your temperament, your education, your IQ, and your stature, keep you from accepting the truth? Let me explain. You marry Jeanine, I say nothing. You go back to church as though you are forgetting your religion—agnosticism, and I say nothing." UH went to question Chu, but Chu raised his palm to UH. "Wait, I'm not finished. You become friends with a priest and bishop, and transfer membership as if it meant something. You give seven hundred and fifty thousand dollars to the local church like good works will make up for your cynical, agnostic, irreligious character—person that you really are. I know, I know that you have tried to escape our covenant, but let me assure you, death is more realistic than a broken covenant with me."

UH began to feel his warm blood circulating as though it was an organ itself.

Chu went on, "I apologize for the wake-up call. I tried, in various ways, to dissuade you by dropping hints, getting angry, and outright straight talk, but you, Mr. Focused on what his brain is desiring, trying to solve a problem, or the grey matter is caught up in plain old human lust.

"Don't look so sad, or down, once you settle in to the overall design which began on May 15th , 2015, you will be greater than your old self, and really focused. Assimilating into a new position can be challenging, but you'll be fine."

UH said, "I am glad to see you still have faith in me."

Chu slowly responded, "Let's just say that I have confidence in you based on the covenant."

As UH left Chu's office, he passed Jamison in the hall, who said, "You look a little better. I'm glad."

UH thanked Jamison, as he was calling Janine, "Sweetheart, I couldn't take your call earlier, because I had a meeting with Eduardo. How may I help my lovely wife?"

Jeanine answered, "Let's go to the special concert at the basilica tonight. Father Summers gave me two tickets for the balcony. There are two piano duets."

"Of course, we can. Is Miss French able to care for Nadine?" asked UH.

Jeanine responded, "Yes, I had asked her before I had called you. She said that she had nothing planned."

"We'll eat, dress for the concert, and after the concert, stop at the Petit bar for a drink," said UH.

At the bar later, UH asked Jeanine if she would like to fly to Nice, and visit their home. We would leave on the 31st, and return on September 3rd. She agreed. UH then called Eduardo, who agreed with their plan.

"When I had taken piano lessons after six months, I became anxious, my instructor would say to me poco por poco, 'ah little Jeanine, learn a little at a time.' Listening to those piano duets made me miss my piano."

UH quickly responded, "We will buy a piano tomorrow. I never knew. Did I tell you that I had learned the violin?"

"No, you hadn't," said Jeanine, "perhaps one day we could play a duet." She smiled and took his hand, and kissed his cheek.

Miss French stayed with Nadine, while UH and Jeanine flew to Nice. Anthony drove them to the house from the airport with a security vehicle in front and one in the back. This was an unannounced and unplanned weekend, but Anthony warned UH that anything bad is possible.

Jeanine whispered in UH's ear, "I will never forget our times here, especially the first time."

"Nor will I my sweet, for it was then you began to be the light of my life, the breath I need, the heart that keeps my heart alive," said UH. He embraced her, soon he carried her to their bedroom.

This was there last time at the house in Nice.

Thursday the 6th was UH's scheduled staff meeting.

Alphonso the Secretary of Finance reported that the Coalition's bank balance was twelve trillion dollars, and no debt. He mentioned the Coalition's WZC Bank was only accepting dollars from regions. Soon after all banks and financial institutions traded in dollars.

VP Barnsfield remarked that he was excited to be on the president's staff, and that he hoped to play more of an active role in coming weeks. (Chu thought otherwise, at least until the staff needed a yes vote.)

David Retsoff, Chief of Staff thanked the president for making his life easy.

Deputy Chief of Staff, Ben Somerville, concurred.

"Everyone except the Senior Advisor had some comment to make," informed UH.

Eduardo smirked, "Well, when the president is doing such a good job, it is in great part due to me."

UH retorted, "That my friends is the crux of my life."

No one accept for Alphonso, who kept his eyes on the papers in front of him as thought he was alone.

In the office of UH, Chu said behind the closed door, "That was poetic, 'light of my life, blah, blah, blah, keeps my heart alive.' You have become a dichotomy. A cynic and a lover.

"Anyway, that was a good short staff meeting. The Coalition is moving in the right direction.

"We took over three very productive gold mines that bring in almost seventy-four trillion dollars annually. We will pay out seven trillion dollars each year for expenses: workers, managers, equipment. Not bad—no worries about Coalition finances. Alphonso was the brains behind this deal. That means that you get a handsome pay raise of one trillion, and the beauty of that is that you don't need a raise. Talk to you later. Bye."

September press conference became mundane, and the Thursday staff meetings, practically became social get-togethers. On the 27th, they did discuss the assassination of three administrators. They were all form Asia. UH said that fortunately, all six perpetrators had been captured, tried, and executed.

Chu met with UH briefly after the staff meeting. Chu said, "We sold the house in Nice, and bought a villa on the Mediterranean five miles from the Port of Nice. I have made arrangements with the port to dock the *Somerville* when you need it. Back to the house, it is thirty-five thousand square feet. You will see it next week. You will fly there to the Nice Airport, but the trip to your new home takes fifteen minutes by way of your helicopter, There is a generous room for you, Jeanine, and Nadine. Next to your living area is a suite for Louisa French, and Nadine when necessary. You have five thousand square feet in your living quarters, and there are rooms in the villa for Chef Franco Russo, Anthony, and the security force.

The security will leave twelve men there, permanently.

"We had to do something with your money," Chu sneered. Next month, after our staff meeting on the 25th, I will have a design meeting with you. Do you understand what I am referring to?" He grinned waiting for UH to respond.

"Yes I do," answered UH.

Chu went on, "You will vacation from October 1st until 20th. From Amsterdam, you sail to Nice. The Port of Nice will dry dock the Somerville for repairs and upgrades. The security force is on the Somerville, at the villa, and at the Port of Nice. I have added fifty more men for our security team. Chef Russo will sail with you, and will remain at the villa with you.

"Have a good time," said Chu. "I'll call you sometime next week." Chu got up and walked out.

"This ship glides through the water. I love it UH," said Jeanine. "So does Nadine. The head butler, Andre Le Shoot, went along this time. He announced that lunch had been served on deck as requested.

UH thought again about how stunning Jeanine was no matter what she was doing. It was a pleasant voyage, and UH thanked Captain Bigalow and crew for their proficient service. They arrived in the Port of Nice on October 20th where Anthony would drive to the house as the rest of the party flew in the helicopter.

Jeanine said to UH and Miss French that the weather was so mild for October. They agreed. Her hair glowed in the sun.

Chu went into the office of Chen, and Jamison was there.

"I'm glad that you are in here," said Chu to Jamison. He went on, "Shit is about to hit the fan. On November 12th a new unavoidable tragedy will happen in Brussels. Be prepared, you know what your duties will be, but after the 12th we will need to be a team with UH."

Chen said, "I am sure you heard Jeanine say to UH when they boarded the plane back to Brussels, that she felt something ominous."

"Yes, but they were interrupted, and UH never had to respond to her concern," said Chu.

UH called Chu, "Eduardo, we are flying back to Brussels. Just thought I'd let you know."

"Thank you UH, I'll see you later this evening. Bye," said Chu.

On Monday, Chu went into UH's office.

"I'm sure your holiday was pleasant. I have been going over the agenda for the director's meeting. There are some points to ponder that is worth emphasizing. Here is the agenda with my notes. Look it over, we have until November 1st to make changes." Chu continued, "I have receives RSVPs that all of the directors and supervisors will attend on the 2nd.

"I have notified the staff at the Europa for lodging, meals, and the meeting."

"Thank you Chu. Who is speaking this year?" asked UH.

Chu retorted, "You are."

"Let me look over the agenda, and I'll put something together. I notice here on line three, that we are having a memorial for the three administrators who were killed this year. Actually Chu, this agenda looks good," concluded UH.

During that week, UH noticed that Jeanine had been more affectionate to him and Nadine. He asked her about it, but she just said that she loved their little family. UH didn't forget this exchange.

For the next two weeks, UH busied himself, practicing his violin, writing out an outline of what he would speak about at the directors meeting, and giving two interviews, one to HNL, and one to Fox News.

One night, Jeanine played the piano, and UH played the violin. The played "Love Story" and later, practiced some other pieces for the Christmas party.

Jeanine said, "We sounded wonderful. I wish I had known all along that you played the violin."

"My sweet, you never told me that you played the piano," said UH.

Eduardo was at the door. Andre let him in, and announced his arrival.

They greeted each other, and then Eduardo said, "I see you found your violin." He looked from UH to Jeanine. "He is a classical violinist."

UH said, "Jeanine is a classical pianist."

"My, what a pair. I think that you mentioned this to me last month before you left on you Voyage. You said that you were planning to present a duet at our Holiday Season party. This will be a grand event again," he said with his usual false flare of happiness.

UH offered Eduardo a drink, but he declined. Eduardo said that he was going to dinner with his brother, Alphonso, and Jamison. Then he said, "This is off the subject, but two of your investments brought in two billion dollars. Well, I must go." Andre accompanied him to the elevator.

Jeanine asked, "How did you earn two billion dollars? Didn't he mean Euros?"

UH smiled at her, "We own two small gold mines, plus my investments with Landerwood from LA. And my love, we no longer use Euros, the world only uses dollars. That was a decision that we came to in the spring at our director's meeting."

"How much are we worth now?" asked Jeanine.

"I don't really know, but I think it around one and a half trillion," UH said, and then tried to change the subject. "What is Franco preparing for tonight's dinner?"

"I think it is a pork tender loin." In walked Nadine with Miss French holding her hand.

"Look at our big girl walking," added Jeanine, as she bent down to pick up Nadine.

Miss French explained that she had to visit her mother at the hospital, but she would be back to spend the night in her apartment.

The Harrisons played with Nadine after dinner, practiced the duet, and put Nadine to bed.

UH did a short news conference on Monday morning.

At the staff meeting on November 1st, UH made reminded them of a memo sent two weeks ago.

"I remind you that tomorrow we have a directors meeting and that from now on, you are all part of that meeting."

"Will we have a vote?" asked Retsoff.

"We decided that you would have a vote, when one is brought to the floor. This will include any policy changes in the WZ Coalition. We will now have quarterly director's meetings here in Brussels. My staff will keep our weekly meetings."

"UH, do you mind if I add additional staff to oversee cybersecurity and satellite development?" asked Military Chief of Staff General Angelo Petit.

"You will have to do so. We have added a trillion dollars to your budget to place generals in oversight positions," responded UH. "Let me know tomorrow who you are appointing to these positions and how many staff members each will require."

After the meeting, Chu said to UH, "Do you agree with the agenda?"

"Yes. It will cost about three trillion dollars to make these changes."

Chu said, "I have talked with Chen, and he stated that it would be five trillion, but we have plenty of money. I'm going to have Chen, ask the WZC to cap your salary at five hundred thousand dollars, because you are now worth two trillion, seventy-five thousand dollars. The richest man in the world. Your bonus from the gold mines could reach another trillion dollars annually.

"See you tomorrow." Chu got on an elevator.

That evening UH and Jeanine sat on the couch and held each other without speaking. Nadine was in bed for the night. Miss French was in her room watching television.Jeanine sat up just enough to look into UH's eyes, and then kissed him. Then she snuggled backinto his arms.

UH felt his blood pumping through his body, which meant Chu was up to something.

He asked Jeanine, "Do you feel my heart beat?"

"No."

He said, "I feel like my blood is pulsing through my body, and you don't feel it"

"No darling. Are you all right?" she asked sitting up.

"Yes of course."

Suddenly Chu spoke to UH, "Don't worry about that feeling. It is part of the design I will be talking to you about, in a few days. Change the subject.

UH said to Jeanine, "Let's have a cup of coffee, and a piece of the cheesecake that Franco made this afternoon."

They got up, went to the kitchen, made coffee to go with the cheesecake, and talked about the weekend.

Jeanine said, "Let's take Nadine to the Planckendael Zoo. They open tomorrow at 10:00, and we could leave here at 9:30. What do you think?"

"That sounds great. It's only 9:00, so I will call Anthony now," said UH.

Jeanine said excitedly, "Nadine is almost a year and a half, so she should enjoy it."

"Yes she should," agreed UH.

In spite of the twelve man security team, they enjoyed the day with Nadine, who seemed to like the giraffe the most, so they purchased a one meter tall stuffed giraffe. She liked that it was taller than she was.

They ate lunch at the zoo, and arrived home at 4:00. Franco had dinner ready at 5:00 and had made a giraffe cake with brown and white butter cream frosting for dessert.

Nadine was tired and went to bed early that night. Later, Jeanine and UH went in to watch her sleep.

The directors, UH's staff, and most of the supervisors were already in their offices in the Europa Building number one. The large conference room had been prepared with finger food, and beverages, for morning meeting.

November 2, 2018 UH walked into the Harrison Conference Room, named after the family when it had been finished. He was early, but had wanted to get his thoughts together and arrange his notes so that he could think more clearly and speak with authority. As members entered, UH felt that feeling of blood moving through his body, this time, like in Beijing, he felt invigorated.

The meeting was about to begin, as UH stated, "I noticed that some men have not come in as yet, so we'll give another five minutes to them."

Rowe came up to the podium and told UH that he looked good, and hoped that all was going well in Brussels, especially Jeanine and Nadine.

He added, "I like the sound of the names of mother and daughter—Jeanine and Nadine."

"Thank you Rowe. We here in Brussels are famously good," said UH.

UH said, "Gentlemen and lady, referring to Schmidt, we are delighted to have you in Brussels." everyone looked around to find Karlene Schmidt, sitting up toward the front, on the far left side.

"I welcome all of you, and as your agenda reads, we have much to discuss before and after lunch. I suggest that we begin. We are called to order.

The new secretary, June Freidan, will read the minutes of the last meeting."

When Freidan finished, the Treasurer was given the floor.

Alphonso stated that due to the our expertise in gold mining, the WZC now owned four gold mines. This meant an additional seventy trillion dollars annually, which meant that the subsidy or underwriting or flat taxes and fees of the twelve regions would be reduced by ten percent. WZC had a net income of sixty-three trillion dollars. He then asked the board to officially cap the president's salary at five hundred thousand dollars, tax free, as UH had requested. This passed unanimously.

Alphonso went on, "It should be noted that UH sold building one and three to the WZC last month. The cost to us was three billion."

There was a motion to accept the treasurer's report pending accounting review.

"The next item on the agenda is the memorial service for the three administrators from the China Region killed by loner terrorists. I have asked Father Summers to present the memorial."

Summers entered from a side door. Chu rolled his eyes, and Chen wondered if Chu had known about this. *Of course he did, he's Chu,* thought Chen. After the service Father Summers existed the room.

There was a call for any reports that had not be sent in advance. There were none.

They broke for lunch at the Petit Restaurant party room that had been arranged for this luncheon.

Chu warned UH that after lunch if he could, "be a little unpredictable."

"What do you mean?" asked UH.

"You will see. If we handle things properly, it won't be as offensive. That is two or three of the district region directors are not going to like the increase in surveillance costs."

"We will now reconvene. Military Chief of Staff, General Angelo Petiti has the floor.

Everyone applauded.

"I will get to the heart of the matter. We have been given a trillion dollars to increase our Staffs and one program. Lieutenant General Paul Johnson will oversee Scott Iverson's office. He will be given a staff of seven to assist his oversight directive. Major General Andrew Robart will oversee Eric Everson's office.

"To really use our satellites, and cybersecurity, we need to increase our satellites to three hundred and five to eliminate a dead spot or blind spots in our current system. We will triple our combat drones. The new drones are better than MQ-9 Reaper drone. Nothing will stand in our way with these combat drones, and no one will avoid our surveillance.

"We will triple the number of administrators. The president selected Karlene Schmidt to be the WZC Security Secretary on his staff. Her job will be to make sure that supervisors and the administrators are working effectively. All directors will have a certain amount of leeway to employ a combat drone. Primarily, they each must call Security Secretary Schmidt first.

"We believe that by hiring civilians to help carry out these strikes, it will satisfy the naysayers and journalists.

"When we install the increased satellites, combat drones, and triple the number of administrators, no one on the planet will perpetrate mayhem, as an individual, or group."

"Any questions?"

Rowe raised his hand.

Angelo acknowledged him.

"CNN keeps repeating their mantra: when will the martial law end. And now that we are more sophisticated in that no one can escape the eye of the WZC, how can I answer their questions about martial law?"

Angelo realized who asked the question, and said, "It is evident that these programs are new, and that it will take ninety days to complete the building of new satellites and new combat drones. Therefore, get back to me in February."

Angelo stepped down. UH took the podium.

UH said, "I would like to say something about Secretary Schmidt's role. She is also in charge of the one hundred security offices we employ for my Europa Building residence which is actually number one in the center. Because the Europa Buildings two and three are also owned by the WZC, the security team must protect the entire complex, as well as my limousine and assistant vehicles, my transport mega trucks, the *Somerville,* and the planes at the airport, she will have a staff of one hundred and thirty-three. This could change . Her new title is Security Chief, and she answers to me and Lt. General Frome Neidert."

Sherman Russel asked, "The treasurer stated that we have more than sixty trillion dollars in our account; our budgets for WZC regions have been cut by ten percent; and our income for the Coalition is increasing annually, will we see a reduction for the subsidy tax from the regions be reduced?"

UH responded, "That is a good question. Yes, we hope to cut your tax next year by another ten percent."

Rowe inquired, "Le Fever and I had been talking about these cuts, does that mean we will be expected to pick up some of the costs for use of drones or satellites?"

UH frankly said to Rowe, "We are not running the WZC like you ran the United States; giving a handout, while taking more taxes; or reducing taxes, and gutting programs. Your congress raised its wages twice, without giving a three percent increase to veterans and social security recipients. Don't imply to lecture the WZC on how to use our funds. We have a surplus of sixty-four trillion dollars, while you had a deficit of twenty-three trillion dollars in your last stint as president. Next question."

Chu and Chen smiled.

UH added, "I hope all of the directors noticed that we increased telecommunications by allowing you to provide better and expanded service for computers, television, cell phones, and land lines—at no additional expense." He looked at Rowe and said, " Rowe there were no fees or hidden taxes."

Rowe was feeling a bit beat up when Director Carlos Rodriquez from Mexico said,

"These are different times, and I hope that we have all learned from our mistakes or difficulties."

Vice President Sidney Barnsfield remarked, "One thing we cannot deny is that there is world peace. At a minor cost to some freedom—yes. Had it been worth that small invasion of privacy—yes. Are we more safe today—yes. Thank you Mr. President for your leadership."

UH gave him a slight nod, as most others applauded.

"I noticed how the press and journalists have been scrambling around, digging here and there for a negative story," stated Director Franklin Pierce of the Europe Region.

Vladimir Nikolin hadn't ever said much, unless asked, but today he had to remark,"Every one of us directors know that we have been better off under the WZC, than running a country. We make more money; we have more security, we don't worry about terrorism, and as a director, we have more latitude and authority than we did as a president or prime minister. I give the president, his staff, and the directors the credit they deserve for their continued leadership." Every one applauded the remarks of Nikolin.

Chu and Chen agreed with UH that he had done a great service to the world. Chu reminded UH that without drastic, calculated, and covert actions, none of these directors would be in place.

You wouldn't have all that you have. We, and Jamison, are a team, part of the design for what is to come. UH listened carefully, as he remembered being in Brussels as president, to director and installing peace, first in Israel, and then the world. As he was thinking about his wealth, Chu asked, "Is everything all right my contemplator?"

"Yes, of course. Much has happened in two and half years to arrive here, self-sufficient, independently wealthy, and president of the WZC.

Wow Chu, I am so happy to have you as a friend and advisor. Oh, and thank you Chen for your assistance, and for watching out for me."

"UH, have a nice weekend," said Chen, as Chu nodded in agreement. When UH arrived at home, Jeanine was playing with Nadine, as Miss French was receiving cooking tips from Franco. UH played with Nadine.

Jeanine said, "What a wonderful life we have darling. Should we fly somewhere, go out to eat?" She quickly added, "Of course Franco would be upset with that last idea."

UH agreed.

He said, "I am having a tad bit of difficulty making changes, even if they are little by little," he went on, "but at least I've accepted what matters."

"My sweet man, you have done marvelously. The cynic is gone, you go to church with me, you are friends with Bishop Biladou and Father Summers, and you treat me and Nadine as though we were queen and princess. I just love you my darling."

Suddenly, Nadine was choking on something, UH took her up and did the child Hymlick maneuver and the chunk of cookie shot out onto the floor.

Jeanine took Nadine in her arms and soothed her small cry. "UH, when did you learn that maneuver?" she asked.

He answered, "On a trip back to China when my son was just a lad."

"I am glad you were knowledgeable, and so is our sweet Nadine," Jeanine softly said in Nadine's ear.

Franco and Miss French were standing in the living room when the Harrisons looked up as Franco announced that dinner was served.

When dinner was over, Franco leaned down to Nadine and said, "I have made a lemon cake with buttercream frosting, with lemon-lime ice cream.

"Do you want some little girl?" She said, "Uh huh."

Jeanine said, "Let's go somewhere for a few days, that's warm."

"We can fly to San Diego, it is sixty-five to seventy degrees at this time of the year," offered UH.

"Let's pack," exclaimed Jeanine.

They told Miss French to pack for five days, and then called Eduardo, who wished them well, and said that he would get the planes readied, and call Anthony, and get the security team in the loop.

Chen called, "UH, I just wanted to let you know that I enjoy working with you, and that you have learned as you should the necessary matters required for the design team."

"Thank you Chen, have good weekend," UH said.

Chen added, "I forgot, have a great five days with your family."

"I will. Take care," UH said.

The Harrisons, Miss French, Anthony and the security detail flew together. The armored limousine, and the other armored vehicles, and the security detail were on the cargo plane that went ahead to San Diego, and to check out the Omni San Diego Hotel.

They spent seven days, and came home on the eighth.

On Monday, November 12th, Jeanine called Nadine's pediatrician to tell him that she must have caught something on the trip to San Diego. She got the sniffles, and was coughing on Saturday evening. The doctor said to bring her in on Thursday, unless she was worse, then go to the ER. Jeanine explained that Nadine did not have a fever, and that Thursday would be fine. Jeanine explained this to UH when he arrived home. He seemed a little tired, so she didn't elaborate.

Nadine acted fine at dinner, but after put to bed, she had a bad night. The next morning, she seemed fine. This went on until Thursday morning.

Anthony had the limo ready. Jeanine brought Nadine down to the vehicle and strapped her in the car seat. Jeanine sat across from her.

Anthony drove down town to a four lane main street and had a green light, as he entered the intersection, a mega truck coming from Anthony's right, had lost its brakes. It hit the limo with such force on the driver's side, that it caused the limo to flip over twice, landing on its side, and then the truck hit the limo on the underneath, and even though the bottom was armored, the huge truck caused the gas tanks to explode, and then it pushed the burning limo on its side for almost a half block. No one could get near the limo because of the fire. The trucker got out of his damaged truck and ran toward the limo. There was not a sound except for fire crackling. The security team behind the limo, had almost hit the second trailer of the tandem. The second in command after Anthony, called UH at his office to tell him what had happened.

"I have to go, Jeanine has been in an accident," UH yelled to Jamison, Elsa, Chu, and Chen. He ran like a sprinter to the elevator. A security team waited in the second limo. They drove UH two blocks to the tragedy. Tears sprang from his eyes as he came up to the burning limo. He stood there, feeling helpless, crying out loud, and screaming that this accident was ridiculous. "This damn thing was staged," he bellowed out, running toward the blazing limo.

By the time the fire trucks arrived, there was nothing much to do, for the limo was badly charred. Stored ammunition had exploded and the artillery weapon blew up as well. The gasoline and the ammunition and guns in the trunk had caused a second explosion minutes before UH had come to the deadly scene.

Chu came over to UH. UH screamed at him, "This is the second time in my life. God, this is not right."

Chu held his arm around UH for a time, when the police came over to inform UH what they had suspected happened.

The police lieutenant told UH that the truck had lost its brakes, and with the tandem trailers behind, they seemed to add to the thrust of the tractor. His brake lines had been severed, and the police suspected foul play. The brake lines were dripping fluid. We could see that it looked like it had been cut."

The lieutenant said, "Eighty-five percent of the citizens in Brussels voted to ban mega trucks from entering the city. This trucker is from Paris, but still knew of the ban, yet missed the proper exit, and thought he could cut through the city. He had noticed that his brakes were not right, and that was another reason that he came in the city. His injuries are not life threatening.

We will complete our investigation this week.

"We are truly sorry Mr. President."

That evening as UH cried, mourned, cursed, and walked the floor, He excused Miss French and Franco, so they could go to their apartments. He was not hungry, and Miss French's presence reminded him of Nadine.

When they had left, UH shuffled around the suite, weeping, remembering his sweet Jeanine. His beautiful, no gorgeous twenty-eight year old wife—was gone.

"This isn't right." He kept saying.

He called Chu, "I know that you have the power to find out who cut the gas lines on that truck that killed my family. Someone is behind this multi murder. Damn it Chu."

Chu offered, "Did you want me to come over now, or wait until tomorrow?"

Chu rang the bell, and the butler answered it and led Chu to the living room where UH was drinking from a snifter of brandy, the one Jeanine had purchased for him.

UH offered Chu a drink, but he declined.

"Oh, I had forgotten that you don't drink alcohol."

"No problem," said Chu, knowing that UH was quite fragile at the time.

"Chu, you know who it was that caused this fucking accident," slurred UH.

Chu said, "Yes, I am able to find out if this accident was intentional or not."

That was exactly what UH needed to hear, and with a sigh, he fell back on the couch where he spend the night.

The next morning as he awakened, the horror of what had happened to his family flooded him with grief. Just then Andre appeared at the arch leading to the living room.

"Please sir, let me know if I am able to serve you."

"Yes Andre, lay out my clothes for the day, and explain to Franco that I will have an extremely light breakfast, preferably, something to drink."

"Will your favorite smoothie be what is in order today?" asked Andre.

UH responded, "Yes, but make it thin."

Chu called, "UH, should I come up to walk with to your office?"

"No. Not necessary. I am a little slow this morning. Give me an hour, and I'll be at the office. I must try to work. Could you call the funeral director back and Father Summers?"

"Yes. I will do both," said Chu.

UH thought, *I'm alone again. I'm alone again. I know that my girls loved me as I love them. God dammit I miss them.* Then he said out loud, "I will find the bastard who took them from me."

Andre asked, "Did you call me sir?"

"No Andre I was just saying something to myself," answered UH.

UH stood in the shower thinking of Sun, William, Jeanine, Nadine, and Anthony, and how much he was missing them, especially his sweet Jeanine.

UH drank his pomegranate-marmalade smoothie, put on his sport coat, said goodbye to his service men who remained at the residence, and went to the office. He didn't feel like talking, and workers kept their heads down except for a quick soft sad glance. When he reached his office, Chu was waiting for him.

"I didn't think that you would mind if Jamison sent out a email blast to your staff, directors, and friends," said Chu.

"Not a problem," said UH, fighting back tears.

A week passed and Chu had found the person who cut the lines, and had him eliminated, according to his standards, he disappeared. UH was very appreciative, but missed Jeanine like a knife turning in his stomach, and a hollow feeling so real that he could not find relief; it was like a bottomless pit of grief, as if it was a part of himself—vanished. He thought, *I need to hold her, make love to her, laugh with her, and watch her soft rest as she sleeps.*

After two weeks he could function more like himself, but a nagging thought plagued him: *Did Chu have something to do with Jeanine's death?*

Chu entered UH's office. "May we talk?" he asked.

"Yes, of course. Sit down," UH pointed to a chair in front of his desk.

"How is everything going for you?" inquired Chu.

"In general, fine, but I have a sense of alienation from life, the church, and the world.

That funeral two weeks ago was bitter, as my two sweet girls laid there. As lifeless as I feel. But I must add. The agnosticism is creeping back in to fill the hollowness." He turned quickly to look outside, and to compose himself.

UH looked away from Chu again, and then added, "After what happened to Jeanine and Nadine, the way they needlessly died, I want nothing to do with the damn Basilica, Bishop Biladou, nor Father Summers—not even their god. This world is seething with violence waiting to erupt—that is the human misery." At that, UH felt a sense of warmth as his blood surged making his physique take on its youthful appearance as well.

Chu sat in silence, quietly listening to his regenerated disciple as he ranted. This was worth the patience, and aggravation of the last two years. The design could now go forward.

Chu said, "UH, my friend, we will talk tomorrow.

Chu called Chen into his office, and said, "Chen the disciple has learned, slowly, and unevenly, but learned. As Eduardo would say 'poco por poco', but he did learn just in the nick of time for us to put the design plan together."

Chen grinned and said, "Well done master Chu. We are the perfect snake salesmen." They both grinned.

The Master Chu's Design

Chu waited another week to begin his project of pain. On Monday, December 3, 2018, Chu presented the first phase of the Design Project: Unrest and Oppression.

UH was in his office, when Chu came in to talk.

"UH, I have a few preliminary matters to discuss. I will be frank, my friend. You have been deceived, as most humans, by your pride because you are attached like an umbilical cord to your ego. You have accepted errors as opportunity which opens doors of deceit. You are not who you think you are. I will help you focus as Chen and Jamison assist you in carrying out our missions.

"It will get gruesome and hideous at times, but it will always be necessary. You have a new voice of authority—use it. What you say, will become law.

"Do you have any questions? You seem to be in a trance, but I think you are in a state of transformation—reinventing yourself. Very good."

"No. I was just thinking. What is it that we must do first?" inquired UH.

Chu thought for a moment, "Are you certain that you are finished with the church and its god?"

UH's eyes squinted and narrowed, "Yes," he said emphatically.

"All right then, let's put phase one, 'Unrest and Oppression', into effect. Chen and Jamison will direct all Christian seminaries, Bible schools, Parochial schools, Christian museums, and Christian bookstores of every kind, to close worldwide, and give them this directive as of January 11, 2019 all shall be closed, and the buildings sold to pay off any debt by February 18, 2019.

"This will send will send a signal to every Christian on the globe, that their time is coming to an abrupt conclusion. We have begun to turn the Christian religion upside down.

"The emails with the first directive are being prepared as we speak. I'm sure that by Friday the 7th, the initial responses will come in. The directors, supervisors, administrators, and your staff will also get this directive today."

Chu went to Chen's office and motioned for Jamison to come with him.

"My friends," said Chu, "the anti-Christ has been established, or should I say selected and completed: Urie Lee Harrison."

The next day, a new directive under martial law was send via email.

By January 31, 2018, it is unlawful to practice the Christian religion, and all Christian Churches shall cease from operating any enterprise:

1. Christian Churches are no longer permitted to function as such.
2. Christian Churches are not permitted to hold services in any building such a theaters, schools, civic edifices, homes, or other rented buildings.
3. Christian Church ministers, deacons, priests, sisters of any order, and all other religious are not permitted to function as any leader, to preach, to speak, or offer any so called sacraments. Only judges, mayors, or other approved civil authorities may officiate weddings, funerals, or other so called ceremonies, sacraments or rites.
4. A Christian Church building can be retained for social services, or sold to relieve debt.
5. No proselyting, evangelism, or attempting to convert another, for this is against the law. The very words "Christian" or "Christ" in public shall be an indictment of guilt, and punishable by fine, imprisonment, or death, or all three in some cases.
6. No free nor at a cost Christian literature shall be offered.
7. Mobile phones, cell phones, computers and other technological devises will be monitored for violations.

8. Exceptions Law: All Sanctuary Areas will exempt these laws
9. All medical care continues to be provided by each region for its constituents and Christian areas in their jurisdiction. In Christian areas all medical supplies will be dropped in by air. Hospitals shall be permitted, if a licensed Christian doctor or nurse is present.
10. No tax deductions for religious churches, mosques, synagogues, other such religions, nor any sect or cult organizations.

EXCEPTIONS LAW: **Sanctuary Areas** will be in all twelve Regions

Please note: Leaving these areas will result in death. No one other than a Christian may enter these areas for any reason. If more Christians need to move into Christian areas, and more room is required, then cities and the other area around them shall be designated for that purpose like the city of Damascus. Christians may petition the WZC through the regional administrator, or director for additional medical supplies or needs.

Christians are expected to be self-sufficient. No Christians may send funds to other Christian areas—anywhere.

Sanctuary Christian Areas are created for Christian safety.

A new Christian convert may request to enter a Sanctuary Christian Area if approved by a director.

All executions will be televised.

Sanctuary Areas:

Asia:

Middle East, China, Malaysia, and India Regions

a. Tibetan Plateau
b. Kunoshima Island off coast of Japan

c. Battleship Island off coast of Japan
d. Tree Island (Group of small islands) South China Sea
e. Palmyra Atoll, Pacific Island off Hawaii
f. Dead Sea Area (Thirty square miles around the Dead sea only)
g. Thirty square miles around Damascus, including Damascus itself.

Australia Region:

a. Antipodes Islands
b. The entire Great Sandy Desert and the city of Uluru.

Europe Region:

a. Belarus and occupy any city
b. Central Siberian Plateau

Mexico Region:

a. Clipperton Island
b. Peninsula of California
c. All of El Salvador

North Africa Region:

a. Nigeria and all cities
b. Cameroon including the city Yaoundé, and all cities

North America:

a. The Arctic from the North Pole down to Alert, Nunavut, Canada
b. North Brother Island East River city blocks, New York City
c. Iron Mountain, and five square miles around it.
d. Death Valley National Park area only

Russia Region:

a. West Siberian Plain
b. New Siberian Islands

South Africa Region:

a. All South Africa
b. All of Botswana

South America Region:

a. South Georgia Island
b. Antarctica
c. All of the state of Belize

Contact other Christians; go onto the internet to select your new location, or simply move to one near you. You will have until February 28th to move, because after that date, all remaining Christians will be imprisoned or executed. No exceptions.

By February 18, 2019, I must have a reply.

President UH

UH sent the email.

On the 12th emails were returned with mixed responses. Islamists were ecstatic, Jews had diverse responses, and directors were worried.

Director Rowe complained, "I don't mind curtailing the onslaught of any religion, but our out-right banning its practice is asking for violence, perhaps even unraveling peace."

Director Carlos Rodriquez was provoked, "This is an outrage. Mexico and Central

America is Christian, as is Spain, Italy, and South America. This is insane. A third of the world is Christian. You are attempting to turn a world inside out."

Director Franklin Pierce remarked, "I quite frankly agree with Rodriquez."

Director Vladimir Nikolin, stated, "This is not a big concern to me."

Director Adam Alon feared the worst and said, "Christians today, Jews tomorrow."

Director Yen Zhang indicated that it would relieve minor tension in China.

Director Aiman Megat said, "Malaysia is highly populated with Muslims, so this decision will not be a difficult one for us."

Director Arnav Kapoor commented, "India is a diverse and highly populated country, so to reduce the population in any fashion would help. I still worry about repercussions and more ferocity."

Director Sherman Russel called the WZC office and exclaimed the he had never heard, read, or had been taught of such aggression with such magnitude. He was resigning immediately. Jeremy Leeds was appointed the new Australian Director

Director Alfredo Colombo was livid. "You are attacking one third of the world. I am stunned and perturbed at this incarceration of Christians.

UH replied to all in an email:

I am not terminating nor exterminating Christians. I am placing them in locations were they may live in large communities and states safely and in fact, in large territories were they have the freedom to do as they wish, practice their faith in any manner, and build their bookstores, churches and the alike. Directors: Any director who is a practicing Christian, like Sherman Russel, should resign, because it will not go well with you after February 28th. I wish you the best.

President UH

Sherman Russel was replaced by Jeremy Leeds as Director of Australian Region.

Carlos Rodriguez was replaced by Felix Santos in the Mexico Region.

Samuel Johnson was replaced by Edward Christianson in the South African Region.

Franklin Pierce was replaced by Rubin Shakes in the European Region.

Alfredo Colombo was replaced by Francisco Silva in the South American Region.

UH had these new directives for Christians published in every large and small newspaper; put on every radio stations; and television stations were told that this would help to use their time up for public service. Billboards were purchased in large cities, and mobile phones were bombarded with messages from the WZC. Computers also spread the news about opening sanctuary areas for Christians.

The directors and supervisors were told to use every means possible to alert Christians, and that administrators would monitor the exodus.

Chu said to Jamison and Chen, "The grand design is now moving into place with unrest, but before the February 28th, oppression will be the norm. I think we should invite UH to join us for dinner at the Petit Restaurant. I'll call Chef Russo, and Le Shoot, the butler, and tell them that they have the afternoon and evening off."

UH called Chu, "I had replaced five directors today."

"Yes, Jamison told me. How about going to dinner with us this evening at the Petit? I called the chef and the butler and gave them the afternoon and evening off. Let's relax."

"Sure, why not? It's been a long morning," said UH. "If I remain busy, I don't think of Jeanine."

Jacobs called UH, "My friend, are you all right? I just heard of this new directive to Christians. My, this seems drastic."

"It is harsh," began UH, "but these are not concentration camps, and we have not executed any of them."

"Well, you take care of yourself UH," concluded Jacobs, still concerned.

Earlier his friend from Paris, Peter LeFever called, "I feel dismayed and betrayed by the WZC. Help me understand why I must move to somewhere in Siberia?"

UH said, "Most Christians are passive, half-hearted, non-committal, serving their personal agendas. Perhaps this will change as they are required to be confined with other Christians, but most likely not. I wish you well as you relocate." UH hung up.

The evening went well, as UH, Chu, Chen, and Jamison talked about the upcoming migration of Christians with the military driving them, the logistics of such a massive move, and how lenient they were to offer such areas of protection, seclusion, and unnecessary misfortune once they arrive.

UH had a passing thought about Jeanine and Nadine, and wondered again if Chu had something to do with their deaths, but didn't dwell on the thoughts. He no longer liked sentimentality nor to worry about something that one cannot change.

UH said that the Bishop Biladou and Father Summers called at different times yesterday and listened to their collective distain for UH and the WZC. The bishop said, "This is unconscionable. What in the world are you thinking?" he asked.

UH responded with, "I refuse to answer the question, except to remind you of the deaths of my wife and my child, that God took from me—twice. Good day!" Then he hung up.

Jamison said, "Keep in mind, neither of the priests have had wives.

"No staff members resigned. That seems odd," UH said.

UH said that he had talked personally with each staff person, and all were in compliance.

Chen responded to Jamison's first comment, "When Christians, and the religious, ponder misfortune of that magnitude, they often buckle beneath it. Of course, there are always martyrs."

Chu added something interesting, "There are many wealthy, non-believers who feel compelled to assist these weary pilgrims as they must go to the designated areas. There are actually four hundred of these well-to-do men and women from around the world who are coordinating an airlift and shipping, and they wish to fly cargo, medical supplies, food, luggage, and other staples to these final destinations. They are also flying the Christians to the spots, and or providing ships to take them to islands, or where ever the Christians wish to go. Of course, these helpers of the longsuffering, realize that after February 28, no help is available to these beleaguered people.

"This will expedite the phase one process by one week. Of course there will be die-hards or anger-filled Christians who refuse to leave the mountains, believing that height, or caves will hide them. I needed to end this fine dinner with this good news."

UH said, "I am glad for this development, but I am not sure why."

Chen, Jamison, laughed, as Chu gave his hearty chuckle and sneer.

When UH got to his suite, he received a call from his new limo driver, Aaron St John.

"Mr. President, I am downstairs in my apartment, if you need me."

"That was kind of you to let me know. Welcome aboard, Aaron," UH responded.

Christians throughout the world were perplexed, as to where to go, what to take, but after the socially conscious wealthy decided to assist, it took a great deal of pressure off of them. Unfortunately, some decided to remain to fight, as loners, or in small groups, or simply facing the wrath of the WZC as pacifists.

"Chu, I would like to fly somewhere tomorrow," said UH.

"How about somewhere that you've never been, Soul, South Korea?"

"That sounds good, but I haven't seen the Taj Mahal in India, or much of India for that matter."

Chu answered, "Sure, I'll call the pilot and crew, and of course, Aaron St. John. Aaron had been a decorated officer with the Navy Seals, and will do a great job protecting you. See you in the morning."

UH flew to Kheria Airport, and was taken to Agra, near the Taj Mahal. He stayed at the Hotel Seven Hills Tower. The next day, he was driven to the Taj Mahal and other sites. It seemed strange to travel alone, but he knew that was to be his future.

February 21st, practically all of the two and a third billion Christians had been settled in the their new sanctuary areas around the world. No Christian chose the Arctic nor the Antarctic. Many of the churches were sold below cost, as well as seminaries, Bible schools, Christian museums, and libraries. Many Christian professors, students, church members, and other laity, packed library books and materials, and museum relics, old parchments, and valuable artifacts, and transported them to their new locations thanks to the airlift by the wealthy. The world wasn't free of Christians, but they were no longer visible. A few former WZC directors, superintendents, and many more administrators departed with the Christians.

"In one week, we round up the last visage of Christians," Chu said happily. "We have replaced all defecting staff members, supervisors and administrators with new ones. It is time to call WZC meeting of all employees from regional directors to those who work for administrators. The weekend of March 1st will do nicely. UH, I will set it up in the Europa Building as usual.

"Welcome to phase one."

On February 8th, the WZC met and announced the second half of phase one: oppression.

UH opened the meeting with an announcement, "There have been twelve administrators killed by Christians. The have been caught and executed. These were Christians who had decided to remain to fight. There are five hundred thousand Christians in the world taking up arms. This will not end without extreme bloodshed, uncalled-for deaths, and a tragic loss for Christians. It is primarily up to administrators and their staffs, and volunteers to find them and address each one accordingly. Pacification in any form will not be recognized as a reason to live. Martial law under the WZC may change, but at this point it is in stone."

"How do we know that there are five hundred thousand taking up arms? They have until the 28th? No?" said Nikolin.

"As you know," UH answered, "we have over two hundred state-of-the-art satellites, various types of drones, and informants. This number could change by the 28th. Good question Vladimir."

"We will have two cruises this year; one for the directors and supervisors, but not as exotic as last year; and one for the administrators. These cruises are to be paid for by the WZC.

"There will not be a memorial service anymore, but we will have a moment of silence for fallen WZC directors and supervisors. We did, and will continue to have our Pledge of Allegiance to the flag of the WZC at the beginning of every bi-annual meeting. Our new flag is flying over every ship, all WZC buildings, and at all director buildings and homes.

"I had received your reports, except for the five directors who had resigned. The Christians have twenty more days, please keep your eyes open, and give your informants credit for what they do, and reward them from time to time, and you will get more information about the renegade Christians.

"It is time for lunch. You will see that the dining room is larger, and that we have more staff for this particularly large group."

Chu said to UH, "I was just informed that the five directors who has resigned will be leading Christians in their chosen respective Christian Sanctuary areas. All five of them were part of the reason the Christians are being airlifted and shipped to these areas, for they knew wealthy do-gooders, but that is nothing to concern ourselves with.

"Muslims in Turkey are stirring, shouting, and complaining about Damascus for Christians. I have informed Nikolin about the matter. He said that troops are already on the way, and will quell the hateful chatter as directed by the WZC. The Damascus International Airport will basically have a skeleton crew after the 28th, but will add personnel as we need them. We do not want Christians to use the airport. He said that he will make it an administrators building, and an office complex for his second director.

"All airports and shipping ports, in Christian areas, will be treated the same, and used only if we should need them. They will be maintained by Christian labor.

"General Petit and Karlene Schmidt will be in control the final days of relocation of Christians, and they will oversee these areas until directors, supervisors, and the expanded number of administrators take over the supervision. Petiti and Schmidt will have senior officers needed will assist our WZC officials.

"We'll talk more about these issues closer to the 28th."

UH said, "It appears that all is going well. I had been sure that three masterminds could work out the details to take care of the Christian population."

"Who are the three masterminds," asked Chu.

"Why, you, Chen, and Jamison."

"You had the number correct, but the names wrong. I am one, Chen is one, and you are the third mastermind. The human anti-Christ must also be an intelligent organizer. Jamison, who speaks in short sentences, and is able to do only what he is told. I remember that you had said one day while entering your office, 'Why did Chu ever hire that idiot?'

"I will meet with you after the meeting," Chu told UH.

UH resumed the meeting.

Nikolin asked to be recognized by the chair. "We have a situation in Damascus. I have killed two hundred protestors that were armed. The rest of them scattered. I explained to the mayor of Damascus that the Christians would be occupying the city, and thirty miles around it. I told him that this area would be a sort of sanctuary or quarantine for Christians around the Dead Sea in Israel. He then said that he couldn't relocate everyone out of that large area. I explained that we could help by transporting all Muslims to Muslim countries, and that we would use cargo planes to move their goods."

UH said, "They do not need to leave Turkey."

Nikolin replies, "Oh, I told them that first."

UH looked at Chu, and then added, "We will keep abreast of this situation. I have received word that this type of issue has occurred already in other regions of the WZC."

General Petiti said, "I have sent a warning to folks in all regions. I told them that there will be no exceptions—the selected areas for Christians had been settled by the WZC. I also stated that if anyone or group interferes with the Christian resettlement, it will not go well for them."

Karlene said, "This transition period is difficult for everyone involved, but what we are doing is good for the world. General Petiti was correct when he said that those who interfere will pay dearly, for we are under time restraints."

UH said, "I and my staff will closely monitor this Christian migration, and we will keep all of you informed regardless of the magnitude of the situation.

"Tomorrow, we will have a night of entertainment. Until then, enjoy your stay in Brussels."

Chu met with UH. They went to the Petit Restaurant, and directly to their private rooms.

They ordered a light meal. Then Chu started the conversation, "We have a tense situation, so beginning on Monday, we begin Phase Two: Oppression. The world is about to see what will be done in the event that anyone attempts to thwart my design. We will begin in Africa, for it has only two hundred million Christians, and this should be an easy migration to Nigeria and Cameroon. South Africa will be more manageable. North Africa is basically Muslim, and South Africa is mostly Christian. I figured that we should get the yelling, shouting, and hating people on the earth—settled first."

"Excellent idea," said UH. "After the Christians are out of the picture, the other religions will continue to fight, bicker, and kill each other. Because man is so self-centered, bigoted, and did you notice that most humans are not questioning us about the so called alien invasion."

Chu responded, "A tiny moon could whirl itself into the earth, and in one generation, most would not concern themselves with the event, and in the next generation, they could not recall where or when it happened.

"As I had said before, we will start in Nigeria and Cameroon. Both directors are not happy. Our reginal district director, Alim Jabir said that his office has had several calls from Nigeria and Cameroon complaining and threatening to 'not move a single Muslim', and will not take in that many Christians. I will talk to Aanuti Tones in Nigeria, and Denzel Allo in Cameroon much like I talked with those leaders in South America last year. I will of course sound like you.

"I will inform you of their decisions," smiled Chu.

"Chu, should I sell the villa in France?" asked UH.

"Not at this time. For one thing, you don't have to sell it. I have to go," said Chu heading for the elevator.

Chu decided to call Aanuti right away, "President Tones, this is UH, and I am calling about your indecision about the new settlement for Christians. I need to address the Christian migration to Nigeria."

"I already told Jabir, that this was not going to happen," shouted Aanuti.

"President Tones, I will make this quite clear. Instead of having until Thursday, February 28th, you now have until the Friday, the 22nd to move all Muslims, and all other religions, out of Nigeria except Christians. Don't interrupt me. Do you hear your heart, it is about to stop, and I will see to it that your family and members of your staff, and their families will die with you as you hit the orange carpet beneath your feet.

"Do you remember what happened in South America last year when all leaders and their families died? I am waiting for a yes," said Chu

Aanuti's heart was racing, perspiration covered his forehead, and he couldn't catch his breath. "All right, all right I will do it." He heart began to beat properly.

"I want you to airlift or truck all who must move. Anyone who remains, will live life under Christian rule. That will not be pleasant. Got it?" Chu asked.

"Yes, by the 22nd," Aanuti said submissively. "Thank you UH."

"I want you to know," said Chu, "that I am calling Allo in Cameroon, with the same demand, because I know that you and he had talked about defying the WZC. He too will leave Cameroon by the 22nd, or I will replace him.

Chu waited until evening to give Aanuti time to talk with Allo.

"Good evening President Allo, I am calling from the World Zone Coalition, and I hoped to convince you to abide by the WZC program for relocating Christians. As I told Aanuti, we would relocate him, his family, and close friends or staff to a new location of his choice, or we would make him an administrator, in a Muslim region. I make this offer to you, but I know that you are a Christian, and this means that you could be an administrator in Cameroon."

Allo responded, "Yes I am a Christian, and yes I'll except the offer to be a WZC administrator."

"Very good, and will you move all other religions out by the 22nd ?" Chu asked.

Allo agreed.

Chu didn't have to do much convincing to Kyuka Jones in the country of South Africa, nor did he with Sidone Kamayou in Batswana, for both were Christians. Africa, as seen from a satellite, was trembling as Christians and other religions migrated, and were transported in and out in all countries. Christians uneasily entered their new homes, and other religions moved to other countries but reluctantly accepted, unless known by, or knew of by a family.

This began to happen all week of the 22nd as the world felt the oppression of quarantining the Christians. On February 28, the demography of the planet had changed.

Chu said, "We have Muslims hiding in Christian areas that could pose a problem. We have five hundred thousand Christians not quarantined. Many of whom have weapons, and about a third belong to a militia. Jamison will send an email to all administrators to be on guard for these terrorists. Chen will email all directors and supervisors to do the same. We are at war again. Welcome to tribulation. It will take a week to identify these groups and individuals. I will talk to you on Monday."

"Thanks Chu for your insight," said UH. "Personally, I don't give a fuck about much."

"That is good," said Chu, "now go enjoy the weekend. Take trip to New York. You haven't been there for a while. I'll call and get everybody readied for the flight tonight."

"I believe that that is a splendid idea," said UH.

UH arrived on New York on Saturday morning, and quite refreshed for he had slept on the plane. He was driven to the Trump Tower in his upgraded armored limousine by new driver Aaron St John.

A person who knew Trump heard that UH was at the Trump Tower, and had just learned that UH was one the world's richest men. He called his concierge and told him to ask UH to come up to his office.

The man said to UH, "I heard that you were interested in purchasing the UN building?"

UH answered, "Yes, I had discussed it with my financial advisor. Why do you ask?"

"I would like to introduce you to a friend of mine who shares your interest in the building," the man remarked. "His name is Ivan Saworski. He had asked me to contact you when he had heard that you were in New York. Here is his card, you can contact him today, if you would like to do that."

"Sure," said UH, "I appreciate your part in this matter. By the way, congratulations on your win in Vegas.

The man said, "Thank you. I spent two years honing my black jack skills," then stood up and led UH to the door.

Chu called UH, "Call Saworski now, he is headed for this office. Remind him that WZC technically owns the building, but we would sell part of it that would put him in a position of remodeling with no expense to us."

UH called Saworski, and set up a meeting for Monday at his Manhattan office.

On Monday, March 4th, the two men met at Saworski's office to discuss the partnership to remodel the former UN building. They reached a tentative agreement, shook hands, and agreed that it is now up to the attorneys to iron out the written details.

In five weeks, they both owned the old UN building. The WZC sold its half for five hundred billion dollars.

"It will be nice working with you UH," said Saworski. "By the way, I heard about the tragedies of your wife and daughter, and I had been and still am very sorry to hear of such misfortunes."

UH responded, "I have opined that sentimentality is not worth the emotional energy. As I've said before, karma can be good, but it also can be a bitch."

UH put his drink down, "I'm sorry if my statements offended you."

"Not at all," said Saworski, "for I am a realist." Saworski smiled.

The named the venture company UH&S, and hired a construction company to begin the remodeling and reconstruction. They decided to use a commercial real-estate broker to handle the leasing.

Chu told UH that his partner could be trusted. Then he told UH that his income went up to seventy-two trillion dollars, and that Saworski was worth fifty-one billion dollars. Saworski had his father to thank for his inheritance, and UH had Chu and the drug cartels, international gangs, and crooked governments to accumulate his wealth.

Chu said, "UH, I am giving three trillion dollars of your income to the WZC to balance our budget. Chen said that this would give the cushion he needed to expand the services we promised to small countries that need medical assistance. He also wanted to improve the living conditions of those outside of the Christian Sanctuaries.

"I believe that anything over sixty-five trillion in my wealth should be given to the WZC," responded UH. "What the hell am I going to do with, even five trillion dollars?"

"That is true. I'll share that with Chen," said Chu. "This year our Appropriation Flat Tax from all of the regions will be more than eighty trillion dollars."

UH dourly responded, "With the regions maintaining their own budgets for infrastructure, medical care, and other financial requirements, I'm interested in what Alfonzo, I mean Chen, will be presenting the WZC Board in June. I'm glad that now we have a June meeting as well."

Chu asked, "I can hear something in your voice, what is it?"

"I feel like a pawn," UH said.

Chu insisted, "Oh, you have never been a pawn, nor will you never be a pawn. You are not the poker chip, you are the game. Must I remind you of this? You had a doting mother until she had died, and a strict father who provided an exceptional education. You had no patience for ignorance in people, and were attracted to intelligent individuals, or those who felt superior like you. For it had been these kind of people who had fed your ego, and nurtured your self-centeredness and over-confidence, and created your futuristic outlook. I required an agnostic like you; someone who had no human shackles like parents, siblings, or a spouse." Chu quickly changed the subject, "There is a requiem for the world, a lament that will cause people to help us continue to dupe all humans into oppression. The positive thinkers will vanish—except us.

"So perk up my genius friend."

"All right," responded UH, "I'll get another drink."

"June may be unpleasant to you, but your temperament understands offensiveness," said Chu as he left.

March and April brought trouble in Christian areas. Some had attempted to leave for various reasons, and were shot dead. Two areas had reported that trucks had broken out of the Christians area in Siberia, and were blown up by missiles delivered by stealth drones.

Overall, the Christian areas were calm, but they felt unrest and oppression like nothing before in their lives. Some became mystics, or wondered off to a secluded place to become an anchorite and meditated most of the time. Churches, synagogues, and mosques were again used, but only for Christian services. Libraries were used for Christian purposes to educate children.

In May, a dozen radical Islamists, were attempting to attack the Christian Sanctuary in Nigeria, but were killed by drone missiles, and WZC snipers had been put into place before the attack.

An administrator's informant passed along the information, and soldiers of the WZC killed everyone who had the slightest inclination to attack a Christian area. There were WZC broadcasts on live television and radio stations every time they executed radical activists . Everyone on the planet had now access to television and/or radio.

The only murders now were caused from domestic violence, road rage, and other heated arguments that left someone dead. All killers were executed. Circumstance was never the issue, only the victims death.

June arrived on a gentle breeze, and the WZC was prepared for their annual meeting at the Europa Building. It had been scheduled for Friday and Saturday, the 7th and 8th, 2019.

UH and his staff met in the morning on the 7th, to discuss any questions that they may have had for the directors.

UH welcomed his staff, regional directors, supervisors, and administrators. This was followed by the pledge of allegiance to the flag of the World Zone Coalition.

The secretaries report was read, amended, and had been unanimously voted on to accept.

Alphonso gave his treasurer's report:

The WZC account had three hundred and fifty trillion dollars from the Regions' Appropriations Flat Tax, their gold mines, and UH's five trillion. Regions at this time functioned like large countries with elite militia, military police departments throughout the region, hospitals with state-of-the-art emergency rooms, medical schools, retirement funds for all citizens, monies set aside for the poor, and of course, salaries for leaders, and their staffs.

All oppression was reserved for the Christians. All debts were paid, and no deficit spending was permitted on any level of the WZC.

Every region had a surplus of funds, which Alphonso scrutinized carefully.

Regional Director Vladimir Nikolin gave a short speech on his Christian situation about the handling of medical needs, clothing, and other extreme cold living requirements. He talked a half hour, often smiling because "I sounding like a humanitarian" he told them.

UH suspended the meeting until after lunch.

The table next to UH had Rowe, Pierce, Nikolin, and Leeds. Kingston said, "The Christians had behaved themselves quite nicely as they were gathered into South Georgia Island and Belize. Of course none of them had chosen the Antarctica. However, many complained about the persecution, and oppression."

Nikolin answered, "As I had said in my speech, no religion or people put in small confined camps or in huge state-like areas will go as easily as the Christians, but the discontented restriction will eventually erupt into a backlash and chaos."

Rowe put in his two cents, "As you know, my mother had been a non-practicing Christian, and my father was a Muslim and progressive socialist." They all looked at him. "I know, but he wasn't a practicing Muslim. I still find the confining of Christians or any group as repulsive, yet understandable. On the one hand, the anti-Islamic flame still flickers in Jewish circles, and Jewish skepticism of Islamists simmer under the radar of WZC, and we have many bigots hiding in corners."

No one responded.

UH had heard Rowe, and walked over to his table, and said, "I appreciate your sentiment." Then he turned to Nikolin, "We are watching

Christian activity, and know about their growing frustration. We allowed Christians to develop a global internet connection, so that we could monitor their activity more efficiently. We will shut them down when or if, necessary.

"We had left the Vatican their tiny walled island in Rome, the old Vatican City, but as of yet, the pope has not really joined them."

Rowe responded, "Why wasn't I informed that the Vatican was a compound?"

UH looked at him with a frown.

"That's right, I had received a memo concerning this small addition to the quarantined Christians, but nothing more," Rowe said looking down at his plate.

The meeting began following lunch.

UH addressed the killing of five administrators in Christian areas, and began a discussion on the subject.

"We found the murderers, tried them the same day, and executed all twelve that were involved. We contacted all administrators, supervisors, and regional directors when each incident occurred. We have decided to militarily equip all administrators beginning with protective gear and Glock firearms. They will be as equipped as a military police officer.

"Each Christian area superintendent had been notified and warned. From today forward, all Christian superintendents are required to support all WZC leaders. They are to employ their own security informants who will work directly with our administrators. The borders of each Christian area, and the area around each Christian island will augment our presence with additional patrols on land and at sea. Currently we have tripled our stealth drone capability.

"Loner attacks have decreased by seventy percent." There was applause.

Shakes asked, "Are we able to send our militias in to quell violence among Christians?"

"No," UH began, "We would prefer to let them kill each other. Your militias are to contain Christians, protect our WZC leaders, and kill any Christian attempting to leave their designated area."

Many of the World Zone Coalition leaders had relatives in the Christian areas, but had been warned by Eduardo, that any sympathy was weakness, and weakness would lead to death.

UH concluded the meeting, "I will see you tomorrow night at our Annual WZC Ballroom for dinner and awards."

Chu said to UH, "Rowe is good at lying about lying. A two term prevaricator-in-chief. He makes me glad that we dispensed with states around the world and formed twelve regions. Rowe is our brilliant regional deceiver. All of the directors are liars, but none as good as Rowe."

UH agreed, and walked with Chu to the elevators.

Chu said, "I see that the last time you were in the states, you met a woman who is quite gorgeous. Helen is a married reporter, but I understand that she is bright, likes you, and is good in bed."

UH responded, "All four observations are correct, but you left one out. I like her.

"I believed you had invited her to the Annual WZC Dinner and Awards," said Chu.

"You know full well that she is in my suite in the Europa Building," retorted UH.

"Yes, I did," Chu said, "but…" He changed his mind. He would not discuss the term love or falling in love concerning Helen. "The awards, entertainment, and dinner have a been arranged with one exception, Franco is under the weather, and he had asked Enrico Petit to step in and handle the dinner, servers, and bar tenders."

"Very good Chu. Thank you for telling me," said UH.

Chu smiled, "Have a nice afternoon." UH caught the reference.

"Helen and I are having a drink at the Petit Bar in an hour," UH smiled back at Chu.

"I understand that she is an agnostic like you," said Chu.

"Yes, she knows her limitations as I do," retorted UH, "I'll talk to you later—tomorrow."

Helen was married, but separated, and her husband was already seeing a blonde twenty-six year old. Helen had reported and covered UH when he had been married to Jeanine, and last year in Brussels. She was as ambitious as UH; didn't care for people who "where a bore or dumb"; and did not like a non-humanist.

They seemed to become the perfect couple.

UH arrived at the suite to pick-up Helen.

"Ah, my manly man," Helen said as UH came through the door.

"Helen, are you ready for a drink?" UH asked.

"Yes. I just got off the phone with the bureau chief in Belgium. He is stationed in Antwerp. He asked if he could meet you, and I told him yes. Is that alright?" UH nodded.

"Good. He is on his way, and if fact, should be here within the hour. I told him to meet us in the Petit Bar."

UH took her by the arm as the suite door closed.

It was odd but Clyde Hemmings, the bureau chief, walked into the Petit Bar, before UH and Helen had been seated.

Helen introduced Clyde to UH and the three sat down at a table.

Clyde started the conversation, "I have wanted to meet the man who brought peace to the middle east, and then the world. Helen and I often talked about your meteor rise to the top of the world. We both were amazed at how quickly the world settled into a peaceful place, but, except for the, I will use a strong phrase, detention of Christians. But we will discuss that at a different time.

"Helen and I worked together in the States for about five years. I worked in New York as she did, but her focus was on getting Rowe reelected, while I traveled around the country talking to Rowe's competition. Nevertheless, it was a great five years. Last week, she resigned as bureau chief in New York.

"I have wanted to meet you for three years, but Washington Times kept me moving around, until I got the assignment in Belgium." Helen gave a look to Clyde who knew it meant he was talking too much. "How is the World Zone Coalition doing?"

UH responded, "It is functioning, not like a well-oiled machine, but as the best political body the world has ever known. Greater than any empire. We have each of the twelve regions operating as though each was an independent country. We monitor their every endeavor. It works like a winning sports steam."

Clyde asked another question, "Is your job less tense now that there is world order?"

UH answered, "Yes for various important reasons. Treating regions as independent countries; collecting a flat tax to make all regions know that we insist on financial equality; and having three WZC meetings each year. The June meeting in now our annual meeting."

They talked about things in general, weather, sports, and the global economy, especially how the regions became financially solvent.

They decided to meet at the Petit Restaurant on Sunday.

Clyde was given authority to officially cover the event. There would also be Fox News, CNN, a local newspaper and local television coverage. UH agreed, and said goodnight.

Helen and UH went to his suite for the night.

"UH I have a hard time believing that you are my lover, and our friendship is blossoming.

You are such a hunk," Helen said taking off her blouse.

Helen's soon-to-be-divorced husband was seven years older, and even though he had played professional football, his physique didn't look like he had played any professional sports. Helen and her husband, Tom, cheated on each other the last four years. He did because he still saw himself as being wanted by young women—and girls. She did not view him as intellectually challenging, and his bedroom prowess had waned—erectile dysfunction was beginning.

UH and Helen embraced each other after their love-making.

"Is that a picture of your daughter on the dresser?" Helen asked.

"Yes. Her name is Nadine, but please, it is too painful to talk about her."

As they dressed, Helen said softly, "You have given me the best fucking I have ever had, or at least, that I can remember, and I've got a good memory. UH, I believe after three months, that I am falling in love with you."

UH said, "You are the most beautiful, dark haired, women I have ever seen. I feel the same way about you," he lied. UH was having a difficulty with love. He feared that each time he had given himself to love, like with Sun and then Jeanine, they tragically died. He wanted to be careful.

They headed for the elevator, and went back to the Petit Bar until 1:00 am. When they were back in his large suite, they repeated the fucking, or making love as Helen believed.

Late that next morning, Helen gathered her belongings from the guest room, and they went to UH's bedroom. They asked Franco to get brunch because he was feeling better.

As Helen walked into the huge kitchen, her eyes widened, "Shit, you must have had great success in recent years. This place blows my mind. I hadn't really looked at your suite yesterday."

UH smiled, "I have had good fortune. Dear, I am going to shower and dress. You may use the guest room, or join me."

She joined UH. He asked his head butler, Le Shoot to lay out clothes, and then wait in another part of the suite.

Helen asked, "How many servants do you have on staff?"

UH said, "Let's see. I have three butlers, five maids, Chef Russo and his staff of two. Oh, don't be startled to see my security team. There are seven who live in the building, and three who sleep in a flex room that adjoins this suite."

"Damn, I feel safe," replied Helen, then said, "All of a sudden, I am feeling a little insecure. I have known presidents, heads of state, and the wealthy, but you are worth trillions and the world president. I also know many things about you because I had done research on you, and Forbes reported that you are the richest man in the world. Listen UH, I forgot about this extravagant life when I had met you, for all I had seen was a tall, handsome, intelligent man who had asked me out. God, I'll leave if you wish me to."

UH held her close to his bare chest, and stroked her dark hair, "Nonsense. You are who I needed, a quick tempered, no-nonsense, intelligent, and absolutely beautiful woman." Then he kissed her passionately—they showered together.

Later that early afternoon, they went to UH's office in his suite to check emails, open mail from last week. He squeezed Helen's waist as she had sat on his leg and knee.

Helen said, "I like how laid-back you are."

"My dear, that is not always the case," countered UH.

"With what I have read about you in Jerusalem, and how you had saved Jacobs from a knife attack, I'm sure that there are times you must summon up a little ire."

"Who reported that story about saving Jacobs life?" questioned UH. "That was to have been kept from the public, and I acquiesced."

"It was reported in a small, and not very well read, Muslim newspaper, I think," said Helen. "What you did was wonderfully brave. That is when I first heard that you had two black belts in martial arts. Wow, now it's all coming back to me. At the time, I had said, 'who is this superhuman?' and I had wanted to meet you, but I couldn't leave Washington."

UH suggested, "All right dear, let's talk about something else, like what are you wearing tonight?"

"Shit, I forgot about the dinner tonight. I was going to buy a dark blue gown I had seen at a store here is Belgium," Helen jumped up and began to tear up.

Chu called UH, "The gown, shoes, and other necessities are in the guest closet. Bye."

"Dear, go look in the guest closet, and tell me if those things are what you had wanted," UH said.

"No, I didn't buy it," Helen said leaving the office.

UH got up, and took her arm, and led her to the guest room closet.

Helen's mouth dropped open after she had opened the closet door. "Holy shit, this is the gown…the shoes… and what are all these accessories? How did you do this?" she said turning to UH and throwing her arms around him. "You were spying on me."

"No," said UH, then offered this explanation: "I had my security team watch over you, and they reported that you talked to the clerk about purchasing these things, when your phone rang. So I asked them to talk to the clerk about purchasing the gown, shoes, and the many accessories."

"You are a sweet man. You make me want to love you more and more, if that is possible," Helen said, pulling his head down to kiss him.

At 3:00 pm, all media outlets were getting set up; Petiti's staff, servers, and bar tenders were given their responsibilities; the security team was reviewing their positions for the evening, and some of the orchestra members were entering the ballroom. Clyde Hemmings was there to station cameras and boom microphones around the ballroom for he was filming as well as reporting.

The Annual World Zone Coalition Award Dinner Program for attendees was delivered at 3:30, and servers placed them on each seat around the table. All media, staff, and security members were given a copy.

UH and Helen came by at 3:45.

"I have been in some beautiful ballrooms before, but this one wins the prize," said Helen.

"The expensive framed art that is placed on the walls between those massive glass panels is spectacular. I can hardly wait for the evening to begin. Besides, I'm not reporting; I am your guest; and I am ecstatic about this event."

They went back to UH's suite to have a drink, copulate, and get ready.

The ballroom appeared to look even more elegant than last year, and when Helen came in, heads turned and men stared like mannequins.

"Wow this ballroom is beyond description in its beauty," Helen remarked. "The original paintings between the floor to ceiling mirrors, and are the chandeliers original too?" she smiled.

UH was glad to have Helen holding his arm as they walked to the front table, greeting people as they passed them.

As UH pulled Helen's chair out for her to sit, he whispered, "You look simply stunning my dear." She tilted her face toward his and smiled.

She leaned over to UH and whispered, "UH, you make that tux you are wearing looks like you belong on the cover of GQ."

Rowe brought his wife, who said, "Isn't UH's date beautiful? I remember that she had helped you win your second term."

Rowe said, "Yes she did, and yes she is lovely."

Chu and UH were always glad to see Mrs. Rowe, because James refrained from making the most meaningless remarks when she was present.

Rowe and his wife sat at the same table as did, his east and west supervisors, and his Canada Region Supervisor, Reed, and all their wives. The four previous tables had Rowe's administrators and a few had brought their wives or dates.

Rowe said to Reed, "I'm glad that the tables are large." Then he smiled at Reed.

The WZC Annual Award Dinner had four hundred and thirty-three in attendance, plus UH's advisory staff, his personal staff, security team of sixty, international media, and Petite's fifty assistants like hosts, two floor managers, servers, and bar tenders for the four bars.

The program went smoothly from the welcoming through the to the dinner. The orchestra played classical music through dinner. Several times UH was interrupted by Clyde and his camera crew. Clyde asked soft ball questions, and other questions about the event itself. UH did not like the interruptions, but tolerated them for the good of the WZC. Off camera, Clyde reminded UH that the coverage was international, and that CNN, HLN, and Fox were also taping.

UH excused himself at the end of the dinner when everyone was eating their desert, because Chu needed to talk with him about something urgent.

As UH stood up he said, "Excuse me dear, and friends, there is an urgent message that I have just received from Eduardo."

Chu told UH, "Our twenty-four hour surveillance over the twelve regions just reveled that three Christian areas have broken through our border security to retrieve medical and food supplies. They have committed several killings. They will be rounded up and executed, or will be shot as they resist. Stealth drones have killed some, and our tanks are moving in to close gaps in the border security. These areas are in the Mexico region of the Christian area in El Salvador; in the Botswana Christian area in South Africa; and in the Damascus Christian area in Turkey."

UH asked, "With our monitoring of cell phones, and computers, how did this occur?"

"They all used word of mouth, primarily, but they had also memorization most of their details. They also used some sort of sign language. We will have to show them that this is unacceptable by killing one hundred and forty-four of them in each of these areas. Kill fifty men, fifty women, and forty-four teens. After which, we will get word out to all other Christian areas that this will be the new standard rule for such breaches. That is, at least this many will die. They seem to be getting restless, so we will show them a little more oppression, that is more effective subjugation.

"Do not announce this during the next part of the program, but call a special meeting of your staff and Regional directors for 10:00 am in the morning."

UH gave out awards to all regional directors, one of which, Vladimir Nikolin, received the highest award: a ten thousand dollar check, an all-expense paid trip to New York, and a larger, two-foot, cut-glass award with "Best of the Best WZC Regional Director", and it had his name cut-in across the base."

The event continued until 12:00 am, and that is when UH and Helen went to his suite.

Helen, said to UH, "I am not tired, so after I change, do you want to go down to the Petit Bar?"

"Sure," he answered.

"On second thought, could we fuck? I'm horny. You are so damn hot," she said taking off her under garments. Helen stood there in her thong as UH hurriedly undressed.

They laid in bed for a few minutes, when Helen said, "I talk like that when I get horny, especially when I look at you. I know that there must be hundreds of women who would willingly take your arm at any event, hop in the sack in a flash, and let you spoil them.

"I love you so much UH," Helen concluded, turning to him; he lifted her into his arms pulling her on top of him, and began kissing, and gently stroking her hair. Helen lifted her head, "Are you falling in love with me?"

UH looked into her eyes that were teared. "Of course I have fallen in love with you. You are a perfect match for me," he lied.

They spent an hour talking, and then decided to go to sleep.

Monday morning, the 10th, UH was in the larger conference room where many of his staff and regional directors had already arrived.

UH called the meeting to order.

UH began, "We have had three tragic incidents as Christians forcibly broke through border guards, killing several in each Christian Sanctuary area." He gave the names of the Christian individuals, the details, and the punishment that is to follow. "I would like to suggest that we build a partial wall around the Christian areas on land where a breach is most likely to occur; increase patrol craft where the area boarders a body of water, or in fact, are an island; and commission an addition three hundred stealth drones. The cost would be defrayed by using Christian labor, and at their financial cost.

"What is your opinion, I have stated mine.?"

"I would suggest that each time that there is such an outbreak, even if no one is killed, double the executions the next time," scowled Nikolin.

Rowe said, "Do they have enough medical and food supplies at this time?"

UH lied, "We had made sure that there would be enough medical and food supplies for a year based upon population. They have computers, cell phones, and administrators to contact if there is a shortage. But what has that to do with our current dilemma? However, we will talk about that for a moment."

Administrators never passed on information from Christian areas because they had been instructed not to do so. Emails from Christians were ignored by administrators. Some Christian areas were unable to grow crops, even if it were possible, the growing season had not produced enough food especially in overcrowded populations. Islands depended on shipping to deliver medicine and food stuffs. Christian areas that could produce an overabundance of food, and were not permitted to transport any goods. In areas that had too few doctors, many died. Hospitals were under-staffed, surgeons were too few, and medical supplies dwindled to a critical level at the end of the first seven months. During the next six months, millions of Christians would suffer, die, and talk of retaliation, for death became a daily occurrence. Unrest led to more cries for their God to step in, and the agony of oppression had become common place.

Felix Santos from the Mexico and Central American Region said, "I know about walls. Israel, Hungary, Kenya, and Norway, to mention just a few in recent years who had walls or were in the process of building walls when the aliens attacked the earth. I agree. We should wall the Christian areas in, where possible."

Yen Zhang from the China region agreed. "We too understand the need for walls. We were the first I believe," he laughed. "I think UH has everything in control. I make a motion that we accept UH's proposal to build these walls around Christian areas an augment our ships to keep them on their islands."

The motion passed.

When asked by Rubin Stakes about the cost, Alphonso, the treasurer, said, "We have the money."

UH said, "We will begin the building as soon as we have construction crews and materials in place this July."

The meeting adjourned, and Chu asked to speak with UH.

Chu said, "I have no patience for the religious. I will instruct administrators and supervisors that they will now have more latitude, that is, they must find informers in the Christian areas, and, secondly, they may interrogate with tools and methods appropriate for these rebellious Christians. If torture fits the particular offense, then employ it. They will now know what persecution is. Unrest and oppression will be a way of life. This information will not go public for some time, for nothing remains a secret long, for humans are the inventors of hush-hush lies."

The Resolution

UH Skyped his staff, regional directors, supervisors, and administrators concerning Christian areas, to give them the dimensions of the walls, the needed increase to patrol boats and ships around islands and water boundaries; he insisted that the need to increase informants and interrogation methods were now indispensable. Supervisors were to inform administrators who had not been able to talk with UH that morning.

During his Skyping that morning he told them, "I had decided after our Annual Award Dinner that everyone, excluding me, will get a ten percent raise in salary. Rowe and Vladimir, you two are the only ones who did not give a three percent monthly increase to the elderly. This was a standard requirement last year. Pay them a lump sum for last year, and begin the three percent beginning in July as had been directed."

Rowe and Vladimir agreed.

UH continued, "I have been financially open with all, and we only expect a flat tax from each region, and this still gives you all more money you need. For god's sake, I pay your salaries.

"One other thing that must be discussed before our August cruise: a chip of a person's personal information will be inserted in the eye brow, or a hand so that a scanner can be used for goods and services. This chip will also have a Nano-chip, so that individuals can be traced. The standard items like name, address, and diseases, but also bank account numbers, government assistance amounts, and local assistance programs. If at any time, a region discovers that the chip has been removed—that person dies.

"I want your input on this chip issue. Talk amongst yourselves, then send in your ideas. We will be compiling a directive for August to institute this project worldwide.

"Keep me, Eduardo, Alphonso, or Jamison informed of any troubling situations."

UH called Helen to tell her that he was on his way back to the suite.

"Helen, the place looks so you. You've done a great job. How could you do all of this in one morning?"

Helen, with a lift in her voice, explained, "I got up, showered, Franco sent breakfast to me by my new maid, Eirene—she is sweet, thank you; and by the time I had dressed and came out it was almost 11:00. I couldn't believe my eyes—the entire suite had been transformed. The movers you had hired, began to bring my things in to your suite from my apartment, that I had only spent two nights in, because I spent nights with you. Is this correct? Am I moving in with you?"

"Dear, the answer to both questions, is yes?" said UH.

Helen excitedly responded, "Wow, we are nearer to a couple; after almost four months, and here we are in the same apartment, I mean gorgeous suite; and, I love you my manly man."

UH said, "I will be there soon."

Chu entered the office of UH, and shut the door, and gave UH a look that said you had better listen.

"UH, I am a bit concerned about this relationship with Helen." UH leaned back in his chair, knowing that hell was about to open its mouth. "You are a fucking idiot at times. You went from fucking the beauty, to friends; then friendlier, when Platonic love blossoms into 'I-love-you-dear' and lovers who move into together, share secrets, past loves, goals, ambitions, futures with each other, money, and current jobs. What the hell are you thinking. I don't care if you screw the women from here to New York and back, but for god's sake—don't fall in love. I can't help that you spent your life trying to please mom and dad, girlfriends, first wife, and second, but Helen will not be the third.

"Either you find a way to prevent this from happening… shit, it is already happening." Chu walked around the office, stroking his goatee, mumbling words that UH could not understand, and cursing."

Chu continued, "I got it. I will initially fix the situation."

UH snapped, "The usual way, by killing someone?"

Chu turned, "You are an impertinent fool. Fuck you. Don't ever question my motives, decisions, or actions. Got it?"

"Sure," UH said weakly.

Chu was going to say something, but in a flash, changed his expression, "UH, just go about your business as president. Begin to plan for your cruise in August. Go home this afternoon," Chu concluded, and he moved to the door. When he closed the door, he looked at a disappointed man. He opened the door and stuck his head in, "UH, go home, have a good fuck, eat dinner, have another fucking experience in your new bed, and screw her after an evening snack and drink. I will see you in the morning."

Chu closed the door with a soft thud, that still made Chen and Jamison turn to look.

"Turn around you imbecilic pledges," said Chu walking to his office.

In the evening, after dinner and the bedroom, Helen received a call from her employer, the Washington Times.

"This is Fred Morgan."

"Yes Fred, what's up?" she asked.

"Helen, I hate to call you this late, but our WT bureau chief in L.A., Frank Rodgers died last night after a short fight with cancer. I don't think that you knew him."

Chu said to Chen, "There was nothing wrong with moving Frank's death up by three days."

"I had met him once in New York at some Times event," commented Helen.

Frank went on, "The owners of the paper, decided to ask you to take the L.A, job. They had asked me to call you about the job."

Helen exclaimed, "I can't believe it. When? How much is my salary?"

Fred answered, "The owners need you there as soon as possible. Your salary is in the six plus figures. I know that Frank was making almost close to one hundred thousand dollars, plus bonuses. And, you could also do that writing you had wanted the freedom to do. Would you consider the job?"

"Of course I will," responded Helen.

Fred explained, "The owners want to meet you on Wednesday, the twelfth in New York. Can you make it. You all will meet in the Rattle N Rum Restaurant that is in the Holiday Inn on 8th Street. I think that it is about a half block from the New York Times offices. They are putting you up at the Holiday Inn for two days. They will pay for dinner on Wednesday evening and the next. They really want to meet with you. The next day, you will go to their offices, and on Friday morning they will make their decision."

Helen inquired, "Do you think that I have a chance to secure this position in L.A.?"

Fred assured Helen, "Don't worry, the job is yours. They have not mentioned anyone else to me. One of the owners, Harriet Simmons, told me that you alone would fill the position well."

Helen was almost beside herself with joy, for she had a premonition, that soon a position like this would open up. She stood for a moment, holding her phone to her cheek. She had clutched so tightly that she pushed on the key pad. When she heard the sound of the key pad, UH looked at her.

She said, "I accidently pushed a button."

UH asked about her phone call. She explained the message had been from Fred, and that she was sorry for not answering him, but that the phone call had been from a colleague who explained to her that a job opportunity had come up, and it is the one she had been working for years—to be an editor-in-chief at a major market.

UH offered, "If anyone deserves this advancement, it is you. I am quite happy for you Helen. Did you want me to take you there on my airplane?"

"Of course, that would be great, but what would you do for three days?" she asked.

"Actually, I was to meet my commercial real estate partner this week. I will call him now to see if Wednesday afternoon or Thursday would be better," said UH. "That way, we could go on Tuesday, to spend some time together."

Helen flung her arms around his neck, and said, "I knew that you loved me."

Chu called UH, "Listen my friend, I will call to have all the arrangements for your flight to New York tomorrow morning. Your partner, Mr. Saworski, will call you later, so there is no need to call him. I figured that the Holiday Inn would do, so I booked a room with a view of New York, with a king-size bed. It isn't where you would have selected, but Helen will be grateful for the nice room she is accustomed to. Bye."

Helen asked UH who that was, and he told her it was Eduardo, and that He would be making the arrangements for the flight to New York and a room at the Holiday Inn.

Tuesday the eleventh, Helen and UH arrived in New York at LaGuardia Airport. St John, the chauffer and body guard, and other security guards drove them to the Holiday Inn, with armored vehicles in front and behind with four security guards in each.

"I don't know if I should take this job in L.A., or live like royalty with you," Helen mused taking his hand and squeezing it. Helen looked out the window, "I haven't seen this part of New York for years."

St John pulled up near the front entrance, and got out to open the door for Helen and UH. They all entered the lobby as the security guards moved the vehicles. Four of them remained with the vehicles.

The next evening, while Helen met with the owners of the New York Times for dinner and discussion of her new position, UH met with Saworski in a conference room provided by the Holiday Inn.

One of the owners said, "Helen, first of all you have the job. We just wanted an informal meeting where we could share some of the past assignments that you think made a difference in your progress to this time in your life. Tomorrow will be the more essential and more specific details about your job as editor-in-chief of the L.A. office. One other issue has to do with salary. It will be the same as Frank's had been, but the bonus program will be increased."

Helen happily said, "Thank you for your confidence in me."

Another owner said, "We know your of dedication, work ethic, and writing skills."

Saworski said to UH, "I like what your attorney had said, and my attorney agreed. I did not realize that your financial advisor worked so closely to your legal team. I was also surprised to know that the World Zone Coalition had owned the building."

UH smiled, "Any time that money is involved, Eduardo is fully engaged. The reason we were able to get a good price on the former UN building was because the WZC had bought it from the former United States for a good price."

They agreed to turn it in to a luxury hotel, with offices, elaborate restaurant, state-of-the- art exercise floor with an Olympic size swimming pool. The renovations and construction would begin in August. UH suggested that he would come to New York when Saworski thought it necessary to meet.

On Thursday, Helen spent the day at the New York Times, and UH spent most of the day on his new laptop computer that had updated for security, which was an ongoing technological necessity. For some reason, when he opened his photos, Jeanine and Nadine popped up. This made him angry, for he had deleted all photos of them so that this would not happen. After he deleted the photos again, he slammed the computer shut with such force that it had broken the screen. He decided to go down to the bar.

Chu tried to Skype UH, but then decided to call him.

Chu said, "I had just tried to Skype you but it didn't go through, so I called you. I hope that you are having a good day."

UH said, "Damnit. Why do you ask me that, when you already know?"

"You are the only one that I allow to talk to me that way. Lucky you," said Chu with a smile.

Chu asserted, "Just trying to be polite. Sorry about your laptop. I'll have another in your room when you return from dinner." He added, "I see that Helen took the position in L.A., that you and Saworski have decided to begin work on the old UN building, and you feel gloomy because Helen will be living in California."

UH ignored Chu's last comment and asked, "Anything happening at the WZC?"

"Plenty: the chip implant program will be ready to implement on July 15th. Christians are dying without proper medical care, and some of them know that the implantation of the chip, is for them as well. A Nigerian Muslim, who had been commanded to leave that country because of new Christian Sanctuary that is now the country of Nigeria, decided to recruit others to attack Lagos at the southern border. He and his small group came in from Porto Novo in Benin. They killed one-hundred and seventy-five Christians, and an administrator and his family."

UH asked, "What are we going to do about this killing in Nigeria?"

"I have already had Chen handle it," said Chu. "The new penalty for killing a WZC official is death to that person and to his family. This will be confirmed at our next meeting. The problem is that Muslims are resentful, for in their minds, these Christian areas were a protective move by the WZC. Their plan is to attack Christians wherever they are found. That is the reason I had sent Chen to Nigeria, and I went to Cameroon. I assure you, this will not be tolerated. Fortunately, as a whole, Muslims are grateful to have Christian separated from them. As usual there are still some who seek world domination at any cost.

"I will give a report to you later, when I turn these responses into your action. Bye."

UH did a three-way call to Chu, Jamison and Chen. "I am calling a staff meeting for Saturday morning at 11:00 am. Is that agreeable to you?" They agreed, and Chen would get in touch with the staff members.

Helen had to fly to L.A. on Friday, so UH flew back to Brussels.

On Saturday the 15th, the staff met in the conference room in the first building of the Europa Buildings.

UH said, "I apologize for calling this meeting on a weekend, but world events have dictated it. I will not keep you long. We have Muslim issues again, Christians are dying because of a lack of medical supplies, and in several Christian areas arguments, fights, and some killing has taken place, like in Iron Mountain in western North American Region, and Belarus area, especially in the inner city. I almost forgot the problems in the North Brother Island East River city blocks, New York City.

"We will not allow either religion to cause more mayhem. Depending on your vote, we will take both, a quick action now, and preemptive strikes in two days."

Karlene Schmidt made a motion to use direct, quick action immediately, and preemptive strikes as soon as intel is available. The motion was seconded by Nikolin, and was passed unanimously.

Eduardo made another motion: "I make a motion to kill all who murder or kill others, and to execute the entire families of those who kill, this includes the Christian Sanctuaries."

This was seconded by Angelo Petiti, Military Chief of Staff.

The motion carried.

UH put forward, as Chu had directed, "Another issue is the implementation of Nano chips that will provide the WZC with complete medical history, personal history, other pertinent info, and can pinpoint where the individual is at all times. This will begin on July 15th and will be completed by the regions, with the help of supervisors, administrators, volunteers. The Christian population will be required to take part in the program, but will be more problematic. They believe that this is an evil mark of some kind. The chip will be placed in the left eyebrow, or the in the left hand. There will be no exceptions. The person must agree or die.

"Do I have a motion?"

There was a motion, a second to the motion, and it passed.

"Thank you. The Operation Nano Chip will begin in two and a half weeks. All of the regional directors and supervisors have started the ground work, and they will be ready."

Chu informed UH, "Vatican City has been as quiet as monks. I'll send Chen to investigate.

"It was a good meeting. I will keep things moving so that each region is properly ready for Operation Nano Chip.

"While you are in L.A. next week, I will make sure that the paper work gets emailed to directors who can make copies for every team implanting the Nano chip. This is a major undertaking.

"Remember who Helen is to you—friend, sex partner, dinner companion. Is that clear?"

UH barely nodded.

On Sunday night, UH talked to Helen about traveling to L.A., but she said that it was going to be extremely busy week, but asked him to please come out if he could. UH called his pilot, Drew Sheets, and ship captain, Dudley Bigalow, for a two week cruise to Nice.

On Monday morning, UH flew in his helicopter, and landed on his ship.

While in Nice, he met an engineer and the engineer's estranged wife. They had been in the casino when UH walked to the bar. He heard them giving snide remarks to one another. He turned his head back to the bar, when he heard another voice at that table. She was the sister of the wife. The engineer got up, and walked to the bar. To order a drink for his sister-in-law.

"You own that huge yacht or ship in the harbor, don't you?"

"Yes," returned UH.

They talked until the drink had been given to the engineer, Bob Harden. Bob asked UH to sit with them at their table. Bob introduced UH to Mrs. Ann Harden, and her younger sister Malory Edwards who was twenty-three. They drank, talked, laughed, until 12:30 am.

"Well I think it's almost time for bed Ann" Bob said to his wife.

"Sure, if you say so," she snapped. "Goodnight UH, it was nice meeting you. Come on Malory,"

"I want another drink," said Malory.

By 1:00 am, Malory and UH were in her room, doing what Chu had suggested—fucking like a whoremonger. Promiscuous, adulterous, or simply a willing woman was now to be the norm for UH, just like the days at college or seven months after Sun died. By morning, while Malory slept, UH walked to his ship, *The Somerville*, and on July 1st, he was in his office.

Chu entered the office of UH, "That woman you had three nights ago was beautiful, and I think that you had enjoyed yourself. I sure hope that this change is here to stay. You haven't been this sexually energetic since Oxford and Cambridge, but now you are rich and free, handsome and available. Take advantage of your situation."

"Let's just say that I'm back to not giving a damn. I've been fated to be this drifter inside," UH complained.

Chu responded, "You accomplish more when you are unhappy because you're an Englishmen, who loves misery brought on by climate and ale. I know that that is not true, but it did sound good, like the times you tried to convince me of some ludicrous notion about love. Wake up UH, love is the verb for sex, fun, and enjoyment."

"All right, all right, you win, shit, I will be me, with no inhibitions," UH raised his voice.

Chu exclaimed, "Damn, that took me three years of painstaking work. Nevertheless, here we are, the duo who will turn this world one more time in pain, tribulation, and suffering.

"Here is my plan:

1. Destroy everyone who opposes me, you, or the WZC.
2. Speed up the implantation of the Nano chip.
3. Make preemptive attacks in the Christian Sanctuaries now to

quell any type of uprising.

4. The same implants given to the general public, will be given to Christians.
5. Increase the number of administrators to seventy-five thousand.
6. Put more administrators in Christian Sanctuaries.
7. Increase the number of volunteers to thirty-three thousand.
8. From this time on, the World Zone Coalition meeting will only include the staff and directors.

"This is just a start," UH seemed to be thinking of something other than what Chu was saying.

"Did you get what I had been saying, for god's sake?" hollered Chu.

"Yes of course I did," UH was uncertain.

"Let's have a little heart to heart, if that were actually possible. I will write and print out these eight points, so focus.

"I had followed you since you were a lad in China. I know everything about you, even the female teen who had awakened your sexuality when you were eleven. Your interest in her was noticeable until she invited you to her bed. Over the years, less and less, you could not keep your body in check, especially you were not able to keep your dick in your pants.

"I know well who you are Urie Lee Harrison. One part of your anatomy is brilliant, for no one could outwit you; another part, is a gift—your tongue, for you have reached the pinnacle of the world through it; and the last one to mention is between your legs." Chu took hold of UH's chin, "You will follow my instruction; you will be my mouth to the world; and that is the sum of it. Got it?"

Chu left the office, leaving UH to think. He went into Chen's office to have him email the eight points to all staff members and World Zone Coalition members including administrators.

Chu said, "Tell everyone the implantation of the Nano chip will commence on the 15th, but start first in the Christian areas. The added volunteers, and administrators who will provide the necessary personnel to complete Operation Nano Chip by the August 5, 2019. This damn process had better be completed on the 5th."

"Chu," said UH, "I am going to lunch at the Petit Restaurant."

"Personally, at this moment, I don't give a damn," retorted Chu.

UH went to lunch, to his clothier, then to Crockett and Jones, and bought two pair of shoes and a pair of Golden Eagle slippers. He was angry with Chu, with himself, with the pseudo intellectuals—the human race in general. He had to disguise the seething of suspicion. Nothing seemed to make sense. He believed that Chu had something to do with the deaths of Sun and Jeanine. Chu seemed to manipulated most situations, accidents, tragedies, and deaths, but he kept all of this to himself. The distrust was based on Chu's handiwork in the Middle East, South America, and in Asia.

Chu called UH, "If you ask silly, mundane, or asinine questions, you get the same response. You should be careful what your lips mouth when you are thinking. Come back to the office, I need to show you a few things. Bye."

UH entered the office and went directly to Chu.

"What is it Chu?"

"I wanted to show you a new map of the twelve regions that will become effective after August 5th. Eight to twelve percent of Christians will refuse the Nano chip, and immediately die. Their deaths, and of course the families deaths, will have most Christians cower in fear, but a few more will join their dead friends. I decided to have Christians surveyed to get the process jump started. Already we are burying bodies of those who will not take the chip, and some of those who have not yet have killed some of our volunteers, but are in the planning stage of doing so.

"The minor changes are in Christian Sanctuaries. We will move Christians from the Dead Sea, Christians in the Asia Region to Central Siberian Plateau in the Europe Region. Central Siberian Plateau is where many Christians have died from the climate and lack of food. Israel will have the

Dead Sea and surrounding area returned.

"Clipper Island Christians who choose to live and take the Nano chip, will be moved to El Salvador. Felix Santos can make this island paradise into whatever he wishes after we move the Christians."

"This sounds good to me," said UH almost absent mindedly.

The weeks moved forward to August 16th, and the staff and directors Skyped that morning.

UH said, "Welcome. We had met our goal of universal implantation of the Nano chip. As you are now aware, there are no Christians around the Dead Sea, nor on the Clipper Island. We will send you a new map of the altered regions.

"The Christians had been depleted by ten percent. The Christians who are left must be observed regularly, for angst is present among those who accepted the Nano chip. Militants within their ranks are already making plans to kill many in the WZC and plan to kill other Christians who don't support them for fear they will inform the local administrator of their plans. As one of these militants said, 'If I am to die for my faith, I am ready kill for my faith.'

"Be on the watch, grill your administrators and the volunteers, for we don't need any of them becoming sympathetic.

"Any questions?"

They all agreed with UH, which is what Chu said would happen more frequently until everyone listened to UH and followed what he desired of them.

After the meeting, Chu looked at UH, "Why not get away? Fly somewhere. Pick up some lovely women, younger than your age, and enmesh them into your charm. I'll protect you from any outcome, negative or indifferent. I see that Helen had called you several times. Fly out to L.A. Perk-up for god's sake. You control the world, remember. There will be great times for you in the next two weeks. Besides, it's mid-summer. Allow me to call Bigalow, and get things moving. St John will drive you anywhere that you land, or you need to go. Now my good man, get the fuck out of here."

UH flew to Rio de Janeiro, found his first lovely in a casino. His second, was a gorgeous rich wife, traveling alone. So it went for almost two weeks. Then he flew to L.A. and had a good time with Helen.

He returned on September 1st, and went to his suite. He talked with his friend Benjamin Singer; he had calls from thee directors; and invited to his suite, and later that evening, a beautiful twenty-three year old married woman he had met in the Petit Bar that evening, and of course, she spent the night.

On Monday morning, the 2nd, he was in his office opening mail, reading emails, and making phone calls. He felt like life was in a downward spiral, but something suddenly made him snap into a good attitude.

"Good morning," Chu said to UH. "How was your mini vacation, and your fun time last night? She seemed to be looking for a good time in the sack before returning to her adoring husband. Was she memorable?"

"Why the hell do you ask me questions that you already know the answer?" asked UH. "I was feeling better until you bounced in here with those idiotic questions. You sure can kill a good mood."

"I know, but why are you so testy?" returned Chu, "That is foolishness. I will not do that again. You poor human."

UH said, "Thank you."

Chu informed UH, "There are five hundred thousand Christians who died for their faith; many with spouses and children. There are three thousand dying from exposure to harsh climate, scarcity of food, and from lack of medical care."

UH asked, "What about other religious organizations outside of the Christians areas?"

Chu answered, "Other killings, and murders, are the same: Muslims kill women, enslave enemies, and seem to find ways to disagree with each other until anger flares up, and one or more of them are dead. The rest of the population is committing murder at a normal percentage rate. Directors and their underlings handle these types of killings.

"Humans will be humans—deadly to each other.

"Bishop Biladou and Father Summers are at the Vatican City compound with a hand full of other Christians who were accepted because of the 'extreme conditions imposed on all of Christendom' said Cardinal Roscoe." There seems to be a situation that is growing. Some are talking about martyrdom. I will go down on Monday the 16th and find out what is going on, and settle the matter."

On the 16th, Chu walked through the guards and tanks that prevented anyone from leaving. A Swiss guard opened the gate. Eduardo and his security detail entered.

I am Eduardo Casus from the WZC, and I am here to see Cardinal Roscoe."

The cardinal approached the entrance.

"How may I help you?" Roscoe asked in Spanish.

Eduardo answered in Spanish, "Speak in English when you answer me. I want to discuss this talk about martyrdom that is being debated in your facility. I know that you and several others have leaned toward a more spiritual position, but I am afraid that a deepened spirituality or any form of mysticism makes no difference. We cannot have murder, or anyone forcing the hand of a WZC official. Do you understand?

"I know who UH is, and I suspect, I know who you are," scowled Roscoe.

"That is grand, but do you understand my statement about attempting to force an officer of the World Zone Coalition in any fashion to kill you, or to get in the face of a volunteer, in an attempt to have him kill you? This may be a form of your martyrdom edict—not mine.

"I have decided to call you our—Satan in the flesh," said Roscoe.

Eduardo looked around at one his security men, and said, "Hand me your pistol."

The guard handed the Glock to Eduardo, who then pointed it at the

Cardinal's forehead.

"Don't worry Roscoe, I will skip the Nano chip. Your impertinence is about to get you shot. Would you like to rephrase your statement?" asked Eduardo.

Cardinal Roscoe looked up and lifted his left hand that had a paper in it, and said, "Forgive me Father." He looked at Eduardo, "You are the Evil One, and your servant, UH is the Antichrist."

Eduardo looked into the eyes of the tearful, but determined cardinal and said, "And you are the dead one." Then he shot Roscoe in the right temple.

As the Roscoe fell to the ground, Eduardo turned, handed the Glock to the security guard, and a Swiss guard went over to check on the cardinal. He retrieved the paper and stuck it in his small pocket.

Later that evening when tensions had waned, the Swiss guard asked to see the Pope's secretary.

"Father Angelo, Cardinal Roscoe had this paper in his hand when he was killed. It is written in English."

Angelo opened the hand written paper and read it:

My brothers and sisters throughout the world and in all Christendom, read this scripture about UH and Eduardo. UH is the antichrist, for he called our Christ an imposter, and called him a deceiver of an third of the earth's population—us. In the book of Daniel it says, "And through his shrewdness, he will cause deceit to succeed by his influence; and he will magnify himself… and will destroy many while they are at ease." UH is a beast, who has been behind the mass murders. Eduardo Casus is the evil one who gives marching orders to UH. Soon this evil one will possess UH and all hell will burst out into the world like an oozing cancerous substance. Goodbye. In the name of the Father, Son, and Holy Spirit.

Chu called UH, "I believe that the death of Cardinal Roscoe will quiet Vatican City. On November 13th, all hell with break out. If anyone had thought that my plan for unrest and oppression had made it difficult for them to live, they will be shocked at my new plan: Cruelty and Tribulation.

"I will bestow on you greater power over life and death. We shall be one in purpose, in planning, and in spirit. I must go. I'll see you tomorrow. You go back to whatever you were doing to Francine, she seems to be enjoying it."

UH stopped his fun, got out of bed, walked from his bedroom to his home office and sat down behind his desk. He felt invigorated more than before, but this time the warmth running through his veins following the pumping heart, never left him again.

"Francine, come here," UH hollered.

She hurried to his office, "What is it?" UH didn't move. "Damn what's wrong?"

"Feel me," he said to her. She went around the desk naked and felt his forehead.

"You don't feel warm," she concluded. "Your eyes look different."

UH asked, "What do you mean, my eyes look different?"

Chu yelled, "I'm back," he said as he walked toward the light in the office.

"Francine, you may leave. Eduardo and I have business to discuss. Sorry, business before absolute pleasure," UH smiled.

www.ingramcontent.com/pod-product-compliance
Lightning Source LLC
Chambersburg PA
CBHW070305260626
47160CB00003B/722

* 9 7 8 0 9 8 6 4 0 1 0 5 3 *